# ABOUT THE WRITERS

**NANCY VARIAN BERBERICK** lives in New Jersey. Her articles have appeared in various small press publications and her short stories have been published in *Beyond, DRAGON®,* and *AMAZING® Stories* magazines.

Born in Salt Lake City, **TRACY HICKMAN** presently resides in Wisconsin in a 100-year-old Victorian home with his wife and two children. When he isn't reading or writing, he is eating or sleeping. On Sundays, he conducts the hymns at the local Mormon church. He is the co-author of the DRAGONLANCE® *Chronicles* and *Legends.*

**MARY KIRCHOFF** has published widely for TSR, including ENDLESS QUEST® books and *Portrait in Blood* for the *AMAZING™ Stories* book series. She edited *The Leaves from the Inn of the Last Home* DRAGONLANCE companion and *The Art of the* DRAGONLANCE Saga, for publication in spring of 1987.

**RICHARD A. KNAAK** lives in Schaumburg, a suburb just northwest of Chicago, Illinois. He is the recipient of a bachelor's degree in rhetoric confirmed by the University of Illinois in Champagne, and is presently working on a novel.

**ROGER E. MOORE** is editor of two fantasy gaming magazines, DRAGON® magazine and DUNGEON® Adventures. A native of Louisville, Kentucky, he is married and the father of a little boy who was named after a hamburger, the J-Boy. His short story originally appeared in the DRAGON magazine issue of May, 1984.

A native Iowan, **NICK O'DONOHOE** has surveyed, jackhammered, and supervised warehouses. Nowadays he writes Nathan P̶̶̶̶̶̶̶̶̶̶, including *April Snow,* ̶̶̶̶̶̶̶̶̶̶̶̶̶ aches at Virginia Tech, a̶̶̶̶̶̶̶̶̶̶̶̶̶ e beer is terrible.

**BARBARA SIEGEL and SCOT SIEGEL** are the authors of 25 books in areas as diverse as fantasy, horror, adventure, sports, self-help, movie tie-in, and celebrity biographies. Barbara and Scott live in a two-bedroom dungeon on the isle of Manhattan with their stuffed polar bear (whose best friend is a runaway dark elf.

**WARREN B. SMITH** is the author of numerous books on a variety of subjects, both fiction and non-fiction. He lives in a small Midwestern community on the west banks of the Mississippi River. He writes with an Apple MacIntosh computer while listening to his extensive collection of rock and roll records.

Born in Independence, Missouri, **MARGARET WEIS** graduated from the University of Missouri and worked for TSR as a book editor before teaming up the Tracy Hickman to develop the DRAGONLANCE novels. Margaret lives in Lake Geneva, Wisconsin, with her two teen-age children, David and Elizabeth Baldwin, and her three cats. She enjoys reading (especially Charles Dickens), opera, and roller-skating. Her short story, "The Test of the Twins,' was published in the DRAGON magazine issue of March, 1984. The published ending, at the insistence of the editor, was more upbeat, but here Margaret presents the story as she originally intended it.

The author of the songs of the DRAGONLANCE novels, **MICHAEL WILLIAMS** has also published poetry and fiction in several national regional magazines. A native Kentuckian, he currently lives in Louisville, where he teaches at the University of Louisville and is at work on a book.

## DragonLance®

### ♣ Tales VOLUME I ♣

# The
# MAGIC
## of KRYNN

### Edited by
### *Margaret Weis and Tracy Hickman*

### featuring "The Legacy"
### by Margaret Weis and Tracy Hickman

Cover Art by LARRY ELMORE
Interior Art by STEVE FABIAN

# DRAGONLANCE® TALES

Volume One

# THE MAGIC
# OF KRYNN

©1987 TSR, Inc.

All Rights Reserved.

Distributed to the hobby, toy, and comic trade in the United States and Canada by regional distributors.

Distributed worldwide by Wizards of the Coast, Inc. and regional distributors.

DRAGONLANCE, DRAGON, AMAZING, DUNGEON, ENDLESS QUEST, and the TSR logo are registered trademarks owned by TSR, Inc.

TSR, Inc. is a subsidiary of Wizards of the Coast, Inc.

Cover art by Larry Elmore.

First Printing: March 1987
Printed in the United States of America.
Library of Congress Catalog Card Number: 86-51591

20 19 18 17 16

ISBN: 0-88038-454-9

T08314-620

U.S., CANADA, ASIA,
PACIFIC, & LATIN AMERICA
Wizards of the Coast, Inc.
P.O. Box 707
Renton, WA 98057-0707
+1-800-324-6496

EUROPEAN HEADQUARTERS
Wizards of the Coast, Belgium
P.B. 2031
2600 Berchem
Belgium
+32-70-23-32-77

Visit our website at **www.tsr.com**

# FOREWORD

"No! No! Please don't leave!" cried Tasslehoff Burrfoot and, before we could stop him, the kender grabbed hold of our magical device that would have transported us out of Krynn and ran off with it down the road!

So here we are, back again, ready for more adventures. If you are one of our long-time fellow travelers, we welcome you along. If you have never journeyed with us through the DRAGONLANCE worlds, we hope this anthology will serve as an interesting and exciting introduction.

A favorite fantasy theme is magic and those who practice it. In these pages, you will find tales of the magic of Krynn. Some were written by us, some written by old friends, and some written by new friends we've met along the way.

*Riverwind and the Crystal Staff* is a narrative poem that describes a haunting search for a magical artifact. *A Stone's Throw Away* is the story of that irrepressible kender, Tasslehoff Burrfoot, and his comic, perilous adventure of the teleporting ring.

*The Blood Sea Monster* tells about "the one that got away." *Dreams of Darkness, Dreams of Light* recounts the tale of Pig-Face William and the magical coin.

Otik the innkeeper has unusual problems in *Love and Ale*. The young mage, Raistlin, faces danger in the Tower of High Sorcery in *The Test of the Twins*. Draconians stumble into a mysterious village of elves in *Wayward Children*.

*Finding the Faith* is a high-adventure tale of the elf maid, Laurana, and her search for the famed dragon orb in Icewall Castle. A young Tanis and his friend, Flint the dwarf, learn about love that redeems and love that kills in *Harvests*.

Finally, in the novella, *The Legacy*, a young mage must face the fact that his evil uncle—the powerful wizard, Raistlin—may be trying to escape eternal torment by stealing his nephew's soul!

Margaret Weis and Tracy Hickman

# TABLE OF CONTENTS

1. RIVERWIND AND THE CRYSTAL STAFF     9
   Michael Williams

2. THE BLOOD SEA MONSTER     27
   Barbara Siegel and Scott Siegel

3. A STONE'S THROW AWAY     49
   Roger E. Moore

4. DREAMS OF DARKNESS, DREAMS OF LIGHT     69
   Warren B. Smith

5. LOVE AND ALE     99
   Nick O'Donohoe

6. WAYWARD CHILDREN     139
   Richard A. Knaak

7. THE TEST OF THE TWINS     161
   Margaret Weis

8. HARVESTS     177
   Nancy Varian Berberick

9. FINDING THE FAITH     215
   Mary Kirchoff

10. THE LEGACY     257
    Margaret Weis and Tracy Hickman

# Riverwind and The Crystal Staff

## Michael Williams

---

## I

*Here on the plains where the wind embraces*
*light and the absence of light,*
*where the wind is the voice*
*of the gods come down,*
*the rumor of song before singing begins,*

*here the People under the winds*
*are wandering ever towards home,*
*forever in movement an old man is singing*
*the song of an absent country,*
*beautiful, heartless as sunlight,*
*cold as imagined winds*
*behind the eye of the rain,*
*and wide before us, my sons and fathers,*
*the song of the country centers and swoops*
*like a hawk in a sleeping land,*
*borne upon hunger and thermals,*
*singing forever, singing:*

---

It was not always
after the wars, it was
a time once when fire
did not rise on its own
out of the dead grass,
a time of waters
and of vanishing light,
when we did not imagine
new country arising
out of the long mirage
of countries remembered
from mother to daughter
in a ruinous dream
that would not have let this happen,
nor did the dance of the moons,
the opened hearts of hawks,
nor did the wind itself
foresee the fires
hot as shrew's blood
in the veins of the land
consuming our dream
while we slept in our journeys,
while these things came to pass.

The outrunners found
the child among waves
of grass and darkness,
on the night when the moon and the moon
wed one another and canceled their light
and the sky was black
except for a wedge of silver
turned like a blade
in the heart of the heavens.

And the night they found him
was his naming night,
and the years unnamed
were the years behind him,
the time among leopards
who must have raised him
in the waves of grass and darkness,
though he did not remember this,
did not recount the graves upon graves
to which he gave infancy,
where he buried the first words of childhood,

And the night they found him
was his naming night.
Riverwind the name he borrowed,
borrowed for him
out of the grass and the darkness moving,
out of their fear of the sky
and the blade of the swallowed moon.

And honored he was among families,
as the source of the blood
was lost in the people,
as the path of the eland,
the high call of the hawk
buried themselves in words
and the long wind died
at the back of his head
as he moved and he moved,
as the Que-Shu contained him,
becoming his country,
as the dream of the Que-Shu
wed to his dreaming

like dark to the moon,
until he remembered
the plains and the wind
and the wandering only.

## II

Riverwind, borrowed from night,
grew as the eyes of the People,
reading the air, the descending wind,
the back of his mind
a prophet, a jackal,
while the cry of the leopard,
unheard by the People
except at the place
where the world falls over, choired
at the back of his head.
And his hand, with the grace
of the falconer's hand
or the falcon herself,
unjessed in the diving air,
was the hand of the People,
the left hand, the off-hand,
the hand that steadies the bow.
And so it would be, my sons and fathers,
until the night
of the dancing moons
when the sky to the east
was silver and black,
red the sky in the westland falling,
the night when we bring forth the daughters.

Robed in the friends of the people,
robed in eland, robed in the fox,
in the falcon's high feathers
ten winters counting,
came forth the daughter of chieftains,
the daughter unwed to man or to sorrow,
unwed to the things she could not be.
Grace of the fathers
dove through her veins
like a wind that the world obeyed.

Heart of the hunter she was
at the heart of the wandering,
gold of the eyes imagining
gold of the moon descended her naming night,
and Riverwind knew that the journey,
the truce with horizons, was ending
in light and the promise of light.
And holy the days he drew near her,
holy the air that carried
his songs of endearment,
the country behind him
a song like a choir of bees
at the edge of hearing, telling him
*here is great sweetness here is pain*
*and you will have to learn about this.*

And seven the summers
in which she eluded him, winters
in which the cold and the country
collapsed on the words *Chieftain's daughter.*
The halved heart of the eland
steamed from the spinning ground below him
and Old Man, Grandfather,

Michael Williams

Wanderer, reader of skies,
reading the face of the boy arising
out of the face of the man,
as the binding of moons on his naming night,
repeating the words like a charm, like a warding,
*Chieftain's daughter*, the old
enduring story of love and of distance,
of the borders at which
the heart bows down.

But the eyes of Wanderer
never the lone eyes watching
as these things came to pass,
in the eyes of the daughter
the leopard's eye reflected
upon reflection, until
it mirrors itself into forever
like the thoughts of a long hall
never the lone eyes watching,
and the eyes of Goldmoon
for the Chieftain looked on
at the dance of the eyes and whispers,
looked on from the place of judgment
deciding this could not be,
and he set for Riverwind
three tasks unapproachable, saying
*Pay court to my daughter only*
*when you can return to my hearthside*
*bearing the moon in your hands,*
*the stars on a dying blanket,*
*and when you can come from the East,*
*bearing the Crystal Staff,*
*the arm of the gods in forgotten country,*
*the source of the magics.*

———

And Wanderer hearing this
heard the *No* and again the *No*
at the heart of the words,
and knew that the magic
was fractured light,
the light at the heart of a crystal,
bending and bending upon itself,
forever becoming nothing.
Knew that the magic was fractured light
when Riverwind spread his cloak on the dew,
when the waters gathered, spangling stars,
and the hunter cupped water
alight in the palms of his hands,
and returned to the Chieftain, bearing
the moon in his hands, the stars
trapped on a dying blanket.
And the third task then
was the terrible one,
for the others were easy, were riddles
set before children
set before huntsmen
set before those
whom the Chieftain could never remember,
and the heart and the mind
of Wanderer bent like the light
of the one true crystal, turning
to words and to whispers,
to the counsel that Riverwind heard
that night at the brink of the journey,
and traveling eastward
under the reeling moons
toward the source of the light
in the heart of the Staff,
again that night was his naming night.

———

Michael Williams

### III

The plains are long as thought, my fathers,
as memory, where the traveler
sees at the edge of the sky
the dead children walking,
and closer, as the sky recedes,
the children accept his name,
in the terrible dust
becoming, as the sky recedes,
the skins of himself
he abandoned in wandering.

Or this is the way it always happens,
the story they tell us of blindness
in the country of leopards
when our eyes say *no more*,
say *we are done with looking*,
*with the children*,
*with skins and with dust and with memory.*

But the time of the Staff was no time,
as Old Man told him it would be,
knowing, reading the hawk's heart,
reading the switch of the wind,
knowing the Staff was calling,
changing the country,
changing the heart and the way
the memory wanders the heart.
And the moons crossed
at impossible angle,
Solinari to rest in the source of the sun,
Lunitari to rest in the dragons.

So Riverwind knew
when the leopard approached him,
skin full of light, of dark,
of darkness boiling in light,
bone and muscle giving way
in imagined tunnels
of plains and movement.
Something behind him
sang with the leopard,
his left eye shining
straight through the leopard
to the edge of the world,
and behind him something saying
*Lie down, give this away at once,*
*give this away before it begins,*
*our son, our young one,*
*for you can learn nothing of this mystery,*
*nothing from this mystery*
*but dry grass but dark but yearning*
*but the graves of your childhood*
*open to moonlight,*
*and the dead*
*the unspeaking dead you see*
*where the sky meets the plains*
*will be always your own, approaching.*

And he knows that he dreams
this story out of wandering
out of night and the long singing he kept
away from the People
from Goldmoon      from the Chieftain
from Old Man himself,
the weaver of blood,
a dream that he cannot remember

---

where the hawk scuttles over the ground,
dragging its wing like a trophy, a kill,
surrendered wind in its eyes.
And as he approaches,
the leopard, the hawk
vanish like water,
reflections of moon over moon
at the heart of the place of the Staff.
He follows each vanishing,
awaiting the snares of the moon,
and *Old Man*, he whispers, *Old Man,*
*I am learning this mapless country.*

But the wanderer travels
through hunger's ambush,
through the thirst of the country
that drives away knowing and knowledge,
and the words of the Old Man
translate the country behind him
but the country before him
is rumors of water,
is crystal arising
distorted by moonlight,
by thought and the absence of thought,
and water arises
like blue crystal before him.
*This time the dreaming is over,* he thinks,
*and this time      and this time*
but the water escapes him
bearing the moons
in its depths like memories,
like the speculations of gods,
until the water is standing before him
and down in the water he sees

himself looking upwards,
the knotted moons at his shoulders,
and kneeling to drink he drinks too long,
for out of the water his arms are rising,
terrible, cold as the wind,
and drawing him downward
to moons and to darkness
to peace past remembering,
peace that whispers
*Join me my brother      my double*
over his vanishing face,
and the words of the Wanderer
returning, drawing him upwards,
the air in the words
sustaining him after belief
falls to the floors
of the waters that never were,
for somewhere the Old Man is saying,
is saying *belief is a facet of crystal*
*that turning, catches the light*
*and bends it to shapes and mirages,*
*bends it to foxfire*
*that lies at the heart of the crystal,*
*where nothing lies but the light*
*that is damaged and broken*
*beyond those things*
*you remember, my son, you remember,*
and Riverwind, doused and redeemed
by the words, by the saving air,
is saying, *Old Man, I have passed this, too,*
*I am learning this mapless country.*

Learning until the red of the moon,
the silver, combine in the air

---

and the light was gold
as the perfumed candles
of Istar, forgotten perhaps terrible,
and Goldmoon walks like a leopard
there at the edge of hearing and faith
saying *Lie down, give this away at once,*
*give this away before it begins,*
*our darling, our young one,*
*for you can learn all of this mystery,*
*all from this mystery*
*dry grass and dark and yearning,*
*the source of the children*
*blossoms for you in the winter.*
*Lie down, my love, lie down.*

Still he walks toward the daughter of the chieftains,
and still she recedes, the story
of days and of years
circles like diving water
and *Old Man,* he whispers, *Old Man,*
*I am learning this mapless country,*
but still she recedes
into the arms and the keeping
of son after chieftain's son
rising like skins of the dead
spangled in stars forever before him,
forever embracing her as she turns,
her eyes green steeples of light,
her eyes his eyes in the twisting moon,
as she smiles, as she gives him to warriors,
and *Old Man,* he whispers, *Old Man,*
*I am giving this knowledge away,*
*this terrible dream of the Staff*
*is a terrible dream when the Staff surrenders,*

and under the moons he follows
his losses until his skin turns against him,
dappling, gold upon black upon gold,
his strong hands remember a nest of knives
and the front of the head bows down
to the hot wind      to the choir of leopards
and in her golden throat
in the throat of her numberless chieftains
the blood is dancing      is rising
like a mirage      like a thermal,
and there are no words for this
as he dreams this dream and the throats unravel.

Forward he moves, remembering nothing,
no movement and cry of the People
no hunt at the head of the movement
no horizons      no crossing moons of the naming
      nights.
He has left them behind him utterly,
surrendering all to the skin full of light,
of dark, of darkness boiling in light,
bone and muscle giving way
in imagined tunnels
of plains and movement.
Something behind him
sings in his ear, his left eye shining
straight through mirages
to the edge of the world,
and the smell of the blood is fading
to the smell of rock      of water
and of things below rock and water
wise and lethal and good beyond thought.
Upright, out of the leopard's salvation
he stalks into light,

his first and his last skin
recalled and surrendered,
robed once more in the long dream shining.
There in a temple of rock,
cold, insubstantial as rain
cold as the silence of stone,
lies the Staff      it is singing, singing
*Arise, you have earned this peace*
*at the edge of the world,*
*behind you a vanishing country.*
*Take me up like a trophy,*
*like a third moon in the sky familiar,*
*and instead of the arm of the Chieftain, become*
*the Chieftain himself,*
*the lord of a land of leopards,*
and Riverwind cold
as the silence of stones,
remembering the edge of the sky,
the dead children walking,
and the staff shines sudden
in the reach of his hand refusing.
There in his grasp the world rolls,
at the back of his head the voice of the leopard
descends into words, is singing
*Lie down, give this away at once,*
*give this away before it begins,*
*our son, our young one,*
*for you can learn nothing of this mystery,*
*nothing from this mystery*
*but dry grass but dark but yearning*
*but the graves of your childhood*
*open to moonlight,*
*and the dead*

*the unspeaking dead you see*
*where the sky meets the plains*
*will be always your own, approaching.*

In the light of the Staff he surrenders the Staff.
More brightly it burns
as it shines on the country of trials,
on the three moons balancing now,
on the night turning in on the heart of the night
creating blue light, the light of the crystal
brought forth by the hand of the warrior
out of the lineage of leopards,
the long heart of the people
remembered past memory,
but Riverwind, cold as the silence of stones,
laughs the first time
since the west has vanished,
for this is the country
he knows he has failed in winning,
for under the plains lies nothing,
and victory walks in the skins of the children
through damaging years of light.

## IV

The rest of the story is known to you,
how Riverwind, bearing the staff,
returned to the People,
the darkness of stones in his eyes,
what the Chieftain ordered,
(I was there to see it
my words this time could not stop them)
what the Staff in the hand of Goldmoon accomplished.

---

Michael Williams

But this you may not know:
that in the pathways of light
from the plains to the Last Home riding
she said to him, *Now are you worthy,*
*no longer in my eyes only,*
*but now in the falcon's eye of the world*
*forever the story is walking forever the story,*

But Riverwind *No,* and *No* again
*No* to the fractured light of the staff,
for caught in the light his hand was fading,
through facet and facet unto the heart of the light,
and not of this earth was the third moon rising,
and the heart of the Staff
was his naming night.

*Here on the plains where the wind embraces*
*light and the absence of light,*
*where the wind is the voice*
*of the gods come down,*
*the rumor of song before singing begins,*

*here the People under the winds*
*are wandering ever towards home,*
*forever in movement an old man is singing*
*the song of an absent country,*
*beautiful, heartless as sunlight,*
*cold as imagined winds*
*behind the eye of the rain,*
*and wide before us, my sons and fathers,*
*the song of the country centers and swoops*
*like a hawk in a sleeping land,*
*borne upon hunger and thermals,*
*singing forever, singing.*

# The Blood
# Sea Monster

## Barbara Siegel and Scott Siegel

*O*ut of breath—and nearly out of hope—I ran across the wet sand, looking for a place to hide. After the terrible storm earlier that day, running along the muddy beach felt like running in a huge bowl of thick mush. But I ran just the same because Thick-Neck Nick, the village baker, was dead-set after me.

I had lost Thick-Neck when I made a quick dash between two buildings and headed down toward the sea. I knew he might realize that I had come this way, but then I saw my salvation: along the shore was a long row of fishing boats.

Clutching the stolen loaf of bread close to my body, I looked back over my shoulder. Thick-Neck hadn't yet reached the beach. I took my chance and dove into the very first boat.

After covering myself with a heavy netting, I took in deep drafts of air, trying to catch my breath. I knew that if Thick-Neck Nick lumbered by, he was sure to hear me.

I don't know how much time passed. When you're scared, breathless, lying in rainwater up to your lower lip, and have heavy fish netting on top of you shutting out the light, nothing moves slower than time. Absolutely nothing.

But my heart started picking up its pace when I heard fast-approaching footsteps. I cringed down at the bottom of the boat. The rainwater covered my mouth. I had to breathe through my nose.

The steps came closer.

It was useless. I raised my mouth up out of the water and took a bite of the bread. If Thick-Neck was going to beat me, at least I wanted to have something in my stomach to show for it.

Despite my dry mouth, I hurriedly began to chew.

The steps came closer. Did he see the netting move? Did he hear my heavy breathing? Did he hear me chewing his bread? Though I hadn't swallowed my first mouthful, I took another bite, and then another, and another, until my cheeks were so puffed out they looked as if they had the wingspan of a dragon. Well, maybe not that big, but there was more bread in my mouth than there was left in my hand—and I hadn't swallowed a single mouthful. At least, not yet.

The footsteps stopped right next to the boat. I closed my eyes, the bread stuck in my throat.

I started to choke!

The netting flew off me. Even as I tried to breathe, I covered my face, hoping to ward off Thick-Neck's blows.

But there were no blows.

I peeked out between my arms as big chunks of bread spewed out of my mouth.

"What is this?" asked a bewildered old man staring down at me. "A young elf, all by himself?"

I didn't answer. I kept coughing, spitting out wads of half-chewed bread into the bottom of the boat.

The old man shook his head with exasperation and began slapping me on the back.

---

When I was finally able to breathe again, I looked past the old man and saw that the beach was empty. Thick-Neck Nick was nowhere in sight.

"You in trouble, elf?" asked the old man, seeing my furtive look.

I nodded my head, figuring to play on the old man's sympathies. "Thick-Neck Nick doesn't like me," I said.

"Thick-Neck Nick doesn't like anybody," agreed the old man with a sigh. Then he looked at me with a sly grin and added, "He especially hates one particular elf who has a habit of stealing his bread."

My face reddened.

"What's your name, elf?" he demanded.

"Duder," I told him.

"That's all? Just Duder?"

"It's enough," I replied, not wanting to say any more on that subject. "What's yours?"

"Folks call me Six-Finger Fiske."

My gaze immediately shifted to his hands.

"Don't expect to see an extra digit, elf," the old man said with a harsh laugh. "Had a drunk doctor at my birthing, and the fool thought he saw six fingers on my hand. My mother didn't know enough to count them herself, and, well, nicknames have a way of catching on. Know what I mean?"

I nodded. What else could I do?

Without warning, the old, leathery fisherman picked me up by my shoulders and set me down on the muddy beach. "You're a funny-looking little fellow," he said. "Don't see too many elves around here. But you can't stay in my boat. I'm heading out to sea now."

"You're going fishing?" I sputtered, astonished. "Everyone stayed in port because of the storm," I pointed out. "And now it's too late to go out. It'll be dark in just a few hours."

"The fish bite best after a heavy rain," replied Six-Finger Fiske. "Besides," he added mysteriously, "there is one fish that I must catch—and my time is running out."

I didn't know what he was talking about. The truth? It didn't really matter to me. All I cared about was keeping out of Thick-Neck's sight; a hard thing to do in such a small fishing village.

"I'll go with you," I quickly offered. "If you head out onto the Blood Sea so late, it'll be dark by the time you come back. I have really good eyes and I'll be able to help you find your way back into port."

The old man laughed. "I don't need you to help me navigate in the Blood Sea," he said. "I've been fishing in these waters since before you were born."

I was sixty-two years old—just an adolescent for an elf—but just the same I didn't doubt that Six-Finger Fiske had outlived me by a good ten or fifteen years. I had to find another way to convince him to take me along.

"If you've been fishing for as long as you say," I said slyly, "then you're not quite as young as you look."—Unlike most elves, I can stretch the truth until it's almost ready to snap.—"But if you're as old as you say, Mr. Fiske, " I continued, "then I'd be glad to offer my rowing services to you for just the modest fee of ten percent of your catch."

"You're a clever one, elf," the old man said with admiration in his voice.

"Please, call me Duder."

"All right, Duder. Though you don't look like you can row worth a damn, your company on a dark night might keep these tired eyes of mine from closing. But if you really want to go with me, you need to know that I'm setting out to catch the Blood Sea Monster."

I couldn't help it. I laughed.

---

"So, you're one of those who doesn't believe it exists," he said without anger.

"I've heard stories," I admitted. "But that's all they are. Everyone knows that. Even kender."

"Just the same," the old man said doggedly, "it's the Blood Sea Monster that I intend to catch. Do you still want to go?"

I certainly didn't want to stay around to face Thick-Neck Nick. So, I bit my tongue to keep from laughing in his face again, and said, "Yes, I still want to go."

Before he could say another word, I started pushing his little fishing boat toward the lapping waves of the Blood Sea, hoping he wouldn't have second thoughts.

Suddenly, he called out to me, "Duder?"

"Yes?"

"You'll get two percent of my catch. And that's final."

I smiled to myself. I was going fishing!

I pulled the oars of the fishing boat until the shore began to shrink out of sight. But our progress was slow because the Blood Sea was still roiling from the storm.

I thought I might get sick from the boat's constant dips into the trough of every wave. Six-Finger must have seen my suffering, but a deal was a deal; he didn't take the oars from me. He offered only one consolation. "Don't worry," he said. "The water will calm down by dusk. It always does."

He was right. As the sun set into the Blood Sea, dazzling crimson lights sparkled on the now-smooth surface of the water. The sea was at peace. And, finally, so was my stomach. Not that there was anything in it, mind you.

It suddenly occurred to me that Six-Finger hadn't cast his line. "You can't catch anything—except your death of cold—without putting your hook in the water," I said.

"Giving orders already, huh?" growled the old man. "I've fished these waters before and I'll not find the Monster hereabouts."

With my stomach calm, I was getting hungry. I'd eaten raw fish before, so I asked, "Do you mind if I use your line and see what I can catch? After all," I reminded him, "I get a percentage of your take."

He shrugged his shoulders. "If you're going to fish," he said gruffly, "give me the oars." Six-Finger heaved on the wooden oars, turning his head away from me as he stared out into the gathering twilight.

My line splashed into the red water, trailing behind the boat as we moved farther out to sea. I closed my eyes, enjoying the steady, rhythmic movement of the old man's rowing.

This is a good way to live, I thought. Someone to row for me, and dinner just waiting to be caught. But then, as always, I started dreaming of more: I'd have a whole fleet of fishing boats with scores of old men bringing in a huge catch every day. I'd be generous and give them ten percent of the profits. Then I stopped and thought, no, I'd give them just two percent.

I smiled to myself and sighed with satisfaction.

I'd be known as Duder, Captain of the Blood Sea. And I'd be the richest elf in the world. The other elves would envy me. They would be sorry they had treated me so badly. I had been expelled from my homeland; punished for a youthful indiscretion; shunned, made to travel all alone—oh, how I hated being by myself. But when the elves needed my fish, needed my money, needed my power and influence . . . they'd come to me then and say, "Duder Basillart, we're sorry. Come home." And I would just grin and tell them—

"Ouch!" The fishing line was nearly torn out of my

hands. My eyes opened wide as I clutched at the line, thinking that though my reverie had come to an end, my dinner was just about to begin.

"Looks like you've got something big," said the old man as he watched me pull on the line.

"I told you I'd be good to have along," I boasted. "This fish will bring in plenty of money. Don't forget," I added, "I get two percent!"

"I remember."

Hand over hand, I pulled on the line. I was counting my money even before my catch broke the surface. But when it did, I stopped my efforts. I had caught a dead man.

"I'm not surprised," said Six-Finger after he helped me haul a drowned sailor up onto the lip of the boat.

"You're not?" I asked, astonished. "Do you catch dead men on your line every day?"

His ancient face showed little emotion. "There is an old folk tale about storms on these waters," he said. "Whenever there's a storm, you can be sure that a ship has been sucked down into the whirlpool at the center of the Blood Sea."

I shivered at the thought; in my lonely travels I had seen so many storms blow across these waves.

"Too bad our fishing expedition had to end like this," I said sadly, figuring that we would head back to shore with the body.

"Don't be silly," said the old man. And with that, he cut the line and let the dead man splash back down into the water.

"What are you doing?" I cried.

"The proper place to bury a sailor is at sea," he calmly explained. "Besides, there is the one fish I've been after all of my life. Tonight, perhaps, I'll finally catch that creature."

It was only then, as I watched the body float away from the boat, that I fully realized the old man's desperation. He was tired—worn out—and he knew he wouldn't have many more chances to catch his fabled Blood Sea Monster.

Six-Finger didn't look back as the sailor's body sunk below the waves.

It wasn't long after I picked up the oars and began to row that I saw wreckage floating nearby from the dead sailor's ship. Cracked and broken pieces of wood were strewn about the water. And then I saw a plaque that must have been part of the ship's bow. In the fading light I read the words, *The Perechon*. And then the plaque tumbled away on a wave and disappeared.

Was it a big ship? Had a great many sailors died? I would never know. To me, it was just another ship that would never see land again, just another crew of sailors who would never see the sun again, just another shipload of souls who would never go home again . . . like me.

It seemed like every passing day took me farther away from my home. And now I was in a little boat, far away from land, somewhere out in the darkness of the Blood Sea in the dead of night. Worse than that, I was sailing with an old fisherman who actually thought he could catch a creature that existed only in the mind of man.

I'm not cruel by nature, but I thought I'd have some sport with Six-Finger. While I rowed, I asked, "What does this Blood Sea Monster look like?"

"I don't know," the old man replied. "No one has ever seen the creature and lived."

"Then how do you know it exists?" I smirked.

"It does," he insisted. "I'm sure of it. Though no one has ever seen it directly, there are stories—hundreds of stories—about the great Blood Sea Monster." He looked away from me, gazing out onto the water. "Some say it's as big as a thousand fishing boats. Others say it isn't the size of the beast, it's the length of its teeth and claws you have to watch out for. But nobody really knows. I knew one man, though, who claimed he saw the beast's reflection in a mirror. He said it had a scaly, blood-stained face that oozed black pus. But it doesn't matter what it looks like. What matters is that I catch it!"

"Why?"

His eye narrowed and his voice grew thick with anger. But he wasn't angry with me. His rage was aimed at the creature he sought. "It killed my father," he said. "And it killed his father, too. It killed my only brother, my sons, my nephews—fishermen, all—it took them to their deaths on this sea of blood. In the end, my wife died of . . . neglect . . . grief. Now I'm alone. No family. Nobody. An old man with nothing in his heart but the desire for revenge." He lifted his head and stared at the sky with a fire in his eyes. "And I'll have that revenge!" he shouted into the night. "I swear it!"

If Six-Finger kept yelling like that, he was going to scare away the fish. He had already scared me.

I forgot all about his ravings when he offered me one of his wheat cakes. I gobbled it down so fast that the old man offered me a piece of fruit from his bag. "What about you?" I asked, not wanting to appear unmindful of my host (and wanting to keep his mind off the Blood Sea Monster). "Aren't you going to eat?"

"My appetite isn't what it used to be," he said with a sigh. "I don't eat half of the things I bring along. Most of the time I throw my leftover food overboard for the fish to eat. A man can't take from the Blood Sea without giving something back," he said reverently. "If the fish live and multiply, then so will the fishermen."

It was a nice thought, but I was hoping he wouldn't

---

throw anything overboard that night, because I was awfully hungry.

He must have been reading my mind, because he took a sweetcake for himself and then handed his food bag over to me, saying, "Take as much as you like."

I took it all.

The moon was halfway across the sky by the time I finished eating. And, then, finally, the old man tossed his fishing line into the water.

We bobbed on the gentle sea, neither one of us talking. I wondered how long we would stay out that night before the old man grew tired and gave up. And I wondered what I would do when we reached shore. Would I move on and steal my bread from another baker, in another town? I wanted more from life than just crumbs. I had a restless craving for . . . experience. That was why I had stolen the elven leader's locket, back in my homeland. I thought that the locket held a secret incantation that would give me power and wisdom. Instead it only brought me misery. When my thievery was discovered, I was banished from my home. Cast out, I had become a dark elf, a renegade. But where was I running *to*?

The boat, as well as the night, drifted along with my thoughts. I had no idea of the time. I liked that about the sea. The timelessness. The old man was intent upon his fishing and I was intent upon my dreaming— until there was a splash in the water!

"I've got something!" Six-Finger exclaimed.

His line went taut. The bow of the boat tipped down as the creature at the other end dove deep with the hook in its mouth.

He didn't really think he had caught the Blood Sea Monster, did he?

Expertly, the old fisherman gave the diving fish

some slack and let him run. Then, as the fish let up, the old man tugged back, reeling him in. When the fish tried to pull away, the old man patiently repeated the process. Yet I could tell that Six-Finger was straining. Whatever was at the end of the line was something powerful, something that wouldn't give up without a terrible fight.

But Six-Finger stayed with the creature until it finally broke the surface again, splashing just off the stern of the boat.

"It's big!" I cried despite myself, seeing the shadow that it cast in the moonlight.

The old man simply scowled. He knew what he had—and it wasn't what he wanted. Still, he reeled the fish in. I helped get it out of the water by using the old man's net.

When I dumped it on the bottom of the little boat, I could see what the old man had caught: a rare—and very feisty—Bela Fish. I had heard of them but had never seen one before because fishermen always throw them overboard. You see, the Bela Fish tastes terrible, and there is no market for it. It's also bad luck to kill a Bela Fish because it's one of the rare fish that can communicate with land creatures.

And the Bela Fish wasn't shy about communicating with us. . . .

"The hook hurts!" it cried. "Take it out of my mouth!"

I immediately got down on my knees and carefully removed the hook.

"Thank you," said the fish. "Now, if you would be so good as to get me back in the water?"

I didn't hesitate. I started putting my hands underneath the body of the Bela Fish, but the old man slapped my wrists. "Leave him be," said Six-Finger. "I think we'll keep him. He'll make good bait."

---

Upon hearing the old man's words, the Bela Fish started flopping all over the bottom of the boat, desperately trying to wriggle over the side. But it was no use. "Please," begged the fish, "let me go!"

I was stunned. I couldn't believe that the old man could be so cruel. How could a man share his food so generously in one moment and then torture an innocent creature in the next?

"Let the Bela Fish go," I demanded. "If he doesn't get back in the water soon, he will die."

"Then he'll die," replied Six-Finger steadfastly. "But I'll give this fish one chance to save his life. And one chance only."

"What is it?" cried the Bela Fish. "I'll do anything."

"Tell me where I can find the Blood Sea Monster," demanded the old man.

The Bela Fish looked at me and then at the old man. "You don't want to know that," it said.

"I do, indeed," insisted Six-Finger. "If you want to live, you will tell me. And you'll tell me right now."

"If *you* want to live, you'll head right back to shore," retorted the fish.

My eyes opened wide at the meaning of the fish's words. "You mean there is such a beast, then?" I cried.

"There is, yes, oh, without question—yes," said the Bela Fish. "And I can tell you that we swim away as fast as we can when we hear that it's near."

"Why?"

The Bela Fish blinked. "You mean you don't know?"

"No."

The fish tried to laugh, but it was quickly losing its strength. Instead, in a weak voice, it said, "There is a reason why no one has ever seen the Blood Sea Monster and lived. It moves through the water like a dark shadow. And the water in its wake is cold, empty . . . dead."

"I don't understand," I said, confused.

"You'll understand all too well if you continue your foolish quest," it replied. "I beg of you, don't—"

"Enough!" exploded the old man, cutting off the Bela Fish. He picked up the fish in his two hands and demanded, "Where is the beast? It's that, or I'll eat you myself, bad taste and all!"

"I was just trying to save you," it gasped. "But if you want to know so badly, I'll tell you."

"Speak up, then, and don't delay," said the old man harshly, leaning close to hear the Bela Fish's words.

"The beast you seek is close by, near the center of the Blood Sea, where a ship was sucked into the whirl-pool's maelstrom. You see, it's the monster's ever-swinging tail that causes the whirlpool, and it's the steam that rises from its body that causes the raging storm that never leaves the center of the sea."

I shuddered, remembering the body and the wooden plaque with the name, *The Perechon*.

The old man grunted with satisfaction. The Bela Fish's words had not frightened Six-Finger Fiske the way they had frightened me. Finally, after all these years, his revenge was at hand.

In fulfillment of his bargain, the old man threw the Bela Fish overboard. Then Six-Finger feverishly took the oars in hand and began rowing toward the deadly center of the Blood Sea. But even as Six-Finger rowed, the Bela Fish swam up close beside the boat and warned, "You're making a mistake. Turn away! Don't go!"

When the old man ignored the fish, the creature turned toward me and cried, "You were kind to me. I want to help you. Listen to what I say, and jump over-board. Save yourself!"

The sea elves are cousins of my people, but that didn't mean that I could swim like a fish. We were miles from shore and the thought of jumping into the middle of the Blood Sea seemed akin to taking my own life. Despite my fear, I chose to stay with the old man.

But I would have stayed anyway. There was something about the old man's fierce determination that hit a nerve inside of me. He was so sure of himself, so unafraid, that it inspired my confidence. I had been impressed by the old man's sureness in the boat—how he caught the Bela Fish and reeled him in so expertly. But, most of all, I thought how wonderful it would be to witness this great feat if the old man really did catch the monster fish. Six-Finger Fiske would be famous, yes, but so would I! I'd be part of the greatest adventure of our time; I'd be the most famous elf in the entire world if I helped catch the Blood Sea Monster.

The old man pulled on the oars for a long time, his breath growing ragged.

"Let me row for a while," I offered. "You'll need your strength if the monster strikes your line."

"That's true," agreed Six-Finger. "I'm glad you came along."

His approval put a smile on my face. I dipped the oars into the water and rowed as hard as I could.

It wasn't long before the moon and stars were obscured by swirling clouds. We were entering the edge of the storm that hovered over the center of the sea. The winds blew raw and cold. And the water itself began to grow rough beneath the boat. We were getting close to the whirlpool . . . close to the monster.

"Pull in your oars," ordered the old man. "I'll cast my line from here."

I was tired from the rowing and was glad to stop. I rubbed my aching arms as I watched the old man cast his line into the dark scarlet sea.

My eyes were fixed on the line dangling out of the boat, figuring that we'd immediately get a strike. But soon my eyes became as tired as my arms and I slumped down into the boat, snuggling into the netting to keep warm. Out of the wind, I felt better, safer. With my excitement ebbing, exhaustion finally crept up on me and I drifted off to sleep.

I don't know how long I dozed, but when I opened my eyes, I heard the old man cough and grumble. I felt sorry for him, sitting up in the cold, damp night, fighting to keep his dream alive of catching this one great fish before he died. It seemed like a dream that would go unfulfilled, for the night was passing and he hadn't had a single bite on his line.

Not a single bite.

My breath caught in my throat. In all that time, it was impossible that the old man hadn't had a single nibble, unless the waters here were *dead*. And if that was true . . .

A terrible fear gripped me, and I wanted to tell the old man to pull up his line. But I didn't get the chance. In that very moment, he shouted, "I've got a strike!"

The fishing line went so taut it almost snapped. And even though the old man was letting out more line to let the fish on the other end run, he couldn't do it fast enough.

The little boat was being pulled through the water!

At first we moved sluggishly across the choppy sea, but then the boat was pulled still faster and, like a dragon in flight, we soon found ourselves soaring across the tops of the waves.

The old man knew better than to hold the line in his bare hands. He had cleverly jammed an oar into the prow of the boat and then wrapped the line around it.

Clever, but not clever enough. The fishing line burned through the wood as the creature on the other

---

end kept pulling farther and farther away.

The old man, fearing that he would run out of line and lose his catch, tied the end of the cord around his body and then held on for the final struggle.

Seeing the old man's bold action, I jumped to the front of the boat to help him. If there was going to be glory, I wanted my share. I took hold of the rope alongside him and tugged at it, trying to stop the fish's run.

Six-Finger Fiske ignored my effort. Instead, he shouted up to the sky, "I've caught the Blood Sea Monster! I've got him, and I'll never let him go!"

I followed Six-Finger's gaze up into the heavens, but all I saw were heavy, ominous clouds. That's when I realized our direction. The great fish was pulling our boat straight toward the maelstrom! If we didn't change direction soon, we'd be sucked into the whirlpool and perish at the bottom of the Blood Sea.

"We've got to turn it!" I cried. "Look where it's taking us!"

The old man heard me and understood what I meant. He took a deep breath and pulled on the line with every ounce of strength in his aged body. And I pulled right along with him.

The line suddenly went slack. It worked!

"We won!" Six-Finger Fiske cried with joy. "Don't you see? It's exhausted, beaten. It's given up the struggle!"

The old man was short of breath. But though weak, his chest heaving from the battle, he hurriedly began reeling in the monster.

I fell back, watching with glee as he pulled in arm's-length after arm's-length of line. We had really done it. The old man would be a legend. And when we hauled the beast up onto shore, I would stand there next to Six-Finger Fiske. People would say, "Look, Duder Basillart was a thieving dark elf, but see what he did? He helped that old fisherman catch the Blood Sea Monster."

I leaned over the side of the boat, anxious to see our catch. After all, I was entitled to two percent. I would remind Six-Finger of his promise when we neared the shore. There was no doubt in my mind that two percent of *this* catch would be worth a fortune.

As I stared down into the water, looking for the fish, the sea began to bubble. And then I heard a roaring sound that seemed to be coming from underneath the boat. No matter what direction I looked, I saw the sea beginning to foam and churn.

"What's going on?" I cried.

The old man didn't say a word. He stopped reeling in his line and just sat there with a look of awe on his face.

The sea started rolling beneath us in a mighty turmoil, and I knew then with a terrible certainty that it wasn't the old man that had caught the Blood Sea Monster. It was the other way around.

"Cut the line!" I screamed. "Let it go!"

The old man seemed undecided. His desire for revenge fought with his desire for life.

The sea began to rage and the little boat was buffeted from wave to wave. And still the old man would not make up his mind. Was it his father he was thinking of? His brother? His sons? Or his poor, unfortunate wife? I didn't know what rooted him in place; I only knew that if he waited any longer, we would surely join his descendants in the darkness of death.

The roaring that I heard from underneath the sea grew even louder, and steam began to rise in a cloud, covering us like a shroud.

The cry of the beast and the enveloping whiteness seemed to finally shake the old man from his moorings. He reached for his knife, intending to cut the

---

line. Except his hands were trembling and he fumbled with the knife, dropping it to the bottom of the boat.

At that moment the sea in front of the boat erupted in a mighty spray. Something hideous thrashed up out of the deep. I couldn't see very much of it because millions of gallons of blood-red water were running down off its massive body. Huge flapping wings made the wind blow so hard I could barely expel my own breath against its awesome force. I could see nothing else except Six-Finger Fiske's huge, shiny metal hook caught between two massive teeth in the beast's otherwise dark, obscured face.

Without his knife, the old man couldn't cut the line. His only hope was to pull the hook free of the monster, and so he wrenched on the line as hard as he could.

The beast's scream of fury made me throw my arms around my face and cower at the bottom of the boat. I heard something clatter down beside me, but I was too afraid to look.

And I'm glad I didn't, because above the thundering sounds of beast and sea, I heard something that I knew I didn't want to see. It was the old man, going mad, calling out to the beast as if he knew him! Six-Finger Fiske actually laughed—a bitter laugh. "Only a fool would seek you out before his time—and I am that fool!" he shouted. And then, calmly, as if in answer to a question that only he could hear, he said, "Yes, I should have known. It isn't I who sought you, but you who sought me." And then he suddenly called out, "The light!"

It was still dark. I didn't know what he meant. But the fact is, I didn't care. I only cared about myself. And in that moment I thought I was going to die.

"It's not your time," a raspy voice rumbled deep in my head, as if in response to my fear. It was a voice that had the weight of countless years upon it.

In the next moment, I heard a huge splash, and a gigantic wave rose up out of the sea and picked up the fishing boat. I clung to the boards at the bottom of the boat, fearing that the wave would crash on top of me and throw me out into the sea. But the boat hung on the crest of that wave, and it rushed headlong for miles and miles, until the wave finally spent itself.

When the boat lolled to a stop, I found the courage to open my eyes.

The old man was gone. Disappeared.

In my fear and confusion, I scanned the waters all around the boat hoping to find some sign of Six-Finger Fiske. But there was none. It was still dark and I was utterly, thoroughly alone.

"It's not my time," I whispered, the great monster's words reverberating in my head.

As I was sitting in the bottom of the boat, my fingers brushed against something sharp. I flinched. The cut went deep into my thumb. I quickly brought my hand up to my mouth to suck away the blood and sooth the wound.

When I looked down to see what had cut me, I was astonished to find a giant, cracked tooth lying near my feet.

At first, I was afraid to go near it. Using an oar, I pushed it to the far side of the little boat. The very thought of the gaping jaws that had held that tooth made me quiver with fear.

I wanted to get away from this cursed Blood Sea and away from the memory of this awful night.

It was still dark, but I could tell by the stars that the night would soon be over. I was desperate for sun to warm my soul.

I grieved for Six-Finger Fiske; I truly did. I couldn't stop thinking of him and his strange words before he vanished beneath the waves. But I had to take care of myself, so I fixed my position by the stars and began rowing toward shore. And the more I rowed, the more joyously grateful I was to be alive. I had survived. And as I slowly rowed the boat back toward the little fishing village where the adventure began, I started to think . . .

I saw it all in my mind's eye. Me, Duder Basillart, had faced the great Blood Sea Monster and I had lived to tell the tale. Dwarves, minotaurs, kender—everyone— would come from all corners of the world to hear me tell how I had valiantly tried to catch the mighty sea beast; how I had heaved on the rope with all my might and turned the monster from its course. How I had tried to save the old man by yelling for him to cut the line. And I would tell them about the evil, awesome creature with its wings and its deep rumbling voice. Yes, I'd tell them how it *spoke to me!* How it spared me because of my bravery. Yes, that's what I'd say.

And who would doubt it?

After all, didn't I have the monster's tooth? Was there another creature's tooth like this anywhere else in the world? No, I had the evidence of my miraculous adventure and my future was now secure. More than secure; it was perfect!

I couldn't afford to lose the Blood Sea Monster's tooth. I realized that, without it, I was nothing. Instead of fearing it, I embraced it, using what was left of Six-Finger's fishing line to hang the broken tooth around my neck. It was so long that it dangled down to my waist. I would let nothing come between me and my glorious find. Nothing.

I became so excited by the thought of my future that I rowed even faster toward port. A whole new life awaited me on the dawning. And then I rowed even harder, thinking about all the presents I would receive, the fine food I'd be served. They would be sorry that they cast me out, made me a dark elf. Yes, they would be sorry, because my name would be on the tongues of millions. I'd be the most envied elf that ever walked Krynn!

The sky was beginning to lighten. The dawn would be approaching soon. There, on the horizon, I could see a dark smudge that could only be land.

Faster and faster I rowed, my mind aflame with thoughts of greatness—until the sea around me suddenly began to churn and foam. The waves rose and fell, and the little boat was buffeted out of my control.

No! Please! Land was so close!

I lost one of my oars. It slipped from my hand and splashed into the heaving water near the side of the boat. I had to get to land. I needed that oar. I reached out over the side of the boat—and saw the Blood Sea Monster storm up out of the depths right in front of me.

"*Now*, it's your time!" I heard the same raspy voice whisper inside my head.

I looked up into its face—and was stunned to see my own face reflected there. The image changed so quickly. It was young, then old, then ravaged by time until only the bones and empty eye sockets remained. Yet it was me. Always me.

I wanted to argue, fight, run. But inside my head the voice said, "Some die old, content with their wisdom. Some die young with silly dreams in their heads. I come for them all."

I clutched at the tooth; it was supposed to change my life. And it did. I had leaned too far over the side, and when the boat rocked from the waves, the weight of the tooth around my neck sent me plummeting overboard.

It was then that I saw the bright, blinding light.

Now I see everything. And nothing.

---

# A Stone's Throw Away

## ROGER E. MOORE

*The* citadel of the Magus sprawled atop the bleakest peak in all of Krynn. A black thunderhead rose in the sky above it, raining lightning down on the barren slopes. The small traces of life and dust that clung to the rocks were buffeted by a cold and endless wind.

For three centuries, no living mortals traveled closer than sighting distance of the peak, their journeys and curiosity warned away by the boiling storm. Lords and kings turned their attention to other matters; great wizards investigated less dangerous secrets.

So it was when, upon finding an intruder within the castle, the citadel's master became at once confounded, enraged, and fascinated. He ordered his unliving servants to bring the intruder to his study for questioning, then retired there to await the arrival.

Catching the intruder was no mean feat, since he was quite skilled at evading pursuit. In due time, however, two of the manlike automatons which served the Magus entered the study, the intruder suspended between them by his arms.

The Magus looked carefully at the intruder, who

stopped kicking the moment he saw the Magus. The intruder was barely four feet in height and thinly built; he had bright brown eyes and the face of a ten-year-old human child. Narrow, pointed ears pressed against his light brown hair, which was pulled into a sort of ponytail on top of his head. The Magus recognized him as a kender, an annoying minor race that shared the world with him.

The Magus was accustomed to seeing terror on the faces of his captives. It disarmed him to see this one look upon him with open-mouthed surprise and lively curiosity. The captive then smiled like a boy caught with one hand in a pastry jar.

"Hey," said the intruder, "you must be one of those necro-guys—necromantics, thaumaturboes, whatcha-callums." He craned his neck and surveyed the study as if it were the living room of a friend. "Nice place you've got here."

Mildly annoyed, the Magus nodded. "I have not had visitors here for many years. Today, I find you here within my fortress. For the sake of courtesy, I will first ask your name before I demand an explanation of how you got in here."

The intruder struggled for a moment, but he accomplished nothing against the grip of his eight-foot-tall captors. With a sigh, he resigned himself to talking his way out.

"My name is Tasslehoff Burrfoot," he began brightly. He almost added, "My friends call me Tas," but decided not to bother. "Could your guards put me down? My arms hurt."

The Magus ignored his request. "Tasslehoff. An unfamiliar name, though I recognize Burrfoot as common among the kenderfolk. How did you get into this fortress?"

Tasslehoff smiled, all innocence, though he was sure

that his arms were getting bruised. "Oh, I dunno, I was wandering by and saw your place up here, so I thought I'd step in, see how you were doing—"

The Magus hissed as if he were a viper that had been stepped upon. Tasslehoff's voice faded away. "That's not going to work, is it?" Tasslehoff finished lamely.

"Wretch!" said the Magus savagely. His pale, skull-like face grew dead white with rage. "I am wasting time on you. Speak plainly!"

Though kender love to infuriate and tease, they can tell when they have pushed someone too far. "Yes, well," Tasslehoff began, "I don't know how I got in here. I mean, uh, I put this ring on"—he nodded toward his left hand, still held tightly by an automaton—"and I teleported in, but, um, I don't know why I did. It just, uh, happened."

A fragile silence reigned. The Magus stared at the kender speculatively. "That ring?" he said, gesturing toward the heavily engraved device with the enormous emerald that rested on the kender's third finger.

"Yes," Tasslehoff said, sighing. "I found it last week, and it looked interesting at the time; well, I put it on, and then I teleported." The kender grinned in mild embarrassment. "I can't seem to stop teleporting now."

For a moment Tasslehoff thought the Magus didn't believe him. "You put it on and appeared here. A ring that teleports the wearer." The Magus appeared to consider this possibility.

Tasslehoff shrugged. "Well, it's got its positive and negative aspec—"

"Take it off," said the Magus.

"Take it off?" Tasslehoff questioned weakly, his grin fading. "Uh, well, I'll try if your big friends will let go of me."

The Magus gestured, and the undead automatons released their grip on the kender's arms, dropping him to the floor. Getting up, the prisoner rubbed his muscles, sighed, then grasped the ring tightly. He pulled and tugged until his face turned red, but his actions had no effect.

"Let me try," said the Magus.

Instinctively, Tasslehoff hid his ringed hand. Though he didn't fear the Magus, he was not eager to have the Magus approach him, either.

The Magus spoke a few words, and the air was suddenly charged with power. A nimbus of light appeared around the Magus's right hand, which he held out in Tasslehoff's direction.

"Show the ring," said the Magus.

Tasslehoff reluctantly held up his hand, hoping the spell would not blast his arm off. With gentle confidence, the Magus reached out and touched the ring.

A blinding flash of green light filled the room, followed by a loud thump. Tasslehoff jerked his hand away in surprise, but he was uninjured. When his vision cleared, Tasslehoff watched as the Magus slowly crawled into an upright position on the other side of the room. The flash had tossed the Magus away like an old stick.

"Wow!" said the kender, his eyes widening. "The ring did that? I had no idea . . ."

A long hiss escaped the Magus's lips. Tasslehoff stopped speaking immediately. For perhaps a minute the Magus said nothing, then he dusted off his robes and looked at the automatons.

"Take him," the Magus whispered. His voice reminded Tasslehoff of the closing of a mausoleum door.

"Well," Tasslehoff said to himself, his voice echoing from the walls of his cell, "I guess I've been in worse predicaments."

Unfortunately, he couldn't think of any worse than

the one he was in now. He almost believed that the gods of Krynn were angry with him and that they were toying with his final punishment even now.

He racked his brain for some sin he may have committed, other than cursing or borrowing things without putting them back where he found them. Other people called it theft, but that term made him wince. It was handling, borrowing, not stealing. There was a difference, though the distinction was rather hazy to Tasslehoff and he'd never quite worked it out.

He rolled over and sat up. The automatons had cast him in the cell after leaving the Magus's chamber, and he had only a low-burning candle for light. Tangled spiderwebs hung from the ceiling. Listlessly, Tasslehoff tapped his hand against the floor, and the ring clicked out a lonely rhythm.

*I should've listened to Mother and gotten into the scribe business,* he mused, *but mapping and traveling were always more interesting than keeping account ledgers.* As a child, he had filled his room with dozens of maps and had memorized the names on each of them. This made it easy to invent unlikely tales about his travels, which always amused and entertained his friends.

Tasslehoff had often tried to make his own maps, but he had no head for the exacting patience it took to draw one accurately. Instead, he thought of himself as an explorer who didn't have to make accurate maps, relying on those who came after him to clear up such details as the direction in which north lay. Being there first, not drawing it up afterward, was what counted.

For years now, he'd walked the world and remembered many sights, great and small. On a high gray mountain, he had watched a golden chimera fight a bloody-tusked manticore to the death. The Qualinesti, the elven people of the high meadows, took him to witness the coronation of a prince of their wooded realms, dressing Tasslehoff in silver and silk of rare design. He'd spoken with wayfarers of a dozen nations and all polite races, and a few races not so polite.

Once in a while, Tasslehoff would run into an old adventuring friend from years ago, and they'd travel together. He'd sketch crude maps of his journeys to show his friends, elaborating on his adventures for effect, waiting for the listeners to smile. He loved storytelling over a map.

Mapmaking was not his only hobby, however. Occasionally, Tasslehoff would see something small and interesting within easy reach. When no one was looking, he'd borrow the item to admire it; oftentimes when he finished looking at it, the owner was gone. With a sigh, he'd drop the item in one of his many pockets and move on. He never meant to steal anything. Things just came out like that.

A week ago, Tasslehoff found the ring.

Tasslehoff scratched his nose in the dim light and remembered. He was in his home town, a farming community called Solace. He'd gotten up early to get hot pastries from a nearby bakery. While waiting for the shop to open, he heard two men having a shouting match in an alley.

Argument turned to scuffling, then came a hideous cry that made the kender jump. Three watchmen walking past immediately rushed toward the alley as the killer fled from it.

The thin-faced murderer was almost too hasty to escape. He stumbled on a loose rock and opened a clenched hand to catch himself. A glittering bauble fell from his palm and bounced beside Tasslehoff, who was hiding behind a wooden box by the bakery door. With a slight move, Tasslehoff covered the ring from view. The murderer hesitated, cursing the ring's loss, but continued fleeing upon seeing the watchmen advance his way. Within seconds, both pursued and pursuers were out of sight. Tasslehoff pocketed the ring with a careless flourish and went off to examine it.

It was very impressive, no doubt about that: solid gold, inlaid with small green emeralds, topped with a great faceted emerald that made Tasslehoff's head spin.

Undoubtedly, the ring was worth a fortune and could alone buy a small mansion or virtually anything Tasslehoff could imagine. Out of curiosity, he compared his left ring finger with the ring's diameter, then put the ring on to admire it.

It was then he discovered that the ring would not come off. He tugged, pulled, and used soap and water, all to no avail. A few minutes after he gave up a last attempt to remove it, the ring flashed, saturating the kender's vision with velvety green light. At the same moment, it teleported him into the ocean, which was supposed to be hundreds of miles away.

The change was so sudden that he almost drowned before he had the presence of mind to paddle to keep himself afloat. He struggled, growing wearier with each passing minute. Then a tall wave slapped him and he choked, and the ring flashed green again and teleported him away—into a woodland full of scratchy briars.

This process continued for days. Every few hours the ring would send him off to a new place he'd never seen before. If danger threatened, the ring would jerk him out of it and carry him elsewhere. He knew that the ring was cursed and uncontrollable and that he'd better find a way to stop the teleporting before he was dropped into a volcano. At least, he was learning to swim quickly enough.

It didn't take long before he noticed the distance between hops was decreasing; eventually, he was teleporting only a mile or so at a time, though more frequently. By making a mental note of landmarks, he also judged that he was moving in a straight line; and this heartened him: the ring was taking him somewhere. An adventure, indeed!

This pleasant feeling was lost completely when the giant thunderhead came into view over the horizon. Below it, illuminated by flickering lightning, was a vast and barren mountain capped by a black stone citadel. He was heading straight for it.

Tasslehoff said a word he'd once heard an angry barbarian use. He liked adventures, but there were limits. As if piqued by his comment, a second later the ring teleported him to within a mile of the mountain itself.

Kender know no fear, but they know a bad thing when they see it. Judging the thunderstorm, mountain, and citadel to be such bad things, Tasslehoff scrambled over rocks and debris in a mad attempt to flee. The ring flashed again, and he reappeared within fifty feet of the pitiless walls of the castle.

"No, no! Stop!" he yelled as he tried to bash the ring with a fist-sized stone. "Whoa! Let's go back to the ocean! I don't wanna g—"

A green flash in his cell cut the kender off in midthought. A spider eyeing Tasslehoff from the safety of the cell's darkened ceiling coiled its legs in surprise. It was now the cell's only occupant.

At first Tasslehoff thought he had teleported into a cave. The flash blinded him as usual, and when the effects wore off, he was still unable to see a thing in the darkness. By feeling about with his hands, he could tell he was in a narrow, square tunnel only three feet high. He crawled slowly in a random direction, testing the floor for traps or deep pits (of which there seemed to be none). Soon he saw a faint light ahead and quickly made for it.

A small, barred opening resembling a window was set in the wall to his right; carefully, he peered through it. Beyond the opening was a vast carved chamber, perhaps a hundred feet across and half as high as it was wide. The window was set two-thirds of the way up from the floor. Logic told Tasslehoff that he was in some sort of ventilation shaft; he had noticed a gentle air current while crawling along but had paid it no heed.

Within the chamber, light flickered from dozens of firepots laid out in a broad circular pattern on the floor. As he stared at the pattern, Tasslehoff realized it was a conjuration circle, such as wizards used to call up spirits from the invisible worlds. Faint traceries of colored chalk faded into the shifting darkness around the motionless flames below.

With a start, Tasslehoff saw that the room was occupied. Far below, striding quietly to the edge of the circle of firepots, was a dark-robed figure. It took but a moment for Tasslehoff to realize that it was the Magus. He briefly considered hiding, but his curiosity got the better of him, so he pressed closer to the bars.

The Magus stopped ten feet from the edge of the circle, within a smaller chalk-drawn circle beside it. For a time he appeared to contemplate the flames before him. Ruddy light played over his drawn face, white like a ghost's; his dark eyes drank in light, reflecting none.

Slowly, the Magus raised his arms and called out to the circle of fire in a language the kender had never before heard spoken. At first the flames crackled and jumped; but as the Magus continued speaking, the fires dimmed and lowered until they were almost invisible. The air grew colder, and Tasslehoff shivered, rubbing his arms for warmth.

Tasslehoff's attention was suddenly drawn to the center of the conjuring circle. Red streaks appeared in crisscross patterns on the floor, within the design of the firepots, as if the floor were breaking apart over red lava. A dull haze clouded the chamber, and the firepots burned more brightly. A strange roaring like a great ocean wave coming in to the shore filled the room by degrees, growing to a thunder that made the very rock tremble. Tasslehoff gripped the bars before him, wondering if an earthquake had been conjured by the sorcerer's powers.

Far below, the Magus called out three words. After each word, light and flame burst from the center of the conjuring circle. Each flash stung the kender's eyes, but he could not look away from the sight. Yellow magma glowed with superheated radiance within the circle, dimming the light from the firepots around it. A wave of heat reddened Tasslehoff's face and arms where the furs he wore did not cover him. The Magus did not seem affected by the heat at all.

One last time the dark figure called out, speaking a single name. Tasslehoff thought his heart would stop when he heard and recognized it. The thundering roar vanished instantly, and an eerie silence filled the air for the space of six heartbeats.

With a screaming whistle, the lava in the circle vanished entirely and was replaced by darkness streaked with an eye-burning violet light, resembling an impossible opening into the night sky. Tasslehoff was straining to see into the pit when a thing of titanic size arose from it, out of the night-pit and into the room.

Tasslehoff had heard rumors about the thing that

stood before him, but he had never truly believed them until now. The thing towered over the Magus, three times the height of a man. Two great tentacles dangled from its shoulders in place of normal arms, and two heads maned with black fur rested where one head should be. Scales glittered over its skin, and in the light of the firepots the kender saw its feet were clawed like those of a bird of prey. Slime and oil fell from it, the droplets smoking when they struck the stony floor.

The heads gazed down upon the Magus. Inhuman mouths spoke, their rasping voices out of time with one another by a fraction of a moment.

"Again," the voices said, "you call me from the Abyss to defile my presence with your own. You summon my divine person to fulfill your petty desires, and you tempt my everlasting wrath. Sorely, I wish to have vengeance on this world for giving you birth, you who toy with the Prince of Demons like a slave. I thirst for your soul like a dying man for water."

"I did not summon you to hear your problems," responded the Magus in a cracked, thin voice. "Bound you are to me, bound by the circle. You shall hear me out."

With screams that made Tasslehoff jerk from the bars and cover his ears, the thing's heads shot down at the Magus—and were thrown back by unseen forces that sparked and flashed like lightning. The thing's tentacles writhed and flailed the air like titans' whips.

"*AAAIIIEEE!!!* Wretch! To speak to me so! Ten thousand times you are cursed should these bonds fade! Ten thousand times will I break you in my coils, until your dark soul rots!" For several minutes the demon roared out its rage. The Magus stood before it, unmoved and silent.

In time the thing ceased to cry out. Its breathing became a slow, ragged thunder.

"Speak," said the heads venomously.

"There is an adventurer in my fortress," said the Magus, "who wears a green-stoned ring. The ring will not leave his hand and defies magical attempts to remove it. It teleported the adventurer into my citadel when it was not his intention to do so. What ring is this? How do I remove it? What are its powers?"

The thing twisted its necks. "You summon me to identify a *ring*?"

"Indeed," said the Magus, and waited.

The twin heads dipped closer to the Magus. "Describe the largest stone."

"An emerald the size of my thumb, rectangular cut with six tiers and no flaws. The face is engraved with a hexagonal sign, with a smaller hexagon set within and another in that one."

Silence filled the darkened room; even the thing's writhing arms were stilled. After a pause, the thing stood upright. Its heads turned about independently of each other. Tasslehoff shrank back against the opposite wall of the tunnel as a head turned his way.

The head stopped when it looked into the barred window of the airshaft. Red fires arose in its eyes and ran through Tasslehoff like spears.

Tasslehoff Burrfoot had never known fear, though he had seen sights that made hardened men shake with terror. When the eyes of the thing were upon him, he shook without breathing, his soul filled with a new emotion.

Something like a smile ran over the lips of the thing's face. The head turned slowly away.

"Magus," said the thing, "concern yourself not with the ring. Turn your pleasure to other matters. You probe the reaches of unseen planes and manipulate the destiny of worlds. Neither the ring nor its wearer will be your concern past the setting of the sun this day."

There was a long silence during which neither monster nor summoner moved.

"That is not the answer I asked of you," said the Magus.

For a time, there was no response from the thing. Then its heads chuckled heavily, and the sound rolled across the room.

"I have spoken," it said, then vanished into the circle of violet light and darkness as if it had been a shadow.

The Magus stood before the circle long afterward, head bowed in thought. Just as it occurred to Tasslehoff that he would have to breathe or explode, the Magus turned and walked to a hidden door that closed quickly behind him.

Tasslehoff, bathed in sweat, leaned against the wall. If the Magus caught him now, he would die. He looked down at the emerald ring and wondered how long he would be able to hide before the Magus found him at last.

Twenty minutes later Tasslehoff arrived at another barred window, this one looking into a musty library lit by candles on a tabletop. Struggling and gasping, the kender squeezed through the bars and dropped onto a bookshelf, climbing down to the floor from there.

He wiped gray dust from his hands and looked around. Shadows flicked against the stone walls. Towering shelves filled with browned volumes bound in exotic leathers and sealed with glyphs surrounded him. As he looked at the tomes, his curiosity got the best of him again.

He cautiously pulled a large volume from a stack on the table before him. A glance at the cover confirmed that the writing was unreadable and probably magical in nature. He opened the book, and ancient pages rustled and fell open in the candlelight.

Tasslehoff flipped the book shut with a gasp. Hesitantly, he reached for another, hoping it was less loathsomely illustrated. To his relief, the next book was written in the common tongue of the land and had no pictures at all.

*"Being a Compendium of Mystic Protections and Sorcerous Inscriptions for the Summoning of Creatures from the Dark Worlds,"* he read aloud. The book appeared to be well used. A thought occurred to him, and he flipped through the volume, his eyes running over the pages in search of the name of the thing he had seen. At the end of the text was a list of creatures one could summon, and the thing's name was among them.

Silently, he read the passage under the list of names, absorbing every word of it. His hand grew cold and damp at the implications of the text. Finished, he closed the book and returned it to the stack with care, arranging the other volumes to disguise his prying.

"Well," he said aloud, wiping his hands. Some of his confidence was returning, though strained by the circumstances. "Summoning is more dangerous than I thought. If the wizard messes up, boof! Off he goes, taken away forever. Demons don't forgive . . ."

His eyes glazed slightly as he thought about some variations on this possibility. Mentally, he crossed off the occupation of sorcerer from those he wished to learn more about. This was better left to people like—

He heard a door, hidden by racks of books, open. Tasslehoff dropped to all fours and crawled under the table.

The floor creaked. Thick robes rustled and fell silent. There was no sound for what seemed like ages of time.

"Tasslehoff," said a wavering voice.

There was no reply.

"You poor wretched puppy, you cannot escape me." The door creaked and thumped shut. "You watched in the Room of Conjurations when I spoke with the demon lord. I knew you were there. Come out now. No use hiding, Tasslehoff."

Robes swished softly and slowly behind a bookcase. His eyes sparkling, Tasslehoff pressed against a table leg.

"You're behind the bookcase, under the table." The wavering voice hardened. "Come out."

A long shadow, stepping from behind the shelves, appeared against a far wall.

"Tasslehoff." The Magus raised his hand and pointed a finger.

Green light burst across the room. Tasslehoff fell back on the floor as the room blinked out and a new one flashed in.

Now he was in the Room of Conjurations. He ran for a corner and tried to climb the wall. Falling back, he ran for the doorway he hoped would be an exit.

The Magus stepped through that very doorway into the chamber. Tasslehoff stopped dead, crouched and ready to jump in any direction.

"Pleased you could join me," said the Magus.

"I must confess," the Magus said, "that I don't understand why the ring you're wearing teleports you about as it does. You're at its mercy, yet it pulls you out of my reach and keeps you safe. It's kept you alive for days and days, bringing you to this castle to me. I don't understand it, and I know I don't like it."

Tasslehoff watched his opponent like a hawk. "I'm not dancing about it either," he said. "I'd rather be home in a tavern."

---

"I don't doubt that," the Magus retorted, walking slowly around the kender. The sorcerer scratched at his cheek with a bony finger. "Circumstances, however, dictate otherwise. I want to finish this now, before the sun sets. You're the first person ever to invade my castle. You deserve a special fate."

"You wouldn't want to be friends and let me go home, would you?" Tasslehoff asked faintly.

The Magus smiled, the skin pulling across his face like dry paper. "No," he said.

Tasslehoff darted for the open door. The Magus gestured, and Tasslehoff slammed into the door as it flew shut. Stunned, he found his nose wasn't broken, though his eyes streamed tears.

Light arose behind him. Tasslehoff turned and saw that the firepots of the conjuring circle were burning. A dark figure with arms stood before the circle, chanting in a low voice.

Tasslehoff felt in his pockets for some last trick, something to pull him out of danger. He found six feet of string, a silver piece with a hole in it, a sugar bun, a crystal button, someone else's tinderbox, a bluejay feather, and a river pebble two inches across. No miracles . . .

He beat and kicked the door until he ached. Thunder rattled his teeth; waves of cold and heat washed over him.

When he heard the Magus call the name of the thing, he gave up. Setting his back to the door, he turned to face the spectacle. If he couldn't escape, he could at least go out like an explorer. He would have lived longer as a scribe, but this was better in a way. Scribes lived such boring lives. That thought comforted him as the scaled shape of the thing arose from the pit of violet lightning and darkness.

The thing's eyes glowed, one head fixed on Tasslehoff and the other on the Magus. "Twice in one day, Magus?" questioned the thing, hissing. "You have company as well. Am I now a circus exhibit?"

"Hear me!" the sorcerer shouted. "There stands an offering to you, a soul you may eat at your leisure! I bind you with words and enchantments of power, under threat of eternal torture and debasement, to take this kender to the Abyss with you until time is no more! Take him away!"

Tasslehoff's mind went blank. His fist, thrust into a pocket, clenched the stone that he had collected some time ago and admired ever since because of its smoothness. In an instant he snatched the stone out of his pocket and threw it.

The Magus gasped and staggered as the stone smacked the back of his skull. Stumbling, his hands clutching his head, he stepped forward. A slippered foot scuffed over the pale chalky lines that surrounded him.

The glowing runes and tracings on the floor went dark like a candle snuffed out. Silently and easily, an oily tentacle reached for the Magus and caught his foot. The Magus screamed.

"Thousands of years ago," said the thing, its voices trembling with peculiar emotion, "it occurred to me that I would need a defense against those who abused my status as Prince of Demons, those who would use me as a footstool on which to rest their pride. Someday, something would be needed to turn the odds in my favor should this ever happen."

The thing's tentacle lifted the Magus high in the air, turning him around slowly as a man would a mouse caught by the tail. "I devised many such defenses, but the one of which I am most proud now is the ring you wear, kender."

Tasslehoff glanced at the ring. The emerald was

ROGER E. MOORE

glowing faintly.

"The ring," the thing continued, "only activates when I need its services. It defends the wearer against death, though it may not make the wearer comfortable. By leaps and bounds it teleports him to my vicinity. It prevents all attempts to remove it until the wearer performs a boon for me, accomplishing what I most desire. You were my tool unknowing, but most serviceable."

Tasslehoff looked at the thing, his mouth dry with the realization of what he'd done.

"Take off the ring," the thing's voices rasped, "and you will be teleported back to your home. I have no more need of you."

Tasslehoff carefully pulled the ring free from his left hand. As it left his finger, it flashed a brilliant, fiery green and dropped to the floor. And in that same instant, Tasslehoff was gone.

The heads of the thing roared with laughter. The Magus screamed, and screamed, and . . .

Tasslehoff finished his drink and pushed it away. Across the tavern table, two old friends, a man and woman, blinked as the thread of the tale snapped and drifted away.

"That," said Kitiara with a shake of her head, "was the most incredible story I've ever heard out of you, Tasslehoff." A grin slowly appeared on her face. "You've not lost your touch."

The kender sniffed, disappointment showing on his face. "I didn't think you'd believe me."

"That was supposed to be true?" Sturm asked, staring at Tasslehoff. His eyes were bright with amusement. "You actually mean to say you met a demon prince, helped destroy a wizard, found and lost a magic ring, and crossed half a world?"

The kender nodded, a playful grin reflected on his face.

For a few seconds, the listeners made no response. The man and woman looked at each other and then at the kender.

"Merciful gods, Tasslehoff," the woman breathed, pushing her chair back. "You could make a goblin believe rocks were valuable." She rose to her feet, tossed a few coins on the tabletop, and waved at kender and warrior. "I think I'll go on to bed with that one."

Sturm groaned in mild embarrassment. Granted, the kender's tale was fantastic, but there was no need to rub his nose in it. He turned back to Tasslehoff with a self-conscious grin, meaning to apologize, and stopped.

Tasslehoff was looking after Kitiara with a strange, wistful gaze. His left hand rested on the tabletop beside the half-melted candle. A pale band was visible around his ring finger, wider than most rings would leave. The skin on either side of the band was scarred and discolored, as if someone had tried to remove a ring once worn there.

Tasslehoff turned to Sturm, missing his gaze, and shrugged. "Well," he said, "maybe it wasn't much of a tale at that. It's about time to turn in, after all." He smiled and pushed his chair back. "See you tomorrow."

Sturm half-waved his hand. The kender left him alone in the inn with his thoughts.

# Dreams of Darkness, Dreams of Light

## Warren B. Smith

William Sweetwater was a short man—five-foot-three, one hundred and eighty pounds, pig-faced, snout-nosed—and he was lost in a universe of nightmares. Eons ago, or so it seemed, the neutral gray mist surrounded his body and drew him into the void. Groping, stumbling, frightened of each step, he wandered through the mysterious fog.

Screams roared through the vapors. Harsh, intermittent, guttural shouts blared out. He heard constant whispers in the mist, low murmurings that were sly, insinuating, often obscene. At other times the mist echoed with the howl of banshees, followed by the grisly noise of feral animals feeding on some bony substance.

An intuitive impulse caused William to stop and assess the nature of his situation. He shivered in the swirling fog and tried to get a sense of direction.

Gradually, he discovered he was standing at the edge of a large, seething pit. He stiffened like a carven stone idol, afraid to move. The mist parted, and his gaze focused on a frothing mass of black slime.

The thick fluid was in a stage of fermentation.

Dark, reptilian forms bubbled to the surface. Their evil, grotesque shapes blocked his vision. They remained in his view for a short time, then vanished as other forms rose to the surface.

The putrifying mixture seemed to engulf the universe. Entrails of odorous steam boiled up from the surface. Images of angry faces were reflected off the sides of giant bubbles. They were dark, resentful faces with eyes glittering with hatred.

A panorama of scenes and sounds assaulted his senses. Here, a disembodied leg stomped endlessly on a bloody face. There, a man in a military uniform snatched an infant from a lace-trimmed crib. The soldier slammed the baby against a stone wall. A band of ghouls rose out of the slime and performed a macabre dance on the black surface. They sank back into the percolating liquid as a fanged lizard wrapped itself around a screaming maiden. An obscene altar flashed into view. A young man and a woman were tied spread-eagled on a filth-strewn slab of stone. A dog-faced priest with minotaur horns raised a dagger to pierce their hearts.

". . . JUMP!"

". . . You belong here! You're like us!" This voice was low, feminine, almost a motherly whisper.

". . . JUMP! JUMP!"

". . . Everyone does it! You're no different," rasped a deep, resonant voice.

". . . JUMP! JUMP! JUMP!"

". . . Roll us over in the slime," sang a guttural chorus.

He wavered.

A part of his being, some ancient reptilian gene, urged him to leap into the abyss and wallow in the slime. As part of the odorous mass, he could act out any evil impulse. He could torture and kill without remorse . . . if only he would accept the pit as his home. The voices knew of his secret hatreds and lusts, knew that William Sweetwater sometimes dreamed of dark deeds.

With the last remnant of his will power, William teetered on the edge of the abyss. He fought the dark urge.

Then, all of a sudden, the rolling mass stopped bubbling. The fermenting halted, images vanished. The voices went silent as the surface of the putrid slime lay still, unmoving.

Out of the pit rose a comely young maiden with platinum blonde tresses and (and this is the strangest thing, William thought) a hideous serpentine monster straining at the end of a chain leash.

The huge monster towered high above the mist and slime, writhing and coiling. William cringed as the reptile's head parted and became five separate entities twisting above the demented maw.

"Oh, pay no attention to that confounded show-off," huffed the maiden in a surprisingly baritone voice. She gave the leash a violent tug and the hideous creature was jerked, choking and sputtering, into an attentive pose.

At least the maiden appeared to be young—and beautiful to gaze upon. But William thought he heard the sound of creaking joints, a sort of arthritic crackle, and there was a frostiness in her smile that made him shudder.

"Your name?"

"William Sweetwater."

She seemed to be perched on a giant mottled toadstool with an ink bottle, quill pen, and sheet of parchment at the ready. She wore a black robe. Two black velvet slippers poked from beneath her garment. A battered wooden staff rested at her side. The hideous serpent creature was trying its hardest to peek over her shoulder as she furiously began to scribble, but she took malicious delight in fidgeting this way and that in order to block its view.

"Race?"

"Human."

The maiden frowned and wrote a strange symbol on the parchment.

"Age?

"Thirty-eight."

"Where were you born?"

"Port Balifor."

The comely maiden hissed a smile. "Ah, one of my favorite areas. Your people have been kind-hearted since the beginning of Krynn. Now, William, do you have any living relatives?"

"No. My mother died when I was a baby."

"And your father?"

"He was a sailor whose ship was lost. That happened when I was eighteen. There were bad storms that year."

"Tragic," said the maiden, though she was still smiling. "Now, William, have you lived a life of grace?"

"What does that mean?"

"Have you worshipped the true gods in a faithful manner?"

William shook his head, negatively. "I've not given much thought to worshipping gods."

The maiden frowned. "Do you have courage?"

"I'm a coward," answered William truthfully. "I dream about doing something brave, but I never do it."

"Follow your instincts in matters of courage," said the maiden in a waspish tone. "Now, are you committed to anyone?"

"What does that mean?"

----

The maiden raised an eyebrow. "You know . . . do you fiddle-faddle around with any females?"

"Women like their men to be handsome. I have a face that only a mother could love." William's hand moved across his porcine features. "Folks say a pig overturned my crib when I was a baby. My face was supposed to have been marked by the experience."

One of the serpent heads left the reptilian cluster and glided forward to inspect William's snouted face. Hard, reptilian eyes examined his features as a long forked tongue darted in and out of the salivating mouth. The mouth of the snake—if indeed, it was a snake—opened wide, exposing two ghastly fangs. Abruptly, the creature began to guffaw, horridly, a foul unearthly noise that shook William's fast-beating heart and prompted him to draw back in horror.

The comely maiden jerked the chain leash, and the serpent monster retreated to its position, hovering silently, for the moment, behind her.

But she too leaned forward and gazed with more intensity upon William. Her breath is not felicitous, thought William. Her eyes grew bold and harsh and glitteringly metallic-like. Reflected in them was a pathetic, shrinking William and the deepening fog and mist.

In general she stinks, thought William, as the maiden drew closer. Perhaps she ought to consider bathing or perfuming.

The maiden had set down the quill pen and now her fingers were closing around her staff. As she spoke again, William remembered thinking how suddenly her face had become distorted and grotesque, how loud and grating her voice had become, like . . . like metal scraping against the sea bottom.

"So, my dear Pig William," she remarked, edging forward, "in other words, you have no relatives, no mate, and nobody fool enough to grieve for you when you are . . . GONE!"

Her voice broke into harsh, strangled laughter which rose in deafening volume. The monstrous five-headed serpent, thrashing at its leash, dove to within an arm's-length of William's face. All five death-heads bared their fangs and slithered closer. William could smell the decay, the venom, the evil. The laughter of the maiden had become hysterical, gibberish, smothering rage. Waves of chillbumps cascaded over poor William's shivering body.

William inched backward toward sanctuary, choking, gasping, sobbing for deliverance.

Encircling him was the mist and the dreadful black pit. Moving with him, glowing in the darkness, were the serpent's five heads. The maiden's screaming was so painful he had to put his hands over his ears.

*The chain leash snapped.*

A hard, tightening force fastened onto his shoulder. A scream started deep down in his throat.


"William, wake up!" The voice was loud, guttural.

Snorting in terror, William Sweetwater opened his eyes and stared up into the face of his friend, Sintk the Dwarf. William made an oinking sound, wrenching himself out of slumber into a moment of confusion before becoming oriented to reality.

William was sitting on a stool behind the polished bar of the Pig and Whistle. Sintk the Dwarf leaned across the bar, his hand firmly gripping and shaking William's shoulder. The dwarf was a muscular man, big in the shoulders, with a blunt, tanned, half-smiling face. His light gray eyes reflected good humor. His thick brown hair had begun to thin on the top. The dwarf and William had known each other since childhood; they shared a love of good conversation and

---

74

good ale.

"You must've been napping," said Sintk, who was the cobbler in Port Balifor. "I came in and heard you snorting like a—" The dwarf paused for dramatic effect "—boar being led to slaughter."

William blinked at the familiar surroundings of his beloved Pig and Whistle. The tavern was a long, wide room with a long mahogany bar and heavy wooden stools. Numerous tables and chairs were in the back of the room overlooking a small stage.

Everything in the Pig and Whistle was in a neat, carefully maintained condition. Woodwork was oiled and polished, the brasswork shiny and free of tarnish. The walls and floors were clean. The neatness of the room was an indication of William's respect and love for his inn.

Except for Sintk and a couple of strangers at a far table, the bar was deserted. Port Balifor had been an occupied town for several months—overrun by armies of the Highlords, whose ships had sailed into the bay and disgorged the hideous draconians and hobgoblins.

The people of Port Balifor, who were mostly human and, like William Sweetwater, mostly meek and cowardly, felt sorry for themselves. The occupation had come without warning. Because of their geographical isolation, most of the citizens had little knowledge of the outside world. They would have counted their blessings if they knew what was happening in other parts of Ansalon.

Not that the Dragon Highlords were particularly interested in this easternmost territory. The land was sparsely populated: a few poor scattered communities of humans like Port Balifor and Kendermore, homeland of the kender. A flight of dragons could have leveled the countryside, but the Dragon Highlords were concentrating their strength elsewhere. And as long as ports such as Balifor remained open, the Highlords had use for the region.

Though business had improved at the Pig and Whistle with the arrival of the troops, the presence of the motley soldiers had caused many of William's old customers to stay away. The draconians and hobgoblins were well-paid, and strong drink was one of their weaknesses. But William had opened the Pig and Whistle to enjoy the companionship of his friends and neighbors. He disliked the repulsive draconian soldiers who snarled and fought like animals once the alcohol had dulled their tiny brains. The hobgoblins were equally obnoxious customers. They were self-centered and arrogant, trying to wheedle free drinks for themselves and their cohorts.

So William had promptly raised the price of his drinks. The Pig and Whistle was three times more expensive than any other inn in Port Balifor. He also watered the ale. As a result, his bar was mostly deserted except for his old friends and the odd traveler, and, once again, William enjoyed being an innkeeper.

Sintk waved a hand in front of William's piggy face. "Are you dozing off again?" he asked. "William, I realize sleep is a good way of forgetting about draconians and those nasty hobgoblins. But, sad it is, a person wakes up and those sculpin are still prowling about town, snooping in everyone's business and acting like they belong here. Which, as a matter of fact, they don't, and I would be the first to say so, if I were so bold. Now, do you feel like yourself, or should I run to the herbalist's shop for a potion?"

William shook his head vigorously to expel the listlessness in his mind. "I'm fine."

"What happened?" The dwarf looked suspicious.

"Business was slow. I fell asleep."

"You must have been daydreaming," the dwarf said. "You were sleeping when I came in for my afternoon pint. You were heaving and snorting like a man possessed by demons."

"I have seen demons and all sorts of things." William opened his hand. A large oval coin was lying in his palm. The polished metal disc glistened in the light. "Remember that coin the Red Wizard used for his tricks?"

"Raistlin?" Sintk looked surprised. "I trust that faker and his gang of misfits aren't back in town. And I hope you're not going to start up with that magic coin business again. . . ."

"But there *is* something magical about it," William insisted. "I traveled from here and had a . . . a . . . strange encounter with a beautiful maiden and a fearsome beast. I journeyed through a mysterious fog and almost fell into a black pit containing demons, snakes, ghouls, and all sorts of bad things."

"Things get confused when you are daydreaming," said Sintk. "But being you're yourself again and not grunting like a boar, I'll have a nice tankard of your finest brew."

"It wasn't a dream," William said sulkily. "It felt more like it was reality and this . . . this . . . is only the shadow of what my life could be."

William drew two tankards of ale and set them across from his friend, Sintk. Then he launched into a detailed account of his daydream—er, vision—while Sintk, parched with thirst, diligently quaffed both tankards. But it was William's story, which was vaguely familiar, that had Sintk yawning presently, not the ale, which was delicious.

"Oh," Sintk rubbed his lips with the back of his hand at a pause in the recounting, "what's that about a black pit?"

---

"The abyss at the end of the universe," replied William.

"Oh, *that* black pit," said the dwarf. "I should have known." He gazed fondly at the row of tankards behind the bar and licked his lips. "You're barmy."

Sighing, William got up from his stool and drew two more tankards of ale.

"I wasn't daydreaming," he declared, setting the drinks on the bar. "Look, touch the coin. It became hot in my hand. Like it was pulsating with life." He held out the large round coin—which truth to tell, looked quite ordinary, resting there in his palm.

"Body heat," said Sintk, wearily. "The coin is nothing. A piece of cast metal."

"Magic!" insisted William.

"Is not," said Sintk.

"Is!" said William, most uncharacteristically raising his voice.

"Why don't you let me be the judge?" said a surly voice behind them.

William and Sintk whirled to see the fiendish countenance of a barrel-chested draconian in smelly armor. It was Drago, captain of the prison guards, who, despised and friendless even among his fellow draconians, took an occasional meal and tankard alone in the Pig and Whistle. The fact that his presence was so repugnant to William Sweetwater and his friends made it all the more pleasurable to Drago.

William remembered too late to close his fist around the magic coin, for it was suddenly gone. Drago held it aloft in his scaly paw, leering. "A magic coin, is it?" he barked to nobody in particular, for there were only a couple of other customers and they were studiously avoiding his gaze. "It looks like a beggar's token to me," he said. Drago bit down on the coin with his yellow, mucousy teeth.

---

Pale with shame, William was staring at his shoes.

"That's right," said Sintk weakly. "It's just a common, worthless . . . " His voice trailed off. His eyes, too, were lowered.

Drago was rubbing the coin against one of his grease-stained sleeves. "I wish . . . I wish . . . " he uttered grandly, "I wish I had a one-year vacation from stinking Port Balifor, and two wives to shine my boots, and . . . and . . . a mountain of gold coins to last a lifetime of ale and mutton."

Everybody in the Pig and Whistle looked up just a little bit, hoping maybe the coin truly was magic. Drago might have his wishes granted, and disappear.

"Bah!" snorted Drago. He reached across the bar and grabbed William by the collar, squeezing until the innkeeper turned pink.

"It was given to him by Raistlin the mage!" blurted Sintk.

Drago squeezed harder.

"He was a faker," gulped William, gasping for breath. "But I am worse. A *fool*. I took the coin as payment in kind, because I believed him when he told me it was magic, but it is . . . nought. You may . . ." He stared directly into Drago's blazing eyes. "You may have it, my friend."

"Bah!" said Drago, and let William go. With a flick of his hand, he sent the coin spinning across the bar. Around and around it spun, sending off glints of light. William grabbed for it and clasped it dearly, feeling its warmth. But Drago had already turned away and settled his bulk at a table.

"Bring me ale and the usual rotten stew!" shouted Drago, without a backward glance. "And be quick about it, Pig-face!"

William bustled about fulfilling Drago's edict, while Sintk unhappily drained two more tankards.

———

*

Later, as the sun was setting, William locked up the Pig and Whistle. It was not unusual for the innkeeper to close early these days. Few honest wayfarers visited Port Balifor. The ominous presence of the Highlords' troops made everyone uneasy.

Besides, William liked to spend the sunset hour walking with Sintk along the harbor. The stroll was the highlight of his day. This particular evening was warm. The sky was cloudless and a light breeze blew in from the bay. The dimming light had that peculiar quality found only in twilight time along the seacoast.

As William and Sintk walked along a street that led to the harbor, they were surprised to see a large sailing vessel tied up at the pier. They stood in the center of the street, looking down toward the wharf, as draconian troops crowded the deck of the unfamiliar ship.

"A supply ship?" asked Sintk.

William shook his head. "Their regular ship was here last week. This must be the patrol boat I heard about. The Highlords are upset because so many citizens are deserting the town and fleeing to the hills."

Draconian crewmen were moving swiftly across the deck of the ship. Then, a door opened and several humans were shoved out of a cabin. The prisoners were linked together with leg chains. Their hands were manacled. They huddled together as the troops pushed them toward the gangplank, which was lowered to the wharf. Several heavily armed draconian guards under the command of a hobgoblin officer waited on the wharf.

Sintk whispered, "Look, the old man in the back. That's Thomas the tailor. Why would Old Tom be in chains? He's a good tailor who wouldn't harm a bug."

Clawed feet on cobblestones sounded behind the two friends. William looked back and saw a group of draconians marching down the street. William and Sintk kept their eyes to the ground. They walked to the front of the Missionary's Downfall, a waterfront bar with a garish facade, where they sat down on a weathered bench in front of the establishment. The tavern was the most notorious dive in eastern Ansalon, not a respectable place like the Pig and Whistle.

They watched as the prisoners shuffled down the gangplank. Faces bruised, shoulders slumped, the manacled men and women moved with a listless step. They were ordered about by a muscular draconian, who carried a short, metal-tipped whip.

Their thoughts were interrupted by a loud creaking noise behind them. A moment later, Harum El-Halup stepped out of the Missionary's Downfall. The minotaur was owner of the tavern, a rugged individual with a bestial face, a massive chest, thick arms and legs.

A fugitive from a sentence of death in his minotaur homeland, Harum El-Halop had found sanctuary in Port Balifor. He had quick wits, fighting ability, and the nerve of someone with nothing to lose. He had quickly gained a reputation as the toughest fighter on the brawling waterfront.

A high-stakes gambler, the minotaur had won the Missionary's Downfall in a card game with the previous owner. Nowadays the tavern was patronized by thieves, cut-throats, and troops from the dragonarmy. It was also the favorite drinking spot for off-duty hobgoblins, who stole supplies from the quartermaster and exchanged the contraband for drinks.

"Why is Thomas being held prisoner?" William asked the minotaur, who stood there, observing the scene with them.

"I told them the plan wouldn't work," sneered Harum. His bestial face looked horrible in the shadowed light. "Thomas and the others wanted to escape by sea. They paid a hobgoblin to steal a boat for them to use at dawn. But hobgoblins are informers, and this one was a low-life who plays everyone off the dragon-army. As soon as the boat was launched, the hobgoblin made his report to the draconians."

William protested. "But Thomas is an honest man. He is no thief."

"He was on the boat," said the minotaur. "Likely he'll end up in the dungeons with the others. The dragonarmy can't allow people to come and go as they please, without permission. Bad for their reputation. Old Tom knew that." The minotaur made a clucking sound with his tongue. "Thomas will be lucky to last a month in that slime pit under the castle."

William shuddered. He had heard tales of the torture of prisoners in the dungeon. Knowing Drago's cruelty as he did, he didn't find the tales hard to believe. Poor Tom. He had always been a good friend to everyone in Port Balifor.

Sintk asked in a forlorn tone, "What can we do?"

"Meat for the dungeon," replied Harum. "Stay out of it."

William looked down, ashamed. If only he had the courage . . . if only he had some idea of how to fight back . . . if only . . .

"Now, William," said Harum, "what the people of Balifor need is a leader. Someone to lead a rebellion against these creatures. You're liked and respected. People will do what you ask of them."

Harum's ugly face took on a quizzical look, and William had the idea he was burrowing into his private thoughts. Or was he teasing him?

"Why don't *you* do it?" William asked the minotaur, thinking, if he were as big and strong as Harum, certainly he'd have little hesitation.

"Oh, I am not a native of Port Balifor," Harum replied nonchalantly, "and I am not sure I care so very much. And people know I serve thieves and scoundrels at the Missionary's Downfall, so they would suspect my motivation. Also, I am a fugitive from my own kind, and people don't follow leaders with such flaws. But they would stand behind someone like you, someone responsible and upstanding. You would have their trust."

"I couldn't do it." William felt weak. He didn't want to look at the minotaur. Instead, he turned his gaze back to the harbor.

The prisoners were being marched off the wharf by the troops and the hobgoblin officer. The last prisoner in the coffle was the tailor, a gray-haired, elderly man with a wrinkled face. His eyes were dull with fatigue. Thin and tall, about six feet in height, the tailor had stooped shoulders from years of leaning over his needles.

The guards may have been careless, for the leg irons around Old Tom's ankles were loose.

Suddenly, without attracting attention, the tailor stepped out of the leg irons and bolted from the shuffling line of prisoners. His escape would have been successful, if he had not stumbled over a rope and fallen to his knees.

"Seize him!" cried the hobgoblin officer.

Now, Tom the tailor was up and running across the weathered boards of the wharf, heading for the street ahead. There was a moment's confusion among the guards before they began running after the old man, so Tom had a head-start.

Even so, one soldier began to overtake the tailor. As William, Sintk, and Harum El-Halop watched helplessly, the grim-faced draconian thrust its hand out to grab the tailor's flapping tunic. The tailor stopped abruptly, spun around, and swung his fist at the draconian.

The force of the blow knocked both the tailor and the draconian off their feet. The tailor fell back on the cobblestones. The draconian weaved to a halt on rubbery legs, its hands clawing at its injured throat.

Within moments, the desperate tailor got to his feet and fled up the street, past the Missionary's Downfall, where William and his friends were still standing, mouths agape. A second later, he vanished into an alley. Two soldiers pursued the fleeing prisoner.

Harum the minotaur grinned in derision as the hobgoblin officer in command bustled past, his fat belly bouncing like jelly above his wide leather belt. The hobgoblin noticed his audience and stopped, his face twisting with anger. Ignoring the powerful minotaur, he focused on poor William and drew his sword, pressing the tip of the blade against the front of William's throat.

"Maybe you'd like to come along with us instead," the hobgoblin snarled.

William trembled. He shoved his shaking hands into his pockets to hide his fear from his friends. His stubby fingers closed over the coin as he prayed fervently for deliverance.

If only . . .

"I'm waiting for your answer," sneered the hobgoblin.

William made a grunting noise like the excited squeal of a frightened piglet. The hobgoblin cocked his head for an instant, looked at Sintk and Harum, then lowered his sword. He chuckled as William's body shivered with fright.

A sudden shout came from the alley. Then, two draconian soldiers came out of the lane with the tailor held fast between them. He jerked and twisted to break free of their grasp. The hobgoblin officer sheathed his sword and walked away to join his troops.

"Close," whispered Sintk.

"Poor Tom," said William.

Harum El-Halup stood quietly with his arms folded over his chest. He watched imperiously as the troops prodded the coffle of prisoners toward the castle. Then the minotaur shrugged and slapped William on the shoulder.

"Every dog has its day," Harum said. "Old Tom should have known better. I told him to mind his own business, keep sewing, and not get ambitious with his thinking. But, my friends, let us slake our thirst and forget about having those reptiles in town. And someday we will throw them over, and you, William, will be our leader." He laughed.

Accompanied by Harum, William and Sintk walked gloomily into the murkiness of the Missionary's Downfall. The bar was crowded with dwarves, humans, hobgoblins, and a group of hard-looking draconians drinking in the back. Several half-elves were noisily testing their mental prowess with a game of riddles. A drunken hobgoblin lay passed out beside his chair. Two bartenders hurried to keep up with requests for drinks. Harum leaned against the end of the bar. He motioned to a bartender, who hastened over with three tankards of ale.

William and Sintk were never completely at ease in the minotaur's establishment. The tavern's reputation for brawls and free-for-all fights was widely known. Bystanders and onlookers were often drawn into melees that ended in what were known as "Harum's wall-bouncing parties." Harum enforced a rule that weapons had to be checked at the door, but it was not completely effective when applied against magic-users and the lowest criminal element.

In addition to fights, the Missionary's Downfall was also widely known for a painting on the ceiling. Some time before, an itinerant artist wandered into Port Balifor with a talent for painting and a yen for ale. The artist hired out to the minotaur for room, board, and all the ale he could drink. The artist erected scaffolds and worked for two years to create an oil mural on the ceiling.

The painting depicted a satyr gamboling with maidens in a pastoral setting. Neither the satyr nor the maidens were particularly shy, a fact that delighted customers of the bar. Some folks claimed the minotaur's regulars could be recognized by the crook in their necks.

Now, after a long drink of ale, William drew the coin from his pocket. It lay coldly in his palm, a lifeless piece of metal.

"What's that?" asked Harum. His thick fingers plucked the coin from William's hand.

"It was a gift from someone special," said William.

Sintk the Dwarf chimed in. "William thinks the coin has magical powers."

The minotaur cocked his head and held the coin up to the light of an oil lamp on the wall. "What does it do?"

"It helps my mind go off to other places." William was pleased that the minotaur had not ridiculed his beliefs about the coin.

Harum asked, "You mean soul-travel?"

William looked startled. "What's that?"

Harum grinned. "Back home, I was given a sentence of supreme shunning. Solitary confinement without contact with anyone. You can't imagine the terrible loneliness. You get crazed from the need for companionship. My mind was becoming quirky and dull, un-

---

til I taught myself to take mental trips. Flights of the imagination. It helped me keep my sanity."

Sintk asked dubiously, "This was all in your mind?"

"Who knows for sure?" The minotaur shrugged his thick shoulders. "But if you can escape this life now and then with such a magic coin, then you are a lucky man, William."

William beamed. "I told you it was magic," he said to Sintk.

Just then, a shout came from the far end of the bar. One man slammed down his tankard, then drove a fist into the stomach of a loud, argumentative drinking companion. The unexpected blow knocked the loud-mouth backward; he crashed into the table where the half-elves were sitting. Their table was upended against the wall.

With wine coursing through their veins, the half-elves leaped up to defend themselves. One fell over the slumbering hobgoblin; another was knocked down by a long-bearded dwarf. The hobgoblin on the floor roused himself, opened his eyes, and rose to a sitting position. A booted foot slammed into his head; he promptly lapsed back into an unconscious state.

Customers rushed from every side of the Missionary's Downfall for a better view of the ruckus. Another half-elf stumbled into a human, who slugged the offender on the chin. Within moments, most of the tavern's patrons were throwing punches, kicking, biting, howling, and exchanging blows in a loud and violent manner.

"Pardon me," growled the minotaur. He handed the coin to William, walked over, and grabbed a half-elf by the neck and trousers. He heaved the elf against a wall of the tavern. Then, Harum grasped the end of a beard and propelled a screaming dwarf into the wall.

William's terror was mixed with awe of Harum.

---

"Let's get out of here," he said in a quavering voice.

"You go." The dwarf was rubbing his hands in glee. "I've never been to a wall-banging before." Sintk dashed into the fight. William pocketed the coin and dashed for the door.

William was sitting behind the bar of the Pig and Whistle. He had been alone most of the evening, turning the coin over and over in his hand. He was thinking about Old Tom the tailor, and how peaceful and carefree life had been before the draconians had overrun Port Balifor. The coin shone in the lamplight as William pondered it. It *is* an unusual and beautiful coin after all, thought William.

"William . . . come quickly!"

The voice was a whispered hiss followed by a light, discreet knocking on the back door of the inn.

He got off his bartender's stool, picked up an oil lamp, and walked to the back of the inn. He unfastened the latch on the door, opened it, and noticed shadowy forms in the gloomy darkness. William stepped back as Sintk and Harum El-Halop entered the room. They stank of too much ale.

"We're going to rescue Tom," said Sintk with unaccustomed fervor. "You'll go with us, won't you?"

"You are drunk," said William.

"We have been drinking," said the minotaur, "but we are not drunk. There is a difference, which you, as a tavern owner, ought to know."

William considered this. "What is your plan?"

"Not much of one," admitted the minotaur.

But he looked at the faces of Sintk and Harum, and decided they were serious. He held the coin very tightly in his hand.

Well, why not?

"I've got a mask and sword for you." The minotaur

---

opened a small cloth bag and pulled out a long piece of black cloth.

William took the short, curved sword and scabbard offered by the minotaur, tied the belt around his waist and the mask around his head. He was feeling . . . positively . . . different. He gazed proudly at his reflection in the curved glass behind the bar and thought to himself, William Sweetwater, you do not need any magic coins to be a hero tonight.

The town was dark and quiet as the three companions slipped out the back door of the Pig and Whistle. Noiselessly, they moved through the back lanes of Port Balifor. They halted on the outskirts of town. Moonlight outlined the dark stone castle a short distance away on the flat plain. There was a grotesque, evil eeriness about the ancient structure. The castle had been abandoned for as long as anyone in Port Balifor could remember.

The companions crept closer to the castle without seeing a single sentry. The draconians were too arrogant; they could not anticipate that anyone would dare storm their fortress. The only light came through a partly open gate leading to the inside of the perimeter. The courtyard was dimly lit by a torch that burned low and cast a glow on a guard sprawled sleeping inside the gate.

"We're lucky," Harum whispered. "They're careless. Stay here. I'll take care of the guard."

The minotaur moved carefully onto a small wooden bridge that spanned the moat. He tested each plank to be certain the old wood did not squeak. Then, Harum entered the courtyard and crept silently into the shadows. Next, the minotaur pulled a strangling rope from his trousers. The short rope had a wooden peg on each end. The strangling rope stretched tautly between thick hands, the minotaur moved close and tapped the guard's arm with his toe.

The guard awakened instantly, fumbling for the sword in its scabbard. The minotaur dropped the rope around the draconian's neck, then wrapped the pegs into a strangler's knot.

The guard clawed at its throat, making tiny strangled gasps. Its mouth went wide open to suck air into its lungs. Its head twisted to and fro, then Harum's heavy boot smashed into the sentry's midsection.

The guard went down on its face. The minotaur looked on without emotion as the draconian died. Then, he motioned for William and Sintk to join him.

William held tightly to the coin as they crossed the bridge. They moved rapidly past the guard, through the courtyard, and then up three massive flights of stone steps at the castle entrance. William pulled on the iron handle of a massive black door, which opened with a loud squeaking sound. His heart was racing, his head pounding with excitement. Emboldened, he drew his sword as he went through the portals, ready for whatever was inside.

They entered an empty room at least fifty paces square, a cold and uninviting area barren of furniture or other decorations. The walls and floor were stone. The room was ill-lit by torches resting in metal holders fastened to the smoke-smeared marble walls. A maze of corridors branched off from this entryroom. The companions moved swiftly and quietly, searching for a stairway leading down into the dungeon.

William discovered a set of stone steps winding down into the bowels of the castle. He made a tiny oinking sound to alert his friends. Sintk and Harum hurried to his side. William grabbed a torch and led the way down the narrow passageway.

The stairs led to a central guardroom that was brightly lit by several flickering torches. Two draconians sat at a battered old table playing a game of blackjack. The two jailers did not look up until William's shadow fell over the cards.

"Who in the Abyss are you?" growled the nearest jailer. It dropped its cards and grabbed the hilt of its sword. The other jailer started to rise out of its chair.

William threw his torch on the floor. He grasped his sword with both hands and rammed the blade deep into the draconian's chest. The ease with which the steel pierced flesh and bone amazed William.

William withdrew the sword, expecting the jailer to fall. The burly draconian's clawed hands grabbed the table for support and, with a low guttural cry, kicked out at William. The innkeeper moved swiftly out of danger, then slashed his blade against his opponent's throat. He tried to pull back his weapon, but the blade seemed stuck into gristle or bone.

"Quick!" snapped Sintk. "Pull it out! He'll turn to stone."

William mustered all his strength with both hands on the hilt and pulled the sword free. Green blood spurted out onto the draconian's tunic. A sidelong glance showed William that the minotaur and Sintk had the other jailer on the floor. The dwarf's blade was buried deep into the draconian's belly.

The draconians made feeble dying motions. William stepped over his victim and grabbed a large ring of keys off a wooden peg on the wall.

"The prisoners are over here!" hissed the dwarf. "Come quick! Bring the keys."

At the end of one of the corridors they found a large cell carved out of solid stone with heavy metal bars and a large locked door.

Dozens of prisoners were crowded up against the front of the cell. Gaunt and skeletal, ragged and hungry, they were the living dead, marked for torture or execution. Their crimes had been petty: pickpocketing, insulting a draconian, trying to escape Port Balifor. Now they stretched out raw, bony fingers, pleading for help.

"Hurry, lads, hurry!" said Tom the tailor, pushing to the front.

"Bless you," husked another prisoner.

"Shut up!" growled the minotaur. "You'll have the whole army down on us."

Everyone was silent as William fumbled with the ring, fitting one, then another of the large metal keys into the lock. Just as he began to think none of the keys would fit, the heavy door swung free. William stepped back as the first prisoner stepped out on wobbly legs into the smoky passageway.

Altogether, there were maybe fifty of them, lucky to be still alive. They bunched together, pathetically, waiting for a command from William.

Old Tom the tailor squinted through the dimness at his masked rescuers. He pointed his finger at William and raised his voice so the others could hear. "That's William of the Pig and Whistle. He had the courage to help us. And Sintk the cobbler. And no one can mistake Halum the minotaur over there."

"Keep moving," snapped Halum, "and save your jabber."

The stone floor of the main guardroom was slippery with green blood from the dead draconians. William almost slipped in the sticky blood, then righted himself and took the lead. Pressing his fingers against his lips for silence, William started up the staircase.

Then he lurched to a halt. Directly above him, coming down, was Drago and three hobgoblin lieutenants. They were armed with swords and battle-axes, which they waved ominously in anticipation of blood-letting. Drago was eagerly walking ahead of his three wary pals. He glared directly at William, but in his eyes was no recognition.

"Come on! Come on!" sneered Drago, his mouth twisted viciously. "We don't often have visitors here. We would like to make your stay a memorable—and long—one."

Hastily, William and the prisoner horde retreated backward into the central guardroom, where they huddled at the bottom of the stairwell. They were trapped. Sintk raised his weapon.

From above, William could hear the troops of the dragonarmy being roused into action. A horn blew in the distance. The thud of heavy boots sounded on stone steps and corridors. Doors slammed, shouts blared and echoed as troops came hurrying into the entry room above. Harum motioned the others to stay back and crept up to stand by the door to the guard-room, his back pressed against the wall.

The first to poke his head in through the doorway was the fierce, eager Drago. The captain of the prison guards held his battle-axe at shoulder height, ready to strike out at anyone who came into view.

As Drago reached the lower stairway, the mino-taur's arm shot out with a quick movement, and his strong fingers fastened on Drago's neck. Harum's powerful arms propelled the draconian brute across the room. Led by Sintk, the prisoners leaped on the draconian, pummeling him with their bare hands. Sintk finished the brute with a swift dagger stroke.

Hearing nothing from their leader, the three hob-goblins hesitated on the stairs, then came to an abrupt halt. The soldiers behind them were bottled up in the stairwell, but they too were not anxious to enter the guardroom and face the aroused minotaur. But it would only be a matter of time . . .

Meanwhile, William had noticed that the torches

on the wall of the guardroom were flickering—and always in the same direction and it wasn't coming from the door! Crawling along the wall, he discovered a draft whistling around a huge block of stone. Pushing against it, he found it opened into a dark passage.

"This way!" he yelled.

Everyone scrambled after him. The passageway was dark and spooky. Maintaining a fast pace, William led them for several hundred yards, until he saw a silver fingernail of moonlight. He gestured for them to pull up.

William crept up to a barred outlet that looked out onto a moonlit landscape. The tunnel exit was near the sea and the wind was directed into the tunnel by a curving stone sea wall. Across the flat plain could be seen the winking lights of Port Balifor, no more than half a mile in the distance.

Unfortunately, their escape was barred by a heavy metal grating that covered the end of the tunnel.

"We're trapped," said Sintk.

Tom the tailor began to moan.

"They're following," warned a kender among the prisoners. The firm voice of the commander could be heard ordering his troops into the tunnels.

"Let me see those bars," said Harum, pushing forward.

The minotaur came up alongside William, and his massive hands began to test the metal barrier. Finally he said, "Stand back." Harum placed his shoulder against one side of the bars. The moonlight gave a thin, gray cast to the top of the minotaur's face. Then, he sucked in a deep breath through his mask.

Harum's shoulder put mighty pressure on the bars. He grunted and strained to tear the metal away from the stone sockets. Once, twice, Harum threw every ounce of his strength against the barrier.

"They're coming this way!" cried Sintk.

Everyone looked back and saw the flare of torches moving into the tunnel.

"To the rear!" exclaimed William bravely to Sintk. He took the dwarf's arm, and they pressed through the prisoners, swords ready for defense.

Now, the minotaur tried the other side of the bars. They were also unyielding. He made several mighty lunges and, once, the metal bent—but still remained fast in the stone.

Exasperated, the minotaur told everyone to get back. "Give me some running room," he spat.

Harum ran back through the tunnel, stopping within sight of the forward line of searching troops. The soldiers sent up a mighty roar of yells and curses. Unmindful of them, Harum El-Halop dropped down into a sprinter's position. Giving of roar of his own, he ran forward, gaining speed with each step. Then, just before he reached the iron barrier, Harum twisted his body and leaped into the air. He flew backward and struck the bars with a sickening thud.

The bars gave a metallic screech and jerked loose from their sockets in the walls. Everyone cheered as the barrier fell out onto the ground. Harum went rolling across the ground, kicking up dust in the pale moonlight. He came up on his feet with a snort.

"Get the bars back in place," William yelled as the fleeing prisoners streamed out of the tunnel.

Sintk led the others in raising the bars, while William and the minotaur raced to grab the end of a large piece of old timber. Everyone helped to wedge the timber so it would hold the bars tight.

Seconds later, the dragonarmy troops came rushing up to the barred exit. They howled and roared, pounding against the bars, as the companions sped off into the night.

---

Outside, William looked up and saw a detachment of mounted draconians ride out of the castle gate. The leader sent his men in a circular direction around the castle. Good, thought William. That will buy some time. His thinking was calm and collected, he was feeling no fear. His eyes swept ahead.

Then, the wedging timber must have given way, because troops came pouring out of the tunnel. Seeing the flare of their torches, William and his group raced on until they came to the water's edge. There, down by the shore, were a dozen oak-ribbed fishing boats with Balifor oarsmen at the alert.

"Your plan?" asked a surprised William.

"Not much of one," replied the minotaur.

One by one, the boats were loaded and pushed off, until there was a small flotilla of prisoners bobbing on the blue-black waves. The last boat was a smaller one and into it climbed William, Sintk, and Harum El-Halop, who had been defending the rear. But they were in no danger; they were out of earshot by the time the first draconians stumbled to the shore.

A mile out to sea, the small vessels hesitated outside Port Balifor.

"You have a head-start on the patrol boats!" shouted William to Tom the tailor over the crashing waves. "You can make a run for it and, with luck, live elsewhere long and happily and free of chains!"

"What about you?" yelled Tom, cupping his hands.

William did not have to ask Sintk, who was already snoring under a cowhide, or Harum, who was doing the rowing of four men. Drago was dead. They could slip into the harbor and never be suspected.

"Port Balifor is our home!" he shouted into the wind. But he doubted if they heard him, as the string of boats had already moved onward, to the west.

Harum and William let Sintk sleep until they had

glided safely into the harbor. The minotaur tied up the boat, and they scrambled to their feet at the end of a small commercial pier. There was frantic activity, fireballs, and shouting from draconian ships at the other end of the harbor, but their dock was practically deserted, and no one was around to pay them any mind.

They slapped each other on the shoulders and Harum hurried away into the fog. Sintk and William kept to the back lanes until the Pig and Whistle hove into view. Sintk continued on to his cobbler's shop.

Inside his inn, William ripped off his mask and tossed the cloth onto a refuse barrel. He hung the sword and scabbard on a wood peg on the wall. Breathing heavily from the night's activities, William went behind the bar and poured himself a tall drink of dwarf spirits.

William came to with a snorting noise. He was sitting on the bartender's stool at his inn. His head ached, and pain was beginning to move deep into his muscles. For an instant, William thought he had caught a case of ague. His thick, short fingers opened and the coin dropped on the bar. The metal was warm to his touch.

What a wonderful dream, he thought. He had been so brave. Sighing heavily, William decided to retire for the night. He pocketed the coin and picked up an oil lamp with a low flame. He yawned as he came around the bar.

Suddenly, a heavy pounding sounded on the front door of the Pig and Whistle. "Open up in the name of the Highlord!" cried a guttural voice.

Shrugging, William headed for the door. Then he stopped, staring in horror.

On a refuse barrel lay a torn black mask . . . ❧

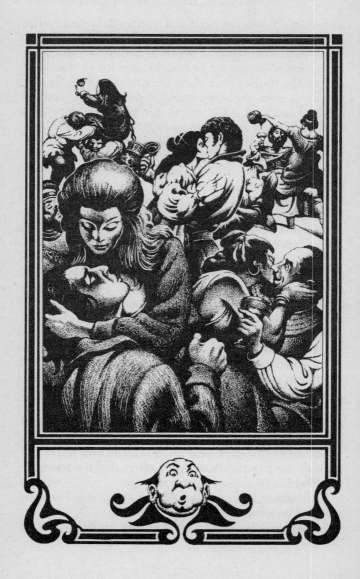

# Love and Ale

## Nick O'Donohoe

"**A**N INN," *Otik puffed, "is blessed or cursed by its* ale." He set the barrow-handles down, noting with approval that the cloth-covered wheel had not marred the lovingly polished Inn floor. "The ale is blessed or cursed by its water and hops."

Tika, staggering in from the kitchen, poured one of her two buckets into the immense brewing tun as Otik pried the top free. "I know, I know. That's why I have to haul fresh spring water up, a bucket at a time, instead of using rainwater from the cistern—which I wouldn't need to pull up." She showed him the rope-marks in her palms. At fifteen, she lacked the patience for brewing.

"Better a bucket than a barrel." Otik slapped the tun. "The innkeeper before me thought cleaning a brewing tun each time was too much work. He just mixed the hops, malt, and sugar into an alewort inside each keg, prying the lids up and recoopering without ever cleaning." He washed the spring water around the sides, checking for the tiniest dirt or stain.

"Well, if we couldn't do that, couldn't we at least not haul the water up?"

"I've tried other ways myself. My very first batch with this tun I made down below, at the foot of the tree."

"Couldn't we do that?" Tika said wistfully. "We could just roll the empty kegs out the garbage-drop with ropes tied to them so they wouldn't smash on the ground. We wouldn't have to haul any water at all, just pipe it to the foot of the tree." She automatically patted the living vallenwood on which the bar was built. The people of Solace were more aware of growing wood than any folk alive. "Then when the ale was all aged and ready, we could fill the kegs—" Her eyes went wide, and she put a hand to her mouth.

"That's right." Otik was pleased that she understood. "I made a batch at ground level, then had nothing to carry it up in but fifty-weight kegs, up forty feet of stairs. Or I could run down a hundred times with empty pitchers, filling the upstairs barrels." He rubbed his back automatically. "I tied safety ropes on the kegs and rolled them up, one at a time. Took the yeast an extra month to settle, and I was in bed for three days with sore muscles."

"Poor Otik." But Tika laughed. "I wish I'd seen it. Nothing exciting happens when we make ale."

"Shame on you, child." He was teasing. "The autumn batch is always exciting. Today, a shipment of hops from the Plains of Abanasinia will arrive. I'm the only innkeeper around who sends far away for rich hops."

"You're the only innkeeper around, in Solace." But she added, "And you'd be the best anyway, if there were a thousand."

"Now, now." Otik was pleased. He patted his belly. "It's a labor of love, and the Inn has loved me back. Now fetch more water."

As if in answer, there came a call from the kitchen.

Otik said, "See? The cook has hauled up more for you. That should make you happier."

"I'm ecstatic. Thank Riga for me." And she went.

Otik, carefully not thinking of the long day ahead, went through the necessary preparations as though they were ritual. First he cleaned a ladle thoroughly and dried it over the fire. While it cooled, he set a tallow candle into another ladle, centered in the bowl so as not to drip, and lowered it into the brewing tun, checking the sides for cracks and split seams. Ale leaking out was not so damaging as air leaking in. He did the same with each of the kegs into which he would pour the fully made wort.

Finally he put down his candle and lowered the cooled, dry ladle into the spring water and sipped, then drank deeply. "Ah." Forty feet below, near the base of the tree that held and shaped the Inn of the Last Home, spring water bubbled through lime rock. Some said the lime rock went down many times farther than a man could dig, and the spring channeled through it all. Otik was not a traveled man, but he knew in his heart that nowhere in the world was there water as sweet and pure as this. Finding hops and malt equal to it was difficult.

As Tika struggled back with the buckets, she panted, "Otik? I've never asked why you named the inn—?"

"I didn't name it, child. The Inn of the Last Home was named by—"

"Why the Last Home?"

"I've never told you?" He glanced around, taking in every scar in the wood, every gouge half-polished out of the age-darkened vallenwood. "When the people of Solace built their homes in the trees, they had nowhere left to go. The Cataclysm left no choices; starving marauders, crazed homeless folk, were destroying villages and stealing everything they could. The folk of Solace knew that if they did not defend themselves well, these trees would be their last home."

"But they survived. Things returned to normal. They could have moved back to the ground."

Otik lifted the barrow-handles. "Follow me."

At the pantry he stopped. "The man who built this inn was Krale the Strong. They say he could tuck a barrel of ale under his arm and climb up the tree itself, one-handed. For all he knew, his inn would be in ruins in a year." Otik tapped the store-room floor. "You've been here a thousand times. Have you ever thought about this floor?"

Tika shrugged. "It's just stone." Then it hit her. "A stone floor? But I thought the fireplace—"

"Was the only stonework. So it is. This is a single stone, set in to keep the ale cool, forty feet above the ground. Krale made a rope harness and hauled it up himself. Then he chopped this chamber out of the living wood, and laid the floor. This was his people's last home, and he built it to last forever."

Otik stamped the floor. The edges were rounded, where the living wooden walls had flowed over the stone, a nail's-breadth a year. "And when the danger was over and the folk of Solace could go back to the ground, they didn't. These were their last homes. In all the world, no place else can be home for them." He finished, a little embarrassed at the speech. "Or for me. Bring out more water, young lady."

As they worked, Tika hummed. She had a sweet, soft voice, and Otik was glad when she finally broke into full song. The ballad was a hill tune, melodic and plaintive; Tika, with great enjoyment, sang it as sadly as she could.

By the second verse she had dropped her scrub-rag and shut her eyes, oblivious to Otik. He listened quietly, knowing that if she remembered his presence, she would blush and fall silent. Lately, Tika had become awkward and shy around men—a bad trait for a bar-maid, but at her age, quite natural. He kept patient, knowing how soon that shyness would end.

Tika sang:

> The tree by my door
> I've watched turn before
> And I've watched as it's branched out and grown;
> When it turns next year,
> Will I still be here,
> And will I be here alone?

> When my love was there,
> Birds sang in the air,
> And they soared like the dreams that we had;
> Now he's off to war,
> They sing like before,
> But all of their songs are sad.

> My good friends, I know,
> Will marry and go,
> And farewell with a kiss and a tear,
> With lovers to tell,
> And children as well,
> While I wait another year.

> Their futures are bright,
> They sing day and night,
> And I'm happy to think them so glad . . .
> The birds that I see
> Still sing back to me,
> But all of their songs are sad.

Otik enjoyed the tune without recognizing it. He

watched Tika, her eyes shut and her arms waving in the air as she sang, and he thought with a sudden ache, "She's old enough for her own place."

Tika had lived with him for a long time; she was as close to a daughter as he would ever have. Before that, for many years, he had lived alone happily. Now he could not imagine how he had stood it.

Finally she finished, and he said, "Nicely sung. What was that?"

"That?" She blushed. "Oh, the song. It's called 'The Song of Elen Waiting.' I heard it last night."

"I remember." The singer had been all of twenty-three, most of his listeners fifteen. He had curly dark hair and deep blue eyes, and by his second song half the girls of Solace were around him. "Some young man sang it, didn't he?"

"You're teasing me." Tika scowled, even when Otik smiled and shook his head. "You don't take me seriously."

"Oh, but I do, I do. This young man that sang—"

"Rian." She said it softly, and the scowl went. "He wasn't so young. Do you know, he had seven gray hairs?"

"Really? Seven, exactly?"

She didn't notice the tease, but nodded vigorously, her own hair bouncing off her shoulders. "Exactly. He let three of us count them after he was done singing, and we all came up with the same number."

"Nice of him to let you."

"Oh, I think he liked it," Tika said innocently. Then she frowned. "Especially when Loriel did it."

"Which one was Loriel?" There'd been a lot of them. After Rian had sung, the young women had walked around the Inn with their heads high, thinking noble thoughts, to Otik's vast amusement. One young man, a red-haired, spindly local with wide eyes, sat in the corner afterward determinedly mouthing lyrics to himself. His friends had seemed afraid he might sing.

Tika scrubbed fiercely at one of the barrels, tipping it. Otik steadied it for her as she said casually, "Loriel? Oh, you know. Turned-up nose, too many freckles, shows her teeth when she laughs—it's a shame they're not straight—and she's the one with all that hair, you know, the yellow stuff?"

"Oh, is she the one with all that pretty blonde hair?" She was around a lot lately. She laughed too often for Otik's taste, but the boys her age seemed to like it. She also had a habit of spinning away from people so that her hair flew straight out and settled back. Otik had twice caught Tika practicing it.

"Do you think it's pretty, then?" Tika tried to look surprised. "That's nice. Poor thing, she'd be pleased." Scrub, scrub.

She began to daub her eyes. "Oh, Otik! He liked *her* and not me."

"There now." Otik put an arm around her, thinking (not for the first time) that if he'd only found a wife, there'd be someone more sensitive to help the poor girl. He barely knew Tika's friends. "There, now. It's not like he's your own true love, just an older lad with a good voice. You don't want him."

Tika laughed and wiped her eyes on her arm. "That's true. But Loriel's supposed to be my friend— what does he see in *her*?"

"Ah." Now he understood. "Well, she's older than you."

"Only a little. A year isn't so much." She sniffed.

"Don't cry again." He added, to get a smile from her, "You'll salt the ale." It almost worked. "You must be patient, like that woman in the song. How did it go again?"

Tika looked wistful, forgetting her own sorrow.

"It's about a man who kisses his love good-bye and goes away forever, only she doesn't know that, and waits for him until she's old and lonely and she dies—"

"Birds sang where she died."

Tika sighed happily. "And all their songs were sad. Otik, am I going to end like that? Do you think I'll end up living all alone, with nobody to love or to live with, sleeping by myself and making meals for one?"

Otik looked for a long time in the mirror at the long bar's end. Finally he turned around. "Sometimes it happens. Surely not to you, though. Now go, pretty young one, and get the last cask."

He scrubbed the tun hard, perhaps harder than it needed.

It was noon, but there were no spiced potatoes cooking, no shouts for ale. Otik had hung a tankard upside down on the post at the bottom steps, so that even the unlettered would know not to climb up needlessly. Otik closed for every brewing, opening only when the alewort was made.

The brewing tun was clean and filled with spring water, waiting behind the bar for the malt syrup. The syrup was warmed and waiting. The yeast, the final addition to the alewort, was in a bowl on the bar.

But the hops had not yet arrived, and Otik was as impatient as Tika before he heard slow, heavy steps on the stairs.

"Tika," he called, "come out." She came from the kitchen, wiping her hands on her apron as he said, "Hear that? Someone carrying a burden. Our hops have come." He cocked an ear, listening with the knowledge of long years. "Not as heavy as I thought. Did Kerwin not bring a full load?"

The Inn door flew open and a burlap bag waddled in, seemingly under its own power, and leaped to the floor before the tun. A kender, still doubled from his load, peered through his arched brows at them and grinned suddenly.

"Moonwick." Otik did not say the kender's name with pleasure. Among men, the short, mischievous kender were famous for practical joking and for disregarding other people's property, and Moonwick Lightfinger was famous among kender. It was said, even by sober travelers, that once when Moonwick was at Crystalmir Lake, the partying crew of a small fishing boat had woken in full gear, on deck, to find their boat lodged thirty feet off the ground between two trees. The topmost tree branches bore pulley marks, but the pulleys had been removed. It took eight men two days to get the boat down.

It was further rumored, in stories possibly started by the kender himself, that Moonwick had on separate occasions stolen the tail from a cat, the blonde hair from a human woman, and, on a night of unexplained eclipse, the moonlight itself—which was how he got his name. Otik subscribed to the more popular theory that the kender's name was a flattering corruption of Moonwit.

Moonwick smiled up at Otik. "Here's your hops, and gods how I prayed a thousand times that they'd hop themselves here. Where's my reward?" He added, "Gold will do."

Otik did not smile back. "Kerwin was bringing the hops. What happened to him?"

"You paid him in advance. He had money. He wanted to gamble." The kender said earnestly, "I said we could do it for anything: buttons, rocks, things in our pockets—but he wouldn't listen. He said he felt lucky."

Otik stared at the kender. "So he gambled for money with you? Lady of Plenty, look after your witling orphans. What happened to him?"

Moonwick looked sad. "He lost."

Otik said dryly, "I'm shocked." As Moonwick opened his mouth in protest, Otik went on, "Never mind. Why are you carrying the hops?"

Now Moonwick did look embarrassed and sincerely angry. "Kerwin said that since I had his wages, I should do his work. I said that was foolish, and we argued, and finally we agreed to gamble for who made this trip."

"Naturally you accepted. Can't pass up a game. And?" Otik suspected, but could not believe, the outcome.

The kender burst out, "He won. I can't imagine how that could have happened. He must have cheated."

"Undoubtedly. Well, you've been paid for your trip, but I'll give you ale for your trouble, and a meal if you wish." Otik knelt and opened the bag, running his hands through the hops.

"I ate on the road. I shared lunch with—well, with another traveler." The kender twiddled at the end of the short hoopak stick angled into his belt. The stick, at once the best weapon and chief musical instrument of kender, seemed to trouble him.

Years of innkeeping had made Otik alive to evasion. "What sort of traveler?"

"Human." Moonwick shrugged, grabbing again at the hoopak stick as it slipped in his belt. "This thing doesn't seem to be balancing properly."

Otik suddenly understood the kender's reluctance to speak of the fellow traveler. "Perhaps that has to do with the purse hooked onto the end of it," he observed.

"Purse?" The kender whirled around. The stick, naturally, whirled with him. "I see no purse."

"Look over your shoulder. No, the other shoulder. The drawstring is twisted over the end of your stick."

Otik sighed as the kender peered this way and that in apparent disbelief that he should ever end up with another man's belongings.

"Why, look at that! A purse, just as you say. Imagine that. How could that happen?"

"Seems incredible," Otik agreed politely.

"And yet . . . Yes, I know exactly how it might have happened. You know how we use hoopaks?"

"Vaguely." Kender could move a hoopak stick, in combat or to make a noise, faster than men could see. Otik had once seen a drunken swordsman lose a fight with an apparently unarmed kender. At the start of the fight, the kender had been five feet from the hoopak.

"Yes. Well, I was singing, and accompanying myself by whirling my hoopak to get a high note—on a dry day with a little wind, I can get two notes at once—and I twisted it with my wrist as I spun it, and I must have caught the purse-string just as I twisted."

"Ah. That must be it."

"You can see how it would happen." Moonwick spun the hoopak over his head and, incidentally, over the bar and nearly against the back wall. "Because it's hard to see exactly where the 'pak-end moves when it twists—"

"I see that." Otik deftly retrieved the tankard which had slipped, seemingly of its own will, over the end of the stick. "Accidents will happen."

"Of course." Moonwick looked at him with insistent innocence. "Because I would never, ever, ever simply steal a purse from someone."

"Of course not."

"Especially from this man. He was so nice, and so knowledgeable." Moonwick leaned on his staff. "We shared our lunches, and traded for variety, and he told the best stories. He'd swum to the bottom of Crystalmir Lake for stonefish, and picked plants from the edge of Darken Wood. He once climbed a dead tree by moonlight, and he told the funniest story about speaking to the ghost of the grandmother that never respected him. His name was Ralf. He was on his way to see his mother, he said." The kender added thoughtfully, "She must like jewelry; he had lots of little gifts for her, and he kept mixing up her name. Said he had a powder to feed Gwendol, then Genna, then Gerria—"

"A mage?" Otik was uneasy near magic.

"Oh, no." Moonwick shook his head violently. "Just a charm vendor: potions, powders, elixirs, amulets— nothing serious. Why, this is probably quite harmless." He held the bag toward Otik. "Probably the poor man will be here any day, looking for this. Would you take—"

"No."

"Just overnight; surely you're not—"

"No."

"What possible harm could there be—"

"I have no idea what harm there could be," Otik said firmly. "I don't intend to find out. I keep away from magic."

The kender looked pityingly. "You miss a lot of excitement that way."

"Long ago I took a vow. I'm devoting my life to missing a lot of excitement."

"All right, then." Moonwick bounced the bag on his palm. "I'll return it myself. Someday."

"Good of you. In the meantime, I'm sorry you don't need a meal. Why don't you take—" With a quick wrist movement, Otik caught Moonwick's arm as it flashed across the bar—"a mug of ale, for your throat."

"Good idea." The kender grabbed a mug. "Maybe I could stay here the night," he said wistfully.

"No." Otik sighed. "I'm still replacing forks from the last time."

Moonwick waved a hand. "Surely you don't blame me— Wasn't that a cry from the kitchen?"

It was. It sounded like a buried cook. Otik grunted. "Pantry shelf's fallen again." He trotted for the kitchen door, then whirled. "Touch nothing without invitation while I'm gone."

"Sound advice," the kender murmured. As Otik disappeared through the door, the kender held his lips still.

The tap on the counter-keg said in a squeaky voice, "Have a refill, Moonwick."

"I will," the kender said happily, "and thank you for the invitation." While he drank, for practice he made the buried-cook sound come from one of the packs at his side.

He stuck his hoopak straight out and spun it, balancing the purse on the end. When the drawstrings came undone he caught the purse neatly, then smelled it. "What an odd odor." He opened it and tilted it sideways. A pinch of powder like cinnamon drifted to the floor. He made a face. "It's a charm. Something terrible, too—icky-sweet and spice-filled. It's not even labeled; it could be anything. How does Ralf expect people who find his purse by accident to know what to do with it?" He sighed. "Magicians are so untrustworthy."

Moonwick poked the purse itself. "Nice bag, though." He looked behind the bar for a place to empty out the useless dust, then saw the loose-lidded tun of alewort. He grinned, lifted the lid and emptied the contents of the pouch inside.

When Otik came back, he checked the bar carefully. Nothing seemed to be missing. He eyed Moonwick, who smiled innocently at him. "Nice ale," the kender said.

"It's my own recipe." The innkeeper added, "Thanks to your contribution, this batch will be even better."

The kender choked. Otik stooped to pat his back, then retrieved an empty purse from the floor. "What's this?"

"Mine." The kender deftly plucked it from the innkeeper's hands. "I hope to fill it someday."

"Not in my inn." Otik added, as the kender rose to leave, "My thanks, Moonwick. Leave the door open, so the brew smell will air out. Come back next full moon, if you wish to taste what you carried."

"Best I hurry on," Moonwick said regretfully. Which was true—sooner or later Ralf might come looking for him. "I do hope I can return to sample that batch." He shook hands with Otik, who checked his ring afterward.

Otik listened to the reassuring thump of the kender's departure down the stairs, and sighed. He said to himself, "There's one source of trouble gone, and no harm done. Now to heat the alewort." He walked to the back, looking for Tika.

While he was away, two fire swallows, a male and a female, flew in the open door and pecked at the fine spicy powder spilled from the purse. The two of them flew out in circles, squawking, billing, and frenziedly pressing against each other's bodies.

After pouring the hops in the tun, Otik cleaned the stream-rounded heating stones and scrubbed the iron tongs he used on them. The whole Inn grew warm as he built up the fire and opened a wind-vent to blow the coals. The stones he laid on a flat clean slab of the hearth; as each stone heated he lowered it with the tongs into the wort. Soon he was sweating freely from the heat. He set the tongs down to wipe his forehead. Without being asked, Tika picked them up, removed several stones from the tun and swung heated ones in, lowering them gently to avoid splashing. Otik puffed and watched, proud of her. When he was younger, he would have needed no rest. For that matter, when Tika was younger, he would not have let her spell him at the heating.

As the tun began steaming, Otik thought again to himself, "She's old enough for her own place." He shook his head, cast the problem from his mind, and tried to think only of the new ale.

After the heating, Tika and Otik poured off the ale into smaller casks. Otik took care to fill each cask only four-fifths full, because the alewort bubbled as it worked, and a full cask could explode. Once, when Otik was young, he had overfilled one; it had taken weeks to get the smell out of the Inn.

Each cask they finished they rolled carefully against the tree and set upright where it would be in sunlight but away from outside walls. For the first seven days, the casks would be warm and working, and the yeast would be settling out of it. After that, they would move the casks, as gently as possible, into the storeroom with the stone floor, and give them until the next full moon to age in cool and quiet. If they had extra casks by then, and if they had the energy, Otik and Tika would pour the beer into freshly washed containers for its final aging. Often, Otik cast about for excuses to avoid that stage; scrubbing twice for each batch, and repouring half-done beer, seemed an awful lot of work for a pleasant drink.

For now, though, the hard part of the brewing process was over, and it seemed to them both that the alewort already smelled delicious. Tika, her troubles forgotten, or at least submerged, sang another verse to 'The Song of Elen Waiting':

*

*Will someone who knows*
*Where all the time goes*
*Come and lead me away by the hand,*
*I know day by day*
*I'm fading away;*
*It's more than my heart can stand.*

*It's not that he knew*
*More than any men do,*
*But he knew all my heart ever had;*
*The birds watch and hear*
*And wait every year,*
*But all of their songs are sad.*

Otik, resealing another cask, felt a shadow of what Tika heard in the song. "That's pretty." He looked at the worn and time-darkened casks. "We had songs like that when I was a lad, too."

"Like that one?" The girl was appalled. Surely no one had ever written a song that deep and meaningful before.

"As good or better." He grinned at her. "Some of them even talked about birds."

Birdsong exploded outside, and Otik glanced out a window near the door. "I wouldn't say that all their songs were sad, though. If this weren't autumn, I'd swear the fire swallows were mating."

"You're teasing me again."

"So I am." Otik sniffed the steam from the alewort, and gave her a quick affectionate hug. "Wonderful, perceptive young lady, would you help me drain the wort into smaller casks?"

Tika did. It was a pleasant, sunny afternoon; afterward it seemed to them both that they had never felt so much like father and daughter.

\*

The next full moon shone through the thick branches, huge and fresh-risen, when Otik rolled the first of the new casks out. It was barely past sunset, and Otik was acting like a bridegroom.

Some innkeepers held back the first cask, only opening it after second or third rounds. Otik despised that: what better way to feel the full flavor of an ale than taste it all evening, uncut and by itself? It was a risk, he knew. Some inns took years for their reputations to recover from bad batches of brew; even strangers who drank little would shun lodging, judging the service and bed to be as poor as the drinks. But, a good house gave its best, and Otik had never failed to open his new casks with the first mug served after sunset.

A slender man in his twenties, a peddler by the look of his bag, stood in the doorway beating road-dust from his clothing. Otik approved silently, but withdrew approval when the tradesman agreeably beat dust from a knight as well—and easily lifted a purse.

Otik coughed loudly. The man in the door looked started, shrugged, and put back the purse. The knight slapped him on the shoulder and drew him in. "I thank you, sir. Now, when you are in your dotage, you may tell your wondering children how you once polished the armor of Tumber the Mighty."

The tradesman rubbed his shoulder and said politely, "I am sure that when I am in my dotage I shall speak of you often." The knight nodded in satisfaction and sat down. The tradesman turned to Otik. "I was cleaning a spot under his purse and neglected to put it back. Thank you for—hmmm—reminding me."

"My pleasure, sir." Otik added, with emphasis, "I like to keep my customers mindful of such things."

"Oh, I don't think I'll be absent-minded again." He was looking back and forth alertly. "Tell me, sir innkeeper—"

"Otik." As always, Otik offered his hand.

"And I am Reger, called Reger the Trader—mostly." He let go of Otik's hand, looked at his own in surprise, and passed Otik's ring back. "Imagine that. I'm forgetful again. And you watching me . . ." He smiled blandly at Otik.

Otik laughed. "Smoothly done. I take your point, Reger. Instead of watching, I ask your cooperation tonight."

"You'll have it." For the first time, he looked tired. "I've traveled long and hard. A good meal and good ale, that's all I want."

"I'll bring the meal out directly. As for the ale—" Otik shrugged nervously. "Well, I think you'll be pleased."

"I'm sure I will." Reger bowed courteously, then leaned forward. "Tell me, since I imagine you know these folk well: Has anyone local complained this fall of poor kitchen goods, little machines that don't do what they are said to, or that break, or that bark the knuckles?"

Otik, mystified, shook his head. "Not one."

Reger straightened again. "In that case," he said more confidently, "do you know any good men or women, even perhaps yourself or your cook, who, troubled with the toil of meal-making, might wish to find their labors light, their peeling paltry, their slicing simple, and all with the amazing, freshly invented, absolutely sworn-to-save-time—" He fumbled in his bag.

Otik said bluntly, "I have a labor-saving device. It's called a cook. The cook has a peeling and slicing device. It's called a knife, and it's very sharp. The cook has a bad temper and a long memory. I don't advise selling here, sir."

"Well." Reger pulled his fingers out of the bag and

drummed them at the bar. "Perhaps I'll merely rest this night. I could use rest."

Otik sighed. "So could we, sir."

Tika, walking by with too much coy tilt to her head, stumbled. Reger's left arm flashed up and caught the tray, balancing it without effort. His right hand caught her elbow. "Are you all right?"

Tika blushed. "I'm fine. I must have caught my foot—" She looked at her dress in dismay. "I stepped on it. It's filthy. I look awful."

"You look lovely." He pulled the tray from her completely. "Far too comely to walk around with a terrible stain, like a patch on a painting."

She blushed as he smiled at her. "You're teasing me."

He winked. "Of course I am. I think I do it well. Go clean off; I'll take this tray around."

Tika looked questioningly at Otik, who nodded. She curtseyed, folding the skirt to hide the dirty streak. "Thank you." She skipped out.

Otik said, "I'll take the tray."

Reger shook his head. A lock of straight hair fell below his cowl, and he suddenly looked young and stubborn. "I told her I'd do it. Best I keep my word." He glanced back at her, smiling again. "Sweet little thing. I have a sister that age, back home."

Otik warmed to Reger. "Take the potato bowls to the far table. Four plates, four spoons to a table, except for the common table. I'll be by with your meal as you finish, and thanks."

"Why, it is my pleasure." Reger, back to being smooth, hoisted the tray over his shoulder and glided between tables, humming. Otik watched him go.

At the first table two men, drovers by the style of their clothes and the faintly bovine look such men get, dove for the potato bowl as Tumber the Mighty, spoon in air, rehearsed a combat for their benefit.

---

"And, sirs, picture it if you will: a mage and two men, tall and steeped in evil, glowing before me, and me fresh out of a stream, armorless and unclad. Picture the mage frowning and preparing to cast his death-bolt, and picture me, sirs." He straightened. Even in armor, his stomach bulged. "Picture me naked."

"Please," the balding drover muttered, "I'm eating." The other snorted and covered his mouth and nose hastily. Tumber the Mighty took no notice.

"What could a man do?" He looked around as though expecting an answer, apparently from the ceiling beams. "Ah, but what might a hero do?" He thumped the table, bouncing the potato bowl. "I dove." He ducked forward, and both drovers ducked back. "I rolled." He swayed to one side, barely missing Reger, who nimbly side-stepped him. "I grabbed my sword, this very sword at my waist, and with bare knuckles and an uncharmed blade, I parried that magic bolt back at him." Tumber folded his arms triumphantly. "He died, of course. I named my sword Death-bolt, in honor of that day."

His triumph became discomfort as the drovers, not applauding, looked at him cynically while they chewed in unison. He glanced around for other listeners and noticed a local woman with striking red hair and well-muscled arms who was staring at him, her mouth open. She said, "Where was this?"

"Ah. Where indeed." He spun to her table and sat. "A land so far from here, so strange to you, that if I spoke of it—"

"Do," she said hungrily. "I love talk about strange places, about heroes and battle and magic. I could listen to it all day, if I hadn't my work to do." She raised a well-scrubbed hand awkwardly. "I am Elga, called Elga the Washer," she half-muttered.

---

He nodded courteously over the hand. "And I am Tumber." He paused for effect. "Called Tumber the Mighty." He made the impression he wanted, and smiled on her. "If you will dine with me, I will give you tales of battle and glory, magic and monsters, journeys and shipwrecks, all of which I have seen with my own eyes." It was quite true. Tumber could read, and had seen and memorized the best tales.

Elga didn't care whether he was a real hero or not. "Tell me everything. I want to hear it all. I wish I could see it all," she added without bitterness. Her eyes shone more brightly than the highlights in her auburn hair.

While Tumber spoke, a slender woman in her forties moved gracefully to the bar. She wore a shawl and carried a small satchel at her waist. "Am I too late for a meal?" Her voice was clear and cultured.

Otik, who had been judging her by the simplicity and travel stains of her clothes, said hastily, "No, lady. There are potatoes, and venison, and cider, and—"

"It smells lovely." She smiled. "And do call me Hillae, which is my name."

Tika stared in awe at the woman's hair. It flowed nearly to her waist and was jet black with a single gray streak to one side. Tika said, "Inns serve late on full-moon nights. People travel longer. I'd think you'd know that, from the road."

Hillae laughed. "So I look road-worn? No, don't blush; I *have* traveled for years, but customs differ." Tika nodded and backed away. The woman turned again to Otik. "I would love a meal."

"Certainly." Otik hesitated, glancing at the drovers and at an arriving stranger with an eye-patch. "If you wish, I could serve your dinner in a private room, Hillae."

She shook her head. "No such luxuries for me now."

She looked Otik in the eye and said frankly, "And I have eaten more meals alone than I care to."

Otik smiled back at her now, suddenly an equal. "I know what you mean, ma'am. I'll seat you in a bright corner; you'll not lack for company."

"Thank you." Hillae looked back at Tika, who was shyly watching the stranger with the eye-patch. He winked at the girl, and she looked away. "The barmaid is lovely. Your daughter?"

"Foster daughter." Otik added suddenly, "If you know much about young women and romance, ma'am, you might have a word with her. If you don't mind, I mean. She's got a broken heart every week, these past few months. I don't know what to say to her, and maybe you—" He spread his hands helplessly.

"She'll learn about broken hearts fast enough without my help. They grow up fast at that age." She patted Otik's hand, though Otik was years her senior. "But send her over when she's free. I'd love the company—as you knew." Hillae glided away, and Otik, for all he felt foolish, was glad he had asked her.

Now the locals were drifting in, for a night of gossip and warmth after their meals at home. First to come were the red-haired, gangly Patrig and his parents. Otik nodded to them. "Frankel. Sareh. Sorry, Patrig; no singers tonight."

"Are you sure?" he croaked. His voice, changing, hadn't come in right yet.

Patrig's mother leaned forward. "He talks all the time about the singers he's heard here. He loves music so."

"Loves it from afar," Frankel said, and chuckled as he mussed Patrig's hair. "Can't sing a note himself."

Patrig ducked and muttered, and the three of them went to sit down. On the way the young man passed

Loriel, newly arriving, who flashed her hair at him as she spun away.

A voice at Otik's elbow crackled, "Music and flirtation. All young folk want now is music and flirtation. It's not like the old days."

Otik nodded respectfully to Kugel the Elder. "I imagine not, sir. Though I did like a dance myself, in my younger days."

Kugelk scowled. "I mean long before then, young man. Back when life was simple and dignified, and there wasn't all this shouting about romance."

"I'm sure, sir. There's a seat waiting for you by the fire. Do you need any help?"

Kugel's wife, a bird of a woman, stepped from behind him. "I'm all the help he's ever needed—though the goddesses know he's needed all of that."

Kugel waved an angry hand at her, but let himself be guided around a huge farmer, who tipped a hat to him reverently but put it back on and drew up a chair not far from Elga and the knight. Otik returned to his work.

Though a few folk stopped for meals at noon, it wasn't until dusk on normal days and well after moonrise that the Inn attracted many weary travelers and locals. Few would waste the light, and fewer still were so desperate to reach destinations that they would travel late. With their meals Otik served hot cider and the old ale, warm spiced potatoes and, by request only, a venison "that warmed winter hearts," as he said. Outside there were already thin patches of ice on the brooks, and the trees were leafless. Early in the evening most of the venison was gone. Otik could scarcely remember an evening when the Inn was so busy and full.

The stranger with the eye-patch, looking more battered than rough, approached the bar. "Ale." He looked at the mugs, then with more respect at the polished tankards on their pegs behind the bar. "Tankard."

"A moment, sir." Otik gestured to Tika, who passed him the tap. He held it and closed his eyes, moving his lips, then pushed it against the side of the cask and hammered it home through the sealer with one sure stroke.

The stranger spun his coin meaningfully, but Otik only smiled. "Put your coin away, sir. The first draw of a new batch is always my gift."

"Thank you kindly." With his good eye, the stranger stared hungrily at the foaming outpouring as Otik turned the tap. "Looks good, it does." He smiled at Tika, who edged behind Otik.

With a polished stick Otik cleared the foam from the tankard. His heart rose as he saw the rich nut-brownness of the ale. Proof was in tasting—which Otik never did until his last guest had tried the new batch—but this ale was rich, eye-catching, as lovely as the gleaming wood of the Inn itself. "You're right, sir. Looks good." He sniffed it, and put an arm around Tika as he felt a wave of affection. "Tika and I made this ourselves, sir. We'd like your opinion."

The stranger took the tankard too hastily, then tried to compensate by judiciously staring at it, smelling it, holding it up to the stained-glass as though moonlight could help him see through pewter. Finally he tipped it up, steeply enough to be staring into his own beer as he drank. He froze there and said nothing, his throat quavering.

Otik froze with him. Ah, gods, was the man choking? Was this Otik's first bad batch?

The one-eyed man slammed his empty tankard down, foam ringing a wide, happy smile. "I love it."

The other patrons applauded. Otik had not even

known they were watching; he waved to them and began drawing off mug after mug after tankard after tankard. Soon he was circulating among a talkative, appreciative, friendly crowd. On the first pass he set ale in front of Tumber the Mighty and in front of Elga the Washer, in front of the bulky farmer (whose name was Mort), and in front of Reger.

The trader was tired and dusty, and looked at his ale longingly. Still, Reger kept to his own tradition of eyeing all the other patrons before drinking. Sometimes a former customer of his was nearby. Once, after nodding absently to a man he should have known, he had been knocked from his chair by a cropper wielding an apple squeezer that worked well as a bludgeon. Since Reger occasionally promised more than his trade goods could deliver, it was better to see such folk before they saw him.

The people of Solace, a pretty rustic bunch, were all he saw. He looked at Farmer Mort drinking in the corner near the door, at the scrawny Patrig near his parents at the central table, last and appreciatively at Elga, the muscled auburn woman at the next table. He thought, briefly, of going over to her, perhaps buying her ale.

On the other hand, Tumber the Mighty was already speaking to her, and she clearly loved his stories, if not him. Besides, she looked to have some anger in her, and as a tradesman, Reger had learned, young as he was, to look for that in people. It didn't look like a good time to interrupt her.

He shrugged. Maybe later. Reger reached for his tankard—

And was shoved back in his chair by a hand in the breastbone. It was the burly farmer, and he was glaring down at him. "None of that."

"None of what?" He squinted at the big man, who

still had farm boots on. From his muscles, Farmer Mort looked to juggle cows for a living.

The farmer ignored the quesiton. "Who do you think you are?"

"Who do you think I am?" Reger asked cautiously.

"Don't wise-mouth. I hate that. I hate it as much as I love her. Stop looking at my woman that way." Farmer Mort glanced, pulled almost helplessly, back toward the woman at the next table, Elga the well-muscled Washer.

"Your woman?" Reger looked back at her. "A moment ago you weren't even with her."

"Well, I love her. I love her more than anything, and you can't look at her that way."

"I wasn't looking at her." The tradesman fingered the short club at his waist. Some nights were for fighting, some weren't; surely this one wasn't, much as Reger loved a good fight. "My friend, you're only reading your own affection for her into all of us. Surely you can't think that I would interfere between you and a woman you've known for—how long did you say you'd known her?"

"Forever and ever." Farmer Mort shook his head wonderingly. "I've known her since I was a little hopper, coming in with Dad's cattle and stopping to get my dress clothes cleaned at her mother's shop before her. Why, I've even had this very shirt cleaned by her. Those hands have washed dirt and dung out of this—" He fingered the material, looking as though he might kiss it.

"Nice of her. How long have you loved her?"

"I don't know. A while, anyway." He scratched his head. "I just noticed after I finished my beer, see. That I loved her, I mean."

"Exactly. And you only just found out that you loved her, even though you've known her forever and—excuse me—you seem a discerning gentlemen." Reger winked in a friendly manner. "Perhaps she's an acquired taste."

"Are you saying she's ugly?" The farmer knotted a huge fist, product of a hand-plow, and waved it in the tradesman's face. "I won't have that now. She's the woman I love, and she's the most beautiful—the loveliest—"

Drunk, then. The tradesman sighed. "Look, just tell me what you want me to say and I'll say it. There's no need to be angry." He took a deep pull from his ale; no sense waiting until this lout spilled it.

Farmer Mort shook his shoulder. "Don't ignore me, and don't make fun of her. Do you want to fight?"

Reger put his tankard down, and the light in his eyes was strange and bright. "I wouldn't make fun of the most beautiful woman in the world."

The farmer squinted piggily at him. "You said you didn't love her."

"I lied." Reger added earnestly, "I do, you know." He took another drink.

"Here now!" The farmer shook him again. "Don't you do it to me." He repeated, "Do you want to fight?"

Reger set down the empty tankard and beamed at the auburn-haired Elga. There was a high buzzing in his ears. "A fight?" He smiled happily and reached for his club. "I *love* fighting."

The first blow caught the slack-jawed farmer in the stomach. Reger dusted his hands, bowed to one and all, and stood gaping at Elga until Farmer Mort, rising, caught him on the chin and sent him backward into the table.

Otik saw their table fall over, but there was no time to do anything. Brawling was to be suffered, now and then, but something even more mysterious was afoot. It seemed as if the entire room was humming with mischief. And those who weren't busy fighting were . . . well, courting and sparking.

Generally, on his rounds, Otik would tactfully bump any couple that was getting too affectionate for the comfort of his other customers. It didn't happen often. Tonight he was moving from couple to couple almost at a run, and some of them he had to pull apart. Everyone seemed to be edging into the private corners created by the irregular trunk of the vallenwood. What was wrong with these people?

He recoiled from the last pair with shock. Kugel the Elder, forced from the arms of his wife, glared up at him and hissed through the gaps where his teeth had once been. "Leave us alone, boy."

Otik backed away, appalled. Kugel was the oldest man in Solace. And to Otik, the fact that Kugel was embracing his own wife only made it worse. *What was wrong with everybody?*

He touched Tika's elbow. "Be freer with the ale. It may be the moon, or something in the air, but we'd best make this bunch sleepy just as quickly as possible." Tika, clearly upset by the goings-on around her, nodded and fairly sprinted toward the bar and the new casks.

In the center of the room, Patrig hopped clumsily onto the common table. He had a slopping tankard in hand, and waved it dangerously over people's heads. They clapped and ducked, stealing kisses from each other as they nearly bumped heads. Sareh stopped embracing her husband long enough to say, "Patrig, get down; you could get hurt."

He ignored his mother, spread his arms, and sang passionately but with little tune:

> No one can love—
> Quite like my love—

*Because her love—*
*Is all I love—*

He coughed and added,
*And in her love—*
*I find my love—*
*And then her love—*
*Is just like love—*

He went on for twenty lines, sipping ale after each line. Otik felt the boy was getting undue applause for his efforts; apparently, his theme had a lot of appeal tonight. Loriel, Tika's young rival, was gaping up at Patrig as though she was seeing the full moon for the first time. Her own mug was empty. Rian, of the seven gray hairs, was temporarily forgotten.

Finally, too excited to sing, Patrig threw up his arms, shouted, "Love, love, live," and crashed off the table. Otik made sure he wasn't hurt or dead, then ran to a corner table where two drovers, swearing fealty to each other, were strangling a stranger.

The raven-haired Hillae was gazing into her half-empty mug thoughtfully. "I wonder about her," Tika said dreamily to the frenzied Otik, who wasn't listening. "She is so beautiful, and perhaps wise. She has gone places. Done things. She has lived a life already. And who knows what secrets she might impart to me, if only we were friends."

Tika moved forward to refill her mug, and Hillae took another sip, set it down, and said aloud, but mostly to herself, "Farin would be thirty-three now. Gods rest him, a body like oak, and it still fell easily enough to fever." There were tears in her eyes. Tika retreated.

Meanwhile, Otik was refilling the mug of Elga the Washer, who was completely absorbed in Tumber's stories. The knight had drunk vast quantities of ale, and seemed most in love with himself; with every second breath he proclaimed his romantic and military prowess, and his adventures grew more outrageous. She didn't seem to notice, any more than she noticed the wobbly attentions of Reger or Farmer Mort whenever they popped up to proclaim their love of her before smashing each other down again.

Elga stared, elbow in hand, at the knight. When her mug was full, she tossed the ale down her throat and threw the empty mug sideways into Tumber's forehead. He didn't seem to notice, just went on describing an improbable epic of love and battle involving an opposing army, two warrior maids, a sea serpent, and a lute.

Elga stood full upright, threw her head back, and shouted, "Gods, goddesses, men and women, I am sick of laundry, cooking, children, and trees!"

Someone shouted approval, and she smashed her fist on the table. "Show me steel. Show me armor. Show me a battle, and something worth fighting for, and never stand between me and those things. I love adventure. I lust for glory. I crave—"

"And you shall have it," Tumber slurred. "All of it and more, in my great person. Come, queen of my battles, and worship my greatness. Thrill to watch my adventures. Glory in my talents, my prowess, my—"

"My god." Heads turned; Elga was no soft speaker. "*Your* battles? *Your* greatness? *Your* adventure?" Tumber almost cringed. "I'll have none of that. *My* battles, *my* conquest, *my* wars. Give me that!"

He gaped at her. She shoved him backward, hit his exposed jaw with her left fist, and caught his sword as he sprawled. She waved it above her head. "Now let all the world forget Elga the Washer and beware Elga the Warrior. I leave Solace, to seek the combat, the adventure, and the glory I love!"

"You can't take my sword," Tumber said from the floor. "It's my honor. It's my only battle companion—before you, of course. It's my *living*." He wavered. "It's borrowed," he finished miserably as he rose.

"Borrowed?" She hefted it, spun it with a supple wrist, pointed it at him.

He put his arms up. "Well, yes. From a knight in financial straits. But I really have used it a little." He added desperately, "Come, love, and we'll seek glory together. Really, I'll let you use it some, if you'll just give it back—"

She pulled the sword away as he reached. "Borrowed, is it? Now it's twice borrowed." She shouted, in a voice that made the tankards vibrate, "Off to fortune and glory!" A few lovers cheered her between kisses. Otik moved to block her exit, but Elga swung the stolen sword menacingly in the doorway. Otik ducked aside, and she was gone.

Tumber the Mighty scuttled past Otik, throwing coins at him. "For her drinks and mine. Really, I don't know what got into her. Wonderful girl, actually; she loved my stories almost as much as I do. Wait, love!" he called down the stairs, and dashed out of sight, knocking Otik sideways.

Otik nearly backed into a raised arm; a middle-aged, peasant couple were waving arms at each other, their eyes locked. "Did you or did you not look at her with pure desire, you great wobble-cheeked fool?" asked the woman.

"Anyone would," the man answered, loud enough to be heard several trees over. "Especially if he were married to a wretched mass of gripes and dimples like you, cow. And you're one to talk, aren't you—ogling that skinny little sly-looking traveler back—" He turned to point at Reger, wavering when all he could see was an occasional flailing fist or arm. "Back there, somewhere. Tramp."

"Pig." They grabbed each other's throats and vanished under the table.

Tika watched, hand to her mouth. Grunts and heavy breathing emerged from under the table. Otik wondered, trotting past to the next crisis, if the two were still fighting, or . . . ?

Tika rushed by him, nearly spilling ale from the pitcher. Otik grabbed her arm as she passed. "Did you give them full-strength ale?"

At first he thought he had grabbed her too hard; then he realized that her tears were from panic. "I did. Strong as can be, straight from the new kegs. But they all get worse, not better. They're not even sleepy."

"Impossible." Otik sniffed at the ale. So did Tika. "Then what's happening?" wondered Otik.

From just the sniffing, Tika's eyes were already bright and restless. Otik knew the answer almost as soon as he had asked the question.

"Moonwick." Otik remembered speaking of magic, and he remembered leaving the kender alone with the alewort. "The empty purse he dropped." A love potion! "If that damned thief-trickster ever returns—"

Just in time he saw the man with the eye-patch raise his tankard, staring directly at Tika. Her eyes leveled in return. Otik gave a start and shoved her hastily behind the bar, setting a barrel in her place. The man licked his lips and came forward, tankard in hand. At the time, setting out the barrel seemed a clever feint, but it opened unforeseen floodgates. Despite Otik's protest—"I'm sorry, there seems to be something wrong with the ale"—the stranger methodically rolled out every last cask. The Inn guests cheered, looking up briefly from their loving and fighting. And the ale continued to pour.

After that, things became confused. The drovers had started several small fights, wandering off and losing interest between drinking rounds, then embracing each other passionately before starting up again. Patrig and Loriel were dancing in the middle of the room. Patrig's mother and father were kissing against the tree trunk. Hillae had disappeared somewhere, and Reger was riding Farmer Mort horseback in circles around the room. Their whoops and cries were indistinguishable from whatever was going on over there, and there, in the shadows.

Tika said, "Can ale do all that?" She looked interestedly at the mug on her tray. "Otik, what if I—"

"No."

"But it looks like so much—"

"No. It looks like too much, that's what it does." Otik pulled her away from a line of dancing old men and women.

"But if Loriel can—"

"No, no, and no. You're not Loriel." Otik made a decision. "Here's your cloak. Wear it. Here's mine; sleep in it. Find a place, go, and don't come back to the Inn tonight."

"But you can't manage without me."

Otik gestured at the room now frenzied with activity. "I can't manage *with* you. Go."

"But where will I sleep?"

"Anywhere. Outside. Someplace safe. Go, child." He cleared her way to the door, pulling her with one hand.

As she stepped into the night, she said in a hurt voice, "But why?"

Otik stopped dead. "Well, we'll talk about that later. Go, child. I'm sorry."

He tried to kiss her good night. Tika, angry, ducked and ran. "I want a place of my own!" she cried. Otik stared after her, then closed the door and tried to get back to the fire.

The best he could do was edge to the bar. The dancers and fighters had split into smaller but more boisterous groups, shouting and singing to each other. Otik, unable even to feed the fire, watched helplessly as the bodies became struggling silhouettes, the silhouettes coupled shadows, the shadows a noisy dark. That night the inn was full of joyous and angry voices, but all he could see, by a single candle held near the mirror, was his own face, alone.

The next morning Otik stepped dazedly over broken mugs and intertwined bodies. Most of the benches lay on their sides, one completely turned over. It was like a battlefield, he thought, but for the life of him he couldn't tell who won. There were bodies on bodies, and clothing hung like banners over chairs, and outflung arms and wayward legs sticking from under the few pieces of upright furniture. Tankards lay on their sides everywhere, and everywhere pieces of pottery rocked on the floor as people snored or groaned.

The fire was nearly out. Not even during the worst nights of Haggard Winter had that happened. Otik put tinder on the last embers, blew them into flame, added splinters, and laid the legs of a broken chair on.

He moved the skillet as quietly as possible, but inevitably the eggs sizzled in the grease. Someone whimpered. Otik tactfully pulled the pan from the fire.

Instead he tiptoed around, gathering dented tankards, pottery shards, and a few stray knives and daggers. A haggard young stranger grabbed his ankle and pleaded for water. When Otik returned, the man was asleep, his arm wrapped protectively around the raven-tressed Hillae. Instead of making him look protective, it made him seem even younger. She smiled in her sleep and stroked his hair.

The steps thudded too loudly; someone was stamping up them. Otik heard more whimpers. The front door boomed against the wall, and Tika, her hair pulled primly back, stepped through and looked disapprovingly at the debris and tangled bodies. "Shall we clean up?" she said too loudly.

Otik winced as the others cringed around her. "In a while. Would you go fetch water? We'll need more than the cistern holds, I'm afraid."

"If you really need it." She slammed the inn door. The thump of her tread down the stairs shook the floor.

"Can't we kill her?" Reger the trader groaned. His right arm was wrapped around both his ears, and his head was cradled on the sleeping farmer's chest. A few weak voices croaked encouragement.

"Even think that again," Otik said quietly, "and I will bang two pots together."

It was quiet after that.

Gradually the bodies disentwined. A few rose, shakily. Hillae approached the bar with dignity and passed some coins. "Thank you," she said quietly. "Not the evening I'd planned, but interesting enough, I suppose."

"Not the evening I'd planned either," Otik agreed. "Will you be all right then?"

"Tired." She pulled her hair back over her shoulders. "It's time I was back home. I have a bird, you know, and it needs feeding."

"Oh, a caged bird, then." Otik realized he wasn't at his sharpest. "Songbird?"

"Lovebird. The mate is dead. You know, I really ought to set it free." She smiled suddenly. "Good day." She bent quietly over, kissed the cheek of her sleeping partner, and walked silently and gracefully out.

---

Tika struggled back in, knocking buckets against the doorframe. A few patrons flinched, but glared at Otik through red-rimmed eyes and said nothing.

He took the water from her. "Thank you. Now go tell Mikel Claymaker that I need fifty mugs." He passed her a handful of coins. "There's my earnest for the order."

She stared at the money. Otik was as casual with his coin today as he was with his help. "Shouldn't I stay here?" she said loudly. "You'll need someone to mop the floor—" She stamped on it to shake the dust for emphasis.

"This is how you can best help me," he said softly. She looked puzzled, but nodded.

A body detached itself from the chair on which it had been draped like a homemade doll. "Tika—"

"Loriel?" Tika couldn't believe it. "Your hair looks like a bird's nest." She added, "Sea bird. Sloppy one."

"It does?" Loriel put a hand up, then dropped it. "No matter. Tika, the most exciting thing. Patrig told me last night that he likes me. He said so again this morning."

"Patrig?" Tika looked around. A pair of familiar boots stuck out from under the main table, toes spread. "Loriel, he spoke this morning?"

"For a while. Then he fell back asleep." Her eyes shone. "He sang so beautifully last night—"

"I remember," Tika said flatly. She couldn't imagine anyone admiring his singing, and Loriel was musical. "Walk with me, and tell me about it."

They ran down the stairs together.

After that, painfully, the patrons gathered their belongings—in some cases their clothes—and paid up. Some had to walk quite a distance to find everything. Purses and buskins and jerkins lay throughout the room, and knapsacks hung from all points and pegs—

one, incredibly, from a loose side-peg in a ceiling cross-beam. For a while Otik watched, attempting to prevent thievery. Eventually he gave up.

Reger the Trader slapped the bar with a snake-embossed foreign coin and said, "This will cover my lodgings, and could I buy a marketing supply of that ale? In this weather it would keep for the road—"

Otik bit the coin and rejected it, dropping it with a dull clank. "Not for sale."

"Oh. Yes, well—" Reger fumbled for real money. "If you change your mind, I'll be back. There." He counted the change, then added a copper. "And give breakfast to my friend there. He may not feel too well." He gestured at Farmer Mort, who had a huge lump behind his right ear.

"I see that. Good day, sir." Otik watched with approval as Reger took the stairs lightly and quickly. On instinct, as when a kender left, he checked the spoons. Some were missing.

Patrig woke healthy and whole, as the young will, and left singing—badly. He asked after Loriel on his way out. Kugel the Elder and his wife tiptoed out bickering, hand in hand. They turned in the door and frowned disapprovingly at the other couples.

The couple that had fought, or whatever, under the tables, left separately. A man whom Otik had barely noticed the night before paid for a room—"so that my friend can sleep if she wishes." When Otik asked when his friend wished to wake up, he blushed and said, "Oh, don't wake her. Not for half a day. Longer, in fact." Otik noticed, as innkeepers will, the circular groove on the man's third finger, where he usually wore a ring.

The rest were sitting up, looking around embarrassedly, testing their heads and tongues. Otik stepped to the center of the common room and said diffidently,

"If the company believes it is ready for breakfast—" he looked through the stained glass to the long-risen sun—"or early lunch—" He nodded at the murmur of assent and put the skillet of eggs back on the fire. At the kitchen door he called to Riga the cook for potatoes, but not too loudly.

By mid-morning he had assessed the night's damage and its profit. After re-hammering the tankards and replacing the mugs, he would still have the greatest profit he had ever made from one night, and not half the lodgings paid up yet. He lifted the pile of coins. It took two hands, and shone in the light from a broken rose windowpane.

All the same, when the man with the eye-patch croaked that he wanted a farewell mug "to guard against road dust," Otik laid hands on the final keg and said firmly, "No, sir. I will never sell this ale full strength again." He added, "You may have a mug of the regular stock."

The man grunted. "All right. Not that I blame you. But it's a shame and a crime, if you intend to water that batch. How can you water ale and not kill the flavor?"

He drained the mug and staggered out. Otik marveled that such a seasoned drinker didn't know the secret of watering ale. You watered ale with ale, of course.

He looked back at his last cask of the only magical brew he had ever made and, gods willing, the only batch he ever would make.

He took his corkscrew in one hand and the pitcher in the other, and he carried the funnel looped by the handle over his belt. Each cask, one by one, he unstoppered, tapped a pint to make room, and poured in a pint of the new ale. It took most of the morning, and almost all of his last fresh cask.

When he finished at midday, every last barrel was forty or fifty parts ale to one part liquid love, and he had one-half pint of the new ale left. He was sweating, and his biceps ached from drawing stoppers and pounding them back. He slumped on the stool back of the bar and turned around to look at the casks.

The store-room was floor to ceiling with barrels. For as long as the barrels lasted, the Inn of the Last Home would hardly have a fight, or a grudge, or a broken heart.

Otik smiled, but he was too tired to maintain it. He wiped his hands on the bar-rag and said hoarsely, "I could use a drink."

The last half-pint sat on the bar, droplets coursing down its sides. Circular ripples pulsed across it as the wind moved the tree branches below the floor.

He could offer it to any woman in the world, and she would love him. He could have a goddess, or a young girl, or a plump helpmate his own age who would steal the covers and tease him about his weight and mull cider for him on the cold late nights. All these years, and he had barely had time to feel lonely.

All these years.

Otik looked around the Inn of the Last Home. He had grown up polishing this bar and scrubbing that uneven, age-smoothed floor. Most of the folk here were friends, and strangers whom he tried to make welcome. He heard the echo of himself saying to Tika, "In all the world no place else can ever be home for them."

He smiled around at the wood, at the stained glass, at the friends he had, and at the friends he hadn't met yet. He raised his glass. "Your health, ladies and gentlemen."

He drank it in one pull.

# Wayward Children

## Richard A. Knaak

"*A* fool's errand, that's what this is!"

Though the words were little more than a hiss, B'rak heard them all too well. He also agreed with them, but it was not his place to say so—especially as he was captain of this patrol.

Others heard the complaint as well. "If you cannot keep your warriors in line, captain, I will be glad to do so for you!"

B'rak hissed angrily at the tall figure wrapped in black cloth. If there was one point on which B'rak agreed with humans, it was that magic-users were not to be trusted, much less liked. But he had no choice: they were assigned to all patrols. He unfurled his wings to emphasize his displeasure at having a mage along on this scouting mission. His metallic silver skin glistened in the light as he pointed a talon at the other.

"The Dragon Highlord commanded that you accompany us, Vergrim, not that you lead us. I will deal with my men as I see fit."

Vergrim's answering smile made even draconians uneasy. Nevertheless, he nodded acceptance of B'rak's words and turned his attention back to the wilderness around them.

They had been wandering for days among the rich woodland just north of the New Sea. Their mission was to assure headquarters that this region was empty of resistance, something that even now made B'rak question the leadership of the Dragon Highlord. He and his men should be fighting for the glory of the Queen. Of what use were his tactical skills against a random elk, several birds, and trees as far as the eye could see?

Sith, his lieutenant, tapped him on the shoulder and pointed to the right. Reptilian eyes narrowed as the patrol captain studied the woods. They widened equally as quickly. Was that an upright figure he saw in the distance? Eagerly, he studied it. That was no animal. An elf or, more likely, a human. Elves were generally more difficult to notice. Secretly, he would prefer a human. Elves were sly, more prone to use tricks than face a warrior one-on-one. Humans knew how to fight. With humans, B'rak could generally assure himself of an entertaining battle.

Some of the warriors in back muttered quietly, their wings rustling. He waved them to silence, though he could well understand their eagerness. This was the first sign of activity they had come across. B'rak fairly quivered with excitement. Had the Highlord known more than the orders had stated? The captain glared at Vergrim, but the draconian magic-user's attention was focused completely on the shadowy figure moving through the trees. If the mage knew something, he was hiding it well. That was not at all like Vergrim.

B'rak dispatched two of his best trackers to follow the figure. The stranger might be just a single hunter, but the captain would not take that chance. There might even be a village up ahead, though how it could have escaped their notice when they were searching earlier was beyond his imagination.

The wait for the trackers to return was long. It was not helped by the constant muttering that arose from Vergrim's need to memorize his spells. More than one warrior was forced to stretch stiffened wings. B'rak tapped his sword impatiently. The day neared its finish.

The trackers returned two hours later. They reported that the figure had led them from one spot to another for no apparent reason. Just when they were convinced that he knew of their presence, the solitary traveler had stepped into the clearing around a small village. The inhabitants of the village were elves.

B'rak was slightly disappointed on hearing this, but he pushed the thought aside. Here, at least, would be some action. One of the trackers handed him a map showing the location of the village. It was some distance to the northeast. They would arrive just before dark.

Vergrim studied the map with great interest, but uttered no comment. B'rak ignored him; this was a possible battle situation and his authority was supreme in that respect. The magic-user could advise, but nothing more.

They moved cautiously through the woods in the general direction of the village. B'rak sent men ahead in order to avoid an ambush. As he walked, he noticed his head beginning to throb. An unusual occurrence, he was not subject to such weakness. Fortunately, the pain was not severe enough to affect his judgment.

. They met no resistance whatsoever. This might have been virgin forest, with the draconians the first intelligent life to pass through it. B'rak's warriors relaxed, their minds turning to thoughts of looting. The captain frowned; discipline was slipping. He avoided looking at Vergrim, knowing the other would be wearing that mocking smile.

The village, when they came to it, was so small as to be almost unbelievable. It couldn't house more than a dozen families. The homes were simple, more like one might have expected humans to live in than elves.

B'rak saw immediately that even with only twenty warriors and the magic-user, he could still have taken it easily. He spat on the ground, the throbbing in his head increasing his anger tenfold. Too simple.

Unrest was spreading through his patrol. Even Sith, always calm and quiet, was shifting impatiently. It had been far too long since any of them had seen action, and now it appeared that they had been deprived of it once more. B'rak finally gave the signal. The patrol advanced into the clearing.

At first, they saw no one. Then, gradually, heads appeared in windows and doorways. Surprisingly, there were no looks of anger, no shouts of hate. The elves stepped out into the openings and stared. Just stared. They seemed to be waiting for something, looking for someone.

The draconians stopped abruptly, alarmed at the unusual reaction of the elves. B'rak turned to Vergrim.

"Well? Are we in any threat of attack here?"

The hooded figure shook his head in distaste. "We have nothing to fear from these weaklings! I read only the desire to help and care for us. Pfah! Even their elven kin would be disgusted at such tolerance as I feel."

Sith leaned close. "Shall we destroy the village?"

B'rak waved him away. "It is not worth the trouble now. If this is an example of what we can expect, the Highlord has little to fear from this region." He studied the elves, frowned, and turned back to his companions. "Where are their young? I see only adults—and most of those are silver-haired."

One of the trackers came up and bowed before him. "We studied the village for a long time before reporting back, captain. Not once did we see any young."

The throbbing in B'rak's head had become little more than a nuisance, but it was just enough to unleash his anger. He shouted to the elves, "I want your leaders here now! If they do not appear, my men will raze this village and kill everyone!"

The elves did not speak, but some of them stepped aside, opening a path for the oldest elf any of the draconians had ever seen. His beard was a sparkling silver and came near to matching his arms in length. He wore only a simple cloth robe, apparently the village's only form of clothing since the other elves were clad in a similar fashion. He carried a long wooden staff, which he also used as a crutch. As he neared the draconian leader, his eyes sparkled. The ancient male wore no sign of authority that B'rak could identify, but the captain had no doubt whatever that this was indeed the village elder.

Vergrim hissed. "Careful, B'rak. He may be a cleric. This whole village smells of a shrine or something. See how they all dress, how they all act."

"Do you detect any threat from this old one? From the look of things, he can barely stand."

"No. As with the others, I detect only the wish to help. Curious." The Black Robe sounded almost disappointed, B'rak noted.

The elder paused before the reptilian warriors. "I am Eliyah, the Speaker for this village. We bid you welcome and offer you our humble hospitality."

The captain waved away the offer for the moment and went immediately to the point that concerned him. "Where are your young? Your children? I warn you, if they do not appear, I shall give the order to have you all put to death."

Eliyah sighed and a sadness seemed to sweep over the entire elven population. B'rak was taken aback by the intensity of the emotion. Had some plague struck down the young? Were he and his patrol in danger? He quickly discarded the thought; no plague he knew of would take the young and strong and leave the old and sickly.

The elder waved a feeble hand at the group of elves that had closed in behind him. "These are all you will find here. Our children have been turned from our ways and no longer recognize us. We pray they will return to us, but our hope grows faint."

Draconians are not known for their sympathy. B'rak, however, found it impossible not to feel some of the hurt the elves bore. Even Vergrim looked downcast for a moment.

The pain in the captain's head brought him back to reality. He cursed harshly, clutching at his head. Eliyah touched his shoulder in a gesture of concern. Sith came to his commander's aid.

"Are you all right, captain?"

"My head pounds, that is all. We will stay here for the night. Secure the area. Post a guard. Secure hostages."

There was a commotion at the back of the patrol. B'rak steadied himself but could not see what was happening. Vergrim, who stood taller, looked at the commotion and then came up to B'rak.

"One of your men appears to have collapsed. Exhaustion, perhaps. I will see to him."

"Captain . . ."

B'rak turned once more to the Speaker. "What is it, old one?"

"You and your companions need food and rest. Come. You have nothing to fear from us. My people will see to your men. Food, shelter—whatever they wish."

Sith jumped on the last statement. "A trick! They will poison the food."

"Unlikely. We will take hostages if necessary. They will not dare harm any of us if their kin are in danger. Any attempt to do so will be answered with the total destruction of this village." B'rak summoned two of his warriors. "You two will come with me." To the elf, he said, "I will accept your hospitality—by staying at your home."

Sith opened his mouth to protest, but decided against it. He merely glared at the elven Speaker and then stalked off to do his duty. Eliyah bowed respectfully and turned, his face having revealed no animosity toward his sudden houseguest. His pace was so slow that the captain had ample time to study the other villagers as they walked along.

As a whole, they were a sorrowful people. B'rak wondered what could have brought elves to such a state. They did not seem to fear draconians and were certainly not hostile to them. There were no signs of plague or destruction. The entire place was an enigma. What had really happened to their children? He chuckled. Boredom, perhaps.

The dwellings of the elves proved to be even more dismal up close. All were constructed from wood and generally consisted of one room. With that in mind, the home of the Speaker appeared comparatively luxurious. It rested against one side of an enormous tree and was no more than a few yards from the main village. Like the others, it was of wood, but large enough to house the entire population. B'rak suspected the structure doubled as a meeting house and contemplated future uses for it.

An elven woman with long, flowing tresses of silver mixed with flakes of gold greeted them at the entrance. Though obviously old, she was still a handsome woman. B'rak, though, could not think of her as anything but someone's grandmother.

"My greetings to our guests."

Eliyah hugged her briefly and then turned back to the draconian commander. "This is my mate, Aurilla Starleaf. She will prepare food for you while I show your men where they may rest. Is that acceptable?"

B'rak blinked. Acceptable? The question made him smile. He was beginning to like these people and their ways. With a flourish that would have done the Highlord justice, B'rak gave his approval. The Speaker left and his mate entered the building. The captain hesitated before following her and turned to the guards.

"See that I am not disturbed. Keep an eye on those two old ones, too. Sith will see to it that you are relieved. Until then, I expect you to be on your guard."

They saluted. B'rak nodded, turned, and sauntered inside, feeling every inch the conqueror.

If the outside appearance of the dwelling hinted simplicity, the inside stated it quite bluntly. There were few pieces of furniture, save a table and two chairs. From the pillows and blankets scattered around, B'rak guessed that the elves here had little use for such things.

The female called Aurilla stepped into the room, a hot bowl in her tiny hands. She gestured to the table. "Please sit. I have made you some broth. I am sure you will find it to your liking."

B'rak purposely displayed long rows of sharp teeth designed for tearing. He much preferred meat to plants and broths. Fresh meat, especially. The elf was unaffected by his act. She smiled and placed the broth on the table. The draconian sniffed. It did smell good.

There was meat in it, too, judging by the aroma. He made his way to the table and sat down in one of the chairs.

The bowl was small, allowing him to swallow the contents in three gulps. He looked up, tongue clearing away the last vestiges of the broth. Aurilla was already there, a second bowl in her hands. B'rak grunted his satisfaction, and she smiled like a mother who had just been complimented by her favorite child. The draconian could not help chuckling at the odd picture that presented.

He took longer with the second bowl. His headache was nagging. Sleep was now becoming an urgent need. He grew impatient for the Speaker's return. One taloned hand gripped the now-empty bowl and crushed it. As if on cue, the ancient elf returned.

"I have prepared sleeping quarters for you with your men. Or you may stay here if you wish."

"I will stay here. My second and the mage will be allowed in here as well. My warriors will be satisfied with whatever they can find." Such are the privileges of rank, the captain added mentally.

There was suddenly a commotion at the entrance. B'rak, hearing draconian voices raised in anger, pulled out his sword. A trap! I've been a fool! They've led me on a leash! He rushed through the doorway.

Vergrim was there, looking very sinister and very upset. The two guards blocked his path. B'rak cursed; he had not meant they should prevent the magic-user from entering. No doubt the only thing holding Vergrim back from retaliating was the fact that he believed they were only following their leader's orders. The patrol leader sheathed his weapon and stepped forward to try and rectify the situation.

"Hold, all of you! What is it, Vergrim? Why do you disturb me?"

---

Richard A. Knaak

The Black Robe straightened his hood and glared at the two guards. "If I may be permitted to speak with you in private?"

B'rak waved the two aside. "Come inside."

"I will not go in there. It is tainted by the weak creatures who live in it."

"I'll remember that when I'm sleeping in there. What is it you want?"

"I said I would speak with you in private. Send these away."

The captain stretched his wings. "You try my patience, Vergrim. Very well. You two, seek out Sith. Tell him you are to be fed. Return here immediately after, however."

The guards responded eagerly. B'rak turned his attention once more to the mage. Vergrim stared past the patrol leader and frowned. B'rak twisted around and discovered both the Speaker and his mate standing in the entranceway. Both wore looks of concern.

"Await me inside. Go!"

They reluctantly stepped back inside the dwelling. B'rak focused on Vergrim and prayed that this time he would hear what the magic-user was so distraught about. Each delay was costing him sleep. To make matters worse, his head was now buzzing worse than before.

"You have three minutes. Speak!"

"I have inspected the warrior who collapsed. His name is S'sira."

"I know him. Quiet but deadly. Go on."

"He is not suffering from fatigue. He complains of headaches and dizziness, but it is not due to a lack of rest. I cannot say for sure, but I believe he may be suffering from some disease."

The captain folded his arms. "You believe it has something to do with the villagers."

"Look for yourself. Where are all the young? The strong? It would explain much."

B'rak laughed harshly. "It explains nothing. I have already thought of that. What disease, pray tell, kills the young and strong while allowing one such as the Speaker to go untouched? Sickness is nothing new to me. If you cannot care for S'sira, it shall be in the Queen's hands."

"You are a fool. Like all warriors. Your own life may be in danger."

"Have a care, mage!" B'rak hissed. Vergrim turned away, thus ending any further conversation. The patrol leader clutched his head; the buzzing was now at a level where it hurt to think. He stalked back into the Speaker's home and shouted for the elf.

Eliyah was already there, a silent spectre. B'rak, already in a foul mood, cursed at him. The elder smiled sympathetically and asked if he wished to rest now. The draconian muttered an affirmative.

The sleeping room proved to be as drab as the rest of the speaker's hovel, though it mattered little to B'rak at this point. He only wanted to lie down and forget the buzzing in his head. He wanted to forget Black Robes and struggles for domination. When Eliyah finally stopped before a pile of pillows and blankets, the captain virtually flung himself to the ground. It was not the most comfortable position for one of his kind, with his wings all crunched up, but he was beyond caring about such trivial things. The Speaker made to leave, but the draconian summoned him back.

"See to it that I rest peacefully, elf. No one, especially the Black Robe, is to disturb my slumber."

Eliyah looked down at him with great seriousness. "You shall not be disturbed, my son. We shall see to that."

B'rak smiled and drifted off, oddly assured by the statement.

Soaring like a bird. High in the heavens. Below him, some of the creatures cursed to a life on one level trudged along their dreary way. He swooped down on them, frightening the lot. They scattered hither and yonder, calling out his name in terror.

He had not meant to frighten them. Not really. They were an interesting group, these small creatures. Dwarves, most likely. He landed gracefully and called to them, telling them that he meant no harm, was only trying to have a little fun.

It took much coaxing to get them to come out of their hiding places. When they did, it was carefully and in small groups of two and three. He smiled in order to reassure them. They smiled back.

When they were close, he let loose the flame.

They shrieked and ran. He could not tell if he had burned any of them. Truly, he had only meant to play with them. He was horrified at himself. With a terrible cry, he shot into the heavens. The clouds were not high enough for him. He flew up and up, seeking the stars and the powers behind them. His cry ripped through the fabric of reality, touching the ears of the gods themselves.

They were there. Opposites. The Queen of Darkness and the brilliant figure clad in platinum armor. Both reached for him. He heard the countless voices crying to him, calling to him as a parent calls for a child who is lost. Almost he came to them.

The light frightened him, though. It wanted to twist him, make him other than he was. B'rak turned and fled, flying to the safety and security of the Queen of Darkness. She welcomed him back.

All turned to black. The voices wailed at the loss

and then faded away.

B'rak woke with a start. He hissed loudly in the darkness, having taken it for part of his dream. Someone stirred nearby. The draconian sniffed. Sith. No one else. Vergrim had apparently decided to seek rest elsewhere.

Sith hissed in his sleep, apparently the victim of dreams not to his liking. B'rak stood up, his eyes now accustomed to the lack of light, and rubbed his head. The buzzing was still there, but at a level barely noticeable. The nightmare was all but forgotten now; the feeling of unease was not. B'rak flexed his wings in thought and then suddenly departed the lodge.

He made his way quietly past the sleeping elves in the other room and stepped outside. The sun was not yet up. The captain hissed to himself. He turned to one of the two guards at the entrance and kicked him. The figure cursed and clutched its leg. B'rak uttered a quiet but direct order—along with the consequences of slow obedience. The warrior quickly stood at attention.

B'rak breathed into his face. "Seek out the trackers and have them report to me. Now!"

The soldier scurried away. B'rak switched to the remaining guard, who now stood poised and ready for battle. The draconian commander moved so that he stood eye-to-eye with the other.

"Where is the Black Robe? Have you seen him or were you asleep all night?"

"He is with the stricken one, captain—S'sira."

"Where would that be?"

The voice floated through the waning night. "There is no need to look for me, captain. I am here."

B'rak whirled. Even in the darkness, he could make out the burning eyes of Vergrim. The magic-user was buried deep within the black cloak which seemed almost an extension of his own form. The mage looked grim.

"It is odd that you should come seeking me, captain. I was just on my way to speak with you. Interesting, don't you think? Tell me, is your headache better?"

"Why do you ask?"

"I shall tell you when you have answered my question. Is your headache better?"

"Yes. It only buzzes slightly now. I found it difficult to sleep."

The hood bobbed up and down as Vergrim nodded. "I suspected as much. You might be interested to know that a number of the men have also complained of headaches and buzzing. S'sira is apparently the only one to have been stricken badly. He babbles like a madman and his form is contorted from pain."

The first rays of light broke through the darkness. B'rak bared his teeth. "He wasn't that sick before. When did this start?"

"Soon after the patrol settled down. Most of those touched were asleep. Shortly after waking, they grew better."

At that moment, the other guard returned with the trackers. They saluted. B'rak ignored them at first, his thoughts on a hundred possibilities. At last, he came to a decision. He turned to the newcomers.

"Did you survey the surrounding forest?"

The two trackers looked at one another. B'rak's eyes narrowed. "That is standard procedure, is it not?"

The senior of the two spoke. "Captain, we did survey the forest. It is just that we found nothing to report. You saw the map. Nothing but trees and grass for miles."

The patrol leader nodded. "I see. Very well, you are

dismissed."

The trackers departed with great haste. B'rak looked at the Black Robe. "You detect nothing from these elves?"

"Only the same as before—the desire to help and care for us. I have not really paid much more attention to them. They are worth less than gully dwarves. At least those creatures know no better. These elves are purely pathetic."

"Then, what do you believe the cause of this—this illness to be?"

"I know not. I felt it necessary to report my feelings and possibly warn you."

B'rak grunted. "Consider me warned."

Vergrim hissed. "I shall see what else I can do for your man. I fear it will not be enough, though."

"May we be of service?"

The elven Speaker and his mate stood behind them. The captain had no idea how long they had been there, but he was pleased to see that the Black Robe was just as startled. He looked from one elf to the other. "How can you help?"

"Our knowledge covers a span of countless generations. It may be that there is something in it that relates to your ill warrior. We only wish to help."

B'rak eyed them skeptically. "Vergrim?"

The mage's voice was barely audible. "I still sense nothing but worry and care for us. I do not understand it, but it is there. They may be of some use. I shall, however, trust them only so far."

"Shall I dispatch a guard to assist you?"

Vergrim scoffed. "I think I can safely handle two aged elves."

The draconian commander nodded. To the elves he replied, "Very well. Go with the magic-user. Be warned—he shall watch your every move! If my warrior dies, you two will follow immediately."

"We understand, captain. We will do what we can."

Vergrim hissed and motioned them to follow him. They did so, maintaining a respectable distance from the magic-user. B'rak watched them depart and rubbed a leathery hand across his chin.

"Sith!"

His second, looking half-dead, stumbled out of the Speaker's dwelling. The captain allowed him a moment to organize himself.

"Captain?"

"You are in charge for now. Organize the patrol for action. I shall return shortly."

"Yes, captain."

B'rak adjusted his sword belt and set out toward the forest himself. Now and then, he would pass one of the elves. All refused to meet his gaze. He hissed softly; there was a difference in their attitude. What it was he could not place. He only knew there was a difference. The sadness was there, but something had changed.

He walked for some time. The woods replaced the village. Eventually he paused at what he estimated to be a fair distance from the community. The land was hilly; another two hours would bring him to one of the lesser mountain ranges in this region. The hills, though, would serve his purpose.

He chose the tallest, most jagged of the hills. One side ended in a sheer cliff. The slight breeze tempted him. Though his wings were of little use for actual flight, he could easily glide some distance. That, however, was not his purpose for being here.

As he had surmised, the hill gave him an excellent view of the surrounding landscape, including the village. Far to the southwest lay what looked like the edge of the New Sea. On either side, vast mountains thrust up from the earth, like great walls protecting the region. The flatter lands consisted only of forest. Virgin forest. Massive trees and lush fields.

His suspicions confirmed, B'rak made his way swiftly down the hill. He prayed Sith had obeyed his instructions and mobilized the patrol. There was still a chance for victory if he had done so. At the very least, the draconians would not be unprepared when the elves made their move.

A trap. Even elves left signs of their existence other than a single, tiny village. B'rak knew of the elaborate dwellings formed from nature, knew of the cities created by the artistic race. A population, though, must eat, and B'rak, a veteran of many battles, knew that even the elves cultivated food and traded with their own kind. Eliyah and his people, though, had no fields, no groves of fruit-bearing trees, no cities coexisting with nature.

In short, the village existed only for the patrol's benefit. A lure. Somehow, they had known his patrol would be coming. After that, it was a matter of waiting.

The draconian cursed his blindness. Sorcery had to be involved. Such colossal errors in judgment were not possible, at least not by a veteran such as himself. Even Vergrim had fallen prey to it. Vergrim with his power, his spells, his ability to read what others felt. All the Black Robe had found was the desire to help.

That was the piece of the puzzle still hidden. They could have killed him, several times over. He had certainly been careless enough, pretending to be the mighty conqueror of a handful of peaceful elves. They could have killed him in his sleep.

They had done nothing.

He reached the outskirts of the village, half-expecting battle. The elves were nowhere to be seen.

Neither was Vergrim. But Sith and the patrol were awaiting him. His second-in-command jumped to attention.

"Your orders, captain?"

B'rak surveyed the village, the trap, and hissed, "I want this village burned to the ground! I want the elves slaughtered, their bodies burned! Start with the hostages! The responsibility is yours. Be prepared for battle! This is a trap! I must seek the Black Robe out before it is too late!"

Sith grinned as the captain hurried by. His teeth glittered in the sun as he barked out orders. Here, at last, was what he had been waiting for. Here was action. He pulled a burning stick out of a fire some of the warriors had built earlier. Others followed his example.

It was then a race to see who would be the one to start the inferno.

B'rak was nearly spent by the time he reached the dwelling where the elves had housed the stricken warrior. It was apart from the rest of the village. Behind him, the shrieks of his warriors could be heard. He hoped they would not accidentally burn down the forest in their enthusiasm. At least, not until the patrol was well on its way.

He was met by Vergrim at the entrance to the hut. The Black Robe, looking drawn, eyed him in a peculiar manner.

"What have you done, B'rak?"

"This is a trap, mage! Just as you originally believed! A very subtle trap!"

The Black Robe continued to stare at him. "What have you done?"

"My patrol is even now burning this village to the ground! I have ordered these elves to be slaughtered before their kinsmen can arrive! They are crafty, Vergrim! Crafty enough to fool the senses of a magic-user!"

The other draconian nodded slowly. "True. It was all for nothing, though. The plan failed. Nothing could be done. The Queen's spell was stronger than we had imagined."

B'rak hissed angrily. "We? What spell? What are you talking about? Where is the elf and his mate? What have they done to you, mage? You're acting even stranger than usual!"

Vergrim moved to one side of the entrance. "You had best see for yourself, captain."

Pushing the mage aside, B'rak burst into the hut. The darkness of the interior prevented him from seeing anything at first and he wondered why there were no windows. Within moments, though, his eyes had adjusted completely.

The draconian backed up a step in horror, every oath to the Queen of Darkness escaping from his mouth as he sought to avoid looking at the thing on the blanket. It was S'sira—and it was not. The form changed constantly, as if two forces sought domination and could not successfully defeat one another, the commander thought.

Disgusted, he pulled the sword from its sheath and forced himself to stand over the shifting mass. One stroke cut off what should have been the head. B'rak picked up a large piece of cloth, intending to use it to clean his weapon. The cloth turned out to be part of a dark robe which had once belonged to Vergrim. The magic-user's charred body lay crumpled in a corner.

"The Queen's hold is too great." The voice was that of the mage, but the form was that of an elf. Looking at him closely, feeling an unreasonable fear creep over him B'rak saw that it was Eliyah . . . and yet it wasn't Eliyah. "We should have never believed she would honor an agreement."

"Some of us refused to believe there was no hope," the elf continued. "We were determined to bring back our children. If the Queen could turn them into hateful monstrosities, we could turn them back."

The draconian captain stepped forward. "You are my prisoner, old one! I have uncovered your trap! Even now, my men are slaughtering your people and burning this mockery of a village."

Eliyah shook his head sadly. "I had hopes for *you*, especially. I knew you for mine when I saw you. The same determination, the same strength. The dream almost caught you. Just as it almost caught the other one." One hand pointed to the still form on the blanket. In the dim light, the elf's hand looked almost leathery.

Eliyah went on. "There was little time to prepare an actual village. Magic did what was necessary, causing you to accept what should not have been acceptable. It was not enough, though. Only one of you truly responded to our spell, despite its intensity. He would not have survived the transformation, however, and was therefore better dead—though I could not bring myself to do it, having come so close to success."

"What transformation?" B'rak backed away. The elf did not act like a prisoner, and his appearance had taken on an odd aspect. The face was broadening, becoming more reptilian.

"You were the next generation. Our pride and joy. Our dear children. Long ago, while we slept, the Queen and her evil dragons stole our eggs and held them hostage, forcing us to swear an oath that we would not interfere in her wicked designs to conquer the world. She promised to leave the eggs unharmed, but she lied. Using her dark arts, she perverted them into creatures such as you. I tell you this, my son, so you know that we do what we now do out of love for what you should have been—if not for the foul Queen."

Wings spread. All vestiges of elf melted away into a towering form of brilliant silver. The draconian fell backward, one hand brandishing the sword in a feeble attempt to defend himself. The walls of the hut, no longer able to hold in the expanding form, burst apart like parchment. B'rak was forced to dodge parts of the roof.

The massive head stared down. A sigh escaped the great jaws.

"Forgive us, your parents, for failing you."

Everything was fire.

The fire was contained in the village. They made sure of that. Not one draconian escaped. Their very act of attempting to burn the village had assured their presence when the moment came.

For three days, the parents mourned the loss. Three days of sorrow, of singing to those twisted by the Queen. When that was done, the dragons—some silver, some gold, some speckled with each—flew off to join their kin in the terrible war.

Behind them, they left only ashes.

# The Test of the Twins

## Margaret Weis

———

The magician and his brother rode through the mists toward the secret place.

"We shouldn't have come," Caramon muttered. His large, strong hand was on the hilt of his great sword, and his eyes searched every shadow. "I have been in many dangerous places, but nothing to equal this!"

Raistlin glanced around. He noticed dark, twisted shadows and heard strange sounds.

"They will not bother us, brother," he said gently. "We have been invited. They are guardians who keep out the unwanted." He did, however, draw his red robes closer around his thin body and move to ride nearer Caramon.

"Mages invited us . . . I don't trust 'em." Caramon scowled.

Raistlin glanced at him. "Does that include me, dear brother?" he asked softly.

Caramon did not reply.

Although twins, the two brothers could not have been more different. Raistlin, frail and sickly magician and scholar, pondered this difference frequently. They were one whole man split in two: Caramon the body,

Raistlin the mind. As such, the two needed and depended on each other far more than other brothers. But, in some ways, it was an unwholesome dependence, for it was as if each was incomplete without the other. At least, this was how it seemed to Raistlin. He bitterly resented whatever gods had played such a trick that cursed him with a weak body when he longed for mastery over others. He was thankful that, at least, he had been granted the skills of a magician. It gave him the power he craved. These skills almost made him the equal of his brother.

Caramon—strong and muscular, a born fighter— always laughed heartily whenever Raistlin discussed their differences. Caramon enjoyed being his "little" brother's protector. But, although he was very fond of Raistlin, Caramon pitied his weaker twin. Unfortunately, Caramon had a tendency to express his brotherly concern in unthoughtful ways. He often let his pity show, not realizing it was like a knife twisting in his brother's soul.

Caramon admired his brother's skill as a magician as one admires a festival juggler. He did not treat it seriously or respectfully. Caramon had met neither man nor monster that could not be handled by the sword. Therefore, he could not understand this dangerous trip his brother was undertaking for the sake of his magic.

"It's all parlor tricks, Raist," Caramon protested. "Riding into that forsaken land is nothing to risk our lives over."

Raistlin replied gently—he always spoke gently to Caramon— that he was determined on this course of action for reasons of his own and that Carmon could come if he so chose. Of course, Caramon went. The two had rarely been separated from one another since birth.

The journey was long and hazardous. Carmon's sword was frequently drawn. Raistlin felt his strength ebbing. They were near the end now. Raistlin rode in silence, oppressed with the doubt and fear that shrouded him as it had when he first decided on this course of action. Perhaps Caramon was right, perhaps he was risking their lives needlessly.

It had been three months ago when the Head of the Order arrived at his master's home. Par-Salian had invited Raistlin to visit with him as he dined—much to the master's surprise.

"When do you take the Test, Raistlin?" the old man asked the young conjurer.

"Test?" Raistlin repeated, startled. No need to ask which Test—there was only one.

"He is not ready, Par-Salian," his master protested. "He is young—only twenty-one! His spellbook is far from complete—"

"Yes," Par-Salian interrupted, his eyes narrowing. "But you believe you are ready, don't you, Raistlin?"

Raistlin had kept his eyes lowered, in the proper show of humility, his hood drawn over his face. Suddenly, he threw back his hood and lifted his head, staring directly, proudly, at Par-Salian. "I am ready, Great One," Raistlin spoke coolly.

Par-Salian nodded, his eyes glittering. "Begin your journey in three months' time," the old man said, then went back to eating his fish.

Raistlin's master gave him a furious glance, rebuking him for his impudence. Par-Salian did not look at him again. The young conjurer bowed and left without a word.

The servant let him out; however, Raistlin slipped back through the unlocked door, cast a sleep spell upon the servant, and stood, hidden in the alcove, listening to the conversation between his master and Par-Salian.

"The Order has never tested one so young," the master said. "And you chose him! Of all my pupils, he is the most unworthy. I simply do not understand."

"You don't like him, do you?" Par-Salian asked mildly.

"No one does," the master snapped. "There is no compassion in him, no humanity. He is greedy and grasping, difficult to trust. Did you know that his nickname among the other students is the Sly One? He absorbs from everyone's soul and gives back nothing of his own. His eyes are mirrors; they reflect all he sees in cold, brittle terms."

"He is highly intelligent," Par-Salian suggested.

"Oh, there's no denying that." The master sniffed. "He is my best pupil. And he has a natural affinity for magic. Not one of those surface users."

"Yes," Par-Salian agreed. "Raistlin's magic springs from deep within."

"But it springs from a dark well," the master said, shaking his head. "Sometimes I look at him and shudder, seeing the Black Robes fall upon him. That will be his destiny, I fear."

"I think not," Par-Salian said thoughtfully. "There is more to him than you see, though I admit he keeps it well hidden. More to him than he knows himself, I'll wager."

"Mmmmm," the master sounded very dubious.

Raistlin smiled to himself, a twisted smile. It came as no surprise to learn his master's true feelings. Raistlin sneered. Who cares? he thought bitterly. As for Par-Salian—Raistlin shrugged it off.

"What of his brother?" Par-Salian asked.

Raistlin, his ear pressed against the door, frowned.

"Ah!" The master became effusive. "Night and day.

Caramon is handsome, honorable, trusting, everyone's friend. Theirs is a strange relationship. I have seen Raistlin watch Caramon with a fierce, burning love in his eyes. And the next instant, I have seen such hatred and jealousy I think the young man could murder his twin without giving it a second thought." He coughed, apologetically. "Let me send you Algenon, Great One. He is not as intelligent as Raistlin, but his heart is true and good."

"Algenón is *too* good," Par-Salian snorted. "He has never known torment or suffering or evil. Set him in a cold, biting wind and he will wither like a maiden's first rose. But Raistlin—well, one who constantly battles evil within will not be overly dismayed by evil without."

Raistlin heard chairs scrape. Par-Salian stood up.

"Let's not argue. I was given a choice to make and I have made it," Par-Salian said.

"Forgive me, Great One, I did not mean to be contradictory," the master said stiffly, hurt.

Raistlin heard Par-Salian sigh wearily. "I should be the one to apologize, old friend," he said. "Forgive me. There is trouble coming upon us that the world may not survive. This choice has been a heavy burden upon me. As you know, the Test may well prove fatal to the young man."

"It has killed others more worthy," the master murmured.

Their conversation turned to other matters, so Raistlin crept away.

The young mage considered Par-Salian's words many times during the weeks that followed while he prepared for his journey. Sometimes he would hug himself with pride at being chosen by the Great One to take the Test—the greatest honor conferred on a magician. But, at night, the words *may well prove fatal* haunted his dreams.

He thought, as he drew nearer and nearer the Towers, about those who had not survived. Their belongings had been returned to their families, without a single word (other than Par-Salian's regrets). For this reason, many magicians did not take the Test. After all, it gave no additional power. It added no spells to the spellbook. One could practice magic quite well without it, and many did so. But they were not considered "true" magic-users by their peers, and they knew it. The Test gave a mage an aura that surrounded him. When entering the presence of others, this aura was deeply felt by all and, therefore, commanded respect.

Raistlin hungered for that respect. But did he hunger for it enough to be willing to die trying to obtain it?

"There it is!" Caramon interrupted his thoughts, reining his horse in sharply.

"The fabled Towers of High Sorcery," Raistlin said, staring in awe.

The three tall stone towers resembled skeletal fingers, clawing out of the grave.

"We could turn back now," Caramon croaked, his voice breaking.

Raistlin looked at his brother in astonishment. For the first time since he could remember, Raistlin saw fear in Caramon. The young conjurer felt an unusual sensation—a warmth spread over him. He reached out and put a steady hand on his brother's trembling arm. "Do not be afraid, Caramon," Raistlin said, "I am with you."

Caramon looked at Raistlin, then laughed nervously to himself. He urged his horse forward.

\*

The two entered the Towers. Vast stone walls and darkness swallowed them up, then they heard the voice: "Approach."

The two walked ahead. Raistlin walked steadfastly, but Caramon moved warily, his hand on the hilt of his sword. They came to stand before a withered figure sitting in the center of a cold, empty chamber.

"Welcome, Raistlin," Par-Salian said. "Do you consider yourself prepared to undergo your final Test?"

"I do, Par-Salian, Greatest of Them All."

Par-Salian studied the young man before him. The conjurer's pale, thin cheeks were stained with a faint flush, as though fever burned in his blood. "Who accompanies you?" Par-Salian asked.

"My twin brother, Caramon, Great Mage." Raistlin's mouth twisted into a snarl. "As you see, Great One, I am no fighter. My brother came to protect me."

Par-Salian stared at the brothers, reflecting on the odd humor of the gods. *Twins! This Caramon is huge. Six feet tall, he must weigh over two hundred pounds. His face—a face of smiles and boisterous laughter; the eyes are as open as his heart. Poor Raistlin.*

Par-Salian turned his gaze back to the young man whose red robes hung from thin, stooped shoulders. Obviously weak, Raistlin was the one who could never take what he wanted, so he had learned, long ago, that magic could compensate for his deficiencies. Par-Salian looked into the eyes. No, they were not mirrors as the master had said—not for those with the power to see deeply. There was good inside the young man—an inner core of strength that would enable his fragile body to endure much. But now his soul was a cold, shapeless mass, dark with pride, greed, and self-ishness. Therefore , as a shapeless mass of metal is plunged into a white-hot fire and emerges shining steel, so Par-Salian intended to forge this conjurer.

---

"Your brother cannot stay," the Mage admonished softly.

"I am aware of that, Great One," Raistlin replied, with a hint of impatience.

"He will be well cared for in your absence," Par-Salian continued. "And of course, he will be allowed to carry home your valuables should the Test prove beyond your skill."

"Carry home . . . valuables . . ." Caramon's face became grim as he considered this statement. Then it darkened as he understood the full meaning of the Mage's words. "You mean—"

Raistlin's voice cut in, sharp, edged. "He means, dear brother, that you will take home my possessions in the event of my death."

Par-Salian shrugged.

"Failure, invariably, proves fatal."

"Yes, you're right. I forgot that death could be a result of this . . . ritual." Caramon's face crumped into wrinkles of fear. He laid his hand on his brother's arm. "I think you should forget this, Raist. Let's go home."

Raistlin twitched at his brother's touch, his thin body shuddering. "Do I counsel you to refuse battle?" he flared. Then, controlling his anger, he continued more calmly. "This is my battle, Caramon. Do not worry. I will not fail."

Caramon pleaded. "Please, Raist . . . I'm supposed to take care of you—"

"Leave me!" Raistlin's control cracked, splintered, wounding his brother.

Caramon fell backward. "All right," he mumbled. "I'll . . . I'll meet you . . . outside." He flashed the Mage a threatening glance. Then he turned and walked out of the chamber, his huge battlesword clanking against his thigh.

A door thudded, then there was silence.

---

"I apologize for my brother," Raistlin said, his lips barely moving.

"Do you?" Par-Salian asked. "Why?"

The young man scowled. "Because he always . . . Oh, can't we just get on with this?" His hands clenched beneath the sleeves of his robe.

"Of course," the Mage replied, leaning back in his chair. Raistlin stood straight, eyes open and unblinking. Then he drew in a sharp breath.

The Mage made a gesture. There was a sound, a shattering crack. Quickly, the conjurer vanished.

*A voice spoke from the nether regions. "Why must we test this one so severely?"*

*Par-Salian's twisted hands clasped and unclasped. "Who questions the gods?" He frowned. "They demanded a sword. I found one, but his metal is white hot. He must be beaten . . . tempered . . . made useful."*

*"And if he breaks?"*

*"Then we will bury the pieces," murmured the Mage.*

Raistlin dragged himself away from the dead body of the dark elf. Wounded and exhausted, he crawled into a shadowy corridor and slumped against a wall. Pain twisted him. He clutched his stomach and retched. When the convulsion subsided, he lay back on the stone floor and waited for death.

*Why are they doing this to me?* he wondered through a dreamy haze of pain. Only a young conjurer, he had been subjected to trials devised by the most renowned Mages—living and dead. The fact that he must pass these Tests was no longer his main thought; survival, however, was. Each trial had wounded him, and his health had always been precarious. If he survived this ordeal—and he doubted he would—he could imagine his body to be like a shattered crystal, held together by the force of his own will.

But then, of course, there was Caramon, who would care for him—as always.

*Ha!* The thought penetrated the haze, even made Raistlin laugh harshly. No, death was preferable to a life of dependence on his brother. Raistlin lay back on the stone floor, wondering how much longer they would let him suffer . . .

. . . And a huge figure materialized out of the shadowy darkness of the corridor.

*This is it,* Raistlin thought, *my final test. The one I won't survive.*

He decided simply not to fight, even though he had one spell left. Maybe death would be quick and merciful.

He lay on his back, staring at the dark shadow as it drew closer and closer. It came to stand next to him. He could sense its living presence, hear its breathing. It bent over him. Involuntarily, he closed his eyes.

"Raist?"

He felt cold fingers touch his burning flesh.

"Raist!" the voice sobbed. "In the name of the gods, what have they done to you?"

"Caramon," Raistlin spoke, but he couldn't hear his own voice. His throat was raw from coughing.

"I'm taking you out of here," his brother announced firmly.

Raistlin felt strong arms slip under his body. He smelled the familiar smell of sweat and leather, heard the familar sound of armor creak and broadsword clank.

"No!" Raistlin pushed against his brother's massive chest with a frail, fragile hand. "Leave me, Caramon! My tests are not complete! Leave me!" His voice was an inaudible croak, then he gagged violently.

Caramon lifted him easily, cradled him in his arms. "Nothing is worth this. Rest easy, Raist." The big man choked. As they walked under a flickering torch, Raistlin could see tears on his brother's cheeks. He made one last effort.

"They won't allow us to go, Caramon!" He raised his head, gasping for breath. "You're only putting yourself in danger!"

"Let them come," Caramon said grimly, walking with firm steps down the dimly lit corridor.

Raistlin sank back, helpless, his head resting on Caramon's shoulder. He felt comforted by his brother's strength, though he cursed him inwardly.

*You fool!* Raistlin closed his eyes wearily. *You great, stubborn fool! Now we'll both die. And, of course, you will die protecting me. Even in death I'll be indebted to you!*

"Ah . . ."

Raistlin heard and felt the sharp intake of breath into his brother's body. Caramon's walk had slowed. Raistlin raised his head and peered ahead.

"A wraith," he breathed.

"Mmmm . . ." Caramon rumbled deeply in his chest—his battle-cry.

"My magic can destroy it," Raistlin protested as Caramon laid him gently on the stone floor. *Burning Hands,* Raistlin thought grimly. A weak spell against a wraith, but he had to try. "Move, Caramon! I have just enough strength left."

Caramon did not answer. He turned around and walked toward the wraith, blocking Raistlin's view.

Clinging to the wall, the conjurer clawed his way to a standing position and raised his hand. Just as he was about to expend his strength in one last shout, hoping to warn off his brother, he stopped and stared in disbelief. Caramon raised his hand. Where before he had held a sword, now he held a rod of amber. In the other hand, his shield hand, he held a bit of fur. He rubbed the two together, spoke some magic words—and a lightning bolt flashed, striking the wraith in the chest. It shrieked, but kept coming, intent on draining Caramon's life energy. Caramon kept his hands raised. He spoke again. Another bolt sizzled, catching the wraith in its head. And suddenly there was nothing.

"Now we'll get out of here," Caramon said with satisfaction. The rod and the fur were gone. He turned around. "The door is just ahead—"

"How did you do that?" Raistlin asked, propping himself up against the wall.

Caramon halted, alarmed by his brother's wild, frenzied stare.

"Do what?" The fighter blinked.

"The magic!" Raistlin shrieked in fury. "The magic!"

"Oh, that," Caramon shrugged. "I've always been able to. Most of the time I don't need it, what with my sword and all, but you're hurt real bad and I've got to get you out of here. I didn't want to take time fighting that character. Don't bother about it, Raist. It can still be your little specialty. Like I said before, most of the time I don't need it."

*This is impossible,* Raistlin's mind told him. *He couldn't have acquired in moments what it took me years of study to attain. This doesn't make sense. Fight the sickness and the weakness and the pain! Think!* But it wasn't the physical pain that clouded Raistlin's mind. It was the old inner pain clawing at him, tearing at him with poisoned talons. Caramon, strong and cheerful, good and kind, open and honest. Everyone's friend.

Not like Raistlin—the runt, the Sly One.

*All I ever had was my magic,* Raistlin's mind

shrieked. *And now he has that too!*

Propping himself against the wall for support, Raistlin raised both his hands, put his thumbs together, and pointed them at Caramon. He began murmuring magic words, but different from those that Caramon had spoken.

"Raist?" Caramon backed up. "What are you doing? C'mon! Let me help you. I'll take care of you—just like always . . . Raist! I'm your brother!"

Raistlin's parched lips cracked in a grin. Hatred and jealousy—long kept bubbling and molten beneath a layer of cold, solid rock—burst forth. Magic coursed through his body and flamed out of his hands. He watched the fire flare, billow, and engulf Caramon. When the fighter became a living torch, Raistlin suddenly knew from his training that what he was seeing simply could not be. The instant that he realized something was wrong with this occurrence, the burning image of his brother vanished. A moment later, Raistlin lost consciousness and slumped to the ground.

"Awaken, Raistlin, your trials are complete."

Raistlin opened his eyes. The darkness was gone; sunshine streamed through a window. He lay in a bed. Looking down at him was the withered face of Par-Salian.

"Why?" Raistlin rasped, clutching at the Mage in fury. "Why did you do that to me?"

Par-Salian laid his hand on the frail young man's shoulder. "The gods asked for a sword, Raistlin, and now I can give them one—you. Evil is coming upon the land. The fate of all this world called Krynn swings in the balance. Through the aid of your hand and others, the balance will be restored."

Raistlin stared, then laughed, briefly and bitterly.

---

"Save Krynn? How? You have shattered my body. I can't even see properly!" He stared in terror . . .

. . . For, as Raistlin watched, he could see the Mage's face dying. When he turned his gaze to the window, the stones he looked at crumbled before his eyes. Wherever he looked, everything was falling into ruin and decay. Then, the moment passed, and his vision cleared.

Par-Salian handed him a mirror. Raistlin saw that his own face was sunken and hollow. His skin was a golden color now, with a faint metallic cast; this would be a symbol of the agony he had endured. But it was his eyes that caused him to recoil in horror, for the black pupils were no longer round— they were the shape of hourglasses!

"You see through hourglass eyes now, Raistlin. And so you see time, as it touches all things. You see death, whenever you look on life. Thus you will always be aware of the brief timespan we spend in the world." Par-Salian shook his head. "There will be no joy in your life, Raistlin, I fear—indeed, little joy for anyone living on Krynn."

Raistlin laid the mirror face down. "My brother?" he asked, his voice barely a whisper.

"It was an illusion that I created—my personal challenge for you to look deeper into your own heart and examine the ways in which you deal with those closest to you," Par-Salian said gently. "As for your brother, he is here, safe . . . quite safe. Here he comes now."

As Caramon entered the room, Raistlin sat up, shoving Par-Salian aside. The warrior appeared relieved to see that his twin had enough energy to greet him, but Caramon's eyes reflected a certain sadness that comes from learning an unpleasant truth.

"I didn't think you would recognize the illusion for what it was," Par-Salian said. "But you did; after all, what magic-user can work spells, carrying a sword and wearing armor?"

"Then I did not fail?" Raistlin murmured hoarsely.

"No." Par-Salian smiled. "The final of the Test was the defeat of the dark elf—truly superb for one of your experience."

Raistlin looked at his brother's haunted face, his averted eyes. "He watched me kill him, didn't he?" Raistlin whispered.

"Yes," Par-Salian looked from one to the other. "I am sorry I had to do this to you, Raistlin. You have much to learn, mage—mercy, compassion, forebearance. It is my hope that the trials you face ahead of you will teach you what you lack now. If not, you will succumb in the end to the fate your master foresaw. But, as of now, you and your brother truly know each other. The barriers between you have been battered down, though I am afraid each of you has suffered wounds in the encounter. I hope the scars make you stronger."

Par-Salian rose to leave. "Use your powers well, mage. The time is close at hand when your strength must save the world."

Raistlin bowed his head and sat in silence until Par-Salian had left the room. Then he stood up, staggered, and nearly fell.

Caramon jumped forward to help him, but Raistlin, clinging to the wooden staff, caught himself. Fighting the pain and dizziness that assailed him, Raistlin's golden-eyed gaze met that of his twin. Caramon hesitated . . . and stopped.

Raistlin sighed. Then, leaning on the Staff of Magius, the young mage pulled himself upright and walked, slowly and with faltering steps, out the door.

Head bowed, his twin followed.

# Harvests

## Nancy Varian Berberick

*F*lint squinted up at the patches of fading blue sky showing through the forest's skeletal cover. Golden light slanted down from a westering autumn sun. The thought of another night in this gloomy woods did nothing to improve his mood, already soured by two restless nights. Wicked whispers and dread-filled moans were this forest's night song. He shivered and caught himself tapping the haft of his battle-axe. There was something wrong in these woods, and thoughts of Solace and home never seemed more welcome to the old dwarf than they had on this journey.

The dwarf glowered at Tanis. Blast the young half-elf's curious nature! So he hadn't been out of his homeland of Qualinesti that long. Did that mean he had to lead them down every cowpath in search of adventure? And wasn't he, Flint Fireforge, a respectable dwarven businessman, old enough to know better?

Flint heaved a disgruntled sigh. He guessed not—or he wouldn't be in this predicament, lost in some gloomy forest that wasn't on his map.

"Are you going to be peering at the dirt much longer," he grumbled, "or can we look for a camp site?"

Tanis, moving on Flint's heels and inspecting the ground to the left of the root-webbed path, gestured for Flint to join him. "Look at this."

The bushes and frost-seared grass to the side of the path were bent and trampled, marking a departure into the forest. A scrap of brown wool still fluttered in the sharp-toothed grasp of a young prickly ash.

"It looks like someone went through here," Flint said. "And recently, at that."

Tanis peered into the forest in the direction the lone traveler had taken. The song of water racing and tumbling over rocks played a faint counterpoint to the whispering rustle of leaves in the cooling breeze. But then from nearer by he heard the soft sound of something or someone breathing in the hard, short gasps that clearly spoke of fear.

"Flint?" he whispered.

"I hear it."

Tanis reached for his bow and nocked an arrow with the quick, almost absent moves of one who has used it with familiarity for years. It took only a gesture and a nod from him to tell the old dwarf to follow quietly.

Elf-silent, making no more noise than a hunted fox, Tanis stepped off the path and into the darkening woods.

Close-growing oaks and then underbrush crowded together, forming a broad wall of trunks and forbidding shadow. Tanis moved quickly from one oak to the next, keeping cover. Several growths thick, the trees ended abruptly in a clearing carpeted with their wide-fingered bronze leaves.

The girl crouched at the edge of the clearing was the most bedraggled creature Tanis had ever seen. Her hair, the color of frost-kissed aspen leaves, tumbled around her shoulders and straggled across her face. It did not hide the scratches and cuts, signs of a careless passage through the prickly ash, that scored her cheeks.

She could not have been more than seventeen and that was young, Tanis thought, even by the standards of short-lived humans. Crouched in the thick shadows of an ancient oak's trunk, she held perfectly still. There was that in her blue eyes that reminded the half-elf of a doe caught in a hunter's aim.

Flint breathed a startled oath. As though the old dwarf's whisper was the impetus she needed, the girl bolted.

"No, wait!" Tanis called. But the girl plunged through the trees, too terrified to cast even a backward look. Tanis leaped after her, slinging his bow and returning the arrow to the quiver as he ran. Behind him he could hear Flint angling toward the stream. Above them a raven screeched hoarsely and took noisy wing from a tall oak.

Tanis caught up with the girl at the stream. "Lady, wait!"

She skittered down the mossy bank. Once there she dropped to her knees, groping along the edge of the water for a rock. Her hand, raw with cold and trembling with fear, clutched a large stone. She hurled it at the half-elf with all her strength and awkward aim.

Tanis ducked and heard the rock drop harmlessly into the brush behind him. Flint breached the woods just a little upstream from the girl. He moved silently down the water's edge. While her attention was still on Tanis, who took the banks in two long leaps, Flint caught her by the elbows. He pinned her arms behind her, and brought her up to her feet.

"That will be enough of that, young woman," he said gruffly. "We've no interest in harming you."

Her eyes wide and wild with terror, the girl looked from the old dwarf to the young half-elf. Gasping, she struggled against Flint's hold. Tanis took another step toward her, showing her his hands, free of weapons.

"He means it, lady. We won't harm you. Flint, you can let her go."

"I'll be happy to—if she promises not to try to break our heads with rocks."

Tanis smiled at the girl. "She'll promise that, won't you, lady?"

Her chin came up, and though her lips trembled, she eyed Tanis defiantly. "And what warrant do you make?"

"I'll make you two," Tanis said gently. "That neither of us will harm you and that we'll offer you a warm fire for the night. Are they acceptable?"

Her whispered "yes" carried such mingled notes of hope and fear that it went right to Tanis's heart. In the twilight gloom now settling on the forest, he saw the sparkle of tears in her eyes. He took her hand and helped her up the bank.

He glanced over her head at Flint, but the dwarf only shrugged. Still, Tanis knew that his friend pondered the same question that he did: what was the girl doing alone in these woods?

Tanis managed to bring down two fat hares while Flint and the girl made camp. Riana, she'd said her name was, but she volunteered no information after that. It was Tanis's thought that she'd speak more willingly once she was fed and warm.

Riana was silent through all the time it took to roast the hares, though some of her fear seemed to leave her as she listened to Tanis's easy banter and Flint's gruff answers. She did not speak during the meal but to thank them for the food and finally to offer to clean the cookware at the stream.

Tanis listened to her careful progress down the bank. A cold wind scampered through the clearing, rustling the leaves and causing the bare branches of the trees to rub and clack together. These were the only sounds in a forest fallen silent before winter's approach.

The sky had been clear at sunset, but now thick clouds crawled up from the north. Though Lunitari's crimson glow had lighted each of their nights before this, it would not tonight; Solinari, could she be seen, was only a slim new curve. Beyond the fire's glow the trees' gnarled hands scratched at the grim sky. Ghostly mist drifted between their dark trunks, obscuring the ground and lowest growths.

In Flint's pack was a small pouch containing nothing but blocks of wood. Tanis smiled as he watched his friend reach into the pouch, taking the first one he touched. The size of his hand, the block was smooth and white, taken from the heart of a maple. Flint's dagger gleamed in the firelight as he made himself comfortable before the fire. In the companionable silence that fell between the two, the little block of wood became a rabbit, one ear dipped, one standing at the alert. The rabbit's nose, nostrils flared as though sniffing the frosty night air, required only a few last cuts when the soft dirge-like moaning that had haunted their nights began again.

Tanis shivered. "In the name of the gods, Flint, why is a child like that traveling alone in this miserable forest?"

But before Flint could answer, Riana's shadow fell across the fire, sharp and black. Her voice trembled. "I was not alone when I set out. My brother and—and Karel were with me." She set the cookware by the fire to dry and came to sit close to the warmth.

Tanis poked at the fire and watched the bright flames lick higher. "Where are they now, Riana?"

The girl shuddered, hunching closer into the poor

shelter of her ragged cloak. "I—I don't know. It happened two nights ago. We were camping farther north, returning from our journey to Haven. Our village lies north of here. You might know it—Winding Vale."

Flint worked at his whittling and did not look up. "We know it," he said quietly. "What happened to your brother and this Karel?"

"Our camp—it was attacked!" The wind mourned long and low in the trees. Riana drew her knees up close to her chest, huddling for warmth. "It was attacked by—things, phantoms, ghosts—I don't know what they were. I only know that they were horrible. And when Karel ran his sword through one it—it didn't die. It laughed and the sound froze the heart in me. I've never seen such fear in Karel before! And I've known him all my life. He looked at me— It was as though he pleaded for my help. Or bade me farewell." She stopped, a sob caught in her throat, grief and an almost witless despair in her wide blue eyes. "And then it touched him, took his hand, and another one took Daryn, my brother, and—and they were gone."

She dropped her forehead to her knees and rocked there in silent misery. Moved by her sorrow, Tanis put his arm around her. She leaned against him, shivering. In the stillness of the black night the fire's crackling seemed too loud.

"And you've been lost these two days, wandering?"

"No!" Her voice was muffled against his shoulder. Tanis could feel her stiffen in anger. "I'm not lost, I'm trying to *find* them!"

"It seems to me," Flint muttered, his eyes still on his whittling, "that it amounts to about the same thing."

"It's not the same thing." Riana pulled away from Tanis and brushed at the hair straggling across her tear-streaked face.

"I see. Then perhaps you have an idea where these

ghosts or phantoms have taken your brother and his friend?"

"If I knew that I'd be going there."

"Lost and wandering."

Before Riana could protest, Tanis took her hand and silenced Flint with a sharp look. "Riana, whatever the case may be, you cannot be alone in these woods. Our way lies northeast to Solace. We would be glad of your company that far."

"No. Thank you, but no. I must find my brother and Karel. Haven't you heard what I've said?" She looked from Tanis to Flint, then suddenly understood the hard line of Flint's questioning. "You don't believe me, do you?"

Tanis shook his head. "No, Riana, it's not that—"

"You don't. What do you think? Do you think I've done away with them? My own brother and the man—who has been a friend to us both for all our lives? Or do you think that I'm fey enough to wander these wretched woods alone for pleasure?" Her voice rose, sharp in the cold dark. "My brother and Karel have *vanished*!"

"Riana, let us help you. Let us take you to Solace."

"I must find them. I'll not find them in Solace." Her tone was bitter, cooling now with disappointment. "But I thank you for your fire tonight and the food. I'll be on my way in the morning."

Tanis took her hand again and suddenly Flint sensed his friend's thought as clearly as he could sense the frost on the night air.

*He's going to take up this foolish girl's quest!*

He sat forward quickly to protest, but before he could speak, Tanis said, "Then you won't go alone, Riana."

The girl's eyes lighted, her lips parted in a genuine smile of surprise and hope. "You'll help me?"

"I will."

Flint watched through narrowed eyes while Riana and Tanis talked together for a short time longer. He made no effort to join their conversation, but sat, brooding before the fire. When Riana, tired at last, bade him goodnight, he answered with only a short nod.

Once the girl was well settled and sleeping, wrapped in Tanis's blanket, Flint sat forward, still grimly silent.

But Tanis did not speak. Long experience had taught him that the best defense against Flint's disapproval was silence. Faced with no argument against which to vent his objections, Flint would, sooner or later, find a way to challenge Tanis's silence. With studied care, Tanis checked the fire and took up the arrows he'd used to bring down the hares. The green and gold fletching that marked them as his own was damaged. Tanis worked over them quietly until Flint at last spoke.

"Well?"

Tanis looked up from his work. "Well?"

"It's late to play word games, Tanis," Flint growled. "What made you offer to take up this foolishness?"

"What are we supposed to do, leave her here?"

"We could escort her to Solace."

"She won't go."

"How do you know that? You didn't press very hard."

Tanis smoothed the stiff feathers of one of the arrows. "It seems clear enough to me."

"What seems clear to me is that you've committed yourself to a hopeless task. Tanis, we don't even know what truth there is in the girl's story. Ghosts? Bandits, I might believe. But phantoms who laugh at cold steel?" The old dwarf shook his head. "The girl is either lying or a lack-wit."

"No, Flint. She's neither."

"You're so sure?"

Tanis wasn't completely certain. He only knew that her determination to go on, to find her brother and their friend, was real. Her eyes had glittered with it, her words held the passion of one who would not be gainsaid. And, too, though he could point to nothing that supported his feeling, Tanis was certain that the girl spoke the truth. He shook his head. At least the truth as she believed it.

"I'm sure, though I can't say why. Flint, the girl is terrified. There is something wrong in this forest. We've both felt it. And still she'll go on, with or without anyone's help. I can't let her go alone."

"I'll not deny that there is an evil feel to this place. I can almost smell it, and it grows stronger every day we journey north. Lad, you're not too old to be reckless, but I am."

Tanis looked from his old friend to Riana, sleeping quietly, one hand pillowing her head, the other fisted as though she clutched her courage even in sleep. Whatever doubts could be had about her story, he knew that she would go on, if she had to, without his help. And likely she would come to quick grief. He couldn't let that happen.

"Flint, I haven't committed you. I don't want to go alone. But I will if I have to."

Smoke drifted up from the fire, a thin veil between them. Even so, Flint could see the regret in his friend's eyes. Despite his words, he knew there was no decision to be made. "No, I noticed you were careful not to do that. Though I wonder that you'd think I would let you go alone." He reached for the arrows Tanis had abandoned. "Here, you'll lose these to the flame if you're not careful."

"Then you'll come with me?"

The wind whispered evil secrets to the night. The

groaning of the trees under the frost might have been the mourning of lost souls. Flint shuddered, remembering the girl's tale of phantoms and ghosts. "I still have little enough faith in the girl's story of ghosts. But it's clear to me that the two of you will need someone with sense along on this fool's errand."

Tanis thanked him gravely, knowing that it would not do now to smile.

On the black stone parapet of his castle, the old mage Gadar turned his face up to a cold sky. Lunitari's red light leaked from behind the clenched fists of crimson clouds. Shadows drifted across the ground. Like dark breaths they twined around the gray trunks of stiffly ranked pines and slid down the mountain's slopes. A night-hawk, talons flashing in the moon's rising light, dropped from her nest: she was an arrow irrevocably launched toward her prey. The rabbit screamed, its first and last voicing, a brief song of the life it had lived and protest of death's agony.

Behind the mage, in a chamber red with the flame of torch and hearth, a raven cawed as though to warn him that time was passing. Gadar turned his back on the mountains and returned to the chamber.

The raven croaked again, cocked its head speculatively, and preened its wings.

"I know," Gadar murmured wearily. "They could be trouble. But they will be dealt with."

The preening stopped then. The raven tilted its head back toward the long table standing before the hearth and eyed with deep mistrust the wooden coffer that lay in its center. Made of finely polished rosewood, hinged and latched with silver, the chest was the one thing that reflected no light from the fire.

"Yes, yes, my friend, you'd best leave while you can."

The bird did not hesitate. It lifted with awkward striving and cleared the window, drifting out into the frost-nipped night.

Alone again, Gadar took up the coffer. With careful movements he released the delicately crafted silver latch and closed his eyes. The words of the summoning spell came quickly, filling him with the power and demanding of him the strength of will needed to direct what it was he summoned.

> *Know who calls you:*
> *He who holds what you have abandoned.*

He lifted the lid of the coffer, hardly feeling the silky wood beneath his fingers, not aware of the soundless swing of the hinges. He opened his eyes, dropped his gaze to the rich amber velvet cushioning the treasure housed within. Cool and bright, silver chased with gold, the four bejeweled sword hilts lay, each touching the other to form a cross.

> *Know who guides you:*
> *He who keeps what you have lost.*

The fire in the hearth leaped, dancing high and roaring with the hollow voices of unhoused spirits. A wind, cold as though it had swept across glaciers, moaned through the room.

> *Know who sends you:*
> *He who owns what you have sold.*

Black as night, insubstantial as the smoke of a funeral pyre, the four phantoms formed before the mage. Their bodies were only shades of what they had once been, living men. Their eyes were red as the flame in the hearth, their hearts as empty as winter's wind.

"Where?" the darkest one, the longest dead, asked.

"A day's journey from here. You should be able to reach them before dawn. A girl, a dwarf, and a half-elf."

"Bring them?"

Gadar hesitated.

The phantom laughed, and the hair shivered along the mage's arms. The spirits were his to control, but he feared them nonetheless. Still, he feared more any interference in his plans. He could not allow himself to be stopped now. Tomorrow was the night when the spell must be cast; tonight the night when one must be chosen from the two young men who waited in his dungeons. He must set these four phantoms prowling again. It must be certain that nothing could occur to thwart the spell.

"Stop them."

"It is done," the leader whispered.

And it was, Gadar thought as he watched the incorporeal bodies of the spirits thin and fade. It was done. These creatures had never failed to serve him before. They would not fail now.

Regret stirred in the old mage's heart. But it never rose strong enough to call him back from the shadowed path he walked. His remorse was bound by chains, made up of links forged by the deaths that he had caused. And those chains were heavy ones, colored red by the fire of his need.

Riana's sleep had been brief. Having wakened just when Flint roused Tanis to take the second of the night watches, she had drawn close to a fire that she kept blazing high with whatever fuel came to hand. She had not been a talkative companion, Tanis thought now as he watched her stirring the fire to greater brightness, but had spent most of the last watch staring into the dancing flames.

Now he stood and gently took the long, smoke-blackened stick from her hands.

"Enough," he said, tossing the stick aside. "You put us in danger of roasting to death." He was sorry to see her flinch. He'd meant his words lightly, for the mist that had made black ghosts of the trees earlier in the night had deepened. And though dawn was only an hour away, warmth and light were welcome.

"Pardon," she murmured. She drew her cloak closer around her shoulders, holding it closed with a hand that trembled. Still she did not take her eyes from the fire.

Tanis could taste the bitterness of her fear. "You do well to be afraid, Riana. If you are considering abandoning your search, you have nothing to be ashamed of."

"No!"

Flint stirred where he lay wrapped in his blankets against the cold, damp ground.

"Hush," Tanis whispered. "He's done his watch. Let him sleep."

When she spoke again Riana's voice was low and trembling. "I will not abandon Karel or Daryn." She bit her lower lip, worrying it until Tanis thought it must bleed. "I hate this forest. I am not the fool your friend thinks I am. I—I would like nothing better than to go with you to Solace. But—I cannot. Can you not see that I must at least try to find them? They are all the family I have . . ." Her words trailed away, as though she did not wish to contemplate a life without her brother or her friend.

In the silence Tanis shivered as the wind grew suddenly sharper. The flames leaped high and then dropped almost to embers. Smoke, thick and acrid, billowed from the campfire, stinging his eyes to quick tears. Above him he could hear a deep-throated roaring, the sound wind makes racing across the treetops. Though for an instant he could not see her, Tanis knew that Riana was on her feet. He heard her coughing, a choking sound filled with ragged gasping. Behind him, Flint was up and complaining bitterly about people who could not keep a simple camping fire from burning down an entire forest.

The wind kicked harder at the fire, scattering bright embers around their feet, sucking at the smoke until it rose in a black column to vanish into the unseen limbs of the trees above their heads. Fear danced up Tanis's spine.

"Riana?" he called.

Her voice was small and pinched, only a whimpering response. Then, as swiftly as it had risen, the wind died as though it had never been. Tanis looked around in the stillness, placed Riana where she stood, frozen, across the fire from him, and Flint who braced just behind him, his axe in his hand. He read the danger in the old dwarf's eyes and spun back, his hand on the hilt of the dagger at his belt.

They might have been creatures of the smoke, so dark and insubstantial were they. But their eyes, four sets of crimson embers, spoke of some kind of unholy life. One separated from the group, taller, darker than the rest, and took a bold step toward where the campfire, now scattered coals, had been.

Riana's gasp was a shuddering sound of terror and dread. Tanis saw his sword lying just out of his reach and felt his heart sink even as he realized that these must be the creatures who had attacked Riana's camp three nights before. If her tale was true, no sword or dagger would prevail against these phantom raiders now.

---

As though he realized Tanis's thought, the leader of the black shadow attackers laughed, a high keening sound that chilled the very bones of those who heard it.

"Do not regret your sword," it said, its voice hollow and fell. "It would do you no good did you have it."

"Who—" Tanis's words caught in his throat, constricting with his fear, and he drew a sharp, tight breath. "Who are you?"

"It cannot matter to you. What matters is that we have been sent to stop you." The phantom's red eyes glowed hotly as it laughed again. "And you are stopped."

Riana's little moan of fear was only a whisper. She bowed her head and covered her face with her hands. "No," she sobbed, "no, not again . . ."

The phantom turned its attention to her, recognition flaring in its bright eyes. "Yes, little one, again. And this time is the last." It reached for her, the motion as smooth as smoke drifting on the wind.

Tanis dove for his sword, scattering the hot coals of the campfire as he ran. He caught up the scabbard and tore the blade from its sheath, whirling just in time to see another of the phantoms flowing toward him. The third, though, swirled away as the glowing embers tumbled like orange jewels at its feet. It feared the fire!

"Flint! Fire! The fire!"

But Flint, faced with attack from the fourth phantom, could not make a move toward the dying fire. Fighting with an instinct that denied Riana's tale of enemies impervious to honest steel, he swung his axe with deadly force at his attacker. It was a blow that would have separated a mortal enemy's head from his shoulders. The blade passed harmlessly through the phantom's neck, whistling in the cold predawn air.

Cursing in both anger and fear, the old dwarf ducked beneath his attacker's reach and dodged to the side, passing close enough to the phantom raider to feel the deathlike chill emanating from its transparent body. He scrambled out of reach, dashed his foot against one of the tumbled stones of the fire ring, and crashed to his knees. As his hand hit the ground to brace for an upward thrust to turn and defend again, burning coals stabbed his palm.

"Flint! Fire!"

"Fire," the dwarf snarled. "I *know* it's fire—"

Tanis stood between Riana and the leader of the phantom attackers, his sword useless as a defense. Suddenly Flint understood what he meant, and knew what was wanted to fend off these ghostly warriors.

Moving quickly, not daring to look behind to see if the creature he had just escaped was moving to renew the attack, Flint grabbed for the largest pieces of wood that still bore traces of the night's fire. Heedless of their burning teeth, he swept them together into the broken fire ring. He snatched up the scattered kindling from their carefully gathered pile, and heaping it onto the smouldering embers and coals, forced himself to gather more than the shallow breaths of fear necessary to fan the sparks into flame.

"Flint!"

"I'm trying, I'm *trying!*" Two of the phantom warriors converged on the dwarf, one from the left and one from the right. Ice was at his back. The wind howled above his head with the threat of fury and a grisly death. And the thing that reached for Tanis was about to lay its blood-freezing hand on his neck.

Riana screamed. It might have been the signal for light.

Flames leaped high, whirling and licking at the brittle kindling, snapping loud on the night air. Flint snatched a brand from the fire and tossed it to his friend. He did not wait to see whether Tanis had it, but caught up another and rounded on his attackers.

But there were none to fight. They were gone, vanishing before the bright flames. Only their high, wailing voices were left, lingering in the graying light of day.

Shuddering, Flint retrieved his axe and went to stand as near the fire as he dared. It was not warmth he sought, however, but light. He lifted his burned fingers to his mouth, eyeing Tanis and Riana over his knuckles.

Tanis drew the girl close into the shelter of his arm, dropped his sword's point, and walked her to the fire. Silently he helped her to sit, gathered up their scattered blankets, and wrapped her in them. He whispered a word to her and waited for her answering nod. When he left the bright circle of the fire, he gestured for Flint to join him. The old dwarf moved away from the light with great reluctance, still nursing his stinging hand.

"Are you all right?" Tanis asked, turning Flint's hand palm upward.

"No," Flint snapped, "I am not! I am burned and scared witless!"

"Badly burned?"

Flint scowled and snatched his hand away. "Badly enough," he growled. But when he saw the real concern in his friend's eyes, he shrugged. "But not so that I can't wield my axe if need be. Though what good that will do us against ghosts, I'd like to know."

"So you revise your opinion of Riana then?"

"That she is a liar? Aye, she's no liar."

"And a lack-wit?"

Flint snorted and shook his head. "I stand by that. And I'll add that we're both lack-wits if we continue on through this cursed forest."

"I'll go on."

"I thought you would. Well, then, so will I." He

glared down at his palms, scowling at the blisters that were already beginning to form there. "I owe someone for this, and I do not like unpaid debts."

Wretched dawn silvered the eastern sky, blighting Gadar's certainty that his work of the coming night would be undisturbed. His phantom warriors had failed in their task, leaving him exposed and vulnerable. They could not be called into service again until darkness swallowed the day's light. By that time the intruders might well have found him.

Or they might not. It was a chance that he would have to take. The time was right for the casting of his spells, the victim had been chosen. One night hence would be too late.

For a moment, regret, sharp and even bitter, touched Gadar's heart. It was ever this way when he was faced with this task. The young man was full of youth's bright flame. The blood ran quick and sparkling in this one, as it had in the others. Youth would dance in his eyes, sing in his veins, and light his face with his golden hopes.

The groaning that had begun with the dawn's coming now increased in persistence, telling of one who struggled against the black prison of unconsciousness, pushing against it with feeble strength and stronger heart. It would have been easier to sink back, rest for a moment, then try again. But this was a strong-willed young man. This, then, would be the one who would give his life's essence.

"Boy," Gadar whispered, "if there were another way—" But there was no other way. Any other way had been lost to him the first time he'd set his foot on this dark path. What was one more life now balanced against the many he had taken and the one he must preserve at the price of even his own soul? There was no profit, and only dangerous distraction, in regret.

Gadar crossed the chamber, stopped at a large table, and checked the components of the spell that he would work tonight. Everything was ready: the wormwood, the powdered dust of a crushed sapphire, the rosemary sprigs, the dark heart's blood of a breeding doe.

Gadar had no intention of trapping the spirit of his chosen victim in any temporal prison, and this was the difficult part of the spell. Were he to simply thrust the spirit of the young man into an en-mazed prison, he would not achieve his purpose. He had a better use for his victim's life.

For that reason he had chosen the stocky young man with the thick chestnut hair. Daryn, his name was, and he seemed strong enough to provide the life essence the mage needed.

At least until he could find someone stronger.

The mage paused, glanced again at the lightening sky. It might be, he thought, testing a new idea, that it was not such a bad thing that his ghostly assassins had failed in their dark charge. It might be that, were he to let the intruders find him, he would be well rewarded. There was no use for the persistent girl or the old dwarf. But a half-elf, young and strong as this one, would give life for many, many more years than the pathetic young humans he'd been using till now.

"Yes," he whispered, running his fingers along the edge of the table, "and peace, for a time, at least, and a rest from this weary work."

He could not send his phantoms for the half-elf now. Not with the sun's bright light shining. But the half-elf would come on his own. Gadar smiled coldly. That persistent girl would see to it. He would let them find him then. He would put no more obstacles in their way than he needed to gain the time to work this spell now.

Daryn's young life would buy him the time he needed. And time was, after all, the purchase he'd always sought to make.

The forest had darkened long before the sun set. The whisperings of the night before became ominous growlings in the underbrush, sobbing wails in the boughs of the trees. A wild wind danced. The little party of three moved upward, carefully picking a barely seen path through the giant pines. They were touched by a chill that put Tanis in mind of winter.

That morning, in grim jest, Flint had suggested that if they simply let the forest's evil feel guide them, they'd no doubt come upon their ghostly attackers.

Tanis had not taken the suggestion seriously until, moving north for lack of any better direction, they each began to feel the same nameless dread.

"Like a foul odor, a clammy touch," Riana had whispered. Her hands, clenched in white-knuckled fists at her sides, trembled when she spoke. Some fearful thing seemed to hover just beyond their sight, breathing in the trees like no wind that Tanis had ever heard before. It groaned piteously, and wept with winter's dying sign.

Shivering in the raw wind, Tanis nodded to Flint. "We could follow this feeling like a well-marked road."

"Aye, well we could," Flint said, running his thumb along the haft of his axe. "But what would we find? Nothing we'd like to, I'll guess." The memory of the phantoms sent more chill through him than the real wind stinging his face now.

The faint path broadened for a while, a rocky trail barren even of dirt, leading them ever upward. It seemed, at times, that the wind's voice really was the wail of dead things keening for life's loss. The trees, naked and stunted, warped as though by some demented hand, were only ugly growths clinging to life by the whim of cruel nature. Then, when no thing grew at all, when the forests had been left far behind and their breath was coming hard and fast in the bitter, thinning air, the path narrowed again, fading to a pass between high peaks. It vanished suddenly at the top of a boulder-strewn cliff. Behind them lay the dark forest, before them, and far below, a narrow vale.

Riana, shivering and exhausted, took the last few yards of the pass with Tanis's help. But the steely determination that had brought her this far still glimmered in her eyes. *She's got more heart than strength,* Tanis thought.

"We'll rest here a moment, Riana. We all need it."

She nodded dumbly, too tired to speak, and sank to a seat on an ice-kissed boulder. Tanis eyed her doubtfully for a moment, then went to join Flint at the cliff's edge.

"She's not going to be able to go much farther, Tanis. The girl's exhausted."

"I know. And she isn't the only one. You've been quiet these few hours, Flint. How are you?"

Flint blew on fingers that were stiff and achingly cold. "My bones are freezing. I suppose this is what comes of listening to the wild stories of pretty young women who lose their brothers and lovers in the forest?"

"Lover? Who, Karel? What makes you say that?"

Flint snorted and shook his head. "Anyone who's heard her story can tell that. Though its likely news to her, too. She's doubtless devoted to her brother, but it's been this young Karel we've heard about time and again, hasn't it? Young girls don't generally blush quite so deeply when they are talking about family friends."

"Flint, you surprise me."

"Why, because I can use my eyes? I'm not so old as all that, youngster. But that's not what concerns me now. What I want to know is where in the Abyss we are."

Tanis looked down into the valley, a deep cleft in the mountains shrouded in a thick mist. "I think we're about where we set out to be. Look." He pointed to a cleared patch in the mist far below.

Black, built from the heart and bone of the mountains, a vast, turreted castle rose, a jagged skeletal finger. The setting sun was a fiery wound in the brittle blue sky, bleeding light across the forbidding dark stone. Around them the sobbing wind mourned and gibbered.

"Can you feel it, Flint?"

The sense of evil that had been their guide to this place seemed to boil and rumble in the vale below as though this were the source of the keening winds and icy fear.

"Aye, I can feel it. And I don't much like it." The dwarf glanced over his shoulder at Riana, who sat hunched and shivering, her eyes on the frozen rocks at her feet. "Tanis, I could well believe that those ghosts came from this vale." He looked out into the valley again and felt the touch of something colder than the bitter wind brush up against his soul. "And I think, too, that something knows we're here."

Were he not so tired, Tanis would have smiled. He'd known the hard-headed old dwarf too many years not to be surprised by the fanciful turn of his thoughts. He looked closely at his old friend. What he saw in Flint's eyes made him shiver. It was sure knowledge that made Flint say what he had. Though the wry twist of his smile told Tanis that he'd no idea where the knowledge came from.

"Just a feeling," the dwarf muttered.

"I think you're right. And I think, too, that whatever knows we're here will not let us turn back now. It will be dark soon, and none of us is up to a trip down to that castle at night. We'd best be going."

"Aye, well, consider this, Tanis: when they attacked her camp, those phantom raiders seemed to have little interest in Riana. It was only Daryn and Karel they ghosted away. And there is something that tells me, too, that they will have small enough interest in an old dwarf."

Tanis did smile then. "Are you claiming to have The Sight, Flint?"

"No. I'm remembering her story."

He remembered it all the way down to the valley. Though it should not have been beyond his skill to find the thin, shale path, Flint, a hill dwarf who'd spent many years in the Kharolis Mountains, thought the trail came too easily to hand. He would not have sworn his oath that it had not been there before. Still, it had the look of a thing misplaced.

"Like it hasn't been here long," he grumbled to Tanis. "But it looks old."

"And it's the next best thing to vertical," Tanis said, catching hold of Riana, who slid on the loose shale. "The sooner we're off it, the safer our necks will be."

Flint had his doubts. And from the look of barely controlled fear in her eyes, he thought Riana shared them. Still, she righted herself with the same hard-eyed purpose that had brought her this far. Flint felt a new and grudging respect for her. He reached back and took her hand.

"This way, Riana. And have a care, the shale gets looser and smaller. I've no wish to tumble down the rest of the path."

"Riana?" *Riana . . . Riana . . . Riana . . .* Karel's whisper echoed in his mind with all the force of thunder crashing overhead. The flags of the stone floor were hard as midwinter's ice beneath his cheek. His leather jerkin was no protection against the chill draft wandering across the floor.

"Daryn?"

Slowly he became aware that he was alone. No chain held him, no manacle bound him to this floor. Still, he was unable to move even a finger. And Riana and Daryn were gone.

Alone! But where? Though he struggled hard with reluctant memory, Karel could not fill in the gap between the icy grasp of the disembodied warrior who'd touched his hand—how long ago? a day? two?—and the chill of this stone floor now. Yet some time had passed. He could see Lunitari riding dark clouds just beyond the window above his head. When he'd last seen the crimson moon she'd been still waning. Now she waxed, though only slightly.

Where was he?

"Where are you?"

Fear raced through Karel then, but so firmly held was he that he could not move. The voice was old but hard and touched with deadly power. Like the whisper of a ghost, he heard an aching answer.

"Here, within your reach."

"Give me your true name."

"Daryn, Teorth's son."

Though it was his friend's voice that answered the formally posed question, Karel barely recognized it. Dull, will-bereft, it held none of the steady confidence he knew as Daryn's. He trembled inwardly, nauseated by the realization that it was not Daryn's will that made his friend answer, but someone else's.

Somewhere, out of his sight, Karel heard the snap and sign of a fire. The bitter scent of burning wormwood tainted the cool air.

"Hear me, Daryn, Teorth's son."

Karel squeezed his eyes shut as that commanding voice dropped to a secret, murmuring chant. He felt the stone floor start to hum and vibrate. Magic!

Tension, so thick and real that he might have been able to reach out and touch it, filled the very air of the chamber. Leaping flames cast black shadow and lurid light through the room. The tension of the magic's power burst and filled the chamber with the dancing rainbows of light.

Daryn moaned. The sound came from deep within his heart, winding and writhing, and touched Karel's soul with dread. He struggled against his invisible bonds. His muscles shrieked with the effort, his head filled to bursting with pain. The sweat of his effort stung his eyes, splintered the shimmering rainbows of magic's light into shards of furious color.

"Daryn!" he gasped. But Daryn did not respond. He could not.

In a bloody circle, stunned with magic, dazed by his own horrified realization that Gadar clutched his soul, Daryn screamed.

Though Tanis scouted carefully once they'd crossed the scree and entered the little valley, he found no sign that the black castle was guarded. But even as he returned to his companions, darkness, thick and black as a mourner's cloak, fell with startling suddenness.

Riana gasped, but Flint only shook his head as though to say that he expected something of the sort. "Night's dark is never this heavy," he muttered. He saw his companions as faint reddish outlines in the unrelieved blackness. Tanis, too, would be able to see. But he knew that Riana, with only her human night vision, weak by the standards of dwarves and elves, must be nearly sightless.

"Tanis, give her a minute," he whispered. To Riana he said, "Close your eyes for a moment, then see if you can't get yourself adjusted to this darkness."

She did, bowing her head in concentration. But when she opened her eyes again she only shook her head.

"It's like being blind!"

"Aye," Flint agreed, "and likely that's how you're meant to feel." He took her hand and guided it to his shoulder. "Get your bearings, girl. Tanis, what did you find out there?"

"Nothing much. There is a postern gate around the north side. We can make for that. The main entry is unguarded, but I'd like to make as quiet an entrance as we can. Let's head for that postern."

"I'll not argue. Lead on then."

The path Tanis led them along was narrow and rocky, curving around the north side of the valley and down through a small decline to a tall, slim tower thrusting up from the main keep. Staying close to the black wall of the tower, Tanis crept slowly toward the weathered wooden door where he waited for Flint and Riana, still clinging to the old dwarf's shoulder, to join him.

The door opened immediately onto a tall flight of dark slippery stairs. Cracked and shattered by age, they were dangerous with sickly gray moss and only wide enough for one to walk.

"Be careful," he whispered. He waited until Riana was between him and Flint, then took the first steps carefully. So dark was the tower that they could make their way up only by slow, cautious steps. Silent as shadows they crept up and up until Flint was certain that the stairs must end on the mountain peaks.

And then, after an endless time of searching blindly for step after step, groping along crumbling stone walls for balance, Flint heard Tanis whisper back that the stairs ended in a corridor.

Light leaked into a high-ceilinged hallway from an intersection several hundred feet to the west. In the barely relieved darkness Flint saw Tanis reach for Riana's hand and help her up the last few steps.

Drawing a long slow breath, glad to be off the treacherous stairs, Flint reached behind him to adjust the balance of his axe, then stepped into the corridor. The dark stone walls wept with moisture, the floor beneath his feet was slick with green-scummed puddles.

It was then he realized that a wind was moaning where no wind should be. And beneath that moaning he heard voices, cold and gibbering.

"Tanis, I don't like this."

Riana turned, fearful questions in her eyes, her hand slipping away from Tanis's grip. Shadows leaped and danced around them as though cast there by a torch in a mad dancer's hand. Like bats smoked from a cave, the hollow, heartless voices of the dead swept round the high vaulted ceiling. The corridor filled with a tomb's chill.

Thickening suddenly, the shadows swirled to form into something black and vaguely manlike.

Before Flint could move or even shout a warning, a dark spectre reached to touch his friend, freezing him to stillness with its grasp. Horrified, he saw Tanis, his eyes suddenly still and glazed, his face like a carved death mask, turn.

Flint leaped, diving for Tanis, thinking to pull him away from the deadly hold of the black ghost. But, fast as he moved, he was too late. He felt for a moment the hard, real warmth of Tanis's arm beneath his hand. Then he felt nothing.

"No!" he howled, hitting out at the clammy stone wall in his fear and anger. "Tanis!" But Tanis was gone, vanished as though he had never been there. "No!" Flint struck the wall again, not feeling the sharp sting of stone tearing at his knuckles. "Tanis! Damn! Where are you!"

He would have hit the wall again in fury and an almost blind need to feel something solid and real, but a slim hand grasped his wrist, pulling his fist down.

"No, please stop!" Riana cried, "Flint, stop."

Flint rounded on the girl, his eyes flashing dangerously.

"Where is he?"

"He's gone—they took him, the way they took Karel and Daryn. I don't know where he is!"

Voices whispered beneath the screams that filled the air, telling of torture and shattering agony. Gone, Flint thought furiously, holding onto his anger to warm the ice of fear from his blood. Gone! And left me here, damn it!

Down the corridor, toward where the gray light straggled in from some unknown source, he saw a dead torch in an old cresset. Flint ran for it, found another, and snatched them both up. Working quickly, he lighted both and shoved one into Riana's hands.

"Hang onto this," he growled, "and don't let it go out. Whatever these demons are, they do their filthy work in the dark. Aye, they had no love for our campfire: they'll keep their distance from our torches. We're going to look for Tanis. And I've no doubt that where we find him we'll find your brother and his friend."

Riana grasped her torch with both hands, to steady it. In the careening shadows Flint's eyes were hard and frightening. "How—how will we find him?"

Flint shifted his own torch to his left hand and hefted his battle-axe in his right. "We'll find him," he growled. "Have no doubt about that, girl. We'll find him." *And when I do,* he thought, still fanning his anger against his fear, *he'll be lucky if I don't kick him from here to Solace for getting me into this nightmare!*

---

*

When they began to find the first bodies, Flint's fury turned to hollow fear. Riana, weeping openly now, stood rooted in the corridor, staring at the lifeless husks that had once been the strong bodies of young men. None of the bodies, some mouldering still, some whitened skeletons bleached by time's passage, showed the marks of a fight: no broken bones, no shattered skulls. Not one of them had battled his way to death.

They littered the corridor like discarded toys, used, broken, and cast aside.

Steeling himself to find what he knew he would not be able to bear to see, Flint moved carefully among them, searching. His blood pounded painfully in his head, his breathing was ragged, whispered fragments of prayers to gods few people acknowledge. Slowly, almost gently at times, he toed over one corpse after another, his hands locked in a death-hold on his axe. But none of the bodies was Tanis, and the most recently dead were still too long gone to have been either Karel or Daryn.

Breathing hard with his relief, he went back to Riana, took her hands in his own, and led her past the dead.

"No, there is no use struggling. You cannot move." Despite his own warning, Karel instinctively tried to reach a hand to the stranger. He grimaced and whispered again, "Don't try, you'll waste your strength. And you'll need it."

The words echoed in Tanis's head, bounding and leaping so that he could barely make sense of them. Where was he? He remembered, with heart-stopping clarity, the touch of hard, cold fingers on his wrist, the grip of a skeletal hand, and a groaning, beckoning voice urging him to follow. And he'd followed, incapable of refusal. Then darkness, bitter as dead hope, covered him, filling him with dread and piercing fear.

Flint? Riana? With a dark and hopeless feeling he recalled Flint's words on the cliff: *Those phantom raiders seemed to have little interest in Riana . . . they will have small enough interest in an old dwarf.* Where are Riana and Flint? Dead? Dead. He heard his own groan of fear and knew, then, that he could speak.

"Who is that? Where are you?"

"Here, beside you." Karel's whispered laugh was sour. "If you could turn your head, you'd see me. As it is, you'll have to be content to stare at the ceiling, friend. Wait until he's deep into the spell again. Then try to move."

Light, splitting and dancing in all the colors of a rainbow, leaped before Tanis's eyes, arcing and splashing across the field of his vision. He squeezed his eyes closed, trying to shut out the needle-sharp pain. "Who are you?"

"Karel. Hush!"

"Daryn." The mage's word was thunder, rolling across the chamber, filling the air with danger. "Rise!"

Beside him, Tanis heard Karel gasp. He gritted his teeth and forced himself to move. The effort should have taken him to his feet. He was only able to turn onto his side. It was enough to allow him to see the whole chamber, and enough to let him shudder with horror at what he saw.

It was a small man who spoke those commands, and very old. He wore his years with little grace. They lay upon him like unholy burdens. His eyes blazed with his magic, his red robes swirled about him as he lifted his hand.

Crimson blood circled a weakly struggling young man. Daryn, Tanis thought, Riana's brother! The soft murmuring of the mage's chant rose and fell in tones that were sometimes coaxing, sometimes commanding.

Then, with jerky, heartless strength, Daryn staggered to his feet. His hands twitched, his legs threatened to buckle, then stiffened as his feet found their purchase upon the stone floor. Dried rosemary leaves rustled in the mage's hand. The fire in the brazier sighed. With a practiced flourish, he sent the dust of a powdered sapphire, blue and sparkling as a high autumn sky, leaping across the distance between him and the bloody circle. It paused in mid-air, an azure halo above Daryn's head, then settled gently, with great precision, inside the blood circle, to form another border.

Imprisoned within Gadar's circles of magic, Daryn stood, his face drawn and white. In that moment, complete understanding rippled through him, carving at his face with the sharp tools of terror.

And in that moment, the door that Tanis could barely see across the wide chamber burst open with a splintering crash. Weird light broke along the finely honed blade of Flint's axe, leaping and dancing.

Karel's sob of fear when he saw Riana standing behind Flint might have been the voice of Daryn, standing mute and terrified in double circles of enchantment. Or it might have been the voice of Tanis's own dread. Gadar spun quickly, his eyes wild and filled with hatred and thwarted purpose. White light leaped from his fingers, deadly arrows of flame.

"Flint! Down!"

But Tanis's cry wasn't needed to send the old dwarf dodging and scrambling for cover, dragging Riana with him. Karel slapped his leg hard and shouted,

"Now! Up, friend, we can move!"

The mage screamed, a mountain cat's howl of rage, and turned on Tanis and Karel. Halfway to his feet,

Tanis dropped again to the stone floor. White-hot arrows of light darted past his face, stinging and burning, filling the air with a sulphurous, acrid stink. Out of the corner of his eye, Tanis saw Karel bolt across the chamber to where Daryn hung, trapped, in the enchanted circle of blood.

Daryn moaned, and Karel, crouched outside the bloody circle, reached out his hand to his friend. He cried out in pain, flung back by the spitting, stinging force of Gadar's magic.

Riana screamed, and Tanis leaped for the mage, caught him around the knees and brought him crashing to the floor. From some hidden place in his sleeve, Gadar found a knife. Its cold blade flashed once, then again in the dancing torchlight, raking along the back of Tanis's hand.

Hardly feeling the pain, Tanis flipped the mage onto his belly and dashed his knife hand against the floor. The steel blade hit stone and rang loudly. Tanis jerked first one hand, then the other tightly behind the mage's back and held him firmly with a knee in the small of his back.

Frightened, filled with terror and despair, Riana's moaning sobs came to the half-elf. A bitter oath in dwarven told him that Flint was unharmed.

"Let Daryn go, mage," Tanis ordered tightly. "It's over. Let him go."

Shuddering and gasping for breath, Gadar twisted his head to glare at his captor. His voice, as hard as ice and steel, was a grating snarl. "It is not over until the spell-caster declares it over. And do not think to try to free him from the magic's circle. Whoever crosses its borders now will not live an instant."

"There is no reason to hold him now. Let him go."

"No reason in your eyes, reason enough in mine." Gadar coughed and shuddered. For a moment Tanis thought he saw the old man's eyes dim, the black glitter of hatred awash with grief. "But even that may be gone now, vanished at last, despite all I have done." Grim purpose darkened the mage's face again. "No! I will fight to the end! Fight as I have always fought!"

Knowing that he must strike before Gadar could begin to work his magic, Tanis raised his fist. But Gadar was an old man! And tired, by the look of him. *Old and weary,* a dry, cracked voice whispered in his mind, *and it will take only one blow, young man, only one if you choose to deal it out against so fragile an opponent. What strength have I against the hard hand of your youth?* Weary age, ancient burdened grief filled the voice, and blurred images of pitiful but valiant striving coalesced into pictures in the half-elf's mind, as clear as though they were his living memories. In the wavering torchlight the shadow of his own fist seemed a black and evil thing. *He is an old man!*

Tanis relaxed his hold on the mage and started to release him. Then, as he turned his head, shamed by the thought of striking so helpless an opponent, he saw Gadar's lips move slowly, silently chanting the words of a deadly spell. His black eyes glittered like those of an ancient snake coiled to strike.

It took only one blow to still the mage. But as magic's rainbow light surged to life again, pulsing and throbbing in the air, Tanis knew he'd struck too late.

Karel hunched his shoulders, his head bowed intending to butt through the wall of Gadar's power.

"No!" Riana screamed.

"Karel!" It was not Riana who cried out then, but Daryn. Something of himself flickered in his eyes. He reached out his hand as though he would stop Karel where he crouched, ready to leap through the blood-etched circle. Daryn's eyes were black with fear, then finally, free of the puppet-master's influence of the mage's will, understanding. At last his own will animated his limbs. He staggered toward Karel, crashed into the pulsing wall of magic, and thrust his hand into the free air of the chamber.

"No, Karel!" His voice was hollow, echoing already with the abandoned agony of the phantoms who haunted the castle.

The chamber shrieked with thwarted power, magic set free of the channels Gadar had forced it into. Daryn grasped his friend's shoulder, shoved him hard, and sent him spinning to the floor.

Writhing in agony so hideous that he could force no sound from his gaping mouth, Daryn collapsed, twitching and hunching against the pain. Then, hissing and spitting, the rainbow lights faded, drifted aimlessly for a moment, and vanished.

There was no longer a life to capture within the enchanted circle.

In the stricken silence, surrounded by the thinning power and the dawning knowledge of the sacrifice Daryn had made, Tanis moved instinctively to Riana.

Stunned, she took a stumbling step toward the now-harmless circle where her brother lay. Tanis caught her back and guided her carefully to Karel. On his knees, his head bowed, Karel reached blindly for her hand.

"Why?" she asked, the question torn painfully from her weeping heart. "Why, Karel?"

Karel held her closely but did not reply. He looked up at Tanis as though to ask the same question. But Tanis had no answer. Behind him he heard the mage groan, stir, and then fall quiet. For all the sound of his own harsh breathing and Riana's weeping, the chamber seemed suddenly silent. The old mage no longer breathed.

There must be answers, but the mage was not going

to give them now. Tanis wondered if he would have found them sufficient or even comprehensible had he been able to hear them.

What twisted purpose, he thought, his head aching with the wondering, would move a man to this warped use of magic?

An old man, his skin the color of parchment, his hands gnarled claws, crawling with thick, twisted veins. Age? Was that the thing the mage had thought to stave off with the life spirit of young Daryn? Had he been pirating the youth of others to keep himself alive? Disgust, empty even of pity, filled Tanis until his stomach knotted.

Wearily he turned, looking for Flint. He found the dwarf in the darkest corner of the chamber, kneeling beside a small, richly clothed bed. In that bed, covered with thick robes and blankets, lay a slim, frail boy.

For one long moment Tanis thought that the boy was dead. His breathing, so slight that it might have been the play of shadows across his chest, made no sound.

"Flint?"

The old dwarf shook his head. "He lives, but only barely."

The boy sighed, then opened his eyes, and Tanis felt an echoing throb of the pain that he saw there. It seemed an ancient pain, long suffered and too long denied. Then, for a moment, the eyes filled with pleading, darkened with fear.

"Father?"

"No," Tanis said, dropping to his knees beside the bed.

"Father, no more."

Tanis looked to Flint, who shook his head. The boy was so weak he could barely see, so weary he could not know that Tanis was not the father he spoke to.

Aching pity filled Tanis then, and he took the boy's hand in his own.

"Be still now," he whispered.

But the boy tried weakly to lift his hand. "No. No more, Father. Please, I cannot. No more."

"Hush, now, lad. Rest."

"Please, Father. I would—I would stay if I could. Please, Father. No more. I—want no more of these stolen lives."

Even as he heard Flint's shuddering gasp, Tanis knew why the mage had fought so bitterly for Daryn's life. It was for the boy! The boy might have been but twelve or thirteen, but his eyes spoke of many more years than that. And those years, Tanis realized suddenly, had all been winters.

"Father? Let me go. I am so weary . . . let me go. Father?"

"Tanis, give him what he wants." Flint sat heavily down on the cold stone floor, his back against the boy's bed. It was as though, Tanis thought, the old dwarf could not look at the boy any longer.

And, in truth, he would have turned away, too. But he could not, though he thought he could drown in the need he saw in the boy's eyes.

"He wants death, Flint."

The boy shivered and stirred again, groping for Tanis's hand. The quiet rustle of his bedclothes was like the sound of Death's soft-footed approach.

"Tanis, help him," Flint whispered. "He thinks you are his father."

Tanis gathered the boy gently in his arms and held him carefully. He wanted to hold the thin spark of life within the boy, as though his pity alone would keep it burning. Across the room he could see Riana, weeping in Karel's arms, one hand stroking her brother's face. Against his neck he could feel the faint breath of the dying boy, warm yet with the life that faded with each moment. He doesn't want death, Tanis realized then, but only permission.

"Yes." Tanis whispered the word the boy wanted to hear, the blessing the mage never gave. Weakly, the boy looked up, searching, and then smiled.

"I love you, Father."

"I know it," Tanis breathed, choking on the words. "But go, now, and go with my love." For one moment he would have taken back his words. Then the boy sighed, a small shudder like the fluttering of a moth's wings. Tanis's arms tightened around the frail body, empty now of life, and he bowed his head.

After a long while, he heard Flint stir beside him. The half-elf did not resist when his friend lifted the boy from his arms and set him gently back on the bed.

"Are you all right, lad?"

Tanis nodded.

"What are you thinking about?"

"That all these people were moved by love to do what they did. Riana and her brother, Karel, and even the mage and his son. But look how bitter the harvests were."

"Aye," Flint said, reaching down to help him to his feet. "Some fruits are bitter."

Tanis touched the peaceful face of the boy on the bed, thinking that it might only have been sleep that smoothed away the sharp lines of pain and not death. "And some are never harvested at all."

Flint was silent for a long moment. Then he smiled, as though to himself. He took Tanis's arm and turned him gently away from the boy's bed. "Bitter, some, and unharvested, others. A harvest depends on the soil in which the seed is planted, lad, and the care it is given." He nodded to Riana, quiet now in Karel's arms. "Don't you think that theirs could yet be sweet?"

# Finding the Faith

## Mary Kirchoff

———

*The heat of the camp's communal peat fire warmed* my old hands, numb from a hard day's work. I, Raggart Knug, true cleric of the Ice Folk, had just completed the long, cold task of forging another frostreaver. Sighing with contentment, I munched on raw fresh fish, wiggling my toes a little closer to the flames.

As the sun dipped below Icemountain Bay, others of the camp came to warm themselves as well.

"Tell us again about the time of the strangers!" Mendor pleaded, his eyes shining with excitement.

Laina, a pretty girl with hair the color of melted walrus blubber, joined in. "Yes, tell us how the beautiful elf woman and her companions charmed an ice bear and fought the wicked Highlord with—"

"Wait a moment! Who's telling this story?" I interrupted her with a chuckle.

Tired though I was, I could not resist the chance to tell my favorite story, about the time I became a true cleric. Wiping greasy hands on the skins of my leggings, I leaned forward to begin the tale, moving away from this time to another, just yesterday it seemed, when . . .

*

———

Nine strangers came from the north, from Tarsis they said. The guards noticed them some distance from the camp, their colorful robes and thin animal skins making them stand out like spring flowers against the whiteness of the glacier.

I did not wish to join those sent to meet the intruders. With the talk of raiding bands of minotaurs, I was forging the Ice Folk's favored weapon, the frostreavers, as quickly as possible. Even so, the making of each one still took many, many days. I was alone in my work since, as cleric of the Ice Folk, I am the only one on Krynn with the knowledge, passed down through my family, of how to forge these remarkable battle-axes from solid chunks of incredibly dense ice. I hoped to complete the one I was working on before the sun left the sky, so I kept my face down when our leader came searching for men to go confront the strangers. It didn't work. For reasons of his own, the Great Harald ordered me to join the party.

Grumbling, I snatched up my staff and pack of curatives before heading for the harbor. Almost absentmindedly, I poked the frostreaver I was working on into the pack. I have no idea why I did that, since I was not strong enough to use it. I had seen sixty winters, and my muscles just weren't what they used to be. Besides, my job would be to moderate with the strangers, not fight them. Although I was once the most knowledgeable guide among the Ice Folk, I saw less and less of the world beyond the camp as the years went by.

My old bones creaked belligerently as I climbed the ladder over the wall of hard-packed snow and made my way to the boats in the harbor. Soon, our lone iceboat, sail extended like a billowing cloud, skittered across the frozen wasteland, carrying twelve Ice Folk toward the dot of color that marked the strangers.

"There are nine," called Wilmar, Harald's lookout, perched on the port bow.

"And a polar bear, a good omen!" Harald exclaimed. "Trim the sail!" Admired for their strength and endurance, polar bears have long been revered by Ice Folk.

The iceboat swept in a wide, graceful arc, stopping about one hundred feet from the group of travelers. With a wave of his hand, Harald ordered us to advance on the strangers.

Harald, his massive form swaying, stepped ahead of us some twenty feet. "I am Harald Haakan, chieftain of the Ice Folk, the people whose land you trespass. Return from wherever you came and we will not harm you."

"Harm *us*?" a young, heavily armored man scowled. His moustache bristled with disdain. "Derek Crownguard, Knight of the Crown, is ordered by no one!"

I watched as irritation swelled Harald's seven-foot frame to full size and weight. In a moment he would order us to attack.

Suddenly, a young, slender elven maiden twisted her way past the knight to stand before the strangers. I must confess, my breath caught in my throat at the loveliness of the woman. Her skin was clean and creamy, not like the soot-stained complexions of the women of the camp. She looked as fragile as an icicle, yet her eyes held the strength of its cousin, the frostreaver.

"I am Laurana, princess of the Qualinesti elves," she began, her voice light, musical, enchanting. She introduced the rest of the party, though I was so entranced by the sound of her voice that I was only half aware of their names. But I knew Harald might ask my counsel, so I forced myself to listen to her words.

There was another elf among them, a quiet, handsome young man Laurana introduced as her brother. He said little, but his eyes flashed with love every time he looked at his sister.

There were three other men dressed like Derek, obviously knights as well, though there the similarity ended. The one named Aran, tall and red-haired, seemed easygoing and affable, though it was only an impression— there was nothing to laugh about in our encounter. Another, a quiet one named Brian, exuded a subtle strength.

The fourth knight was more interesting than the rest, mainly because he was not so easy to read. Laurana called him Sturm. There was something unsettled and mysterious about the knight with the double moustache. He stood tall and proud, and honesty shone from his eyes. But surrounded by people, he seemed oddly alone.

"We mean you no harm," Laurana continued. "We are traveling from Tarsis to Icewall Castle on a mission vital to the safety of Krynn."

Harald's chest stopped heaving with anger, but he remained cautious. "You did not bring the bear from Tarsis," he growled.

The maiden paled at his accusatory tone. "No, he was being tortured by minotaurs, so we freed him," she explained hastily. "We released him, but—"

"He's fallen in love with Laurana!" a small, childlike creature with a long tassle of hair cried, leaping forward with delight.

Completely undaunted by Harald, the creature started forward, small hand extended. "How do you do? My name is Tasslehoff Burrfoot and . . ."

"Hush up, you doorknob," a stocky dwarf growled, yanking the excited kender back by the arm, "or I'll feed you to a minotaur myself!"

Laurana smiled embarrassedly and glanced at the massive white bear. "He does seem rather fond of me."

Like Harald, I found the presence of the ice bear intriguing. I knew the bear was young from its awkward, clumsy gait. I'd seen many of these lumbering creatures on the glacier, but never had I seen one willingly serve any master, human or otherwise. An iron collar strained at the bear's thick neck and deep red welts marred its white fur, witness to the elf woman's story of the minotaur's tortures.

But Harald's interest turned to the talk of minotaurs. "How many bull-creatures were there? Did you kill them?"

I could see the elf woman trying to gauge Harald's reaction. Perhaps the Ice Folk were friendly with minotaurs. "There were seven—and yes"—she gambled, watching him closely—"we killed them all. We've seen no others since."

Though Harald's wide face spread into a grin, I could see that he did not trust these strangers yet. "Bull-men have long plagued us. We owe you a great debt. Come to our camp and rest. We will feed and clothe you properly before you continue across the glacier."

This was not just mere politeness. I knew that Harald wanted to question the strangers further and he felt more comfortable back on his own ground. And, if he did not like their answers . . . they would never leave our village alive.

The sour-faced dwarf stepped forward and hitched up his gear. "Well, I certainly could use some warm food and clothing," he grumbled. "This wild-goose chase the kender has us on for some silly dragon orb we know nothing about is enough to freeze a man's bones!"

The knight, Derek, could hold himself in check no

longer. "We can't waste time in revelry! Besides, how do we know we can trust these barbarians? I say we leave immediately!" Reaching out, Derek grabbed hold of Laurana, intending perhaps to emphasize his point by forcing her to look him in the eyes.

It didn't work.

The huge white bear had been standing calmly next to Laurana. When Derek caught hold of the elf maid, the bear roared in anger and suddenly stood up on its hind legs. Its massive frame stretched to a height that dwarfed even Harald, and it swayed menacingly over the knight, snarling and growling as if daring him to move again. All color drained from Derek's face; he hastily dropped the maiden's arm. The Ice Folk around me fell back slightly, knowing the bear's sharp, protruding claws had the power to rip out Derek's throat in a second. The frigid air fairly crackled with tension, broken only by Derek's ragged breathing.

"D-d-down, bear," the elf maiden finally managed to stammer. But the creature remained suspended over Derek. Realizing that she alone had the power to persuade it, Laurana bravely reached up a slender hand to pat the beast reassuringly. "Down!" she commanded more firmly. The bear hesitated for a moment, then, reluctantly, it dropped back to all fours, eyeing Derek and giving one last snarl. Though obviously relieved that the bear no longer threatened him, Derek's face burned red with humiliation.

So *that's* why this slender young female is a leader of men, I thought to myself. The bear has chosen her. I saw Harald take note of this, too.

At that moment, a bearded man whose presence I had overlooked stepped gingerly past the bear. I judged him to be older than most of his companions but younger than myself. He spoke to the elf maid in mild, firm tones and I could tell, from her respectful attitude, that he had long been her counselor. "Derek is right about one thing, Laurana, my dear: we have no time to waste. Tanis may already be waiting for us in Sancrist."

"I have not forgotten, Elistan," Laurana said softly, a strange, almost wistful look in her eyes.

She turned to Harald slowly. "We regretfully decline your kind offer of hospitality," she began. "My . . . that is . . . friends wait for us." Coughing, she cleared her throat. There was a note of pain in her voice. "And we have an important mission to fulfill before we can join them," she explained.

"I'm afraid you misunderstood me, princess," Harald said, his friendly tone gone. "It was not an offer, but a demand. You see, we Ice Folk are at war—we cannot afford to trust anyone." He gave a tight-lipped smile. "You will return with us." Accustomed to being obeyed, Harald turned to leave. He did not, therefore, see Derek draw his sword or Laurana grip the knight's arm, forcing him to put the sword back to its sheath.

"What can I do to convince you we mean you no harm, that we are not spies?" she demanded of Harald's back. "Our mission is vital—it cannot wait!"

Harald swung around slowly, irritation turning his face even redder than its normal shade. He did not like complications—and this maiden was proving stubborn. Suddenly, his expression brightened as an idea struck him.

"You have my leave to go on this 'mission' of yours, then," he said. "But leave several of your number here as—"

"As hostages?" Laurana finished for him coolly.

"No, I prefer to think of them as a sign of good faith." Harald smiled slightly. "And as a sign of our good faith, I vow to spare their lives for the seven days

I give you to return, as long as we meet with no harm during that time. That is fair, I think?

"I would, of course, prefer that you leave your fighters," he added, his eyes going to the well-armed knights, "and the bear, as a token of luck."

Laurana's mouth twisted in shock and outrage. Her thin frame shook as she struggled for control. "Without knowledge of the glacier, it is impossible for us to know how long it will take us to reach Icewall Castle. And without fighters, what chance have we of retrieving that which we seek?"

Harald shrugged. "I did not say I wanted *all* of your fighters. These two will do," he said, pointing to Aran and Brian. "And the ones called Flint and Gilthanas must stay behind. You will be more inclined to return for your brother and your friend." He eyed Derek. "You may keep the sulky one."

"This is an outrage!" Derek snarled, once again putting his hand on the hilt of his sword. "There are only twelve of them. I say we take our chances and—"

But Laurana cut his words off, her voice clipped. "When it comes to retrieving the orb, I will take no chances. If you insist on fighting, Derek, then you will fight alone." The knight called Sturm moved nearer to her, nodding in support. "I suggest you instruct your men to join Harald," Laurana added, her voice breaking, "as I will my friends and my brother."

The dwarf glowered at this. "No, Laurana," he said stubbornly. "I won't allow you to traipse across this frozen wasteland looking for Reorx-knows-what without me! It's too dangerous!" Realizing his voice had risen, Flint eyed the bear warily and dropped his tone. "Tanis would never forgive me!"

"Nor would our father," Laurana's brother added grimly. "I'd rather we turned around and forgot that orb than to let you go off unprotected!"

With a sad smile, Laurana placed her hands in theirs. "You both know retrieving the dragon orb may be Krynn's only hope, and everyone is counting on us. Besides, I won't be alone—Sturm, Elistan, and Derek will be with me. If there were any other way," she added, "I'd take it. But we have no choice but to accept their terms, it seems. Please don't make this more difficult for me than it is already."

Flint searched her eyes, sighing heavily. "Very well," he said gruffly. "Besides, you don't want a grumpy old dwarf slowing you down."

Gilthanas nodded slowly, but I could tell he wasn't happy. He started to argue, but she continued to look at him intently, pleadingly, until he shrugged angrily. "I'll stay, if that's what you want," he said.

Sighing, Laurana turned back to Harald.

"What proof have we that you'll keep your end of the bargain and will not harm them?" she asked.

Scratching his bearded chin, Harald thought about that for a moment. Propped up against my staff, I watched absently as the old man called Elistan came over to stand beside Laurana.

It was then that I noticed the medallion around the old man's neck. My breath caught in my throat, though this time in fear—the hazy winter sun glistened off a golden medallion in the shape of a platinum dragon, the symbol of the true god, Paladine. I could not believe my eyes. Long ago, right before the Cataclysm, all clerics of the true gods had vanished from the world, my own great-great-great grandfather among them. With them vanished the ability of the clerics to work the will of the gods in the world, to perform healing and other magical spells. Many said that this was because the true gods themselves had forsaken Krynn, but my family did not believe this. Since that day, we had pledged ourselves to wait for some sign of the return of the true gods. None had lived to see that day. Nervously, I rubbed at my eyes with grubby fists, hoping to erase the image.

But when I looked up again, the medallion still hung from Elistan's neck. A sickness grew in my stomach. I had always prayed that I would be the one to discover a true cleric—one who could perform miracles—as a sign that the true gods had returned. But in my heart of hearts, I never really believed I would. Face to face with the symbol heralding that discovery, I still did not—could not—believe it! He must be a charlatan, and I wanted nothing more than to escape someone who would try to trick us.

"You drive a hard bargain, elf woman," Harald finally said to Laurana. "I like you—I don't trust you entirely—but I like you." His laughter pounded against the frozen glacier. "As a sign of our good faith, and to aid you in returning within seven days, we will send with you a guide." He clapped me on the back. "Our cleric is the best one among us. He will accompany you to the castle."

Harald's words echoed in my aching head, echoed across the glacier. Could the fates be so cruel? Had I heard right? Harald's beefy hand on my shoulder assured me that I had. My words came to my ears as if spoken by another.

"I cannot—I mean, I don't want to guide them," I mumbled, avoiding Harald's eyes. "I don't trust them."

Harald's huge face turned as red as his hair. "Just so!" he bellowed. "They will not attack us without their fighters, and they will not harm you while we hold their friends." He swung his face down to meet mine, his fishy breath fanning my face. "Do you question my judgment?"

My cheeks drained of color as I struggled to force words from my throat. "No—no. It's just that—"

Could I tell him of my fears?

"Spit it out, man," Harald roared impatiently. "Men freeze while you sputter!"

I forced down the lump in my throat. "The human, Elistan—he wears the symbol of the true god, Paladine! He is a charlatan!"

Harald's features relaxed from anger to a look of confusion. "But, Raggart, surely you and every member of your line have pledged your life to meet one such as this!" he said. "This is your chance!"

The simple logic of Harald's words turned my fear to dogged stubbornness. "That is why I am suspicious!" I whispered. "Would such an important person just appear on the glacier one day?"

My eyes narrowed. "What is this dragon orb, anyway? And if it's so valuable, who would keep it in a frozen, abandoned castle at the farthest edge of the glacier? Someone with something to hide, that's who!"

Harald shook his head firmly. "I cannot say. The gods move in mysterious ways." He shook me slightly. "But whether he is a true cleric or an enemy scout sent to determine our strength, we need our best guide to watch them. That someone is you."

I, Raggart Knug, cleric of the Ice Folk, looked into my chieftain's icy blue eyes and knew that only death would save me from guiding the strangers to Icewall Castle.

We were just preparing to depart when the kender, who had been standing next to Laurana, shifting impatiently from one foot to the other, said cheerfully, "Well, who wants me?"

"They do!" both sides cried, pointing to the other.

It seemed tempers were going to flare again, Derek refusing to take Tasslehoff and the dwarf insisting that the kender be packed off to Icewall Castle without delay. In the end, it was Harald who decided Tasslehoff's fate.

"The kender goes!" he said firmly.

I thought even Laurana appeared a bit downcast at this decision.

The ice bear also proved difficult. He refused, quite violently I might add, to leave Laurana until she spoke with him at length. I wonder how much he understood; I think her tone convinced him. The bear accompanied Harald, and I noticed that our leader kept his distance from the sulking bear as he led the search party back to the ice boat.

Finally my party and I started off in search of this dragon orb or whatever they were after. Using my staff to propel my old bones along, my body slowly adjusted to the rigors of exploring the glacier. Though time and the elements had changed the landscape, I still knew what to look for, how to avoid snow-covered crevasses. Despite the nature of the trek across the glacier, I enjoyed the feeling of the cold, icy wind across my leathery cheeks, the sight of swirling eddies of snow. I had been cooped inside my hut forging frostreavers for too long.

Remembering my situation, I looked back at my wards and was grateful that Harald had insisted we take peat for nighttime fires on the open glacier and that we dress in the Ice Folk pelts of bear and otter. The strangers' borrowed furs made them much less conspicuous than their colorful robes against the snowy backdrop.

I did not mind the danger. Everyday life at our camp held dangers. Besides, I had lived a full life and did not particularly fear the possibility of death. Still, I did not want my life to end accompanying a band of tricksters in the name of the true god! The irony of the situation nearly made me chuckle; fate had a wry sense of humor.

Unfortunately, Derek did not. Nothing I did pleased him. I walked too slow. I walked too fast. It was too cold. The furs made him hot. I had no love for the knight, but I knew that answering his complaints would only provoke him further. I remained silent, my head bent against the swirling snow as I picked our path across the glacier toward Icewall Castle.

Krynn's sun rose and set on three cold days as we crossed the snowy wastelands. Each day, five travelers from warmer lands struggled behind me through bitter winds and man-swallowing drifts.

The kender proved as much a handful as any ten children from the village. More than once did I catch sight of him in the corner of my eye as he wandered off the path I had chosen. Once I collared him just as the snow beneath his little feet slid away, revealing a crevasse.

"Wow, would you look at that?" he marveled. "I wonder what's down there? Perhaps I'll make a map of this—maybe it's a shortcut to the other side of Krynn!" Tasslehoff reached into a pouch for some paper.

"Don't be any sillier than you can help," Derek grumbled, trudging through snow that reached his knees. "I'd be the first to fall down it if it led to someplace warmer!"

Tasslehoff's face fell only slightly. "I suppose," he mumbled.

Though I vowed to keep to myself and merely guide them as ordered, I could not help but wonder about the others. I had a lot of time to observe them, after all.

My first impressions of Sturm Brightblade never changed; he was a man alone. For some reason, the older knight, Derek, seemed determined to break the

younger knight's will, but Sturm never wavered in his
loyalty to Laurana. And though provoked enough for
ten men, he never raised his voice to the older knight.
Some dark secret rode Sturm's shoulder like a black
beast, but I never discovered what it was.

Though Elistan was silent most of the time and
never complained—or maybe because of those
things—I still did not trust him. Every now and then
he smiled serenely to himself for no obvious reason as
his eyes scanned the bleak horizon. He couldn't be enjoying the trip, I reasoned. Was he laughing at me, at
tricking a gullible old cleric who waited for the return
of the true faith? The thought made my legs move
faster, to hasten the moment when I would leave him
behind.

But I must confess that, much as I tried, I could not
look forward to the time when I would leave Laurana.
When we'd first met, I'd thought it strange that a slight
young woman would lead eight men, four of whom
were knights. Then I'd believed, as Derek did, that her
power over the group came from the bear.

"My quest is to retrieve that orb," the knight
growled one night after he'd lost another debate to
Laurana. "That bear is no longer here to fight your
battles!"

Derek's threat struck me as foolishly hollow, marking in my mind the moment when I first knew Laurana
had enchanted me, though not in a romantic way.
Each night when we stopped and lit a small fire to
warm ourselves and eat our meager rations, Elistan
sat whispering to Laurana, advising her, giving her the
moral strength to go on. The sight filled me with jealousy. I wanted to be the one whose advice she sought,
to receive her grateful smile. Beyond her physical
beauty was an inner strength that made me want to
follow her even without the bear.

We were all grateful when, on the morning of the fourth day, the sun rose behind the distant silhouette of Icewall Castle, shining upon the jagged promontory of Icewall. Before the Cataclysm, the castle, made of stone, stood upon a rocky island in the seas south of Tarsis. But the Cataclysm turned those seas to ice and snow, as well as the island below the castle, creating Icewall. Wordlessly, our pace quickened, each of us heartened by the sight. Soon I would be free of the strangers . . .

Within a few hours we stood at the base of Icewall. Forty or so paces to our right, icy remnants of a stairway snaked up the cliff face as far as the eye could see. Perched on the top of Icewall was our goal, Icewall Castle.

"That's it—the mighty Icewall Castle?" the kender's high-pitched voice screeched loudly in the chill air. Terrified, I tried to clap a hand to his mouth, but I was too late. "Why, it's nothing but a big block of ice, not nearly as attractive as other castles I've seen!" he shouted.

As I had feared, a slow groaning sound shook Icewall, sending a snowy avalanche thundering down toward us.

"Run!" I shrieked. Pumping as fast as my legs and deep snow would allow, I could only hope that the others followed my lead. When Icewall finally quieted down, only the kender, to his own delight, had been swallowed by snow up to his neck.

"Oh, my, did I cause that?" he asked innocently as Sturm plucked him out by the armpits. "Look!" he gasped abruptly. "The avalanche opened up a cave or something!" He pointed skyward to a dark, shadowy spot halfway up the face of Icewall. "It must be a shortcut into the castle—I'm sure of it! And I found it," he added proudly.

Derek's face twisted into a grim smile. "That's precisely why we should avoid it. To say nothing of the fact that it's foolish to climb toward a dark spot that may or may not be a cave opening—which may or may not lead into the castle." His eyes narrowed as he leaned menacingly toward the kender. "And suppose it is an opening—who do *you* suppose made it?"

"I'm sure I don't know," said the kender, shrugging. His eyes lit up. "But it would be interesting to find out."

Derek snorted. "'Interesting' isn't a word I would use to describe whatever's guarding a powerful artifact such as this orb!"

Laurana's brow creased with concern. "I hadn't even considered that!" she said, looking chagrined. "I assumed that since it was stuck out here on the glacier, Icewall Castle would be deserted. But Derek's probably right. Raggart, you know this area better than any of us. What do you think? Is there likely to be someone or something inside the castle?"

I hesitated for a moment to determine what I *did* think. I did not wish to alarm her unnecessarily, but she had to know the truth.

"There have been reports of a white dragon coming and going from the castle," I told her reluctantly. "Any number of other creatures may have taken up residence—you have already met the minotaurs."

"I don't know why I did not think of that before!" She sighed, then squinted up at the icy cliff. "What route should we take?"

I followed her gaze. "I believe the kender is right— that is a cave opening which may lead into the castle. Though we don't know what awaits us inside, we chance the same thing climbing to the top, with half the risk of being spotted from above. Whatever you decide, the climb would be safer if we rope ourselves together."

"The old barbarian doesn't know what he's saying," Derek scoffed, "though his idea about the rope seems reasonable enough. Let's waste no more time—an orb awaits us above!" He tied a length of rope to his waist and held the end to Sturm. "Come, Brightblade, link yourself to me and we'll find the base of that stairway!"

Sturm's brows lifted in question. "Laurana?"

"Raggart is our guide," she said confidently. "We'll climb to the opening."

Suddenly her expression changed to fear. Like a curtain falling, we were engulfed in shadows. Startled, I followed her gaze. There, high above Icewall, I saw the massive underbelly of a white dragon as it soared from the castle's balustrade.

"Get down!" I hissed. Thankfully, everyone dropped to his stomach without question, even the kender. They knew, as did I, what would happen if the dragon spotted us. I shuddered at the thought and prayed that with our light-colored furs, we blended in with the snow.

Without a backward glance, the dragon sped away in the direction we'd just come, pulling its massive shadow along. A sudden fear knotted my stomach. When the dragon was a mere dot in the distant horizon, I stood up and, turning, started heading back.

"Wait, Raggart! Where are you going?" Laurana shouted, stumbling after me to catch hold of my arm.

"Now we know that the reports about a dragon are true. Given its general direction, I'm afraid it's headed for my village. I have to go back immediately!"

Laurana looked sympathetic, but she shook her head. "We cannot abandon our search for the orb, especially when we're this close to it," she said.

"What is this dragon orb? How can it be more important than the lives of my kinsman?" I demanded.

"I understand your concern," Laurana said, "but a lone dragon would scarcely attack an entire village. And *if* it wanted to, it would have long before this. Think, Raggart," she commanded, grasping my shoulder. "Even if we left immediately, we would reach your village days behind the creature, too late to help anyone. Then we would neither save your village nor retrieve the orb."

"Then what about our lives? Are they worth nothing?" I shouted. "The presence of the dragon convinces me that Icewall Castle is far more dangerous than any of us imagined." Even to my own ears, I sounded like a frightened old man. That only made me angrier. "I am not an old coward, but neither am I a young fool!"

"Of course you're not!" Laurana's eyes glittered brilliantly. "The orb we seek has the power to control dragons. Though you may not understand or believe me, Raggart, more people will suffer if we do not find it before someone who would use it for evil gains."

Laurana grasped my hand. "I know Harald instructed you to watch—I mean guide us, but I would not blame you if you chose to return without us." Her voice picked up momentum. "But, Raggart, time is of the essence if we are to save our friends—save Krynn. We—*I* need your help. Will you continue on with us?"

Derek snorted with disgust and began looking for footholds in the icy cliff face.

I was momentarily torn with indecision. Though her words had convinced me my fears were largely unfounded, I still hesitated. In the end, I decided to continue with them for three reasons: for good or bad, I needed to know the truth about Elistan; Laurana wanted me to go; and Derek did not.

I did not like the thought that my life in any way depended on Derek, but lashed to him as I was, it did. After me came Laurana, then Elistan, then Tas; Sturm pulled up our rear. Though Derek had complained heartily on the glacier, he took too much pride in his physical strength to give in to the exhaustion that plagued us all on the back-breaking climb up Icewall. His tenacity may well have saved our lives more than once. Whenever I faltered or lost my footing, Derek's hand was there to pull me to safer ground.

The cliff face provided even less protection from the elements than the open glacier. Forced to look up to find our way, our faces were exposed to icy, blistering winds that blasted flesh till it was raw. Fingers permanently bent, my arms ached from the strain, my toes throbbed from struggling to find new footholds. Even my jaws hurt from being clenched too long.

But as much as I suffered, at least I was used to the cold. I knew the rest must feel it tenfold. Behind me, Laurana struggled to swallow involuntary whimpers of pain. Below her, Elistan wheezed until I thought his lungs would burst.

"I don't mean to complain," I heard the kender say wearily, "but is anyone else tired? I'm all for adventures, and I know we have to find the orb, but I haven't been this exhausted since that time with the woolly mammoth. I *have* told you about that, haven't I?"

"Yes, Tas, we've all heard it," was Sturm's patient reply. "Save your energy for climbing now."

"I'm quite sure Raggart hasn't heard it," Tas said a bit petulantly, "but perhaps you're right," he added, gasping for breath.

Hours, seeming more like days, passed as we slowly made our way up the glassy crags of Icewall. Behind me, the cleric, Elistan, sighed loudly. Though I was still suspicious of him, he seemed a kind enough man, not at all inclined to jokes or tricks. What had I—what had Knugs for generations—expected? Since I seldom left the village anymore, let alone the glacier, just where was I expecting to find this messenger from the gods if not on the glacier?

"Aren't we nearly there?" Tas spoke the words everyone else longed to ask. "I feel as though we've climbed to the top and back down again!"

"It *is* getting near sunset," Laurana pointed out. "Perhaps we should stop."

I, too, had noticed our lengthening shadows upon the cliff face. Soon the moons would rise.

"If we're not likely to reach that opening soon," Sturm called up to us, "I say we find a ledge on which to spend the night and rest."

"For once I agree with Brightblade," Derek said, finally giving in to the strain. Wiping his brow with his fur-covered arm, he stopped climbing, prompting everyone else to do the same.

We'd used up all the peat crossing the glacier. The thought of a night spent clinging to this frigid mountain, the wind whistling louder than Harald's snoring, did nothing to raise my spirits. I squinted up Icewall past Derek. Though twilight turned every icy crag dark, one not very far off was larger and blacker than all the rest.

I cleared my throat, for I had not spoken since we started our climb that morning. "I think we're almost there. Look," I said, pointing to what I believed to be the cave opening.

"You're just saying that because I suggested we stop!" Derek barked without looking up, exhaustion making him even more churlish.

"You know, Derek," Tasslehoff said shrilly, "people would be more inclined to listen to you if you were pleasant, like Laurana or Sturm—"

"Not now," Sturm warned the kender in a low tone.

"I'm sure Derek appreciates being told this," Tassle-hoff continued, unperturbed. "Flint once called me a thief. It was all a terrible misunderstanding, of course, something about a bracelet. Anyway, he explained to me that people might mistake my motives, you know, think I'm a thief when I'm really just protecting their interests. Now I know not to take it personally. Derek understands what I mean," the kender finished confidently.

"*Not now, Tas!*" Sturm hissed, eyeing Derek's purple face, noting his clenched fists.

"Yes . . . well . . ." Laurana coughed uncomfortably, perhaps swallowing a laugh. "I think we'd better hurry if we intend to continue."

Derek's hands slowly unclenched as he struggled for control. With a grim glance at the oblivious kender, he turned and squinted into the growing darkness, then continued up the cliff face, practically jerking the rest of us along in his wake.

Fortunately, we hadn't far to go.

"Well, what do you know?" Derek breathed up ahead of me. Scrambling over a jagged crag, he disappeared from sight. Frowning, I forced my reluctant muscles to move faster. When I reached the spot where I'd last seen him, I stopped and caught my breath.

We'd found the cave.

And it was beyond all imaginings. Walls, ceiling, and floor were made of ice smooth as glass. Though the cave should have been pitch-black, a rainbow of muted colors glowed from inside the glassy surfaces, colors I'd never seen in my whole life danced on the bleak, black-and-whiteness of the glacier. I stood rooted to the spot.

"Raggart, what is it?" Laurana pushed past me to

climb onto the ledge. "Oh, my!" she gasped. "It's beautiful!"

"It's also magical," Elistan said uneasily, as we helped him onto the ledge. Tas and Sturm followed. "And of the Black Robes, I believe."

"What does that mean?" the kender asked.

"I'm afraid it means we're probably not alone up here," Sturm said grimly. "Someone possessed of very powerful—and evil—magic created this effect."

"I know some very powerful magic-users," Tas chimed in. "There's Raistlin—have you heard of him?" he asked me, not waiting for an answer. "Then there's Fizban, although he's not very powerful," the kender's brow wrinkled, "or alive for that matter."

Derek glanced at Tasslehoff as he would an irritating fly. "We can't afford to rest here, then," he said decisively. "This could be that dragon's lair, for all we know!"

"I don't think so, Derek, this cave's too small. Besides, we're exhausted!" Laurana said wearily. "What good will we be if we're too tired to defend ourselves should the need arise?"

But I was scarcely aware of their debate. Inside my head a question went round and round, louder with each revolution. Elistan had not indicated that he was a magic-user. Though I knew what the answer would be, I had to ask my question aloud.

"How does he know the effect is magical?" I asked, pointing to the old man.

Laurana shrugged, unconcerned. "Elistan is a true cleric of Paladine. His god has told him that this place is created by magic." She turned to Elistan. "Do you think it's safe to rest here for a while?"

I looked into the calm, though weary face of one who claimed to be a true cleric. I saw his love for Laurana—for everyone—and I began to dare to believe.

"I think it safe to rest for a few moments, but then I think we should press on, as Derek suggests," Elistan said diplomatically.

Derek snorted derisively at his partial victory. Refusing the walrus blubber I offered him, he began to pace about the cave. Laurana, on the other hand, calmly laid down a skin and curled up like a kitten to nap in what precious time there was.

I divided the remainder of our blubber between the other three and myself. Sturm stood alone, chewing absently on his, watching Derek pace.

Elistan found a distant corner and assumed a meditative pose. Was he praying to Paladine—or some false god instead? I longed for the ability to read minds. If Paladine really did exist and Elistan was his cleric, why didn't he give me a sign?

"If you don't mind my saying so," Tasslehoff interrupted my thoughts, "this stuff is awful. Don't get me wrong—I truly appreciate you sharing your food—but do your people really eat this all the time?"

"No," I said, grinning. "Sometimes we eat raw fish."

The kender's small face wrinkled with distaste. "Really? No spiced potatoes, no dwarf spirits?" He shuddered. "I guess you can't help being what you are—but I'm glad I was born a kender and not an Ice Folk!"

I did not tell him so, but I was glad as well.

Derek paced till he could stand it no more. "May we please continue looking for the orb now?" he asked with sarcastic politeness. Laurana jerked awake.

"What?" she mumbled, dazed. "How long have I been asleep?" With a grimace, she forced herself to her feet.

"Not long enough," Sturm muttered, giving Derek an irritated glance.

Wincing, Laurana rubbed at the knotted muscles of her lower back. "Never mind." She tried to sound energetic. "Let's see if this cave leads anywhere."

"It had better," Derek said pointedly, glaring at me before storming off toward the back of the cave. "Hurry up, Brightblade."

Smothering a grin, Sturm clapped me encouragingly on the back and strode after the impatient knight. Assuming his usual, disturbingly serene expression, Elistan gathered his furs closer and joined Laurana.

Thankfully, the cave did lead to a tunnel, though where the tunnel led to was anyone's guess.

We would soon find out.

"You know, I get the feeling we're overlooking something," Tasslehoff muttered, dashing between us to press his face to the cold, glassy walls. "I get this creepy feeling we're being watched."

"You are," Sturm said, fondly tugging the kender's topknot, "by me."

Tasslehoff frowned. "Make fun if you like, Sturm, but my Uncle Trapspringer says—"

Sturm clapped his hands to his ears and snorted. "Not an Uncle Trapspringer story!"

Derek's head jerked around. "Hush!" he snarled. Suddenly his face contorted in surprise. "Whoa!" The tunnel had ended abruptly in a deep, dark chasm! One foot over the edge, Derek swung his arms wildly to keep from sliding over entirely.

Instinctively, Laurana reached for his out-flung arm, and Sturm grabbed her. Together they pulled the struggling knight back from the edge. Wheezing and panting, he collapsed momentarily in a heap. Then, remembering himself, he struggled to his feet, brushing off the helping hands.

"Great! Now where do we go?" he demanded.

Laurana frowned. "I don't see any reason—or way—to cross the chasm. There's nothing but an icy wall on the other side. I guess we'll have to retrace our steps and continue up the cliff face after all," she finished wearily.

"Not necessarily!" sang out Tasslehoff, whom I must confess I'd forgotten. He was on his knees, tapping on the left wall with his knuckles. Suddenly he looked up at Elistan, reaching for the mace hanging from the cleric's belt. "May I borrow this?" he asked politely. Without waiting for an answer, he grabbed the mace and smashed it into the icy wall, sending glassy shards flying about the tunnel.

"Tasslehoff, what on Krynn are you doing?" Laurana demanded, reaching out to prevent his next swing. She stopped abruptly as the kender's blows revealed a hole into another area. Before she could say more, Tasslehoff hopped through the jagged opening.

"Tas, wait!" she cried, hurrying after him.

"Oh, no," Sturm muttered, as if this scene were nothing new to him. Hitching up his gear, he followed the golden-haired elf. The rest of us hastily followed.

Stepping through the opening, I found the others in a vast room formed of rough-hewn stone blocks. In one corner was stacked a pile of dried peat, ready for burning. In another were huge wooden barrels in neat rows. Weapons and tools hung from racks on the walls. A dilapidated door swung from one hinge on the wall opposite me. We seemed to be in some sort of storeroom—but for whom? A shiver of apprehension raised the hair on my scalp.

"I knew we were overlooking something!" Tasslehoff cried, scurrying about the room in excitement.

Elistan strode up to the kender, his palm outstretched. "Yes, you were. . . . My mace, please," he reminded Tas.

"Oh, this?" Tas asked, pulling the mace from his pack, where he'd obviously placed it for safe-keeping. "Yes, well, I was talking about something else. Listen."

The kender's voice hushed, the room became strangely, uncomfortably quiet. Tasslehoff crept slowly toward the center, cocking his head from side to side. As if frozen, we all stood watching him. "Do you hear it, Sturm?" he asked softly. "It sounds like . . . like clicking, or scratching. Raggart?"

All eyes turned to me as if I should somehow know the source of the strange noise. I reached up to pull down my fur hood so that I could hear better, when Derek bellowed in sudden fury, his sword flashing from its sheath. Before any of us had time to comprehend what was happening, the room exploded into snarling, screaming chaos. Minotaurs, creatures with the bodies of men and the heads of bulls, and thanoi, another bizarre mix of human and walrus, burst through the doorway and fell on the two knights and the kender.

Surprised, Sturm had barely time enough to draw his weapon from under his furs. Surging forward with Derek, he strove to push the gruesome creatures back to the door. But the thanoi, hungry for the blood of intruders, were crazed. Swinging wildly with axes and clubs, they forced the two knights back into the center of the room.

My eye caught sight of Laurana's flaxen hair as she drew her blade and lunged forward to join the attack. The sight of the plucky fighter made me realize I'd done nothing to help. But what could I—a tired old man—do?

Tormented with indecision, I saw the kender disappear among the rows of barrels. It wasn't like him to hide from something this exciting. What was he up to? I wondered.

Suddenly, a blood-thirsty roaring filled my ears. Jerking my head around, I saw a minotaur press past the warriors, bent for Elistan and me. But the creature's face changed from delight to surprise as he tripped and fell at my feet for no apparent reason. From among the barrels I heard a childish giggle, and the reason became clear. "Now!" shouted the kender, and I guess he was talking to me, for suddenly I knew what to do.

First, I raised my staff and bashed the minotaur over the head with it as hard as I could. Then I dashed over to the first row of barrels and tugged on the rim of one of the heavy things until whatever was inside sloshed, swaying the barrel ever so slightly.

"Elistan, help me!" I called to the cleric, who stood on the edge of the battle, mumbling prayers. Seeing my intention, he drew his hands from his cuffs and pulled on the rim of the barrel with me, until, with a ground-jarring thump, the cask dropped onto its rounded side on the floor. Wordlessly, we stepped back and ran at the barrel full-tilt, sending it rolling like a loosened boulder at the prone minotaur.

Groggy from his fall and my bashing, the creature looked up just in time to see a spiraling wooden barrel about to smash into the tips of his horns. Then the minotaur's eyes saw no more, squashed as they were by the mammoth barrel.

But my triumph was shortlived as I quickly realized my error. The barrel was still rolling, headed straight for Laurana, Sturm, and Derek. Still engaged with thanoi and minotaurs in the center of the room, they did not see their danger. I panicked and yelled to the only one who faced me.

"Sturm!"

The knight's blood-spattered face jerked up, his eyes widened slightly. Without missing a beat, he slashed viciously at the thanoi before him. Leaning to his right, he shoved Derek away from the minotaur he fought, then bowled Laurana over to his left, not a second ahead of the swiftly turning barrel. It knocked the remaining minotaur and thanoi to the floor, then the barrel stopped, pinning or squashing whatever happened to get in its way.

Unfortunately, that included Derek's foot. Surprised by Sturm's shove, the stubborn knight had tried to stand his ground, apparently slipped in a pool of blood, and crashed to the floor, just as the barrel arrived. Though obviously in great pain, the knight hacked at the furry thanoi fingers that desperately groped at him from under the barrel.

Raising her sword, Laurana strode forward and ended the lives of the struggling creatures, as Sturm hoisted the end of the barrel pinning Derek's foot.

"This is your fault, Brightblade," Derek growled, nearly spitting on Sturm's proffered hands. He struggled to stand alone, though the effort cost him. Sturm caught the Knight of Solamnia by the armpits as he slumped toward the floor.

As the cleric of my tribe, it was my duty to heal, as best I could, the wounds of my people. I rushed to Derek's side to examine his foot. Even with his boot on, I could see that it was twisted unnaturally. Gently slipping the furry glove off, my hand touched the jagged edge of a bone. Blood flowed freely from the purple, swollen wound. Swallowing a gasp of revulsion, I searched my mind for an answer. But I had none. I hadn't the power to heal this man.

Derek, thankfully, had passed out from the pain. I gently maneuvered the bone back to what I thought was its intended position, then let Derek's foot slide from my hand to rest on the cold ground. Looking up suddenly, I found Sturm's eyes on me.

"Great job, Raggart," he said, smiling warmly. "Your trick with the barrel was an excellent idea."

My mouth dropped in shock. How could he say that? Not only had I crushed Derek's foot, but I'd given Sturm's enemy more cause to hate him. Derek would never forgive Sturm for my mistake! I couldn't bare the shame anymore. I spun around to flee, but a firm hand gripped my shoulder.

"Do not blame yourself, Raggart." Elistan's soothing voice enveloped me. "Sturm is right. Your quick thinking saved our lives—including Derek's." He knelt down next to the unconscious knight and laid a hand to his forehead.

Though his words were intended to reassure me, they only increased my shame. I hung my head and turned away, my face burning. No matter what anyone said, I knew that my thoughtless, though well-intended action had caused Derek's injury. Not only had I caused it, I couldn't even cure him! Some cleric I was!

"Laurana, Sturm!" the kender squealed. I'd forgotten all about him again. "I think I know where the orb is!"

"Tasslehoff Burrfoot, what have you been up to?" Laurana demanded sternly. "You haven't been off exploring by yourself, have you?"

"Well, not exactly." The kender looked sheepish. "I thought I saw one of those walrus-looking men running out the door, so I thought I'd better find out what mischief he was up to. When I realized I'd lost sight of him, I looked up and found myself in a library—here in this frozen castle!" His face was flushed with barely contained excitement. Though I said nothing, I noticed that his pack had new bulges.

"That does it," Laurana said firmly. "Our battle here will likely draw more attention. Let's get moving." She brushed a tangle of hair from her face. "Will Derek be able to travel, or must we carry him?"

"I will carry myself!" Derek growled. To my surprise, he pushed past Elistan to pull himself to his feet. "Never let it be said that Derek Crownguard slowed anyone down!"

"No one would ever accuse you of that," Laurana muttered, the double edge in her words lost to Derek. "Let's go find this library of Tas's."

Gingerly, Derek placed his weight on his foot. I waited for him to crumble like softened snow. But as he headed for the door, a slight limp was the only indication that he'd hurt his foot. Having seen the extent of his wound, I was stunned! Could sheer force of will allow Derek to walk on the bloody stump I had just examined?

What startled me almost as much was that no one else was surprised. I was about to demand an explanation when Elistan caught my eye. That serene, half-smile lit his face as he winked at me knowingly. My mind balked at the only possibility. Could it be true? . . . Elistan . . .?

"Come on, Raggart!" Tasslehoff's high-pitched voice prodded me. Shaking my head, I looked around the storeroom to find I was alone with dead minotaurs and thanoi. Everyone waited for me at the doorway at the far side of the room. I'd think about Elistan and Derek's foot later, I told myself as I hurried to join them.

Sturm poked his head out the door and peered about for signs of life. With a jerk of his head, he signaled us to follow him into the area beyond.

We stepped into what must have been the central courtyard of a once-beautiful castle. Five or more doors led off in a semi-circle to the right, and three more curved around to our left. The courtyard was otherwise empty, save for a massive fountain shaped of water-spurting dragons. The fountain immediately struck me as strange— Why hadn't it frozen?

"Magical," Elistan said abruptly, as if reading my thoughts. "The water has curative properties."

But instead of thrilling me, for I had many aches and pains a few swallows might cure, Elistan's prediction made me apprehensive. Someone or something very magical and intelligent was at work in Icewall Castle.

"The library's over here!" Tasslehoff whispered loudly, slipping off to one of the rooms to our left. "There was a trap on this door," he added proudly, his hand on the knob, "but I fixed it." He disappeared through the opening, only to thrust his head back out again. "By the way," he chimed, pointing to a spot before the door, "don't step on this big, flat stone."

"Kender!" muttered Derek, but I noticed he stepped across the stone before continuing into the room beyond. Sturm and Laurana followed, with Elistan and me behind.

Several candles, nearly burned to their bases, lit the small room that was filled with racks and shelves of books, scrolls, and loose papers. Tasslehoff was everywhere at once, ducking under tables and peering between shelves.

"What makes you think the orb is in here, kender?" asked Derek. "We shouldn't stay long. We can't afford to get caught in here. I can barely turn around, let alone fight."

"Derek's right, Tas," said Laurana. "Let's search quickly and get out of here," Derek cast a surprised glance at Laurana, caught off guard by her support. "Raggart, keep an eye on the courtyard." Following her instructions, I moved back to stand in the doorway, an eye on both areas.

"I didn't say the orb was in here," Tasslehoff said defensively, "I only said it *might* be. Whoever owns this library must certainly read a lot, though how he finds the time . . . Of course, what else has he to do in the middle of all this boring ice and snow—no offense, Raggart."

I smiled to let him know none was taken. Frankly, I found the landscape a bit dull at times, too. But my smile slipped as I read the spines of several books— spellbooks, I noted with growing apprehension.

"I've not felt such all-consuming evil since . . . since Pax Tharkas." Elistan shuddered, though I didn't understand the reference. "I think we're near the orb, but I do not believe it is in this room."

Abruptly, Laurana stopped pulling books from shelves. Looking resolute, she said grimly, "Then we'll just have to search every room in this frozen castle until we find it."

"I knew better than to trust a kender," Derek scoffed, striding toward the door.

"You're the one who insisted back in Tarsis that I come along," Tasslehoff pointed out, his little chin thrust forward.

"A demand I've come to regret more than once," Derek muttered.

"Then I don't suppose you want to know about the room hidden behind this wall?" the kender asked coyly.

Derek's face turned dark.

Laurana stepped up between them. "What room, Tas?" she asked in that sweet voice of hers.

Tasslehoff shot a triumphant glance at Derek before turning an excited grin on Laurana. "I think there's one behind this bookcase," he said, striding up to the shortest wall in the room, directly opposite the doorway I stood in. Tas knocked twice on the middle support of the bookcase. The whole wall swung back, almost knocking the kender off his feet in the process. "See?"

"I see," Derek said, pushing past the startled kender to peer into the room beyond. "I see another empty, orbless room!"

Derek took a few steps into the room, disappearing from my view. "Whoa—what the—?" He gasped suddenly. "Hey!" It was a shriek of frustration, not pain. Everyone pressed forward. Though I knew I should stay by the door no matter what, I could not resist looking too.

There, in a bedchamber the same size as the library, stood Derek, his hands frozen to his sides. I could not understand it until I saw the slender form of an elf in chainmail and black robes, a black longsword gleaming in his hand. He wore a strange helmet with horns over his head. I did not know it then, but I was getting my first glimpse of a Dragon Highlord.

"He's a dark elf wizard and he's put some kind of hold on Derek!" Elistan cried. "Keep him from casting spells!"

Before anyone could reach the dark elf, he slammed the hilt of his sword into Derek's face. The knight crumpled into what I hoped was only unconsciousness.

Instantly, Laurana and Sturm ran into the room, their arrival drawing the dark elf wizard away from the helpless Knight of Solamnia. The Highlord started to attack them, but he hesitated for a moment at the sight of Laurana.

"An elf, and a woman yet, dares invade the castle of Feal-Thas, Dragon Highlord of the White Wing?" the wizard snarled, and suddenly began slashing at her with his sword.

Ducking his blow, Laurana lost her footing and fell,

hitting her head on a wooden desk. For a moment, she could not move, but crouched on the floor, holding her head in her hands. Seeing his opening, Feal-Thas closed in, his sword raised.

"It was high and mighty elves like you who cast me out!" Feal-Thas cried. "You will pay!" But in his thirst for Laurana's blood, the wizard had forgotten Sturm.

The knight lunged forward to strike the sword from the dark elf's hand. But with a speed and agility unknown to most humans, the Highlord read Sturm's intentions and whirled about, slashing the knight's own sword hand. Sturm's gasped, holding his bleeding wrist. His moment of weakness cost him dearly. In a single, lightning-swift motion, Feal-Thas snatched a dagger from his sleeve and hurled it toward the knight. A hideous shriek gurgled out of Sturm's mouth as he clutched at his throat, and blood streamed down his fur cloak. He collapsed.

"Sturm!" Laurana cried out at the sight of her fallen friend. Her beautiful face contorted with rage as she whirled on Feal-Thas. With grim determination, Laurana wiped the blood from her eyes and fought her enemy, though it was easy to see that each blow drained her by half. Feal-Thas appeared to enjoy playing with her, seeming to delight in parrying her waning blows without striking back.

Elistan, whose strategy so far had been to stay out of the way of the fighters in the small chamber, could hold back no longer. Seeing Laurana alone, he hurled himself at the wizard, bashing him repeatedly in the back with his mace. Though the attack caught him unaware, Feal-Thas used his magic to toss the cleric from him as he would a fly. A huge, phantom hand reached out, grabbed the cleric, and threw him aside. Elistan slammed into the far wall and slid silently to the floor.

And there I stood, rooted to the spot, useless as a

dwarven doorknob. What had my strategy—my excuse—been? I wasn't even watching our rear anymore. What could I do? I remembered the kender—where was he? He'd come through for me before, tripping the minotaur. But he was nowhere to be seen. There weren't any barrels here to save my unworthy life.

I watched in despair as Laurana, exhausted from her lone struggle, dropped to one knee. She tried desperately to regain her footing, but Feal-Thas leaned forward and plucked the sword from her blood-stained, aching hands. Eyes dim with angry tears, she swung desperately at him with her fist. The dark elf grabbed her wrist and laughed.

"What a pity," he murmured, the patronizing sound of victory in his voice. He held the tip of her own sword to the throbbing vein in her throat. "You appear to be an elf of some breeding—not entirely unattractive either. I could spare your life if you gave me good reason," he offered suggestively.

Laurana, breathing heavily from her struggles, turned her gaze from the knife in Sturm's throat and his blood-soaked chest to look at the Highlord. She swallowed hard. "Are you suggesting I join you as a Highlord?" she asked in a seductively coy tone I would never have thought her capable of using.

I was shocked. Why on Krynn was she toying with this evil Highlord while her friend lay dying at her feet? Suddenly, I saw the knuckles of her hands, clenched and white with anger, and I knew she must be stalling for time, hoping to regain her strength.

"What I'm suggesting has nothing to do with being a Highlord," the wizard said, leering. Encouraged that she might entertain the thought, confident that she no longer had the strength to fight, and obviously discounting me completely, the wizard lowered his sword. "If we cleaned you up a bit, you might be worthy."

Laughing, he looked over at the bed and even reached out his hand to smooth the silken sheets.

I thought I might choke on the bile in my throat, as I longed to strangle the life from the evil creature. Suddenly, I remembered my frostreaver! (I know now that the thought came from Paladine himself.) But I was not strong enough to wield it—only fighters were. I looked at the bent form of the courageous woman warrior. Could Laurana . . . ? No one but Ice Folk had ever been allowed to use frostreavers. But these were extraordinary people I traveled with. Faith overcame tradition.

Sliding the axelike weapon from my pack ever so quietly, I crept forward. Time seemed to grind to a halt. The wizard was still pawing the bed and laughing, his foul suggestions of what he intended to do to the elven maid burning my heart.

Softly, I tip-toed up behind Laurana and slipped the glistening frostreaver to the princess of the Qualinesti elves, praying to Paladine to give her strength that I did not have.

Laurana's fingers curled around the haft of the icy 'reaver. Raising it over her head, she sprang up like a wolf and lunged at the unsuspecting elf wizard just as he turned around for his answer. Candlelight glinted off the frigid edge of my painstakingly crafted frostreaver as it bit into Feal-thas's throat. A scream, the wizard's last on Krynn, pierced the air. The floor of the small chamber ran red with the blood of the dead Highlord.

Dry, wracking sobs shook Laurana's body as she stumbled over to kneel beside Sturm. Self-consciously, I moved forward to wrench the icy weapon from her shaky fingers. She laid her hands awkwardly on the knight's bloody chest, not quite knowing what to do. Biting her lip, she forced her right hand forward to close around the hilt of the dagger in his throat. A heart-breaking moan escaped her lips as, mustering all her strength and courage, she pulled the dagger out. Blood welled from the wound; she pressed a small cloth to it timidly, uselessly. My throat grew thick with tears as I watched the life drain from her friend.

Somehow I became aware of other sounds in the room. Derek stirred slowly, then spun onto his back.

"Be careful, Laurana!" he cried, jumping to his feet as if pulled by a rope, his sword aloft. "He's a magic-user!" Spinning about, the Knight of Solamnia blinked in bewilderment. His eyes traveled from the dead body of the Highlord to Laurana as she knelt at Sturm's side. Understanding and admiration lit his eyes. He bowed his head respectfully for the dying knight.

Suddenly there came a muffled pounding on the wall behind Elistan, rousing the unconscious cleric. Shaking his head to clear it, he stood slowly and stepped away from the wall.

Oh, no! I thought. The wizard's allies! We are doomed!

Brows narrowed in a frown, Derek raised his weapon as a small crack spread on the wall in the shape of a door.

Suddenly, out popped the kender!

"Who's been blocking the door?" he demanded testily. "I've been pounding and pounding, but you've all been too busy doing who knows what to notice!" He saw Laurana's tear-stained face, then the bloody pool on the floor. His eyes widened in disbelief.

"Sturm!" he cried, dropping to the floor by Laurana. "Sturm, wake up! Flint would never forgive me if

I let anything happen to you while he was away!" The kender choked. "You know how grouchy he can be when he thinks I've fouled things up again! Oh, Sturm!" The kender's voice trailed away into sobs.

Wringing my hands helplessly, I searched my mind for some way to comfort them. I felt even more useless than I had when Derek's foot had been crushed.

Then, "Elistan!" Laurana cried, motioning for the cleric.

I stared at her in sorrow. Now we would see Elistan for the fake he was. I wished, for her sake alone, that he was what he claimed to be.

Furry robe rustling softly on the floor, Elistan's face was composed as he knelt beside the dying knight.

"We will ask for Paladine's aid, but it may be that this man's life has been fulfilled. If so, we must give thanks that he died as he would have wished, defending those he loved." Drawing the golden medallion from under his furs, Elistan held it tenderly and mumbled words I could not understand. Moments passed and nothing happened. I held my breath, hoping, and yet not daring to believe. I kept my eyes on Sturm. Elistan continued to pray, his voice gathering intensity and momentum.

Suddenly, blood stopped oozing from Sturm's throat. Fear grabbed me. Was this the end? Had the knight's heart simply given up?

And then a miracle happened. I can close my eyes and, to this day, see again what I saw in that small room in Icewall Castle. Color returned to Sturm's cheeks. Slowly, so slowly I couldn't be certain of my eyes, the wound sealed shut. Sturm moaned as life again flowed through him.

"He will live," Elistan pronounced heavily, obviously drained. Tears flowing from my eyes, I bowed my head and dropped to my knees before Paladine's cleric.

But Elistan pulled me to my feet. "Do not worship me. I am but Paladine's messenger on Krynn, as you will soon be."

I heard the words of promise as if in a dream I could scarcely believe.

"Hey, I almost forgot!" Tasslehoff hiccuped, his tears drying. "I found it!"

"Found what?" Laurana asked, preoccupied with Sturm.

A look of extreme patience crossed the kender's face. "What have we been looking for? The orb, that's what! I must say, it doesn't look like much compared to the picture I saw in the book in the Great Library. Oh, it's round and carved and all that, but it's awfully small. It looks like there's something red inside it— I'd love to break it and find out what it is!"

"Don't you dare!" Derek shouted, heading for the small door Tas had just used. He returned a few moments later holding a small crystal globe that randomly shifted in color from misty white to blue.

It didn't look like much to me either, but almost instantly, fighting broke out over it. Laurana wanted to hold it, for she intended to give it to her people, the elves. Derek demanded to keep it to return it to the council of the Knights. They agreed only to disagree— and to let me, as a disinterested third party, hold it until we reached the Ice Folk camp, where they would rejoin their friends.

With Paladine's help, Sturm slowly returned from death's grip. We spent the rest of the night in Feal-Thas's library, warmed there by the fire, protected from minotaur and thanoi. But we were not attacked. After we deposited the remains of the Highlord's body in the courtyard, his former minions did not disturb us. I think they fled. I didn't blame them. He didn't appear to have been a kindly master.

Or perhaps they sensed that in the next room, while a courageous elf maiden, a precocious kender, and two very different knights slept, Good struck another blow in its battle against Evil. Elistan and I discussed this, as we prayed and talked all through the night. When the two moons gave way to the sun that morning, I, Raggart, cleric of the Ice Folk had became a long-awaited true cleric of Paladine.

I settled back from the flames, my voice scratchy from the lengthy tale. Though tired, I was reluctant to leave the warmth of the fire and my memories. Closing my eyes, I breathed deeply.

"Did the great chief Harald keep his promise to not harm Laurana's friends?" Laina asked, though she knew the answer from previous tellings of the tale.

"He did, but while we fought minotaurs and thanoi in Icewall Castle, others of their races attacked our village in what has become known as the Battle of the Ice Reaches. Many of our people were killed, as well as the knights Aran and Brian. I'm told they fought valiantly."

"And Laurana and Sturm and the others?" Mendor asked. "What became of them?"

My eyes flew open. This was a new question. "The woman who could charm an ice bear . . ." I said at last. "I can only hope Laurana joined her Tanis, as I've come to think of him.

"Derek and Sturm . . . both driven by some dark secret," I mumbled, my eyes narrowing. "Though I believe Sturm conquered his, I fear Derek's had grown too powerful."

I rubbed my chin. "I don't know for certain," I continued more slowly. "But I imagine Flint growing to a ripe old age under a shady tree somewhere, grumbling happily.

"The kender?" I chuckled. "It's anyone's guess with a kender. But before our adventure in Icewall Castle was over, Tas uncovered yet another secret in the castle—the dragonlance. Tas told me more than he was supposed to, of course. But I must confess the details are lost to me . . ."

I stared, unblinking, into the flames. "Elistan spent his life in the work of Paladine," I continued with certainty. "And if he has not already left Krynn to join the true god, he will one day soon."

With that, I, Raggart Knug, true cleric of Paladine, rose to my feet. Looking for the constellations in the sky, I thought wistfully of the day I, too, would join Paladine. Straightening my weary back, I left the fire for my hut and sleep. Tomorrow I would begin forging another frostreaver.

# The Legacy

## Margaret Weis and Tracy Hickman

---

## CHAPTER ONE

Caramon stood in a vast chamber carved of obsidian. It was so wide, its perimeter was lost in shadow, so high its ceiling was obscured in shadow. No pillars supported it. No lights lit it. Yet light there was, though none could name its source. It was a pale light, white—not yellow. Cold and cheerless, it gave no warmth.

Though he could see no one in the chamber, though he could hear no sound disturb the heavy silence that seemed centuries old, Caramon knew he was not alone. He could feel the eyes watching him as they had watched him long ago, and so he stood stolidly, waiting patiently until they deemed it time to proceed.

He guessed what they were doing and he smiled, but only inwardly. To those watching eyes, the big man's face remained smooth, impassive. They would see no weakness in him, no sorrow, no bitter regret. Though memory was reaching out to him, its hand was warm, its touch gentle. He was at peace with himself, he had been for twenty-five years.

---

As if reading his thoughts—which, Caramon supposed, they might well have been—those present in the vast chamber suddenly revealed themselves. It was not that the light grew brighter, or a mist lifted, or the darkness parted, for none of that happened. Caramon felt more as though he were the one who had suddenly entered, though *he* had been standing there upwards of a quarter hour. The two robed figures that appeared before him were a part of this place just like the white, magical light, the ages-old silence. He wasn't—he was an outsider and would be one forever.

"Welcome once again to our Tower, Caramon Majere," said a voice.

Caramon bowed, saying nothing. He couldn't—for the life of him—remember the man's name.

"Justarius," the man said, smiling pleasantly. "Yes, the years have been long since we last met, and our last meeting was during a desperate hour. It is small wonder you have forgotten me. Please, be seated." A heavy, carved, oaken chair materialized beside Caramon. "You have journeyed long and are weary, perhaps."

Caramon started to state that he was just fine, a journey like this was nothing to a man who had been over most of the continent of Ansalon in his younger days. But at the sight of the chair with its soft, inviting cushions, Caramon realized that the journey *had* been rather a long one—longer than he remembered it. His back ached, his armor appeared to have grown heavier, and it seemed that his legs just weren't holding up their end of things anymore.

Well, what do you expect, Caramon asked himself with a shrug. I'm the proprietor of an inn now. I've got responsibilities. Someone's got to sample the cooking. . . . Heaving a rueful sigh, he sat down, shifting his bulk about until he was settled comfortably.

"Getting old, I guess," he said with a grin.

"It comes to all of us," Justarius answered, nodding his head. "Well, most of us," he amended, with a glance at the figure who sat beside him. Following his gaze, Caramon saw the figure throw back its rune-covered hood to reveal a familiar face—an elven face.

"Greetings, Caramon Majere."

"Dalamar," returned Caramon steadily with a nod of his head, though the grip of memory tightened a bit at the sight of the black-robed wizard. Dalamar looked no different than he had years ago—wiser, perhaps, calmer and cooler. Ninety years of age, he had been just an apprentice magic-user, considered little more than a hot-blooded youth as far as the elves were concerned. Twenty-five years mattered no more to the long-lived elves than the passing of a day and night. Now well over one hundred, his cold, handsome face appeared no older than a human of thirty.

"The years have dealt kindly with you, Caramon," Justarius continued. "The Inn of the Last Home, which you now own, is one of the most prosperous in Krynn. You are a hero—you and your lady-wife both. Tika Majere is well and undoubtedly as beautiful as ever?"

"More," Caramon replied huskily.

Justarius smiled. "You have five children, two daughters and three sons—"

A sliver of fear pricked Caramon's contentment. No, he said to himself inwardly, they have no power over me now. He settled himself more solidly in his chair, like a soldier digging in for battle.

"Your two eldest sons, Tanin and Sturm, are soldiers of renown"—Justarius spoke in a bland voice, as though chatting with a neighbor over the fence. Caramon wasn't fooled, however, and kept his eyes closely on the wizard—"bidding fair to outdo their famous father and mother in deeds of valor on the field. But the third, the middle child, whose name is . . ." Justarius hesitated.

"Palin," said Caramon, his brows lowering into a frown. Glancing at Dalamar, the big man saw the dark elf watching him intently with slanted, inscrutable eyes.

"Palin, yes." Justarius paused, then said quietly, "It would seem he follows in the footsteps of his uncle."

There. It was out. Of course, that's why they had ordered him here. He had been expecting it, or something like it, for a long time now. Damn them! Why couldn't they leave him alone! He never would have come if Palin hadn't insisted. Breathing heavily, Caramon stared at Justarius, trying to read the man's face. He might as well have been trying to read one of his son's spellbooks.

Justarius, Head of the Conclave of Wizards, the most powerful magic-user in Krynn. The red-robed wizard sat in the great stone chair in the center of the semicircle of twenty-one chairs. An elderly man, his gray hair and lined face were the only outward signs of aging. The eyes were as shrewd, the body appeared as strong—except the crippled left leg—as when Caramon had first met the archmage twenty-five years ago.

Caramon's gaze went to the mage's left leg. Hidden beneath the red robes, the man's injury was noticeable only to those who had seen him walk.

Aware of Caramon's scrutiny, Justarius's hand went self-consciously to rub his leg, then he stopped with a wry smile. Crippled Justarius may be, Caramon thought, chilled. But only in body. Not in mind or ambition. Twenty-five years ago, Justarius had been the leading spokesman only of his own Order, the Red Robes, those wizards in Krynn who had turned their backs upon both the Evil and the Good to walk their own path, that of Neutrality. Now he was Head of the

Conclave of Wizards, ruling over all the wizards in the world, presumably—the White Robes, Red Robes, and the Black. Since magic is the most potent force in a wizard's life, he swears fealty to the Conclave, no matter what private ambitions or desires he nurses within his own heart.

Most wizards, that is. Of course, there had been his twin Raistlin . . .

Twenty-five years ago.

Par-Salian of the White Robes had been Head of the Conclave then. . . . Caramon felt memory's hand clutch him more tightly still.

"I don't see what my son has to do with any of this," he said in an even, steady voice. "If you want to meet my boys, they are in that room you magicked us into after we arrived. I'm sure you can magic them in here anytime you want. So, now that we have concluded social pleasantries— By the way, where is Par-Salian?" Caramon demanded suddenly, his gaze going around the shadowy chamber, flicking over the empty chairs next to Justarius.

"He retired as Head of the Conclave twenty-five years ago," Justarius said gravely, "following the . . . the incident in which you were involved."

Caramon flushed, but said nothing. He thought he detected a slight smile on Dalamar's delicate elven features.

"I took over as Head of the Conclave, and Dalamar was chosen to succeed Ladonna as Head of the Order of Black Robes in return for his dangerous and valiant work during—"

"The incident," Caramon growled. "Congratulations," he added.

Dalamar's lip curled in a sneer. Justarius nodded, but it was obvious he was not to be distracted from the previous topic of discussion.

"I would be honored to meet your sons," Justarius said coolly. "Palin in particular. I understand that the young man is desirous of becoming a mage someday."

"He's studying magic, if that's what you mean," Caramon said gruffly. "I don't know how seriously he takes it, or if he plans to make it his livelihood, as you seem to imply. He and I have never discussed it—"

Dalamar snorted derisively at this, causing Justarius to lay his hand on the dark elf's black-robed arm.

"Perhaps we have been mistaken in what we have heard of your son's ambition, then?"

"Perhaps you have," Caramon returned coolly. "Palin and I are close. I'm certain he would have confided in me."

"It is refreshing to see a man these days who is honest and open about his love for his sons, Caramon Majere," began Justarius mildly.

"Bah!" Dalamar interrupted. "You might as well say it is refreshing to see a man with his eyes gouged out!" Snatching his arm from the old wizard's grasp, he gestured at Caramon. "You were blind to your brother's dark ambition for years, until it was almost too late. Now you turn sightless eyes to your own son—"

"My son is a good boy, as different from Raistlin as the silver moon and the black! He has no such ambition! What would you know of him anyway, you . . . you outcast?" Caramon shouted, rising to his feet in anger. Though well over fifty, the big man had kept himself in relatively good condition through hard work and training his sons in the arts of battle. His hand went reflexively to his sword, forgetting as he did so, however, that in the Tower of High Sorcery he would be as helpless as a gully dwarf facing a dragon. "And speaking of dark ambition, you served your master well, didn't you, Dalamar? Raistlin taught you a lot. Perhaps more than we know—"

"And I bear the mark of his hand upon my flesh still!" Dalamar cried, rising to his feet in turn. Ripping his black robes open at the neck, he bared his breast. Five wounds, like the marks of five fingers, were visible on the dark elf's smooth skin. A thin trickle of blood trailed down each, glistening in the cold light of the Chamber of Wizards. "For twenty-five years, I've lived with this pain. . . ."

"And what of my pain?" Caramon asked in a low voice, feeling memory's hand dig sharp nails into his soul. "Why have you brought me here? To cause my wounds to open and bleed as well as your own!"

"Gentlemen, please," said Justarius softly. "Dalamar, control yourself. Caramon, please sit down. Remember, you two owe your lives to each other. This establishes a bond between you that should be respected."

The old man's voice penetrated the shouts that still echoed in the vast chamber, its cool authority silencing Caramon and calming Dalamar. Clasping his torn robes together, the dark elf resumed his seat next to Justarius.

Caramon, too, sat down, ashamed and chagrined. He had sworn he would not let this happen, these people would have no power to shake him. And already he'd lost control. Trying to assume a relaxed expression, he leaned back in the chair. But his hand clenched over the hilt of his sword.

"Forgive Dalamar," Justarius said, his hand once again on the dark elf's arm. "He spoke in haste and anger. You are right, Caramon. Your son, Palin, *is* a good man—I think we must say *man* and not *boy*. He is, after all, twenty—"

"Just turned twenty," Caramon muttered, eyeing Justarius warily.

The red-robed archmage waved it aside. "And he is,

as you say, different from Raistlin. How not? He is his own person, after all. Born to different parents, under different, happier circumstances than faced you and your twin. From all we hear, Palin is handsome, likeable, strong, and fit. He does not have the burden of ill health to bear, as did Raistlin. He is devoted to his family, especially his two elder brothers. They, in turn, are devoted to him. Is all this true?"

Caramon nodded, unable to speak past the sudden lump in his throat.

Looking at him, Justarius's mild gaze suddenly became sharp and penetrating. He shook his head. "But in some ways you *are* blind, Caramon. Oh, not as Dalamar said,"—seeing Caramon's face go red with anger—"not the way you were blinded to your brother's evil. This is the blindness that afflicts all parents, my friend. I know"—Justarius smiled and gave rueful shrug—"I have a daughter . . ."

Glancing at Dalamar out of the corner of his eye, the archmage sighed. The handsome elf's lips twitched in a hint of a smile. Dalamar said nothing, however. He simply sat staring into the shadows.

"Yes, we parents can be blind," Justarius murmured. "But that is neither here nor there." Leaning forward, the archmage clasped his hands together. "I see you growing impatient, Caramon. As you guessed, we have called you here for a purpose. And, I'm afraid it does have something to do with your son, Palin."

This is it, Caramon said to himself, scowling, his sweating hand clenching and unclenching nervously around the hilt of his sword.

"There is no easy way to say this, so I will be blunt and direct." Justarius drew a deep breath, his face became grave and sorrowful, touched with a shadow of fear. "We have reason to believe that the young man's uncle—your twin brother, Raistlin—is *not* dead."

# CHAPTER TWO

"This place shivers my skin!" Tanin muttered, with a sideways glance at his youngest brother.

Slowly sipping a cup of tarbean tea, Palin stared into the flames of the fire, pretending not to have heard Tanin's remark, which he knew was addressed to him.

"Oh, in the name of the Abyss, would you sit down!" Sturm said, tossing pieces of bread at his brother. "You're going to walk yourself right through the floor, and the gods only know what's beneath us."

Tanin only frowned, shaking his head, and continued his pacing.

"Reorx's beard, brother!" Sturm continued almost incomprehensibly, his mouth full of cheese. "You'd think we were in a draconian dungeon instead of what might pass for a room in one of the finest inns in Palanthas itself! Good food, great ale—" he took a long pull to wash down the cheese— "and there'd be pleasant company if you weren't acting such a doorknob!"

"Well, we aren't in one of the inns in Palanthas," said Tanin sarcastically, stopping in his pacing to catch a hunk of thrown bread. Grinding it to bits in his hand, he tossed it on the floor. "We're in the Tower of High Sorcery in Wayreth. We've been spirited into this room. The damn door's locked and we can't get out. We have no idea what these wizards have done with Father, and all you can think of is cheese and ale!"

"That's not *all* I'm thinking of," Sturm said quietly with a nod of his head and a worried glance at their little brother, who was still staring into the fire.

MARGARET WEIS AND TRACY HICKMAN

"Yeah," Tanin snapped gloomily, his gaze following Sturm's. "I'm thinking of him, too! It's *his* fault we're here in the first place!" Moodily kicking a table leg as he walked past, Tanin resumed his pacing. Seeing his little brother flinch at his older brother's words, Sturm sighed and returned to his sport of trying to hit Tanin between the shoulder blades with the bread.

Anyone observing the older two young men (as someone was at this very moment) might have taken them for twins, although they were—in reality—a year apart in age. Twenty-four and twenty-three respectively, Tanin and Sturm (named for Caramon's best friend, Tanis Half-Elven, and the heroic Knight of Solamnia, Sturm Brightblade) looked, acted, and even thought alike. Indeed, they often played the part of twins and enjoyed nothing so much as when people mistook one for the other.

Big and brawny, each young man had Caramon's splendid physique and his genial, honest face. But the bright red curls and dancing green eyes that wreaked such havoc among the women the young men met came directly from their mother, who had broken her share of hearts in her youth. One of the beauties of Krynn as well as a renowned warrior, Tika Waylan had grown a little plumper since the days when she bashed draconians over the head with her skillet. But heads still turned when Tika waited tables in her fluffy, low-necked, white blouse, and there were few men who left the Inn of the Last Home without swearing that Caramon was a lucky fellow.

The green eyes of young Sturm were not dancing now, however. Instead, they glinted mischievously as, with a wink at his younger brother—who wasn't watching—Sturm rose silently to his feet and, positioning himself behind the preoccupied Tanin, quietly drew his sword. Just as Tanin turned around, Sturm stuck the sword blade between his brother's legs, sending him to the floor with a crash that seemed to shake the very foundation of the Tower.

"Damn you for a lame-brained gully dwarf!" roared Tanin, falling flat on his face. Clambering to his feet, he leaped after his brother, who was scrambling to get out of the way. Tanin caught him and, grabbing hold of the grinning Sturm by the collar of his tunic, sent him sprawling backward into the table, smashing it to the floor. Tanin jumped on top of his brother, and the two were engaged in their usual rough and tumble antics that had left several bar rooms in Ansalon in shambles when a quiet voice brought the tussle to a halt.

"Stop it," said Palin tensely, rising from his chair by the fire. "Stop it, both of you! Remember where you are!"

"I remember where I am," Tanin said sulkily, gazing up at his youngest brother.

As tall as the older two young men, Palin was well-built. Given to study rather than sword-play, however, he lacked the heavy musculature of the two warriors. He had his mother's red hair, but it was not fiery red, being nearer a dark auburn. He wore his hair long—it flowed to his shoulders in soft waves from a central part on his forehead. But it was the young man's face—his face and his hands—that sometimes haunted both the dreams of mother and father. Fine-boned, with penetrating, intelligent eyes that always seemed to be looking right through one, Palin's face had the look of his uncle, if not his features, the unseen observer noted. Palin's hands were Raistlin's, however. Slender, delicate, the fingers quick and deft, the young man handled the fragile spell components with such skill that his father was often torn between watching with pride and looking away in sadness.

Just now, the hands were clenched into fists as Palin glared grimly at his two older brothers lying on the floor amid spilled ale, pieces of bread, crockery, a half-eaten cheese, and shards of broken table.

"Then try to behave with some dignity, at least!" Palin snapped.

"I remember where I am," Tanin repeated angrily. Getting to his feet, he walked over to stand in front of Palin, staring at him accusingly. "And I remember who brought us here! Riding through that accursed wood that damn near got us killed—"

"Nothing in Wayreth Forest would have hurt you," Palin returned, looking at the mess on the floor in disgust. "As I told you if you'd only listened. This forest is controlled by the wizards in the Tower. It protects them from unwanted intruders. We have been invited here. The trees let us pass without harm. The voices you heard only whisper to you the fears in your own heart. It's magic—"

"Magic! You listen, Palin," Tanin interrupted in what Sturm always referred to as his Elder Brother voice. "Why don't you just drop all this magic business? You're hurting Father and Mother—Father most of all. You saw his face when we rode up to this place! The gods know what it must have cost him to come back here."

Flushing, Palin turned away, biting his lip.

"Oh, lay off the kid, will you, Tanin?" Sturm said, seeing the pain on his younger brother's face. Wiping ale from his pants, he somewhat shamefacedly began trying to put the table back together—a hopeless task considering most of it was in splinters.

"You had the makings of a good swordsman once, little brother," Tanin said persuasively, ignoring Sturm and putting his hand on Palin's shoulder. "C'mon, kid. Tell whoever's out there"—Tanin waved his hand somewhat vaguely—"that you've changed your mind. We can leave this cursed place, then, and go home—"

"We have no idea why they asked us to come here," Palin retorted, shaking off his brother's hand. "It probably has nothing to do with me! Why should it?" he asked bitterly. "I'm still a student, it will be years before I am ready to take my Test . . . thanks to Father and Mother," he muttered beneath his breath. Tanin did not hear it, but the unseen observer did.

"Yeah? And I'm a half-ogre," retorted Tanin angrily. "Look at me when I'm talking, Palin—"

"Just leave me alone!"

"Hey, you two—" Sturm the peacemaker started to intervene when the three young men suddenly realized they were not alone in the room.

All quarrels forgotten, the brothers acted instantly. Sturm rose to his feet with the quickness of a cat. His hand on the hilt of his sword, he joined Tanin, who had already moved to stand protectively in front of the unarmed Palin. Like all magic-users, the young man carried neither sword nor shield nor wore armor. But his hand went to the dagger he carried concealed beneath his robes, his mind already forming the words of the few defensive spells he had been allowed to learn.

"Who are you?" Tanin asked harshly, staring at the man standing in the center of the locked room. "How did you get in here?"

"As to how I got here"—the man smiled broadly—"there are no walls in the Tower of High Sorcery for those who walk with magic. As for who I am, my name is Dunbar Mastersmate, of Northern Ergoth."

"What do you want?" Sturm asked quietly.

"Want? Why—to make certain you are comfortable, that is all," Dunbar answered. "I am your host—"

"You? A magic-user?" Tanin gaped, and even Palin

seemed slightly startled.

In a world where wizards are noted for having more brains than brawn, this man was obviously the exception. Standing as tall as Tanin, he had a barrel of a chest that Caramon might well have envied. Muscles rippled beneath the shining black skin. His arms looked as though he could have picked up the stalwart Sturm and carried him about the room as easily as if he had been a child. He was not dressed in robes, but wore bright-colored, loose-fitting trousers. The only hint that he might have been a wizard at all came from the pouches that hung at his waist and a white sash that girdled his broad middle.

Dunbar laughed, booming laughter that set the dishes rattling.

"Aye," he said, "I am a magic-user." With that, he spoke a word of command, and the broken table, leaping to its legs, put itself back together with incredible speed. The ale vanished from the floor, the cracked pitcher mended and floated up to rest on the table, where it was soon foaming with brew again. A roasted haunch of venison appeared, as did a loaf of fragrant bread, along with sundry other delicacies that caused Sturm's mouth to water and cooled even Tanin's ardor, though they did not allay his suspicions.

"Seat yourselves," said Dunbar, "and let us eat. Do not worry about your father," he added, as Tanin was about to speak. "He is in conference with the heads of the other two Orders. Sit down! Sit down!" He grinned, white teeth flashing against his black skin. "Or shall I make you sit down? . . ."

At this, Tanin let loose the hilt of his sword and pulled up a chair, though he did not eat but sat watching Dunbar warily. Sturm fell to with a good appetite, however. Only Palin remained standing, his hands folded in the sleeves of his white robes.

"Please, Palin," said Dunbar more gently, looking at the young man, "be seated. Soon we will join your father and you will discover the reason you have been brought here. In the meanwhile, I ask you to share bread and meat with me."

"Thank you, Master," Palin said, bowing respectfully.

"Dunbar, Dunbar . . ." The man waved his hand. "You are my guests. We will not stand on formalities."

Palin sat down and began to eat, but it was obvious he did so out of courtesy only. Dunbar and Sturm more than made up for him, however, and soon even Tanin was lured from his self-imposed role of protector by the delicious smells and the sight of the others enjoying themselves.

"You . . . you said the heads of the *other* Orders, Mast—Dunbar," Palin ventured. "Are you—"

"Head of the Order of the White Robes. Yes." Dunbar tore off a hunk of bread with his strong teeth and washed it down with a draught of ale which he drank in one long swallow. "I took over when Par-Salian retired."

"Head of the Order?" Sturm looked at the big man in awe. "But—what kind of wizard are you? What do you do?"

"I'll wager it's more than pulling the wings off bats," Tanin mumbled through a mouthful of meat.

Palin appeared shocked, and frowned at his older brother. But Dunbar only laughed again. "You're right there!" he said with an oath. "I am a Sea Wizard. My father was a ship's captain and his father before him. I had no use for captaining vessels. My skills lay in magic, but my heart was with the sea and there I returned. Now I sail the waves and use my art to summon the wind or quell the storm. I can leave the enemy becalmed so that we can outrun him, or I can cast bursting flame onto his decks if we attack. And, when necessary"—Dunbar grinned—"I can take my turn at the bilge pump or turn the capstan with the best of them. Keeps me fit." He pounded himself on his broad chest. "I understand you two"—he looked at Sturm and Tanin—"have returned from fighting the minotaurs who have been raiding the coast up north. I, too, have been involved in trying to stop those pirates. Tell me, did you—"

The three were soon deeply involved in discussion. Even Tanin warmed to the subject, and was soon describing in vivid detail the ambush that had stopped the minotaurs from leveling the city of Kalaman. Dunbar listened attentively, asking intelligent questions, making comments, and appearing to enjoy himself very much.

But though the wizard's shrewd gaze was concentrated on the warrior brothers, his attention was in truth on the younger.

Seeing the three deep in conversation and himself apparently forgotten, Palin thankfully gave up all pretence of eating and went back to staring into the fire, never noticing Dunbar watching him.

The young man's face was pale and thoughtful, the slender hands twisted together in his lap. So lost in his thoughts was he that his lips moved and, though he did not speak aloud, one other person in the room heard the words.

"Why have they brought me here? Can they read the secrets of my heart? Will they tell my father?"

And, finally, "How can I hurt him, who has suffered so much already?"

Nodding to himself as if he had found the answer to some unasked question, Dunbar sighed and turned his complete attention back to fighting minotaurs.

## CHAPTER THREE

"You're wrong," said Caramon calmly. "My brother is dead."

Raising his eyebrows, Justarius glanced at Dalamar, who just shrugged. Of all the reactions they had been prepared for, this calm refutal by the warrior-turned-innkeeper had not been one of them, apparently. His expression grave, seeming uncertain what to say, Justarius looked back at Caramon.

"You talk as though you have proof."

"I have," said Caramon.

"May I ask what?" Dalamar inquired sarcastically. "The Portal to the Abyss closed, after all—closed *with your brother's help*—leaving him trapped on the other side." The dark elf's voice dropped. "Her Dark Majesty would not kill him. Raistlin prevented her entry into this world. Her rage would know no bounds. She would take delight in tormenting him eternally. *Death* would have been Raistlin's salvation—"

"And so it was," said Caramon softly.

"Sentimental drivel—" Dalamar began impatiently, but Justarius once again laid his hand upon the dark elf's arm, and the black-robed mage lapsed into seething silence.

"I hear certainty in your voice, Caramon," Justarius said earnestly. "You have knowledge, obviously, that we do not. Share this with us. I know this is painful for you, but we face a decision of grave importance and this may influence our actions."

Caramon hesitated, frowning. "Does this have something to do with my son?"

"Yes," Justarius replied.

Caramon's face darkened. His gaze went to his sword, his eyes narrowed thoughtfully, his hand absently fingering the hilt. "Then I will tell you," he said, speaking reluctantly, yet in a firm, low voice, "what I have never told anyone—not my wife, not Tanis, not anyone." He was silent a moment more, collecting his thoughts. Then, swallowing and brushing his hand across his eyes, keeping his gaze on the sword, he began.

"I was numb after . . . after what happened in the Tower in Palanthas. After Raistlin . . . died. I couldn't think. I didn't want to think. It was easier to go through the day like a sleepwalker. I moved, I talked, but I didn't feel. It was easy." He shrugged. "There was a lot to do to keep me occupied. The city was in ruins. Dalamar"—he glanced briefly at the dark elf—"was nearly dead, Revered Daughter Crysania hurt badly. Then there was Tas—stealing that floating citadel." Caramon smiled, remembering the antics of the merry kender. But the smile soon faded. Shaking his head, he continued.

"I knew that someday I'd have to think about Raistlin. I'd have to sort it out in my mind." Raising his head, Caramon looked at Justarius directly. "I had to make myself understand what Raistlin was, what he had done. I came to face the fact that he was evil, truly evil. That he had jeopardized the entire world in his lust for power, that innocent people had suffered and died because of him."

"And for this, of course, he was granted salvation!" Dalamar sneered.

"Wait!" Caramon raised his hand, flushing. "I came to realize something else. I loved Raistlin. He was my brother, my twin. We were close, no one knows how close." The big man could not go on, but stared down at his sword, frowning, until, drawing a shaking breath, he lifted his head again, proudly. "Raistlin did some good in his life. Without him, we couldn't have defeated the dragonarmies. He cared for those who . . . who were wretched, sick . . . like himself. But even that, I know, wouldn't have saved him at the end." Caramon's lips pressed together firmly as he blinked back his tears. "When I met him in the Abyss, he was near to victory, as you well know. He had only to reenter the Portal, draw the Dark Queen through it, and then he would be able to defeat her and take her place. He would achieve his dream of becoming a god. But in so doing, he would destroy the world. My journey into the future showed that to me—and I showed the future to him. Raistlin would become a god—but he would rule over a dead world. He knew then that he couldn't return. He had doomed himself. He knew the risks he faced, however, when he entered the Abyss."

"Yes," said Justarius quietly. "And, in his ambition, he chose freely to take those risks. What is it you are trying to say?"

"Just this," Caramon returned. "Raistlin made a mistake—a terrible, tragic mistake. And he did what few of us can do—he had courage enough to admit it and try to do what he could to rectify it, even though it meant sacrificing himself."

"You have grown in wisdom over the years, Caramon Majere. What you say is convincing." Justarius regarded Caramon with new respect, even as the archmage shook his head sadly. "Still, this is a question for philosophers to argue. It is not proof. Forgive me for pressing you, Caramon, but—"

"I spent a month at Tanis's, before I went home," Caramon continued as if he hadn't heard the interruption. "It was in his quiet, peaceful home that I thought about all this. It was there that I first had to come to grips with the fact that my brother—my companion since birth, the person that I loved better than anyone else on this world—was gone. Lost. For all I knew, trapped in horrible torment. I . . . I thought, more than once, about taking the edge off my pain with dwarf spirits again. But I knew that was only a temporary situation." Caramon closed his eyes, shuddering.

"One day, when I didn't think I could live anymore without going mad, I went into my room and locked the door. Taking out my sword, I looked at it, thinking how easy it would be to . . . to escape. I lay down on my bed, fully intending to kill myself. Instead, I fell into an exhausted sleep. I don't know how long I slept, but when I woke up, it was night. Everything was quiet, Solinari's silver light shone in the window, and I was filled with a sense of inexpressible peace. I wondered why . . . and then I saw him."

"Saw who?" Justarius asked, exchanging quick glances with Dalamar. "Raistlin?"

"Yes."

The faces of the two wizards grew grim.

"I saw him," said Caramon gently, "lying beside me, asleep, just like when . . . when we were young. He had terrible dreams sometimes. He'd wake, weeping, from them. I'd comfort him and . . . and make him laugh. Then he'd sigh, lay his head on my arm, and fall asleep. That's how I saw him—"

"A dream!" Dalamar scoffed.

"No." Caramon shook his head resolutely. "It was too real. I saw his face as I see yours. I saw his face as I had seen it last, in the Abyss. Only now the terrible lines of pain, the twisted marks of greed and evil were gone, leaving it smooth and . . . at rest—like Crysania said. It was the face of my brother, my twin . . . not the stranger he'd become." Caramon wiped his eyes again, running his hand down over his mouth. "The next day, I was able to go home," he said huskily, "knowing that everything was all right. . . . For the first time in my life, I believed in Paladine. I knew that he understood Raistlin and judged him mercifully, accepting his sacrifice."

"He has you there, Justarius," boomed a voice from out of the shadows. "What do you say to faith like that?"

Looking around quickly, Caramon saw four figures materialize out of the shadows of the vast chamber. Three he recognized and, even in this grim place with its storehouse of memories, his eyes blurred again, only these were tears of pride as he looked upon his sons. The older two, armor clanking and swords rattling, appeared somewhat subdued, he noticed. Not unusual, he thought grimly, considering all they had heard about the Tower both in legend and family history. Then, too, they felt about magic the way he himself felt—both disliked and distrusted it. The two stood protectively, as usual, one on either side of Caramon's third son, their younger brother.

It was this youngest son that Caramon looked at anxiously as they entered. Dressed in his white robes, Palin approached the Head of the Conclave with his head bowed, his eyes on the floor as was proper for one of his low rank and station. Having just turned twenty, he wasn't even an apprentice yet and probably wouldn't be until he was twenty-five at least. That is the age when magic-users in Krynn may choose to take the Test—the grueling examination of their skills and talents in the Art which all must pass before they can acquire more advanced and dangerous knowledge. Because magicians wield such great power, the Test is designed to weed out those who are unskilled or who do not take their art seriously. It does this very effectively—failure means death. There is no turning back. Once a young man or woman of any race—

elven, human, ogre—decides to enter the Tower of High Sorcery with the intent of taking the Test—he or she commits body and soul to the magic.

Palin seemed unusually troubled and serious, just as he had on their journey to the Tower—almost as if he was about to take the Test himself. But that's ridiculous, Caramon reminded himself. The boy is too young. Granted, Raistlin took the Test at this age, but that was because the Conclave needed him. Raistlin was strong in his magic, excelling in the art, and—even so—the Test had nearly killed him. Caramon could still see his twin lying on the blood-stained floor of the Tower. . . . He clenched his fist. No! Palin is intelligent, he is skilled, but he's not ready. He's too young.

"Besides," Caramon muttered beneath his breath, "give him a few more years and he may decide to drop this fool notion. . . ."

As if aware of his father's worried scrutiny, Palin raised his head slightly and gave him a reassuring smile. Caramon smiled back, feeling better. Maybe this weird place had opened his son's eyes.

As the four approached the semicircle of chairs where Justarius and Dalamar sat, Caramon kept a sharp eye on them. Seeing that his boys were well and acting as they were supposed to act (his oldest two tended to be a bit boisterous on occasion), the big man finally relaxed and studied the fourth figure, the one who had spoken to Justarius about faith.

He was an unusual sight. Caramon couldn't remember having seen anything stranger and he'd traveled most of the continent of Ansalon. He was from Northern Ergoth, that much Caramon could tell by the black skin—the mark of that sea-faring race. He was dressed like a sailor, too, except for the pouches on his belt and the white sash around his waist. His voice was the voice of one accustomed to shouting commands over the crashing of waves and the roaring of the wind. So strong was this impression that Caramon glanced around somewhat uncertainly. He wouldn't have been the least surprised to see a ship under full sail materialize behind him.

"Caramon Majere, I take it," the man said, coming over to Caramon, who rose awkwardly to his feet. Gripping Caramon's hand with a firmness that made the warrior open his eyes wide, the man grinned and introduced himself. "Dunbar Mastersmate of Northern Ergoth, Head of the Order of White Robes."

Caramon gaped. "A mage?" he said wonderingly, shaking hands.

Dunbar laughed. "Exactly your sons' reaction. Yes, I've been visiting with your boys instead of doing my duty here, I'm afraid. Fine lads. The oldest two have been with the Knights, I understand, fighting minotaurs near Kalaman. We came close to meeting there, that's what kept me so long." He glanced in apology at Justarius. "My ship was in Palanthas for repairs to damage taken fighting those same pirates. I am a Sea Wizard," Dunbar added by way of explanation, noticing Caramon's slightly puzzled look. "By the gods, but your boys take after you!" He laughed, and, reaching out, shook Caramon's hand again.

Caramon grinned back. Everything would be all right, now that these wizards understood about Raistlin. He could take his boys and go home.

Caramon suddenly became aware that Dunbar was regarding him intently, almost as if he could see the thoughts in his mind. The wizard's face grew serious. Shaking his head slightly, Dunbar turned and walked across the chamber with rapid, rolling strides, as though on the deck of his ship, to take his seat to the right of Justarius.

"Well," said Caramon, fumbling with the hilt of his

sword, his confidence shaken by the look on the wizard's face. All three were staring at him now, their expressions solemn. Caramon's face hardened in resolve. "I guess that's that," he said coldly. "You've heard what I've had to say about . . . about Raistlin. . . ."

"Yes," said Dunbar. "We *all* heard, some of us—I believe—for the first time." The Sea Wizard glanced meaningfully at Palin, who was staring at the floor.

Clearing his throat nervously, Caramon continued. "I guess we'll be on our way."

The wizards exchanged looks. Justarius appeared uncomfortable, Dalamar stern, Dunbar sad. But none of them said anything. Bowing, Caramon turned to leave and was just motioning to his sons when Dalamar, with an irritated gesture, rose to his feet.

"You cannot go, Caramon," the dark elf said. "There is still much to discuss."

"Then say what you have to say!" Caramon stated angrily, turning back around to face the wizards.

"I will say it, since these two"—he cast a scathing glance at his fellow wizards—"are squeamish about challenging such devoted faith as you have proclaimed. Perhaps they have forgotten the grave danger we faced twenty-five years ago. I haven't." His hand strayed to the torn robes. "I never can. My fears cannot be dispelled by a 'vision,' no matter how touching." His lip curled derisively. "Sit down, Caramon. Sit down and hear the truth these two fear to speak."

"I do not fear to speak it, Dalamar." Justarius spoke in rebuking tones. "I was thinking about the story Caramon related, its bearing upon the matter—"

The dark elf snorted, but—at a piercing look from his superior—he sat back down, wrapping his black robes around him. Caramon remained standing, however, frowning and glancing from one wizard to the other. Behind him, he heard the jingle of armor as his

two older boys shifted uncomfortably. This place made them nervous, just as it did him. He wanted to turn on his heel and walk out, never returning to the Tower that had been the scene of so much pain and heartbreak.

By the gods, he'd do it! Let them try to stop him! Caramon clasped the hilt of his sword and took a step backward, glancing around at his sons. The two older boys moved to leave. Only Palin remained standing still, a grave, thoughtful expression on his face that Caramon could not read. It reminded him of someone though. Caramon could almost hear Raistlin's whispering voice, *"Go if you want to, my dear brother. Lose yourself in the magical forest of Wayreth as you most surely will without me. I intend to remain . . ."*

No. He would not hear his son say those words. Flushing, his heart constricting painfully, Caramon seated himself heavily in the chair. "Say what you have to say," he repeated.

"Almost thirty years ago, Raistlin Majere came here to take his Test," Justarius began. "Once inside the Tower, taking his Test, he was contacted by—"

"We know that," Caramon growled.

"Some of us do," Justarius replied. "Some of us do not." His gaze went to Palin. "Or at least, they do not know the entire story. The Test was difficult for Raistlin—it is difficult for all of us who take it, isn't it?"

Dalamar did not speak, but his pale face went a shade paler, the slanted eyes were clouded. All traces of laughter had vanished from Dunbar's face. His gaze went to Palin and he almost imperceptibly shook his head.

"Yes," Justarius continued softly, absently rubbing his leg with his hand as though it pained him. "The test is difficult. But it is not impossible. Par-Salian and the Heads of the Orders would not have granted Raistlin permission to take it—as young as he was—if they had not deemed it likely that he would succeed. And he would have! Yes, Caramon! There is not a doubt in my mind or in the minds of any who were present that day and witnessed it. Your twin had the strength and the skill to succeed on his own. But he chose the easy way, the sure way—he accepted the help of an evil wizard, the greatest of our order who ever lived— Fistandantilus."

"Fistandantilus," Justarius repeated, his eyes on Palin. "His magic having gone awry, he died at Skullcap Mountain. But he was powerful enough to defeat death itself. His spirit survived, on another plane, waiting to find a body it could inhabit. And he found that body. He found Raistlin."

Caramon sat silently, his eyes fixed on Justarius, his face red, his jaw muscles stiff. He felt a hand on his shoulder and, glancing up, saw Palin, who had come to stand behind him. Leaning down, Palin whispered, "We can go, father. I'm sorry. I was wrong to make you come. We don't have to listen . . ."

Justarius sighed. "Yes, young mage, you do have to listen, I am afraid. You must hear the truth!"

Palin started, flushing at hearing his words repeated. Reaching up, Caramon gripped his son's hand reassuringly. "We know the truth," he growled. "That evil wizard took my brother's soul! And you mages let him!"

"No, Caramon!" Justarius's fist clenched, his gray brows drew together. "Raistlin made a deliberate choice to turn his back upon the light and embrace the darkness. Fistandantilus gave him the power to pass the Test and, in exchange, Raistlin *gave* Fistandantilus part of his life force in order to help the liche's spirit survive. *That* is what shattered his body—not the Test. Raistlin said it himself, Caramon! 'This is the sacrifice I made for my magic!' How many times did you hear him say those words!"

"Enough!" Scowling, Caramon stood up. "It was Par-Salian's fault. No matter what evil my twin did after that, you mages started him down the path he eventually walked." Motioning to his sons, Caramon turned upon his heel and walked rapidly from the chamber, heading for what he hoped (in this strange place) was the way out.

"No!" Justarius rose unsteadily to his feet, unable to put his full weight upon his crippled left leg. But his voice was powerful, thundering through the chamber. "Listen and understand, Caramon Majere! You must, or you will regret it bitterly!"

Caramon stopped. Slowly, he turned around, but only half-way. "Is this a threat?" he asked, glaring at Justarius over his shoulder.

"No threat, at least not one we make," Justarius said. "Think, Caramon! Don't you see the danger? It happened once, it can happen again!"

"I don't understand," Caramon said stubbornly, his hand on his sword, still considering.

Like a snake uncoiling to strike, Dalamar leaned forward in his chair. "Yes, you do!" His voice was soft and lethal. "You understand. Don't ask for us to tell you details, for we cannot. But know this—by certain signs we have seen and certain contacts we have made in realms beyond this one, we have reason to believe that Raistlin lives—much as did Fistandantilus. He seeks a way back into this world. He needs a body to inhabit. And you, his beloved twin, have thoughtfully provided him with one—young, strong, and already trained in magic."

Dalamar's words sank into Caramon's flesh like poisoned fangs. "Your son . . ."

---

## CHAPTER FOUR

Justarius resumed his seat, easing himself into the great stone chair carefully. Smoothing the folds of his red robes about him with hands that looked remarkably young for his age, he spoke to Caramon, though his eyes were on the white-robed young man standing at his father's side. "Thus you see, Caramon Majere, that we cannot possibly let your son—Raistlin's nephew—continue to study magic and take the Test without first making certain that his uncle cannot use this young man to gain entry back into the world."

"Especially," added Dunbar gravely, "since the young man's loyalties to one particular Order have yet to be established."

"What do you mean?" Caramon frowned. "Take the Test? He's long way from taking the Test. And as for his loyalties, he chose to wear the White Robes—"

"You and Mother chose that I wear the White Robes," Palin said evenly, his eyes avoiding his father. When only hurt silence answered him, Palin made an irritated gesture. "Oh, come now, Father. You know as well as I do that you wouldn't have considered letting me study magic under any other conditions. I knew better than to even ask!"

"But the young man must declare the allegiance that is in his heart. Only then can he use the true power of his magic. And he must do this during his Test," Dunbar said gently.

"Test! What is this talk of the Test! I tell you he hasn't even made up his mind whether or not to take the damn thing. And if I have anything to say about it—" Caramon stopped speaking abruptly, his gaze going to his son's face. Palin stared at the stone floor, his cheeks flushed, his lips pressed tightly together.

"Well, never mind that," Caramon muttered, drawing a deep breath. Behind him, he could hear his other two sons shuffling nervously, the rattle of Tanin's sword, Sturm's soft cough. He was acutely aware, too, of the wizards watching him, especially of Dalamar's cynical smile. If only he and Palin could be alone! Caramon sighed. It was something they should have talked about before this, he supposed. But he kept hoping. . . .

Turning his back on the wizards, he faced his youngest son. "What . . . what other loyalty would you choose, Palin?" he asked belatedly, trying to make amends. "You're a good person, son! You enjoy helping people, serving others! White seems obvious . . ."

"I don't know whether I enjoy serving others or not," Palin cried impatiently, losing control. "You thrust me into this role, and look where it has gotten me! You admit yourself that I am not as strong or skilled in magic as my uncle was at my age. That was because he devoted his life to study! He let nothing interfere with it. It seems to me a man must put the magic first, the world second . . ."

Closing his eyes in pain, Caramon listened to his son's words, but he heard them spoken by another voice—a soft, whispering voice, a shattered voice—*a man must put the magic first, the world second. By doing anything else, he limits himself and his potential—*

He felt a hand grasp his arm. "Father, I'm sorry," Palin said softly. "I would have discussed it with you, but I knew how much it would hurt you. And then there's Mother." The young man sighed. "You know mother . . ."

"Yes," said Caramon in a choked voice, reaching out

and grasping his son in his big arms, "I know your mother." Clearing his throat, he tried to smile. "She might have thrown something at you—she did me once—most of my armor as I recall. But her aim is terrible, especially when it's someone she loves. . . ."

Caramon couldn't go, but stood holding his son. Looking over his shoulder at the wizards, he asked harshly, "Is this necessary, right now? Let us go home and talk about it. Why can't we wait—"

"Because this night there is a rare occurrence," Justarius answered. "The silver moon, the black, and the red are all three in the sky at the same time. The power of magic is stronger this night than it has been in a century. If Raistlin has the ability to call upon the magic and escape the Abyss—it could be on a night like this."

Caramon bowed his head, his hand stroking his son's auburn hair. Then, his arm around Palin's shoulder, he turned to face the wizards, his face grim.

"Very well," he said huskily, "what do you want us to do?"

"You must return with me to the Tower in Palanthas," said Dalamar. "And there, we will attempt to enter the Portal—"

"The Tower? Let us ride as far as the Shoikan Grove with you, Father," Tanin pleaded.

"Yes!" added Sturm eagerly. "You'll need us, you know you will. The road to Palanthas is open, the Knights see to that, but we've had reports from Porthios of draconian parties, lying in ambush—"

"I am sorry to disappoint you, warriors," said Dalamar, a slight smile upon his lips, "but we will not be using the roads between here and Palanthas. Conventional roads, that is," he amended.

Both the young men looked confused. Glancing warily at the dark elf, Tanin frowned as though he suspected a trick.

Palin patted Tanin's arm. "He means magic, my brother. Before you and Sturm reach the front entryway, Father and I will be standing in Dalamar's study in the Tower of High Sorcery in Palanthas—the Tower my uncle claimed as his own," he added softly. Palin had not meant anyone to hear his last words, but— glancing around—he caught Dalamar's intense, knowing gaze.

"Yes, that's where we'll be," muttered Caramon, his face darkening at the thought. "And you two will be on your way home," he added, eyeing his older sons sternly. "You have to tell your mother—"

"I'd rather face ogres," said Tanin gloomily.

"Me, too," Caramon said with a grin that ended in a sigh. Leaning down suddenly to make certain his pack was cinched tightly, he kept his face carefully in the shadows. "Just make certain she's not standing where she can get hold of the crockery," he said, keeping his voice carefully light.

"She knows me. She's been expecting this. In fact, I think she knew when we left," Palin said, remembering his mother's tender hug and cheery smile as she stood at the door to the Inn, waving at them with an old towel. Glancing behind him as they had been riding out of town, Palin recalled seeing that towel cover his mother's face, her friend Dezra's arms going around her comfortingly.

"Besides," said Caramon, standing up to glare at his older two sons, his tone now severe, "you both promised Porthios you'd go to Qualinesti and help the elves handle those draconian raiding parties. You know what Porthios is like. It took him ten years to even speak to us. Now he's showing signs of being friendly. I won't have sons of mine going back on their word, especially to that stiff-necked elf. No offense," he said, glancing at Dalamar.

"None taken," said the dark elf. "I know Porthios. And now—"

"We're ready," interrupted Palin, an eager look on his face as he turned to Dalamar. "I've read about this spell you're going to cast, of course, but I've never seen it done. What components do you use? And do you inflect the first syllable of the first word, or the second? My Master says—"

Dalamar coughed gently. "You are giving away our secrets, young one," he said in smooth tones. "Come, speak your questions to me in private." Placing his delicate hand upon Palin's arm, the dark elf drew the young man away from his father and brothers.

"Secrets?" said Palin, mystified. "What do you mean? It doesn't matter if they hear—"

"That was an excuse," Dalamar said coldly. Standing in front of the young man, he looked at Palin intently, his eyes dark and serious. "Palin, don't do this. Return home with your father and brothers."

"What do you mean?" Palin said, staring at Dalamar in confusion. "I can't do that. You heard Justarius. They won't let me take my Test or even keep on studying until we know for certain that Raistlin is . . . is . . ."

"Don't take the Test," Dalamar said swiftly. "Give up your studies. Go home. Be content with what you are."

"No!" Palin said angrily. "What do you take me for? Do you think I'd be happy entertaining at country fairs, pulling rabbits out of hats and golden coins out of fat men's ears? I want more than that!"

"The price of such ambition is great, as your uncle discovered."

"And so are the rewards!" Palin returned. "I have made up my mind . . ."

"Young one"—Dalamar leaned close to the young man, placing his cold hand upon Palin's arm. His voice dropped to a whisper so soft that Palin wasn't certain he heard its words spoken or in his mind— "why do you think they are sending you—truly?" His gaze went to Justarius and Dunbar, who were standing apart, conferring together. "To somehow enter the Portal and find your uncle—or what's left of him? No"—Dalamar shook his head—"that is impossible. The room is locked, one of the Guardians stands constant watch with instructions to let no one in, to kill any who tries. *They* know that, just as they *know* Raistlin lives! They are sending you to the Tower—*his* Tower—for one reason. Do you know the old legend about using a young goat to net a dragon?"

Staring at Dalamar in disbelief, Palin's face suddenly drained of all color.

"I see you understand," Dalamar said coolly, folding his hands in the sleeves of his black robes. "The hunter tethers the young goat in front of the dragon's lair. While the dragon devours the goat, the hunters sneak up on him with their nets and their spears. They catch the dragon. Unfortunately, it is a bit late for the goat. . . . Do you still insist on going?"

Palin had a sudden vision of his uncle as he had heard of him in the legends—facing the evil Fistandantilus, feeling the touch of the bloodstone upon his chest as it sought to draw out his soul, suck out his life. The young man shivered, his body drenched in chill sweat. "I am strong," he said, his voice cracking. "I can fight as *he* fought—"

"Fight him? The greatest wizard who ever lived? The archmage who challenged the Queen of Darkness herself and nearly won?" Dalamar laughed mirthlessly. "Bah! You are doomed, young man. You haven't a prayer. And you know what I will be forced to do if Raistlin succeeds!" Dalamar's hooded head darted so near Palin that the young man could feel the touch of his breath upon his cheek. "I must destroy him—I *will* destroy him. I don't care whose body he inhabits. That's why they're giving you to me. *They* don't have the stomach for it."

Unnerved, Palin took a step back from the dark elf. Then he caught himself, and stood still.

"I . . . understand," he said, his voice growing firmer as he continued. "I told you that once. Besides, I don't believe my uncle would harm me in . . . the way you say."

"You don't?" Dalamar appeared amused. His hand moved to his chest. "Would you like to see what harm your uncle is capable of doing?"

"No!" Palin averted his eyes, then, flushing, he added lamely, "I know about it. I've heard the story. You betrayed him—"

"And this was my punishment." The dark elf shrugged. "Very well. If you are determined—"

"I am."

"—then I suggest you bid farewell to your brothers—a final farewell, if you take my meaning. For I deem it unlikely that you will meet again in this world."

The dark elf was matter-of-fact. His eyes held no pity, no remorse. Palin's hands twitched, his nails dug into his flesh, but he managed to nod firmly.

"You must be careful what you say." Dalamar glanced meaningfully at Caramon, who was walking over to Justarius. "Your brothers mustn't suspect. *He* mustn't suspect. If he knew, he would prevent your going. Wait"—Dalamar caught hold of the young man—"pull yourself together."

Swallowing, trying to moisten a throat that was parched and aching, Palin pinched his cheeks to bring the color back and wiped the sweat from his brow with the sleeve of his robe. Then, biting his lips to keep them steady, he turned from Dalamar and walked over to his brothers.

His white robes rustled around his ankles as he approached them. "Well, brothers," he began, forcing himself to smile as his brothers turned to face him, "I'm always standing on the porch of the Inn, waving good-bye to you two, going off to fight something or other. Looks like it's my turn now."

Palin saw Tanin and Sturm exchange swift, alarmed glances and he choked. The three were close, they knew each other inside out. How can I fool them? he thought bitterly. Seeing their faces, he knew he hadn't.

"My brothers," Palin said softly, reaching out his hands. Clasping hold of both of them, he drew them near. "Don't say anything," he whispered. "Just let me go! Father wouldn't understand. It's going to be hard enough for him as it is."

"I'm not sure *I* understand," Tanin began severely.

"Oh, shut up!" Sturm muttered. "So we don't understand. Does it matter? Did our little brother blubber when you went off to your first battle?" Putting his big arms around Palin, he hugged him tightly. "Good-bye, kid," he said. "Take care of yourself and . . . and . . . don't be gone . . . long. . . ." Shaking his head, Sturm turned and walked hurriedly away, wiping his eye and muttering something about "those damn spell components make me sneeze!"

But Tanin, the oldest, remained standing beside his brother, staring at him sternly. Palin looked up at him pleadingly, but Tanin's face grew grim. "No, little brother," he said. "You're going to listen."

Dalamar, watching the two closely, saw the young warrior put his hand on Palin's shoulder. He could guess what was being said. The dark elf saw Palin drawn away, shaking his head stubbornly, the young

MARGARET WEIS AND TRACY HICKMAN

man's features hardening into an impassive mask that Dalamar knew well. The wizard's hand went to the wounds in his chest. How like Raistlin the young man was! Like, yet different, as Caramon said. Different as the white moon and the black. . . . The dark elf's thoughts were interrupted when he noticed that Caramon had observed the conversation between his two sons, and was taking a step toward them. Quickly, Dalamar interceded. Walking over to Caramon, he placed his slender hand on the big man's arm.

"You have not told your children the truth about their uncle," Dalamar said as Caramon glanced at him.

"I've told them," Caramon retorted, his face flushing, "as much as I thought they should know. I tried to make them see both sides of him. . . ."

"You have done them a disservice, particularly one of them," Dalamar replied coldly, his glance going to Palin.

"What could I do?" Caramon asked angrily. "When the legends started about him—sacrificing himself for the sake of the world, daring to go into the Abyss to rescue Lady Crysania from the clutches of the Dark Queen—what could I say? I told them how it was, I told them the true story. I told them that he lied to Crysania. That he seduced her in spirit, if not in body, and led her into the Abyss. And I told them that, at the end, when she was of no more use to him, he abandoned her to let her die alone. I told them. My friend Tanis has told them. But they believe what they want to believe. . . . We all do, I guess," Caramon added with an accusing glance at Dalamar. "I notice you mages don't go out of your way to refute those stories!"

"They've done us good," Dalamar said, shrugging his slender shoulders. "Because of the legends about Raistlin and his 'sacrifice,' magic is no longer feared, we wizards no longer reviled. Our schools are flour-

ishing, our services are in demand. The city of Kala-
man has actually invited us to build a new Tower of
High Sorcery there." The dark elf smiled bitterly.
"Ironic, isn't it?"

"What?"

"By his failure, your brother succeeded in what he
set out to accomplish," Dalamar remarked, his smile
twisting. "In a way, he *has* become a god. . . ."

"Palin, I insist on knowing what's going on." Tanin
laid his hand on Palin's shoulder.

"You heard them, Tanin," Palin hedged, nodding toward Dalamar, who was talking with his father.
"We're going to travel to the Tower of High Sorcery in
Palanthas, where the Portal is located, and . . . and
look in. . . . That's all."

"And I'm a gully dwarf!" growled Tanin.

"Sometimes you think like one," Palin snapped, losing his patience and thrusting his brother's arm away.

Tanin's face flushed a dull red. Unlike the easygoing Sturm, Tanin had inherited his mother's temper
along with her curls. He also took his role of Elder
Brother seriously, too seriously sometimes to Palin's
mind. But it's only because he loves me, the young
man reminded himself.

Drawing a deep breath, he sighed and, reaching
out, clasped his brother by the shoulders. "Tanin, you
listen to me for a change. Sturm's right. I didn't 'blubber' when you went off to battle that first time. At
least not when you could see me. But I cried all night,
alone, in the darkness. Don't you think I know that
each time you leave may be the last time we ever see
each other? How many times have you been
wounded? That last fight, that minotaur arrow missed
your heart by only two fingersbreadth."

Tanin, his face dark, stared down at his feet. "That's

different," he muttered.

"As Granpa Tas would say, 'A chicken with its neck wrung is different from a chicken with its head cut off, but does it matter to the chicken?' " Palin smiled.

Swallowing his tears, Tanin shrugged and tried to grin. "I guess you're right." He put his hands on Palin's shoulders, looked intently into his pale face. "Come home, kid! Give this up!" he whispered fiercely. "It isn't worth it! If anything happened to you, think what it would do to Mother . . . and Father. . . ."

"I know," Palin said, his own eyes filling despite all his best efforts to prevent it. "I have thought of that! I must do this, Tanin. Try to understand. Tell Mother I . . . I love her very much. And the little girls. Tell them I'll . . . I'll bring them a present, like you and Sturm always do . . ."

"What? A dead lizard?" Tanin growled. "Some moldy old bat's wing?"

Wiping his eyes, Palin smiled. "Yeah, tell 'em that. You better go. Dad's watching us."

"Watch yourself, little brother. And him." Tanin glanced at his father. "This will be pretty tough on him."

"I know." Palin sighed. "Believe me, I know."

Tanin hesitated. Palin saw one more lecture, one more attempt to dissuade him in his brother's eyes.

"Please, Tanin," he said softly. "No more."

Blinking rapidly and rubbing his nose, Tanin nodded. Cuffing his little brother on the cheek and ruffling the auburn hair, Tanin walked across the shadowy chamber to stand near the entryway with Sturm.

Palin watched him walk away, then, turning, he went the opposite direction, toward the front of the great hall, to bid his parting respects to the two wizards.

"So Dalamar has spoken to you," Justarius said as

the young man came to stand before him.

"Yes," said Palin grimly. "*He* has told me the truth."

"Has he?" Dunbar asked suddenly. "Remember this, young one. Dalamar wears the Black Robes. He is ambitious. Whatever he does, he does because he believes it will ultimately benefit him."

"Can you two deny what he told me is true? That you are using me as bait to trap my uncle's spirit if it still lives?"

Justarius glanced at Dunbar, who shook his head.

"Sometimes you have to look for the truth here, Palin," Dunbar said in answer, reaching out his hand to touch Palin gently on the chest, "in your heart."

His lip curled in derision, but Palin knew what respect he must show two such high-ranking wizards. So he simply bowed. "Dalamar and my father are waiting for me. I bid you both farewell. The gods willing, I will return in a year or two for my Test, and I hope I will have the honor of seeing you both again."

Justarius did not miss the sarcasm, nor the bitter, angry expression on the young man's face. It made him recall another bitter, angry young man, who had come to this Tower over thirty years ago. . . .

"May Gilean go with you, Palin," the archmage said softly, folding his hands in the sleeves of his robes.

"May Paladine, the god you are named for, guide you, Palin," Dunbar said. "And consider this," he added, a smile creasing his black face, "in case you never see the old Sea Wizard again. You may learn that—by serving the world—you serve yourself best of all."

Palin did not reply. Bowing again, he turned and left them. The chamber seemed to grow darker as he walked back across it. He might have been alone, he could see no one for a moment, not his brothers, not Dalamar and his father. . . . But as the darkness deepened, the white of his robes gleamed more brightly, like the first star in the evening sky.

For an instant, fear assailed Palin. Had they all left him? Was he alone in this vast darkness? Then he saw a glint of metal near him—his father's armor, and he breathed a sigh of relief. His steps hurried and, as he came to stand beside his father, the chamber seemed to lighten. He could see the dark elf, standing next to Caramon, pale face all that was visible from the shadows of his black robes. Palin could see his brothers, could see them lift their hands in farewell. Palin started to raise his, but then Dalamar began chanting, and it seemed a dark cloud covered the light of Palin's robes, of Caramon's armor. The darkness grew thicker, swirling around them until it was so deep that it was a hole of blackness cut into the shadows of the chamber. Then there was nothing. The cold, eerie light returned to the Tower, filling up the gap.

Dalamar, Palin, and Caramon were gone.

The two brothers left behind shouldered their packs and began the long, strange journey back through the magical Forest of Wayreth, thoughts of breaking this news to their red-haired, fiery-tempered, loving mother hanging around their hearts with the weight of dwarven armor.

Behind them, standing beside the great stone chairs, Justarius and Dunbar watched in grim silence. Then, each speaking a word of magic, they, too, were gone, and the Tower of High Sorcery at Wayreth was left to its shadows, only memories walked the halls.

## CHAPTER FIVE

" 'He came in the middle of a still, black night,' " Dalamar said softly. " 'The only moon in the sky was one his eyes alone could see.' " The dark elf glanced at Palin from the depths of the black hood that covered his head. "Thus runs the legend about your uncle's return to this Tower."

Palin said nothing—the words were in his heart. They had been there, secretly, ever since he was old enough to dream. In awe, he looked up at the huge gates that barred the entrance, trying to imagine his uncle standing where he now stood, commanding the gates to open. And when they did— Palin's gaze went farther upward still to the dark Tower itself.

It was daylight in Palanthas, it had been mid-morning when they left the Tower of High Sorcery in Wayreth, hundreds of miles to the south. And it was mid-morning still, their magical journey having taken them no more than the drawing of a breath. The sun was at its zenith, shining right above the Tower. Two of the blood-red minarets atop the Tower held the golden orb between them, like blood-stained fingers greedily grasping a coin. And the sun might well have been nothing more than a coin for all the warmth it shed, for no sunshine ever warmed this place of evil. The huge black stone edifice—torn from the bones of the world by magic spells—stood in the shadow of the spell-bound Shoikan Grove, a stand of massive oak trees that guarded the Tower more effectively than if each tree had been a hundred knights-at-arms. So powerful was its dread enchantment that no one could even come near it. Unless protected by a dark charm, no one could enter and come out alive.

Turning his head, Palin glanced from the folds of his white hood at the Grove's tall trees. They stood unmoving, though he could feel the wind from the sea blowing strong upon his face. It was said that even the terrible hurricanes of the Cataclysm had not caused a leaf to flutter in the Shoikan Grove, though no other tree in the city remained standing. A chill darkness flowed among the trunks of the oaks, reaching out snaking tendrils of icy fog that slithered along the paved courtyard before the gates, writhing about the ankles of those who stood there.

Shivering with cold and a fear he could not control, a fear fed by the trees, Palin looked at his father with new respect. Driven by love for his twin, Caramon had dared enter the Shoikan Grove, and had very nearly paid for his love with his life.

He must be thinking of that, Palin thought, for his father's face was pale and grim. Beads of sweat stood upon his forehead. "Let's get out of here," Caramon said harshly, his eyes carefully avoiding the sight of the cursed trees. "Go inside, or something. . . ."

"Very well," replied Dalamar. Though his face was hidden once again by the shadows of his hood, Palin had the impression the dark elf was smiling. "Although there is no hurry. We must wait until nightfall, when both the silver moon, Solinari, beloved of Paladine, the black moon, Nuitari, favored by the Dark Queen, and Lunitari, the red moon of Gilean, are in the sky together. Raistlin will draw upon the black moon for his power. Others—who might need it— may draw upon Solinari—if they choose. . . ." He did not look at Palin as he spoke, but the young man felt himself flush.

"What do mean—draw upon its power?" Caramon

demanded angrily, grabbing hold of Dalamar. "Palin's not a mage, not yet. You said you would deal with everything—"

"I am aware of my words," Dalamar interrupted. He wrenched his arm free of Caramon's grip with an ease astonishing in the slender elf. "And I will deal with . . . what must be dealt with. But things strange and unexpected may happen this night. It is well to be prepared." Dalamar regarded Caramon coolly. "And do not interfere with me again or you will regret it. Come, Palin. You may need my assistance to enter these gates." Dalamar held out his hand.

Glancing back at his father, Palin saw his eyes fixed on him. "Don't go in there," his anguished gaze pleaded. "If you do, I will lose you . . . ."

Lowering his own eyes in confusion, pretending he hadn't read the message that had been as clear as the very first words his father taught him, Palin turned away and laid his hand hesitantly upon the dark elf's arm. The black robes were soft and velvety to the touch. He could feel the hard muscles and, beneath, the fine, delicate bone structure of the elf, almost fragile to the touch, yet strong and steady and supportive.

An unseen hand opened the gates that had once, long ago, been made of fluted silver and gold but were now black and twisted, guarded by shadowy beings. Drawing Palin with him, Dalamar stepped through them.

Searing pain pierced the young man. Clutching his heart, Palin doubled over with a cry.

Dalamar stopped Caramon's advance with a look. "You cannot aid him," the dark elf said. "Thus the Dark Queen punishes those not loyal to her who tread upon this sacred ground. Hold on to me, Palin. Hold on to me tightly and keep walking. Once we are inside, this will subside."

Gritting his teeth, Palin did as he was told, moving forward with halting footsteps, both hands gripping Dalamar's arm.

It was well the dark elf led him on for, left on his own, Palin would have fled this place of darkness. Through the haze of pain, he heard soft words whisper, "Why enter? Death alone awaits you! Are you anxious to look upon his grinning face? Turn back, foolish one! Turn back. Nothing is worth this. . . ." Palin moaned. How could he have been so blind? Dalamar had been right . . . the price of ambition was too high. . . .

"Courage, Palin . . ." Dalamar's voice blended with the whispering words.

The Tower was crushing him beneath the weight of its dark, magical power, pressing the life from his body. Still Palin kept walking, though he could barely see the stones beneath his feet through a blood-red film blurring his eyes. Was this how *he* felt when *he* first came? Palin asked himself in agony. But no, of course not. Raistlin had worn the Black Robes when he first entered the Tower. *He* came in the fullness of his power, Master of Past and Present. *For him, the gates had opened. . . . All dark and shadowy things bowed in homage.* Thus went the legend. . . .

For him, the gates had opened. . . .

With a sob, Palin collapsed upon the threshold of the Tower.


"Feeling better?" Dalamar asked as Palin raised himself dizzily from the couch on which he lay. "Here, a sip of wine. It is elven. A fine vintage. I have it 'shipped' to me from Silvanesti, unknown to the Silvanesti elves, of course. This was the first wine made following the land's destruction. It has a dark, faintly bitter taste—as of tears. Some of my people, I am told, cannot drink it without weeping." Pouring a glassful, Dalamar held the deep purple hued liquid out to Palin. "I find, in fact, that even when I drink it, a feeling of sadness comes over me."

"Homesick," suggested Caramon, shaking his head as Dalamar offered him a glass. Palin knew by the tone of his father's voice that he was upset and unhappy, frightened for his son. He sat stolidly in his chair, however, trying to appear unconcerned. Palin cast him a grateful glance as he drank the wine, feeling its warming influence banish the strange chill.

Oddly enough, the wine *was* making him think about his home. "Homesick," Caramon had said. Palin expected Dalamar to scoff or sneer at this statement. Dark elves are, after all, "cast from the light" of elven society, banned from entering the ancient homelands. Dalamar's sin had been to take the Black Robes, to seek power in dark magic. Bound hand and foot, his eyes blindfolded, he had been driven in a cart to the borders of his homeland and there thrown out, never more to be admitted. To an elf, whose centuries-long lives are bound up in their beloved woods and gardens, to be dismissed from the ancestral lands is worse than death.

Dalamar appeared so cool and unfeeling about everything, however, that Palin was surprised to see a look of wistful longing and swift sorrow pass over the dark elf's face. It was gone as quickly as a ripple over quiet water, but he had seen it nonetheless. He felt less in awe of the dark elf. So something could touch him, after all.

Sipping the wine, tasting the faint bitterness, Palin's thoughts went to *his* home, the splendid house his father built with his own hands, the inn that was his parent's pride and joy. He thought about the town of Solace, nestled among the leaves of the great vallen-

wood trees, a town he had left only to attend school as
must all young, aspiring magic-users. He thought of
his mother, of the two little sisters who were the bane
of his existence—stealing his pouches, trying to peek
under his robes, hiding his spellbooks. . . . What
would it be like—never seeing them again?

. . . never seeing them again . . .

Palin's hand began to tremble. Carefully, he set the
fragile glass down upon the table near his chair, fearing he might drop it or spill his wine. He looked
around hurriedly to see if either his father Dalamar
had noticed. Neither had, both being engaged in a
quiet discussion near the window overlooking the city
of Palanthas.

"You have never been back to the laboratory since?"
Caramon was asking, his voice low.

Dalamar shook his head. He had removed the hood
of his robes, his long, silky hair brushed his shoulders.
"I went back the week you left," he replied, "to make
certain all was in order. And then I sealed it shut."

"So everything is still there," Caramon murmured.
Palin saw his father's shrewd gaze turn to the dark elf,
who was staring out the window, his face cold and ex-
pressionless. "It must contain objects that would grant
a tremendous power to a wizard, or so I would guess.
What is in there?"

Almost holding his breath, Palin rose from his chair
and crept silently across the beautiful, luxurious car-
pet to hear the dark elf's answer.

"The spellbooks of Fistandantilus, Raistlin's own
spellbooks, his notes on herb lore and, of course, the
Staff of Magius—"

"*His* staff?" Palin said suddenly.

Both men turned to look at the young man, Caramon's face grave, Dalamar appearing faintly amused.

"You told me my uncle's staff was lost!" Palin said to

his father accusingly.

"And so it is, young one," Dalamar answered. "The spell I put upon that chamber is such that even the rats do not come anywhere near it. None may enter on pain of death. If the famed Staff of Magius were at the bottom of the Blood Sea, it could not be more effectively lost to this world than it is now."

"There's one other thing in that laboratory," Caramon said slowly in sudden realization. "The Portal to the Abyss. If we can't get in the laboratory, how are we supposed to look inside the Portal or whatever fool thing you wizards want me to do to prove to you my twin is dead?"

Dalamar was silent, twirling the thin-stemmed wine glass in his hand thoughtfully, his gaze abstracted. Watching him, Caramon's face flushed red in anger. "This was a ruse! You never meant it, any of you! What do mean, bringing us here? What do you want of me?"

"Nothing of you, Caramon," Dalamar answered coolly.

Caramon blenched. "No!" he cried in a choked voice. "Not my son! Damn you, wizards! I won't allow it!" Taking a step forward, he grabbed hold of Dalamar . . . and gasped in pain. Yanking his hand back, Caramon flexed it, rubbing his arm that felt as though he had touched lightning.

"Father, please! Don't interfere!" begged Palin, going to his father's side. The young man then glanced angrily at Dalamar. "There was no need for that!"

"I warned him," Dalamar said, shrugging. "You see, Caramon, my friend, we cannot open the door from the outside." The dark elf's gaze went to Palin. "But there is one here for whom the door may open from the *inside*!"

## CHAPTER SIX

*For me, the gates will open. . . .*

Palin whispered the words to himself as he climbed the dark and winding stairs. Night had stolen in upon Palanthas, sealing the city in darkness, deepening the perpetual darkness that hung about the Tower of High Sorcery. Solinari, the silver moon beloved of Paladine, shone in the sky, but its white rays did not touch the Tower. Those inside gazed upon another moon, a dark moon, a moon only their eyes could see.

The stone stairs were pitch-black. Though Caramon carried a torch, its feeble, wavering flame was overwhelmed by the darkness. Groping his way up the stairs, Palin stumbled more than once. Each time, his heart pulsed painfully, and he pressed himself close against the chill wall, closing his eyes. The core of the Tower was a hollow shaft. The stairs ascended it in a dizzying spiral, protruding from the wall like the bones of some dead animal.

"You are safe, young one," Dalamar said, his hand on Palin's arm. "This was designed to discourage unwelcome intruders. The magic protects us. Don't look down. It will be easier."

"Why did we have to walk?" Palin asked, stopping to catching his breath. Young as he was, the steep climb had taken its toll. His legs ached, his lungs burned. He could only imagine what his father must be feeling. Even the dark elf appeared to be at a loss for breath, though Dalamar's face was cold and impassive as ever. "Couldn't we have used magic?"

"I will not waste my energies," Dalamar replied.

"Not on this night of all nights."

Seeing the slanted eyes observing him coolly, Palin said nothing, but began climbing again, keeping his eyes staring straight ahead and upward.

"There is our destination." Dalamar pointed. Looking up the stairs, Palin saw a small doorway.

*For me, the gates will open. . . .*

Raistlin's words. Palin's fear began to subside, excitement surged through him. His steps quickened. Behind him, he heard Dalamar's light tread and his father's heavier one. He could also hear Caramon's labored breathing, and felt a twinge of remorse.

"Do you want to rest, father?" he asked, stopping.

"No," Caramon grunted. "Let's get this foolishness over with. Then we can go home."

His voice was gruff, but Palin heard a strange note in it, a note he had never heard before. Turning slowly around to face the door, Palin knew it for what it was—fear. His father was afraid. Palin knew then a secret feeling of joy—one his uncle must have known. His father, Hero of the Lance, the strongest man he knew, who could—even now—wrestle the brawny Tanin to the ground and disarm the skilled swordsman, Sturm. His father was frightened, frightened of the magic.

He is afraid, Palin realized, and I am not! Closing his eyes, Palin leaned back against the chill wall of the Tower and, for the first time in his life, gave himself up to the magic. He felt it burn in his blood, caress his skin. The words it whispered were of welcome, of invitation. His body trembled with the ecstasy of the magic and, opening his eyes, Palin saw his exultation reflected in the dark elf's glittering gaze.

"Now you taste the power!" Dalamar whispered. "Go forward, Palin, go forward."

Smiling to himself, cocooned in the warmth of his

euphoria, Palin climbed the stairs rapidly, all fear forgotten. For him, the door would open. He had no doubts. Why or by whose hand, he did not speculate. It did not matter. Finally, he would be inside the ancient laboratory where some of the greatest magic upon Krynn had been performed. He would see the spellbooks of the legendary Fistandantilus, the spellbooks of his uncle. He would see the great and terrible Portal that led from this world into the Abyss. And he would see the famed Staff of Magius. . . .

Palin had long dreamed of his uncle's staff. Of all Raistlin's arcane treasures—this intrigued Palin most. Perhaps because he had seen it portrayed so often in paintings or because it always figured prominently in legend and song. Palin even owned one such painting of Raistlin in his black robes, the Staff of Magius in his hand, battling the Queen of Darkness. If my uncle had lived to teach me, and I had been worthy of him, perhaps he might have given me the staff, Palin thought wistfully every time he looked at the painting of the wooden staff with its golden dragon claw clutching a shining, faceted, crystal ball.

Now I will get to see it, perhaps even hold it! Palin shivered in delicious anticipation at the thought. And what else will we find in the laboratory? he wondered. What will we see when we look into the Portal?

"All will be as my father said," Palin whispered, feeling a momentary pang. "Raistlin is at rest. It must be! Father would be hurt, so terribly hurt otherwise. . . ."

If Palin's heart was whispering other words, the young man ignored them. His uncle was dead. His father had said so. Nothing else was possible, nothing else was to be wished for. . . .

"Stop!" hissed Dalamar, his hand closing about Palin's arm.

Starting, Palin halted. He had been so lost in his

thoughts, he had scarcely noticed where he was. Now he saw that they had come to a large landing, located directly below the laboratory door. Looking up the short flight of stairs that led to it, Palin drew in his breath with a gasp. Two cold, white eyes stared at them out of the darkness—eyes without a body, unless the darkness itself was their flesh and blood and bone. Falling back a step, Palin stumbled into Dalamar.

"Steady, young one," the dark elf commanded, supporting Palin. "It is the Guardian."

Behind them, the torchlight wavered. "I remember them," Caramon said hoarsely. "They can kill you with a touch!"

"Living beings," came the spectre's hollow voice, "I smell your warm blood, I hear your hearts beating. Come forward. You awaken my hunger!"

Shoving Palin to one side, Dalamar stepped in front of him. The white eyes glistened for an instant, then lowered in homage.

"Master of the Tower. I did not sense your presence. It has been long since you have visited this place."

"Your vigil remains undisturbed?" Dalamar asked. "None have tried to enter?"

"Do you see their bones upon the floors? Surely you would, if any dared disobey your command."

"Excellent," Dalamar said. "Now, I give you a new command. Give me the key to the lock. Then stand aside, and let us pass."

The white eyes flared open, a pale, eager light shining from them.

"That cannot be, Master of the Tower."

"Why not?" Dalamar asked coolly. His hands folded in the sleeves of his black robes, he glanced at Caramon as he spoke.

"Your command, Master, was to 'Take this key and keep it for all eternity. Give it to no one,' you said, 'not even myself. And from this moment on, your place is to guard this door. No one is to enter. Let death be swift for those who try.' Thus were your words to me, Master, and—as you see—I obey them."

Dalamar nodded his hooded head. "Do you?" he murmured, taking a step forward. Palin caught his breath, seeing the white eyes glow even more brightly. "What will you do if I come up there?"

"Your magic is powerful, Master," said the spectre, the disembodied eyes drifting nearer Dalamar, "but it can have no effect on me. There was only one who had *that* power—"

"Yes," said Dalamar irritably, hesitating, his foot upon the first stair.

"Do not come closer, Master," the eyes warned, though Palin could see them shining with a lust that brought sudden visions of cold lips touching his cringing flesh, drinking away his life. Shuddering, he sagged back against the wall. The warm feeling was gone, replaced by the chill of this horrible creature, the chill of death and disappointment. He felt nothing inside now, just empty and cold. Perhaps I will give it up, it isn't worth it. Palin's head drooped. Then his father's hand was on his shoulder, his father's voice echoing his thoughts.

"Come, Palin," Caramon said wearily. "This has all been for nothing. Let's go home—"

"Wait!" The gaze of the disembodied eyes shifted from the dark elf to the two figures that huddled behind him. "Who are these? One I recognize—"

"Yes," said Caramon, his voice low, "you've seen me before—"

"*His* brother," murmured the spectre. "But who is this? The young one. Him I do *not* know. . . ."

"C'mon, Palin," Caramon said gruffly, casting a fearful glance at the eyes. "We've got a long journey—"

Caramon's arm encircled Palin's shoulders. The young man felt his father's gentle urging and tried to turn away. But his gaze was fixed on the spectre, who was staring at him strangely.

"Wait!" the spectre commanded again, its hollow voice ringing through the darkness. Even the whispers fell silent at its command. "Palin?" it murmured softly, speaking questioningly, it seemed, to itself . . . or to someone else. . . .

A decision was reached, apparently, because the voice became firm. "Palin. Come forward."

"No!" Caramon grasped his son.

"Let him go!" Dalamar ordered, glancing around with a furious look. "I told you this might happen! It is our chance!" He gazed coldly at Caramon. "Or are you afraid of what you might find?"

"I am not!" Caramon returned in a choked voice. "Raistlin is dead! I have seen him at peace! I don't trust you mages! You're not going to take my son from me!"

Palin could feel his father's body trembling near his, he could see the anguish in his father's eyes. Compassion and pity stirred within the young man. There was a brief longing to stay safe within his father's strong, sheltering arms. But these feelings were burned away by a hot anger that surged up from somewhere inside of him, an anger kindled by the magic.

"Did you give Tanin a sword, then bid him break it?" Palin demanded, breaking free of his father's grip. "Did you give Sturm a shield and tell him to hide behind it? Oh, I know!" Palin snapped, seeing Caramon, his face flushed, about to speak. "*That* is different. *That* is something *you* understand. You've never understood me, have you, Father? How many years was it before I persuaded you to let me go to school, to study with the Master who had taught my uncle?

When you finally relented, I was the oldest beginning student there! For years, I was behind the others, working to catch up. And all the time, I could sense you and mother watching me anxiously. I could hear you talking at night, saying that maybe I'd outgrown this 'fancy.' *Fancy*!" Palin's voice grew agonized. "Can't you see? The magic is my *life*! My *love*!"

"No, Palin, don't say that!" Caramon cried, his voice breaking.

"Why not? Because I sound like my uncle? You never understood him, either! You aren't intending to let me take the Test, are you, Father?"

Caramon stood without moving, refusing to answer, staring grimly into the darkness.

"No," said Palin softly. "You aren't. You're going to do everything in your power to stop me. Maybe even this!" The young man turned to look at Dalamar suspiciously. "Maybe this is some foul stew you and your friends here have cooked up to feed to me so that I'll quit! It gives you all the perfect excuse! Well, it won't work." Palin's cold gaze went from Dalamar to his father. "I hope you choke on it!"

Stepping past the dark elf, Palin put his foot on the first step, his eyes on the spectre above him.

"Come, Palin"—a pallid hand appeared from nowhere, beckoning—"come closer."

"*No*!" Caramon screamed in rage, jumping forward.

"I will do this, Father!" Palin took another step.

Caramon reached out his hand to grasp his son. There came a spoken word of magic, and the big man was frozen to the stone floor. "You must not interfere," Dalamar said sternly.

Glancing back, Palin saw his father—tears streaming down his face—still struggling in impotent fury to break free of the spell that bound him. For a moment,

Palin's heart misgave him. His father loved him. . . . No. Palin's lips tightened in resolution. All the more reason for letting me go. I will prove to him I am as strong as Tanin and Sturm. I will show him I am not a child, needing his protection.

Palin saw Dalamar start to ascend the stairs behind him. But then the dark elf himself came to a halt as two more pairs of disembodied eyes suddenly materialized out of the darkness.

"What is this?" Dalamar demanded furiously. "Do you dare stop me—the Master of the Tower?"

"There is only one true Master of the Tower," the Guardian said softly. "He who came to us long ago. For him, the gates opened."

As the Guardian spoke, it held out its hand to Palin. A silver key lay within its skeletal palm.

"Palin!" Dalamar shouted, fear and anger tightening his voice. "Don't enter alone! You know nothing of the Art! You have not taken the Test! You cannot fight him! You could destroy us all!"

"Palin!" Caramon begged in agony. "Palin, come home! Can't you understand? I love you so much, my son! I can't lose you—not like I lost him. . . ."

The voices dinned in his ears, but Palin didn't hear them. He heard another voice, a soft, shattered voice whispering in his heart. "Come to me, Palin! I need you! I need your help . . ."

A thrill tingled in his blood. Reaching out, Palin took the key from the spectre and, his hand shaking with fear and excitement, finally managed to insert the silver key into the ornate silver door lock.

There was a sharp click. Placing the tips of his five fingers on the oaken panel, Palin gave a gentle push.

For him, the door opened.

## CHAPTER SEVEN

Palin entered the dark laboratory, slowly, exultantly, his body shaking in excitement. He glanced back to see if Dalamar was behind him (to gloat a little, if the truth must be told) when the door slammed shut. There was a click, a snap. Sudden fear assailed Palin, trapped alone in the darkness. Frantically, he groped for the silver door handle, his fingers trying desperately to fit the key in the lock—a key that vanished in his hand.

"Palin!" On the other side of the door, he heard his father's frantic shout, but it sounded muffled and far away. There was a scuffling sound outside the door, muttered words of chanting and then a thud, as though something heavy had struck it.

The thick oaken door shivered, light flared from beneath it.

"Dalamar's cast a spell," Palin said to himself, backing up. The thud was probably his father's broad shoulder. Nothing happened. From somewhere behind him, Palin noticed a faint light beginning to glow in the laboratory. His fear diminished. Shrugging, the young man turned away. Nothing they did could open that door. He knew that, somehow, and he smiled. For the first time in his life he was doing something on his own, without father or brothers or Master around to "help." The thought was exhilarating. Sighing with pleasure, Palin relaxed and looked around, a tingle of joy surging through his body.

He had heard this chamber described to him only twice—once by Caramon and once by Tanis Half-

Elven. Caramon never spoke about what had happened that day in this laboratory, the day his twin had died. It had been only after much pleading on Palin's part that his father had told him the story at all—and then only in brief, halting words. Caramon's best friend, Tanis, had been more elaborate, though there were parts of the bittersweet tale of ambition, love, and self-sacrifice about which Tanis could not even talk. Their descriptions had been accurate, however. The laboratory looked just as Palin had pictured it in his dreams.

Walking slowly inside, examining every detail, Palin held his breath in reverent awe.

Nothing and no one had disturbed the great chamber in twenty-five years. As Dalamar had said, no living being had dared enter it. The gray dust lay thick on the floor, no skittering mice feet disturbed its drifted surface, as smooth and trackless as newfallen snow. The dust sifted from the window ledges where no spider spun its web, no bat flapped its leathery wings in anger at being awakened.

The size of the chamber was difficult to determine. At first, Palin had thought it small, logic telling him it couldn't be very large, located as it was at the top of the Tower. But the longer he stayed, the larger the chamber seemed to grow.

"Or is it me that grows smaller?" Palin whispered. "I am not even a mage. I don't belong here," said his mind. But his heart answered, "You never really belonged anywhere else. . . ."

The air was heavy with the odors of mildew and dust. There lingered still a faint spicy smell, familiar to the young man. Palin saw the light glint off rows of jars filled with dried leaves, rose petals, and other herbs and spices lining one wall. Spell components. There was another smell, too; this one not so

pleasant—the smell of decay, of death. The skeletons
of strange and unfamiliar creatures lay curled at the
bottoms of several large jars on the huge, stone table.
Remembering rumors of his uncle's experiments in creating life, Palin looked hurriedly away.

He examined the stone table, with its runes and polished surface. Had it really been dragged from the bottom of the sea as legend told? Palin wondered,
running his fingers lovingly over the smooth top,
leaving behind a spidery trail in the dust. His hand
touched the high stool next to the table. The young
man could picture his uncle sitting here, working,
reading. . . .

Palin's gaze went to the rows of spellbooks lining
shelf after shelf along one entire wall of the chamber.
His heart beat faster as he approached them, recognizing them from his father's description. The ones with
the nightblue bindings and silver runes were the books
of the great archmage, Fistandantilus. A whispering
chill flowed from them. Palin shivered and stopped,
afraid to go nearer, though his hands twitched to
touch them.

He dared not, however. Only mages of the highest
ranking could even open the books, much less read the
spells recorded therein. If he tried it, the binding
would burn his skin, just as the words would burn his
mind—eventually driving him mad. Sighing with bitter regret, Palin turned his gaze to another row of
other spellbooks, these black with silver runes—his
uncle's.

He was wondering if he should try to read, what
would happen if he did, and was just starting to examine them closer when he noticed, for the first time, the
source of the light illuminating the laboratory.

"His staff!" he whispered.

It stood in a corner, leaning up against a wall. The

Staff of Magius. Its magical crystal burned with a cold, pale light, like the light from Solinari, Palin thought. Tears of longing filled his eyes and ran, unheeded, down his cheeks. Blinking them back so that he could see, he drew nearer the staff, hardly daring to breathe, fearful the light might go out in an instant.

Given to Raistlin when he successfully completed his Test by the wizard, Par-Salian, the staff possessed untold magical power. It could cast light at a word of command, Palin recalled. According to legend, however, no hand but his uncle's could touch the staff or the light would extinguish.

"But my father held it," Palin said softly. "He used it—with my dying uncle's help—to close the Portal and prevent the Dark Queen from entering the world. Then the light went out and nothing anyone said could make it glow again."

But it was glowing now. . . .

His throat aching, his heart beating so it made him short of breath, Palin reached out a trembling hand toward the staff. If the light failed, he would be left alone, trapped, in the smothering darkness.

His fingertips brushed the wood.

The light gleamed brightly.

Palin's cold fingers closed around the staff, grasping it firmly. The crystal burned brighter still, shedding its pure radiance over him, his white robes glowed molten silver. Lifting the staff from its corner, Palin looked at it in rapture and saw, as he moved it, that its beam grew concentrated, sending a shaft of light into a distant corner of the laboratory—a corner that had previously stood in deepest darkness.

Walking nearer, the young man saw the light illuminate a heavy curtain of purple velvet hanging from the ceiling. The tears froze on Palin's face, a chill shook his body. He had no need to pull the golden, silken cord that hung beside the velvet, no need to draw aside those curtains to know what lay behind.

The Portal.

Created long ago by wizards greedy for knowledge, the Portals had led them to their own doom—into the realms of the gods. Knowing what terrible consequences this could have for the unwary, the wise among all three Orders of wizards came together and closed them as best they could, decreeing that only a powerful archmage of the Black Robes and a holy cleric of Paladine acting together could cause the Portal to open. They believed, in their wisdom, that this unlikely combination could never come about. But they had not counted upon love.

So Raistlin was able to persuade Crysania, the Revered Daughter of Paladine, to act with him to open the Portal. So he had entered and challenged the Queen of Darkness, thinking to rule in her stead. The consequences of such ambition in a human would have been disastrous—the destruction of the world. Knowing this, his twin brother, Caramon, had risked all to enter the Abyss and stop Raistlin. He had done so, but only with his twin's assistance. Realizing his tragic mistake, Raistlin had sacrificed himself for the world—according to legend. He closed the Portal preventing the Queen from entering, but at a dreadful cost. He himself was trapped upon the Other Side of this dread doorway.

Palin came nearer and nearer the curtain, drawn to it against his will. Or was he? Was it fear making his steps falter and his body shake—or excitement?

And then he heard that whispering voice again, "Palin . . . help . . ."

It came from beyond the curtain!

Palin closed his eyes, leaning weakly upon the staff. No! It couldn't be! His father had been so certain. . . .

Through his closed eyelids, the young man saw another light begin to glow, coming from in front of him. Fearfully, he opened his eyes and saw the light radiating from around and above and beneath the curtain. A multicolored light, it welled out in a fearsome rainbow.

"Palin . . . help me . . ."

Palin's hand closed over the golden drawstring of its own volition. He had no conscious thought of moving his fingers, yet found himself holding onto the cord. Hesitating, he looked at the staff in his hand, then glanced back behind him at the door leading into the laboratory. The thudding had stopped, no lights flashed. Perhaps Dalamar and his father had given up. Or perhaps the Guardians had attacked them. . . .

Palin shivered. He should go back. Abandon this. It was too dangerous. He wasn't a even a mage! But as the thought crossed his mind, the light from the crystal atop the staff dimmed—or so it seemed to him.

No, he thought resolutely. I must go on. I must know the truth!

Gripping the drawstring with a palm wet with sweat, he pulled it hard, watching, holding his breath as the curtain slowly lifted, rising upward in shimmering folds.

The light grew more and more brilliant as the curtain lifted, dazzling him. Raising his hand to shade his eyes, Palin stared in awe at the magnificent, fearful sight. The Portal was a black void surrounded by the five metallic dragon's heads. Carved by magic into the likeness of Takhisis, Queen of Darkness, their mouths gaped open in a silent scream of triumph, each head glowing green, blue, red, white, or black.

The light blinded Palin. He blinked painfully and rubbed his burning eyes. The dragon's heads only shone more brilliantly, and now he could hear them each began to chant.

The first, *From darkness to darkness, my voice echoes in the emptiness.*

The second, *From this world to the next, my voice cries with life.*

The third, *From darkness to darkness, I shout. Beneath my feet, all is made firm.*

The fourth, *Time that flows, hold in your course.*

And finally, the last head, *Because by fate even the gods are cast down, weep ye all with me.*

A magical spell, Palin realized. His vision blurred and tears streamed down his cheeks as he attempted to see through the dazzling light into the Portal. The multicolored lights began to whirl madly in his vision, spinning around the outside of the great, gaping, twisting void.

Growing dizzy, Palin clutched the staff and kept his gaze on the void within the Portal. The darkness itself moved! It began to swirl, circling around an eye of deeper darkness within its center, like a maelstrom without substance or form. Round . . . and round . . . and round . . . Sucking the air from the laboratory up in its mouth, sucking up the dust, and the light of the staff. . . .

"No!" Palin cried, realizing in horror that it was sucking him in as well! Struggling, he fought against it, but the force was irresistible. Helpless as a babe trying to stop his own birth, Palin was drawn inside the dazzling light, the writhing darkness. The dragon's heads shrieked a paean to their Dark Queen. Their weight crushed Palin's body, then their talons pulled him apart, limb by limb. Fire burst upon him, burning his flesh from his bones. Waters swirled over him, he was drowning. He screamed without sound, though he could hear his voice. He was dying and he was thankful he was dying for the pain would end.

His heart burst.

# CHAPTER EIGHT

Everything stopped. The light, the pain. . . .
Everything was silent.

Palin opened his eyes. He was lying face down, the Staff of Magius still clutched in his hand. Opening his eyes, he saw the light of the staff shining silver, gleaming cold and pure. He felt no pain, his breathing was relaxed and normal, his heartbeat steady, his body whole and unharmed. But he wasn't lying on the floor of the laboratory. He was in sand! Or so it seemed. Glancing around, slowly rising to his feet, he saw that he was in a strange land—flat, like a desert, with no distinguishing features of any type. It was completely empty, barren. The landscape stretched on and on endlessly as far as he could see. Puzzled, he looked around. He had never been here before, yet it was familiar. The ground was an odd color—a kind of muted pink, the same color as the sky. His father's voice came to him, *As though it was sunset or somewhere in the distance, a fire burned. . . .*

Palin closed his eyes to blot out the horror of realization as fear surged over him in a suffocating wave, robbing him of breath or even the power to stand.

"The Abyss," he murmured, his shaking hand holding onto the staff for support.

"Palin—" the voice broke off in a choked cry.

Palin's eyes flared open, startled at hearing his name, alarmed by the sound of desperation in the voice.

Turning around, stumbling in the sand, the young man looked in the direction of that terrible sound and saw, rising up before him, a stone wall where no wall had been only seconds previously. Two undead figures walked toward the wall, dragging something between them. The "something" was human, Palin could see, human and living! It struggled in its captor's grasp as though trying to escape, but resistance was useless against those whose strength came from beyond the grave.

As the three drew nearer the wall, which was, apparently, their destination, for one pointed to it and laughed, the human ceased his struggles for a moment. Lifting his head, he looked directly at Palin.

Golden skin, pupils the shape of hourglasses . . .

"Uncle?" Palin breathed, starting to take a step forward.

But the figure shook its head, making an almost imperceptible movement with one of its slender hands as though saying, "Not now!"

Palin realized suddenly that he was standing out in the open, alone in the Abyss, with nothing to protect him but the Staff of Magius—a magical staff whose magic he had no idea how to use. The undead, intent upon their struggling captive, had not noticed him yet, but it would only be a matter of time. Frightened and frustrated, Palin looked about hopelessly for some place to hide. To his amazement, a thick bush sprang up out of nowhere, almost as if he had summoned it into being.

Without stopping to think why or how it was there, the young man ducked swiftly behind the bush, covering the crystal on the staff with his hand in an attempt to keep its light from giving him away. Then he peered out cautiously into the pinkish, burning land.

The undead had hauled their captive to the wall that stood in the middle of the sand. Manacles appeared on the wall at a spoken word of command. Hoisting their captive up into the air with their incredible strength, the undead fastened Raistlin to the wall by his wrists. Then, with mocking bows, they left him there, hanging from the wall, his black robes stirring in the hot breeze.

Rising to his feet, Palin started forward again when a dark shadow fell across his vision, blinding him more completely than the brilliant light, filling his mind and soul and body with such terror and fear that he could not move. Though the darkness was thick and all encompassing, Palin saw things within it—he saw a woman, more beautiful and desirable than any other woman he had ever seen before in his life. He saw her walk up to his uncle, he saw his uncle's manacled hands clench. He saw all this, yet all around him was such darkness as might have been found on the floor of the deepest ocean. Then Palin understood. The darkness was in his mind, for he was looking upon Takhisis—the Queen of Darkness herself.

As he watched, held in place by awe and horror and such reverence as made him want to kneel before her, Palin saw the woman change her form. Out of the darkness, out of the sand of the burning land, rose a dragon. Immense in size, its wing span covered the land with shadow, its five heads writhed and twisted upon five necks, its five mouths opened in deafening shrieks of laughter and of cruel delight.

Palin saw Raistlin's head turn away involuntarily, the golden eyes close as though unable to face the sight of the creature that leered above him. Yet the archmage fought on, trying to wrench himself free of the manacles, his arms and wrists torn and bleeding from the futile effort.

Slowly, delicately, the dragon lifted a claw. With one swift stroke, she slit open Raistlin's black robes. Then, with almost the same, delicate movment, she slit open the archmage's body.

Palin gasped and shut his eyes to blot out the dreadful sight. But it was too late. He had seen it and he would see it always in his dreams, just as he would hear his uncle's agonized cry forever. Palin's mind reeled and his knees went limp. Sinking to the ground, he clasped his stomach, retching.

Then, through the haze of sickness and terror, Palin was aware of the Queen and knew that she was suddenly aware of him! He could sense her searching for him, listening, smelling. . . . He had no thought of hiding. There was nowhere he could go where she would not find him. He could not fight, not even look up at her. He didn't have the strength. He could only crouch in the sand, shivering in fear, and wait for the end.

Nothing happened. The shadow lifted, Palin's fear subsided.

"Palin . . . help . . ." The voice, ragged with pain, whispered in the young man's mind. And, horribly, there was another sound, the sound of liquid dripping, of blood running.

"No!" The young man moaned, shaking his head and burrowing into the sand as though he would bury himself. There came another gurgling cry, and Palin retched again, sobbing in horror and pity and disgust at himself for his weakness. "What can I do? I am nothing. I have no power to help you!" he mumbled, his fist clenching around the staff that he held still. Holding it near him, he rocked back and forth, unable to open his eyes, unable to look. . . .

"Palin"—the voice gasped for breath, each word causing obvious pain—"you must be . . . strong. For your own . . . sake as well as . . . mine."

Palin couldn't speak. His throat was raw and aching, the bitter taste of bile in his mouth choked him.

Be strong. For his sake . . .

Slowly, gripping the staff, Palin used it to pull himself to his feet. Then, bracing himself, feeling the touch of the wood cool and reassuring beneath his hand, he opened his eyes.

Raistlin's body hung limply from the wall by its wrists, the black robes in tatters, the long white hair falling across his face as his head lolled forward. Palin tried to keep his eyes focused on his uncle's face, but he could not. Despite himself, his gaze went to the bloody, mangled torso. From chest to groin, Raistlin's flesh had been ripped apart, torn asunder by sharp talons, exposing living organs. The dripping sound Palin heard was the sound of the man's life blood, falling drop by drop into a great stone pool at his feet.

The young man's stomach wrenched again, but there was nothing left to purge. Gritting his teeth, Palin kept walking forward through the sand toward the wall, the staff aiding his faltering footsteps. But when Palin reached the gruesome pool, his weak legs would support him no longer. Fearing he might faint from the horror of the dreadful sight, he sank to his knees, bowing his head.

But the voice came again. "Look at me . . . You . . . know me . . . Palin?"

The young man raised his head, reluctantly. Golden eyes stared at him, their hourglass pupils dilated with agony. Blood-stained lips parted to speak, but no words came. A shudder shook the frail body.

"I know you . . . uncle. . . ." Doubling over, Palin began to sob, while in his mind, the words screamed at him. "Father lied! He lied to me! He lied to himself!"

"Palin, be strong!" Raistlin whispered. "You . . . can free me. But you must . . . be quick. . . ."

Strong . . . I must be strong. . . .

"Yes." Palin swallowed his tears. Wiping his face, he

rose unsteadily to his feet, keeping his gaze on his uncle's eyes. "I—I'm sorry. What must I do?"

"Use . . . the staff. Touch the locks around . . . my wrists. . . . Hurry! The . . . Queen . . ."

"Where—where is the Dark Queen?" Palin stammered. Stepping carefully past the pool of blood, he came to stand near his uncle and, reaching up, touched the glowing crystal of the staff to the first of the manacles that held Raistlin bound to the wall.

Exhausted, near death, his uncle could speak no longer, but his words came to Palin's mind. "Your coming forced her to leave. She was not prepared to face one of the White Robes such as you. But that will not last long. She will return. Both of us . . . must be gone. . . ."

Palin touched the other manacle and, freed of his chains, Raistlin slumped forward, his body falling into the arms of the young man. Catching hold of his uncle, his horror lost in his pity and compassion, Palin gently laid the torn, bleeding body on the ground.

"But how can you go anywhere?" Palin murmured. "You are . . . dying."

"Yes," Raistlin answered wordlessly, his thin lips twisting in a grim smile. "In a few moments, I will die, as I have died countless mornings before this. When night falls, I will return to life and spend the night looking forward to the dawn when the Queen will come and tear my flesh, ending my life in tortured pain once more."

"What can I do?" Palin cried. "How can I help you?"

"You are helping already," Raistlin said aloud, his voice growing stronger. His hand moved feebly. "Look . . ."

Reluctantly, Palin glanced down at his uncle's terrible wound. It was closing! The flesh was mending! The young man stared in astonishment. If he had been a high-ranking cleric of Paladine, he could have performed no greater miracle. "What is happening? How—" he asked blankly.

"Your goodness, your love," whispered Raistlin. "So might my brother have saved me if he had possessed the courage to enter the Abyss himself." His lip curled in bitterness. "Help me stand."

Palin swallowed but said nothing as he helped the archmage rise to his feet. What could he say? Shame filled his soul, shame for his father. Well, he would make up for it.

"Give me your arm, nephew. I can walk. Come, we must reach the Portal before the Queen returns."

"Are you sure you can manage?" Palin put his arm around Raistlin's body, feeling the strange, unnatural heat that radiated from it warm his own chilled flesh.

"I must. I have no choice." Leaning upon Palin, the archmage gathered his torn black robes about him, and the two walked forward as fast as they could through the shifting sand toward where the Portal stood in the center of the red-tinged landscape.

But before he had gone very far, Raistlin stopped, his frail body wracked by coughing until he gasped for air.

Standing beside him, holding him, Palin looked at his uncle in concern. "Here," he offered. "Take your staff. It will aid your steps—"

Raistlin's hourglass eyes went to the staff in the young man's hand. Reaching out his slender, golden-skinned hand, he touched the smooth wood, stroking it lovingly. Then, looking at Palin, he smiled and shook his head.

"No, nephew," he said in his soft, shattered voice. "The staff is yours, a gift from your uncle. It would have been yours someday," he added, speaking almost to himself. "I would have trained you myself, gone with you to watch the Testing. I would have been proud . . . so proud . . ." Then, he shrugged, his gaze going to Palin. "What am I saying? I *am* proud of you, my nephew. So young, to do this, to enter the Abyss—"

As if to remind them where they were and the danger they were in, a shadow fell upon them as of dark wings, hovering overhead.

Palin looked up fearfully. Then his gaze went to the Portal that seemed farther away than he remembered. "We can't outrun her!" he gasped.

"Wait!" Raistlin paused for breath, color coming back to his face. "We don't need to run. Look at the Portal, Palin. Concentrate on it. Think of it as being right in front of you."

"I don't understand—" Palin looked at Raistlin, confused.

"Concentrate!" the archmage snarled.

The shadow was growing increasingly darker. Looking at the Portal, Palin tried to do as he was told, but he kept seeing his father's face, the dragon ripping his uncle's flesh. . . . The shadow over them grew still darker, darker than night, dark as his own fear.

"Don't be afraid." His uncle's voice came to him through the darkness. "Concentrate."

The disciplined training in magic came to Palin's aid. Thus was he forced to concentrate on the words to a spell. Closing his eyes, the young man shut everything out—his fear, his horror, his sorrow—and envisioned the Portal in his mind, standing directly before him.

"Excellent, young one," came Raistlin's soft voice.

Palin blinked, startled. The Portal was right where he had envisioned it, just a step or two away.

"Don't hesitate," Raistlin instructed, reading the young man's mind. "The way back is not difficult, not like coming through. Go ahead. I can stand on my own. I will follow. . . ."

Palin stepped inside, feeling a slight sensation of dizziness and a momentary blindness, but it passed quickly. Looking around, he drew a deep breath of relief and thankfulness. He was standing in the laboratory once more. The Portal was behind him, though he had no clear remembrance of how he got through it, and, beside the Portal, he saw his uncle. But Raistlin was not looking at him. His eyes were on the Portal itself, a strange smile played on his thin lips.

"You are right! We must close it!" Palin said suddenly, thinking he knew his uncle's mind. "The Queen will come back into the world—"

Raising the staff, the young man stepped forward. A slender, golden-skinned hand closed over his arm. Its grip hurt, the touch burned him. Catching his breath, biting his lip from the pain, Palin looked at his uncle in confusion.

"All in good time, my dear nephew," whispered Raistlin. "All in good time. . . ."

## CHAPTER NINE

Raistlin drew the young man nearer, smiling slightly as Palin flinched, noting the look of pain in the green eyes. Still Raistlin held him, regarding him searchingly, studying the features, probing the depths of his soul.

"There is much of myself in you, young one," Raistlin said, reaching up to brush back a lock of hair that had fallen across Palin's pale face. "More of me than of your father. And he loves you best for that, doesn't he? Oh, he is proud of your brothers"—Raistlin shrugged, as the young man started to protest—"but you he cherishes, protects. . . ."

Flushing, Palin broke free of Raistlin's grip. But he might have spared his energy. The archmage held him fast—with his eyes, not his hands.

"He'll smother you!" Raistlin hissed. "Smother you as he did me! He will prevent you taking the Test. You know that, don't you."

"He—he doesn't understand," Palin faltered. "He's only trying to do what he thinks—"

"Don't lie to me, Palin," Raistlin said softly, placing his slender fingers on the young man's lips. "Don't lie to yourself. Speak the truth that is in your soul. I see it in you so clearly! The hatred, the jealousy! Use it, Palin! Use it to make you strong—as I did!"

The golden-skinned hand traced over the bones of Palin's face—the firm, strong chin, the clenched jaw, the smooth, high cheekbones. Palin trembled at the touch, but more still at the expression in the burning, hourglass eyes. "You should have been *mine*! My son!" Raistlin murmured. "I would have raised you to power! What wonders I would have shown you, Palin. Upon the wings of magic we would have flown the world—cheered the winner of the fights for succession among the minotaur, gone swimming with the sea elves, battled giants, watched the birth of a golden dragon. . . . All this could have been yours, *should* have been yours, Palin, if only they—"

A fit of coughing checked the archmage. Gasping, Raistlin staggered, clutching his chest. Catching hold of him in his strong arms, Palin led his uncle to a dusty, cushioned chair that sat near the Portal. Beneath the dust, he could discern dark splotches on the fabric—as though it had, long ago, been stained with blood. In his concern for his uncle, Palin thought little of it. Raistlin sank down into the chair, choking, coughing into a soft, white cloth that Palin drew from his own robes and handed to him. Then, leaning the staff carefully against the wall, the young man knelt down beside his uncle.

"Is there something I can do? Something I can get for you? That herbal mixture you drank." His glance went to the jars of herbs on a shelf. "If you tell me how to fix it—"

Raistlin shook his head. "In time . . ." he whispered as the spasm eased. "In time, Palin." He smiled wearily, his hand reaching out to rest on the young man's head. "In time. I will teach you that . . . and so much more! How they have wasted your talent! What did they tell you, young one? Why did they bring you here?"

Palin bowed his head. The touch of those slender fingers excited him, yet he caught himself cringing, squirming beneath their burning caress. "I came— They said . . . you would try . . . to take . . ." He swallowed, unable to continued.

"Ah, yes. Of course. That is what those idiots would think. I would take your body as Fistandantilus tried to take mine. What fools! As if I would deprive the world of this young mind, of this power. The two of us . . . There will be two of us, now. I make you my apprentice, Palin." The burning fingers stroked the auburn hair.

Palin raised his face. "But," he said in amazement, "I am of low rank. I haven't taken the Test—"

"You will, young one," Raistlin murmured, exhaustion plain upon his face. "You will. And with my help, you will pass easily. Just as I passed with the help of another . . . Hush. Don't speak anymore. I must rest." Shivering, Raistlin clutched his tattered robes about his frail body. "Bring me some wine and a change of clothes or I will freeze to death. I had forgotten how damp this place was." Leaning his head back against the cushions, Raistlin closed his eyes, his breath rattling in his lungs.

Palin stood up slowly, casting an uneasy glance behind him.

The five heads of the dragon around the Portal still glowed, but their colors were faded, less brilliant. Their mouths gaped open, but no sound came out. It seemed to Palin, though, that they were waiting, biding their time. Their ten eyes watched him, glittering with some secret, inner knowledge. He looked inside the Portal. The red-tinged landscape stretched into the distance. Far away, barely discernible, he could see the wall, the pool of blood beneath it. And above it, the dark, winged shadow. . . .

"Uncle," Palin said, "the Portal. Shouldn't we—"

"Palin," said Raistlin softly, "I gave you a command. You will learn to obey my commands, apprentice. Do as I bid."

As Palin watched, the shadow grew darker. Like a

cloud covering the sun, the wings cast a chill of fear over his soul. He started to speak again, but at that moment glanced back at Raistlin.

His uncle's eyes appeared to be closed, but Palin caught a slit of gold gleaming beneath the lids, like the eyes of a snake. Biting his lower lip, the young man turned hastily away. Taking hold of the staff, he used its light to search the laboratory for that which his uncle had requested.

Dressed once more in soft black velvet robes, Raistlin stood before the Portal, sipping a glass of elven wine that Palin had discovered in a carafe far back in a corner of the laboratory. The shadow over the land within had now grown so dark that it seemed night had fallen over the Abyss. But no stars shown, no moons lit that dread darkness. The wall was the only object visible, and it glowed with its own, horrid light. Raistlin stared at it, his face grim, his eyes haunted by pain.

"Thus she reminds me of what will happen should she catch me, Palin," he said softly. "But, no. I am not going back." Looking around, the archmage glanced at the young man. Raistlin's eyes glittered within the depths of his black hood. "I had twenty-five years to consider my mistakes. Twenty-five years of unbearable agony, of endless torment. . . . My only joy, the only thing that gave me strength to meet each morning's torture was the shadow of you I saw in my mind. Yes, Palin"—smiling, Raistlin reached out and drew the young man nearer—"I have watched you all these years. I have done what I could for you. There is a strength—an inner strength—in you that comes from me! A burning desire, a love for the magic! I knew, one day, you would seek me out to learn how to use it. I knew *they* would try to stop you. But they could not.

Everything they did to prevent your coming must only bring you closer. Once in here, I knew you would hear my voice. You would free me. And so I made my plans . . ."

"I am honored that you take this interest in me," Palin began. His voice broke, and he cleared his throat nervously. "But you must know the truth. I—I didn't seek you out to . . . to gain power. I heard your voice, pleading for help, and I—I came because . . ."

"You came out of pity and compassion," Raistlin said with a twisted smile. "There is still much of your father in you. That is a weakness that can be overcome. As I told you, Palin. Speak the truth—to yourself. What did you feel upon entering this place? What did you feel when you first touched the staff?"

Palin tried to look away from his uncle's gaze. Though the laboratory was chill, he was sweating beneath his robes. Raistlin held him tightly, however, forcing the young man to look into the golden, glittering eyes.

And there see a reflection of himself. . . . Was what he said true? Palin stared at the image in the archmage's eyes. He saw a young man, dressed in robes whose color was indeterminate, now white, now red, now darkening. . . .

The arm Raistlin held jerked spasmodically within the archmage's grasp.

He can feel my fear, Palin realized, trying to control the tremors that shook his body.

Is it fear? the golden eyes asked. Is it fear? Or exultation?

Palin saw the staff he held in his hand reflected in those eyes. He stood within the pool of its bright light. The longer he held the staff, the more he could sense the magic within it—and within himself. The golden eyes shifted in their gaze slightly, and Palin followed them. He saw the black-bound spellbooks standing upon the shelf. He felt once again the thrill he had experienced upon entering the laboratory, and he licked his dry, parched lips like a man who has been wandering long in a vast desert and who has, at last, found the cool water to ease his burning thirst. Looking back at Raistlin, he saw himself as in a mirror, standing before the archmage dressed in black robes.

"What—what are your plans?" Palin asked hoarsely.

"Very simple. As I said, I had long years to consider my mistake. My ambition was too great. I dared become a god—something mortals are not meant to do—as I was painfully reminded every morning when the Dark Queen's talon ripped my flesh."

Palin saw the thin lip curl for a moment and the golden eyes glint. The slender hand clenched in anger and remembered agony, its grip tightening painfully around the young man's arm. "I learned my lesson," Raistlin said bitterly, drawing a rasping, shuddering breath. "I have trimmed my ambition. No longer will I strive to be a god. I will be content with the world." Smiling sardonically, he patted Palin's hand. "We will be content with the world, I should say."

"I—" The words caught in Palin's throat. He was dazed with confusion and fear and a wild rush of excitement. Glancing back at the Portal, however, he felt the shadow cover his heart. "But, the Queen? Shouldn't we shut it?"

Raistlin shook his head. "No, apprentice."

"No?" Palin looked at him in alarm.

"No. This will be my gift to her, to prove my loyalty—admittance to the world. And the world will be her gift to me. Here she will rule and I . . . I will serve." Raistlin bit the words with his sharp teeth, his lips parted in a tight, mirthless grin. Sensing the hatred and the anger surging through the frail body, Palin shuddered.

Raistlin glanced at him. "Squeamish, nephew?" He sneered, letting loose of Palin's arm. "The squeamish do not rise to power—"

"You told me to speak the truth," Palin said, shrinking away from Raistlin, relieved that the burning touch was gone, yet longing—somehow—to gain it back. "And I will. I'm frightened! For us both! I know I am weak—" He bowed his head.

"No, nephew," said Raistlin softly. "Not weak. Just young. And you will always be afraid. I will teach you to master your fear, to use its strength. To make it serve you, not the other way around."

Looking up, Palin saw a gentleness in the archmage's face, a gentleness few in the world had ever seen. The image of the young man in the black robes faded from the glittering golden eyes, replaced by a yearning, a hunger for love. Now it was Palin who reached out and clasped hold of Raistlin's hand. "Close the Portal, uncle!" the young man pleaded. "Come home and live with us! The room my father built for you is still there, in the Inn. My mother has kept the plaque with the wizard's mark on it! It is hidden in a chest of rosewood, but I've seen it. I've held it and dreamed of this so often! Come home! Teach me what you know! I would honor you, revere you! We could travel, as you said. Show me the wonders your eyes have seen. . . ."

"Home." The word lingered on Raistlin's lips as though he were tasting it. "Home. How often I dreamed of it"—his golden-eyed gaze went to the wall, shining with its ghastly light—"especially with the coming of dawn. . . ."

Then, glancing at Palin from within the shadows of his hood, Raistlin smiled. "Yes, nephew," he said softly. "I believe I will come home with you. I need time to rest, to recover my strength, to rid myself of . . . old dreams." Palin saw the eyes darken with remembered pain.

Coughing, Raistlin motioned the young man to help him. Carefully, Palin leaned the staff against the wall and assisted Raistlin to the chair. Sinking into it weakly, Raistlin gestured for the young man to pour him another glass of wine. The archmage leaned his head back wearily into the cushions. "I need time . . ." he continued, moistening his lips with the wine. "Time to train you, my apprentice. Time to train you . . . and ..o train your brothers."

"My brothers?" Palin repeated in astonishment.

"Why, yes, young one." Amusement tinged Raistlin's voice as he looked at the young man standing by his chair. "I need generals for my legions. Your brothers will be ideal—"

"Legions!" Palin cried. "No, that's not what I meant! You must come home to live with us in peace. You've earned it! You sacrificed yourself for the world—"

"*I?*" Raistlin interrupted. "I sacrificed myself for the world?" The archmage began to laugh—dreadful, fearful laughter that set the shadows of the laboratory dancing in delight like demons. "Is that what they say of me?" Raistlin laughed until he choked. A coughing fit seized him, this one worse than the others.

Palin watched helplessly as his uncle writhed in pain. The young man could still hear that mocking laughter dinning in his ears. When the spasm passed, and he could breathe, Raistlin lifted his head and, with a weak motion of his hand, beckoned Palin near.

Palin saw blood upon the cloth in his uncle's hand, blood flecked Raistlin's ashen lips. Loathing and horror came over the young man, but he drew nearer anyway, compelled by a terrible fascination to kneel down beside his uncle.

"Know this, Palin!" Raistlin whispered, speaking with great effort, his words barely audible. "I sacrificed . . . *myself* . . . for . . . *myself!*" Sinking back into his chair, he gasped for breath. When he could move, he reached out a shaking, blood-stained hand and caught hold of Palin's white robes. "I saw . . . what I must . . . become . . . if I succeeded. *Nothing!* That . . . was . . . all. Dwindle . . . to . . . nothing. The world . . . dead. . . . This way"—His hand gestured feebly at the wall, the gruesome pool beneath it. His eyes gleamed feverishly—"there was . . . still . . . a chance . . . for me . . . to return . . . ."

"No!" Palin cried, struggling to free himself from Raistlin's grasp. "I don't believe you!"

"Why not?" Raistlin kept hold of the young man. His voice grew stronger. "You told them yourself. Don't you remember, Palin? 'A man must put the magic first, the world second . . . ' That's what you said to them in the Tower. The world doesn't matter to you anymore than it does to me! Nothing matters— your brothers, your father! The magic! The power! That's all that means anything to either of us!"

"I don't know!" Palin cried brokenly, his hands clawing at Raistlin's. "I can't think! Let me go! Let me go . . ." His fingers fell nervelessly from Raistlin's wrists, his head sank into his hands. Tears filled his eyes.

"Poor young one," Raistlin said smoothly. Laying his hand on Palin's head, he drew it gently into his lap and stroked the auburn hair soothingly.

Wracking sobs tore at Palin's body. He was bereft, alone. Lies, all lies! Everyone had lied to him—his father, the mages, the world! What did it matter, after all? The magic. That was all he had. His uncle was right. The burning touch of those slender fingers; the soft black velvet beneath his cheek, wet with his tears;

the smell of rose petals and spice. That would be his life. . . . That and this bitter emptiness within. An emptiness that all the world could not fill.

"Weep, Palin," Raistlin said softly. "Weep as I wept once, long, long ago. Then you will realize, as I did, that it does no good. No one hears you, sobbing in the night alone."

Palin lifted his tear-stained face suddenly, staring into Raistlin's eyes.

"At last you understand." Raistlin smiled. His hand stroked back the wet hair from Palin's eyes. "Get hold of yourself, young one. It is time for us to go, before the Dark Queen comes. There is much to be done—"

Palin regarded Raistlin calmly, though the young man's body still shuddered from his sobs and he could see his uncle only through a blur of tears. "Yes," he said. "At last I understand. Too late, it seems. But I understand. And you are wrong, uncle," he murmured brokenly. "Someone *did* hear you crying in the night. My father."

Rising to his feet, Palin brushed his hand across his eyes, keeping his gaze steadfastly on his uncle. "I am going to close the Portal."

"Don't be a fool!" Raistlin said with a sneer. "I won't let you! You know that!"

"I know," said Palin, drawing a shivering breath. "You will stop me—"

"I will kill you!"

"You will . . . kill me. . . ." Palin continued, his voice faltering only slightly. Turning around, he reached out his hand for the Staff of Magius that stood leaning against the desk beside Raistlin's chair. The light of the crystal beamed white and cold as his hand closed over it.

"What a waste!" Raistlin hissed, twisting out of his chair. "Why die in such a meaningless gesture? For it will be meaningless, I assure you, my dear nephew. I will do all I planned. The world will be mine! You will be dead—and who will know or care?"

"You will," said Palin in a low voice.

Turning his back upon his uncle, Palin walked with firm, steady steps over to stand before the Portal. The shadow was deeper and darker, making the wall within the Abyss stand out by hideous contrast. Palin could feel the evil now, feel it seeping through the Portal like water flowing into a wrecked ship. He thought of the Dark Queen, able to enter the world at last. Once more, the flames of war would sweep across the land as the forces of good rose to stop her. He saw his father and mother die by his uncle's hand, his brothers fall victim to their uncle's magical charm. He saw them dressed in dragonscale armor, riding evil dragons into battle, leading troops of hideous beings spawned of darkness.

No! With the help of the gods, he would stop this if he could. But, raising the staff, Palin realized helplessly that he hadn't the vaguest idea how to close the Portal. He could sense the power in the staff, but he could not control it. Raistlin was right—what a stupid, meaningless gesture.

Behind him, Palin heard his uncle laugh. It wasn't mocking laughter this time, however. It was bemused, almost angry.

"This is senseless, Palin! Stop! Don't make me do this!"

Drawing a deep breath, Palin tried to concentrate his energy and his thoughts upon the staff. "Close the Portal," he whispered, forcing himself to think about nothing else, though his body quivered with fear. It was not a fear of dying, he could tell himself that with quiet pride. He loved life, never so much as now, he realized. But he could leave it without regret, though the thought of the grief that his death would cause those who loved him filled him with sorrow. His mother and father would know what he had done, however. They would understand. No matter what his uncle said.

And they'll fight you, Palin knew. They will fight you and your Dark Queen as they fought once before. *You will not win.*

Palin gripped the staff, his hand sweating, his body trembling. He wasn't afraid of dying. He was afraid of . . . of the pain.

Would it hurt . . . very much . . . to die?

Shaking his head angrily, the young man cursed himself for a coward and stared hard at the Portal. He had to concentrate! To put this out of his mind. He must make fear serve him! Not master him. There was a chance, after all, that he might close the Portal before his uncle . . . before . . .

"Paladine, help me," said Palin, his gaze going to the silvery light gleaming atop the staff with steadfast, unwavering brilliance in the shadowy darkness.

"Palin!" Raistlin shouted harshly. "I warn you—"

Lightning crackled from Raistlin's fingertips. But Palin kept his eyes upon the staff. Its light grew brighter, shining with a radiance whose beauty and clarity eased Palin's last fears.

"Paladine," he murmured.

The name of the god mercifully obliterated the sound of magical chanting Palin heard rising behind him.

The pain was swift, sudden . . . and soon over.

## CHAPTER TEN

Raistlin stood alone in the laboratory, leaning upon the Staff of Magius. The light of the staff had gone out. The archmage stood in darkness as thick as the dust that lay, undisturbed, upon the stone floor, upon the spellbooks, upon the chair, upon the drawn, heavy curtain of purple velvet.

Almost as deep as the darkness was the silence of the place.

Raistlin stilled his breathing, listening to the silence. The sound of no living being disturbed it—neither mouse nor bat nor spider— for no living being dared enter the laboratory, guarded by those whose vigilance would last unto the end of the world and beyond. Almost Raistlin thought he could hear one sound—the sound of the dust falling, the sound of time passing. . . .

Sighing wearily, the archmage raised his head and looked into the darkness, broke the ages-long silence. "I have done what you wanted of me," he cried. "Are you satisfied?"

There was no answer; only the gently sifting dust drifting down into the perpetual night.

"No," Raistlin murmured. "You cannot hear me. And that is just as well. Little did you think, Dalamar, that when you conjured my illusion for this purpose, you would conjure *me*! Oh, no, apprentice"—Raistlin smiled bitterly—"do not pride yourself. You are good, but not that good. It was not your magic woke me from my sleep. No, it was something else. . . ." He paused, trying to remember. "What did I tell the young man? 'A shadow on my mind'? Yes, that's what it was.

"Ah, Dalamar, you are lucky." The archmage shook his hooded head. For a brief moment, the darkness was lit by a fierce glint in the golden eyes, gleaming with their inner flame. "If he had been what I was, you would have found yourself in sad straits, dark elf. Through him, I could have returned. But as his compassion and his love freed me from the darkness into which I cast myself, so it binds me there still."

The light of the golden eyes faded, the darkness returned.

Raistlin sighed. "But that is all right," he whispered, leaning his head against the staff that supported him. "I am tired, so very tired. I want to return to my sleep." Walking across the stone floor, his black robes rustling about his ankles, his soft unheard footsteps leaving no trail at all in the thick dust, the archmage came to stand before the velvet curtain. Placing his hand on it, he stopped and looked around the laboratory that he could not see except in his memories, in his mind.

"I just want you to know," Raistlin cried, "that I didn't do this for you, mages! I didn't do it for the Conclave. I didn't do it for my brother! I had one more debt to pay in my lifetime. Now I have discharged it. I can sleep in peace."

In the darkness, Raistlin could not see the staff he leaned upon, but he didn't need to. He knew every curve of the wood, every tiny imperfection in the grain. Lovingly he caressed it, his delicate fingers touching the golden dragon's claw, running over each facet of the cold, dark crystal it held. Raistlin's eyes stared into the darkness, stared into the future he could glimpse by the light of the black moon.

"He will be great in the Art," he said with quiet pride. "The greatest that has yet lived. He will bring honor and renown to our profession. Because of him, magic will live and flourish in the world." The archmage's voice lowered. "Whatever happiness and joy was in my life, Palin, came from the magic.

"To the magic, I give you. . . ."

Raistlin held the staff an instant longer, pressing the smooth wood against his cheek. Then, with a word of command, he sent it from him. It vanished, swallowed up by the endless night. His head bowed in weariness, Raistlin laid his hand upon the velvet curtain and disappeared, becoming one with the darkness and the silence and the dust.

# CHAPTER ELEVEN

Palin came slowly to consciousness. His first thought was one of terror. The fiery jolt that had burned and blasted his body had not killed him! There would be another. Raistlin would not let him live. Moaning, Palin huddled against the cold stone floor, waiting fearfully to hear the sound of magical chanting, to hear the crackle of the sparks from those thin fingertips, to feel once again the searing, exploding pain. . . .

All was quiet. Listening intently, holding his breath, his body shivering in fear, Palin heard nothing.

Cautiously, he opened his eyes. He was in darkness, such deep darkness that nothing whatever was visible, not even his own body.

"Raistlin?" Palin whispered, raising his head cautiously from the damp, stone floor. "Uncle?"

"Palin!" a voice shouted.

Palin's heart stilled in fear. He could not breathe.

"Palin!" the voice shouted again, a voice filled with love and anguish.

Palin gasped in relief and, falling back against the stone floor, sobbed in joy.

He heard booted footsteps clambering up stairs. Torchlight lit the darkness. The footsteps halted, the torchlight wavered as though the hand holding it shook. Then the footsteps were running, the torchlight burned above him.

"Palin! My son!" and Palin was in his father's arms.

"What have they done to you?" Caramon cried in a choked voice. Dropping the torch, he lifted his son's body from the floor and cradled it against his strong breast.

Palin could not speak. He leaned his head against his father's chest, hearing the heart beating rapidly from the exertion of climbing the Tower stairs, smelling the familiar smells of leather and sweat, letting—for one last moment—his father's arms shelter and protect him. Then, with a soft sigh, Palin raised his head and looked into his father's pale, anguished face.

"Nothing, Father," he said softly, gently pushing himself away. "I'm all right. Truly." Sitting up, he looked around, confused in the feeble light cast by the torch flickering on the floor. "But where are we?"

"Out—outside that . . . that place," Caramon growled, letting go of his son, but watching him dubiously, anxiously.

"The laboratory," murmured Palin, puzzled, his gaze going to the closed door and the two, white, disembodied eyes that hovered before it.

The young man started to stand up.

"Careful!" said Caramon, putting his arm around him again.

"I told you, father. I'm all right," Palin said firmly, shaking off his father's help and getting to his feet without assistance. "What happened?" He looked at the sealed laboratory door.

The two eyes of the spectre stared back at him unblinking, unmoving.

"You went in . . . there," Caramon said, his brow creasing into a frown as his gaze shifted to the sealed door as well. "And . . . the door slammed shut! I tried to get in . . . Dalamar cast some sort of spell on it, but it wouldn't open. Then more of those . . . those *things*"—he gestured at the eyes with a scowl—"came and I . . . I don't remember much after that. When I came to, I was with Dalamar in the study. . . ."

———

"Which is where we will return now," said a voice behind them, "if you will honor me by sharing my breakfast."

"The only place we're going now," said Caramon in a stern, low voice as he turned to face the dark elf, who had materialized behind them, "is home. And no more magic!" he snarled, glaring at Dalamar. "We'll walk, if need be. Neither my son nor I are ever coming back to one of these cursed Towers again—"

Without a glance at Caramon, Dalamar walked past the big man to Palin, who was standing silently next to his father, his hands folded in the sleeves of his white robes, his eyes downcast as was proper in the presence of the high-ranking wizard.

Dalamar reached out his hands and clasped the young man by the shoulders.

"*Quithain, Magus,*" the dark elf said with a smile, leaning forward to kiss Palin on the cheek as was the elven custom.

Palin stared at him in confusion, his face flushed. The words the elf had spoken tumbled about in his mind, making little sense. He spoke some elven, learned from his father's friend, Tanis. But, after all that had happened to him, the language went right out of his head. Frantically, he struggled to remember, for Dalamar was standing in front of him, looking at him, grinning.

"*Quithain* . . ." Palin repeated to himself. "Means . . . congratulations. Congratulations, *Magus* . . ."

He gasped, staring at Dalamar in disbelief.

"What does it mean?" demanded Caramon, glaring at the dark elf. "I don't understand—"

"He is one of us now, Caramon," said Dalamar quietly, taking hold of Palin's arm and escorting him past his father. "His trials are over. He has completed the Test."

"We are sorry to have put you through this again,

Caramon," Dalamar said to the big warrior. Seated opposite the ornately carved desk in the dark elf's luxuriously appointed study, Caramon flushed, his brow still lined with the signs of his concern and fear and anger.

"But," Dalamar continued, "it was fast becoming apparent to all of us that you would do your best to prevent your son from taking the Test."

"Can you blame me?" Caramon asked harshly. Rising to his feet, he walked over to the large window, staring out into the dark shadows of the Shoikan Grove below him.

"No," said Dalamar. "We could not blame you. And so we devised this way of tricking you into it."

Scowling angrily, Caramon turned, jabbing his finger at Dalamar. "You had no right! He's too young! He might have died!"

"True," said Dalamar softly, "but that is a risk we all face. It is a risk you take every time you send your older sons to battle. . . ."

"This is different." Caramon turned away, his face dark.

Dalamar's gaze went to Palin, who sat in a chair, a glass of untasted wine in his hand. The young mage was staring dazedly around as though he could still not believe what had occurred.

"Because of Raistlin?" Dalamar smiled. "Palin is truly gifted, Caramon. As gifted as his uncle. For him, as for Raistlin, there could have been only one choice—his magic. But Palin's love for his family is strong. He would have made the choice, and it would have broken his heart."

Caramon bowed his head, clasping his hands behind him.

Palin, hearing a muffled choke behind him, set his wine glass down and, rising to his feet, walked over to stand beside his father. Reaching out his hand, Caramon drew his son close. "Dalamar's right," the big man said huskily. "I only wanted what was best for you and—and I was afraid . . . afraid I might lose you to the magic as I lost him. . . . I—I'm sorry, Palin. Forgive me."

Palin's answer was to embrace his father, who wrapped both his great arms around the white-robed mage and hugged him tight.

"So you passed! I'm proud of you, son!" Caramon whispered. "So proud—"

"Thank you, father!" Palin said brokenly. "There is nothing to forgive. I understand at last—" The rest of the young mage's words were squeezed from him by his father's hug. Then, with a clap on the back, Caramon let his boy go and returned to staring out the window, frowning down at the Shoikan Grove.

Turning back to Dalamar, Palin looked at the dark elf, puzzled.

"The Test," he said hesitantly. "It—it all seems so real! Yet, I'm here. . . . Raistlin didn't kill me . . ."

"Raistlin!" Caramon glanced around in alarm, his face pale.

"Be at ease, my friend," Dalamar said, raising his slender hand. "The Test varies for each person who takes it, Palin. For some, it is very real and can have real and disastrous consequences. Your uncle, for example, barely survived an encounter with one of my kind. Justarius's Test left him crippled in one leg. But, for others, the Test is only in the mind." Dalamar's face grew tense, his voice quivered in remembered pain. "That, too, can have its effects. Sometimes worse than the others . . ."

"So—it was all in my mind. I didn't go into the Abyss? My uncle wasn't really there?"

"No, Palin," Dalamar said, regaining his composure. "Raistlin is dead. We have no reason to believe otherwise, despite what we told you. We do not know for certain, of course, but we believe that the vision your father described is a true one, given to him by Paladine to ease his grief. When we told you we had signs that Raistlin was still alive, that was all part of the ruse to bring you here. There have been no such signs. If Raistlin lives today, it is only in our legends. . . ."

"And our memories," Caramon muttered from the window.

"But he seemed so real!" Palin protested. He could feel the soft black velvet beneath his fingertips; the burning touch of the golden-skinned hands; the cool, smooth wood of the Staff of Magius. He could hear the whispering voice, see the golden, hour-glass eyes, smell the rose petals, the spice, the blood. . . .

Lowering his head, he shivered.

"I know," said Dalamar with a soft sigh. "But it was only illusion. The Guardian stands before the door, the door is still sealed. It will be, for all eternity. You never even went inside the laboratory, much less the Abyss."

"But I saw him enter—" Caramon said.

"All part of the illusion. I alone saw through it. I helped create it, in fact. It was designed to be very real to you, Palin. You will never forget it. The Test is meant to judge not only your skill as a magic-user but, more importantly, to teach you something about yourself. You had two things to discover—the truth about your uncle, and the truth about yourself."

*Know the truth about yourself* . . . Raistlin's voice.

Palin smoothed the fabric of his white robes with his hands. "I know now where my loyalties lie," he said softly, remembering that bitter moment standing before the Portal. "As the Sea Wizard said, I will serve the world and, in so doing, serve myself."

Smiling, Dalamar rose to his feet. "And now, I know you are eager to return to your home and your family, young mage. I will detain you no longer. I almost regret that you did not make another choice, Palin," the dark elf said with a shrug. "I would have enjoyed having you as my apprentice. But you will make a worthy adversary. I am honored to have been a part of your success." Dalamar extended his hand.

"Thank you," said Palin, flushing. Taking Dalamar's hand in his, he clasped it gratefully. "Thank you . . . for everything."

"Yeah," mumbled Caramon, leaving the window to come stand beside his son. He, too, gripped Dalamar's hand in his, the elf's slender fingers completely engulfed in the big man's grip. "I—I guess I will let you use . . . that magic of yours . . . to send us back to Solace. Tika'll be worried sick—"

"Very well," Dalamar said, exchanging smiles with Palin. "Stand close together. Farewell, Palin. I will see you at the Tower of Wayreth."

There came a soft knock upon the door.

Dalamar frowned. "What is it?" he asked irritably. "I gave instructions that we were not to be disturbed!"

The door opened by itself, apparently. Two white eyes gleamed from out of the darkness. "Forgive me, Master," said the spectre, "but I have been instructed to give the young mage a parting gift."

"Instructed? By whom?" Dalamar's eyes flashed. "Justarius? Has he dared set foot in my Tower without my permission—"

"No, Master," said the spectre, floating into the room. Its chill gaze went to Palin. Slowly it approached the young mage, its fleshless hand outstretched. Caramon moved swiftly to stand in front of his son.

"No, Father," said Palin firmly, putting a restraining hand on his father's sword-arm. "Stand aside. It means me no harm. What is it you have for me?" the young mage asked the spectre, who came to a halt only inches from him.

In answer, the fleshless hand traced an arcane symbol in the air. The Staff of Magius appeared, held fast in the skeletal fingers.

Caramon gasped and took a step backward. Dalamar regarded the spectre coldly. "You have failed in your duties!" The dark elf's voice rose in anger. "By our Dark Queen, I will send you to the eternal torment of the Abyss for this—"

"I have not failed in my duty," the guardian replied, its hollow tone reminding Palin fearfully of the realm he had entered—if only in illusion. "The door to the laboratory remains locked and spellbound. The key is here, as you can see." The Guardian held out its other hand, showing a silver key lying in the bony palm. "All is as it was, undisturbed. No living being has entered."

"Then who—" Dalamar began in fury. Suddenly, his voice dropped, his face went ashen. "No living being . . ." Shaken, the dark elf sank back into his seat, staring at the staff with wide eyes.

"This is yours, Palin, as was promised," the spectre said, handing the staff to the young mage.

Reaching out, Palin took hold of the staff with a shaking hand. At his touch, the crystal on the top flared into light, blazing with a cool, clear radiance, filling the dark room with a bright, silvery light.

"A gift from the true Master of the Tower. With it," the spectre added in its chill tones, "goes his blessing."

The white eyes lowered in reverence, then they were gone.

Holding the staff in his hand, Palin looked wonderingly at his father.

Blinking rapidly, Caramon smiled through his tears. "Let's go home," he said quietly, putting his arm around his son. ✍

## Bridges of Time Series

This series of novels bridges the thirty-year span between the Chaos War and the Fifth Age DRAGONLANCE® novels.

### Spirit of the Wind
*Chris Pierson*
Riverwind the Plainsman answers a call for help from the besieged kender in their struggle against the great red dragon Malystryx.

### Legacy of Steel
*Mary H. Herbert*
Sara Dunstan, an outcast Knight of Takhisis, risks a perilous journey to Neraka to found a new order of knighthood in the land of Ansalon.

### The Silver Stair
*Jean Rabe*
As the Fifth Age dawns, Goldmoon, Hero of the Lance, searches for a new magic and founds the great Citadel of Light, linked to the heavens by an endless stair.

### The Rose and the Skull
*Jeff Crook*
When Lord Gunthar, head of the Solamnic Knights, dies mysteriously, the order must make an alliance with their deadliest enemy, as a troop of gully dwarves races across Krynn to unmask treachery.

### Dezra's Quest
*Chris Pierson*
The daughter of Caramon Majere brings aid to the centaurs, as they try to escape a terrible pact made with Chaos.

*Edited by Margaret Weis and Tracy Hickman*

An anthology of short stories from prominent DRAGONLANCE authors, describing the terrible battles and brave exploits of heroes during the first decades of the Fifth Age.

Contributors include Margaret Weis and Don Perrin, Nancy Berberick, Richard A. Knaak, and Douglas Niles.

# The Raistlin Chronicles

The story of Raistlin Majere, Ansalon's greatest mage, told by the person who best knows his tale.

## The Soulforge

*Margaret Weis*

A mage's soul is forged in the crucible of magic. Now, at last, Margaret Weis reveals the hidden story of Raistlin Majere's early years, from his first brushes with magic to his Test in the Tower of High Sorcery. His life, and those of the people near to him, will be changed forever.

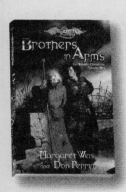

## Brothers in Arms

*Margaret Weis and Don Perrin*

As the shadows of war gather across Krynn, Raistlin and his brother Caramon offer their services to a commander. Half a continent away, their sister Kitiara also enlists in an army and begins her rise to power among the Dark Knights of Takhisis.